STUCK WIDE OPEN

SUMMER SHULTZ

Published by High Country Publications
Denver, Colorado
Copyright © 2021 by Summer Shultz. All rights reserved.
www.summershultz.com

"Again" reproduced by permission of Trampled By Turtles and Terrorbird Publishing, LLC

Publisher's Cataloging-in-Publication data

Names: Shultz, Summer, author.
Title: Stuck wide open / by Summer Shultz.
Description: First trade paperback original edition. | Denver [Colorado] : High Country Publications, 2021. | Also published as an ebook.
Identifiers: ISBN 978-0-9986509-6-8
Subjects: LCSH: Romance fiction. | Travel Fiction.
BISAC: FICTION / Romance / New Adult.
Classification: LCC PS3619 | DDC 813.6–dc22

Cover and Interior Design by Victoria Wolf
Cover photographs © Summer Shultz
Editing by Bobby Haas
Author photo © PBMedia, LLC

Printed in the United States of America.

STUCK WIDE OPEN

prologue

DESERT DA(Y)ZE: SAHARA DESERT – MERZOUGA, MOROCCO

WE RESTED IN THE SHADE beneath what looked like a large circus tent, sprawled out on ornate camel-hair rugs. We'd been lying like this, barely moving, for hours. Waves of heat rose from the desert floor, making the air around us sparkle and crackle. All I wanted out of life in this moment was to sink into the lazy oblivion of a mid-afternoon nap. Sadly, the flies made sleep impossible. I covered as much of my body as I could with my scarf, but these flies were relentless, moisture-seeking missiles. So I tossed and turned and fidgeted and swatted. Swatting at the flies was the only movement I really felt capable of. Mostly, I was content with doing nothing at all.

This amount of free time left Liam and Nate bored and restless. They sat a few feet away from me at one of the tables, attempting to play a game of cards, but the heat was infuriatingly distracting. Every few minutes, one or the other of them would set down his hand of cards and stare off into space for a while. More often than not, Nate was the first to break the silence. He repeated everything that he said many times and spoke in general terms, never quite seeming to get to any real point. He'd shake his head and repeat something along the lines of, "Fuck, man. ... Shit got real out there this morning. We sure as hell got our Sahara experience, huh?" Nate's favorite line to repeat was the joke about the Germans in their desert yoga camp. I'd heard this line too many times, so I did my best to tune him out.

Since joining Liam and Nate in Morocco, I noticed this trend of how much we seemed to talk around and avoid truth. I didn't know how to interact in this casual, airy sort of way. I oscillated between over-talking to compensate for my nervousness and falling into long stretches of silence in which I withdrew further into myself. This journal and these words were my lifeline to making myself understood, at least by myself. For it felt as if I was inhabiting a space so entirely my own that Liam and Nate were just a mirage, as I imagine I appeared to them. Thinking like this, loneliness came crashing over me in a dark wave. A part of me yearned for a physical aloneness to match how I felt internally. Already, I dreamed of being back in the dunes, lost among mountains of sand. How strange it is to feel so at home in such a hostile, threatening environment. Yet, to me, the desert represented all that I was experiencing in physical form. The rise and fall of the dunes stretching out before me mirrored the rise and fall of my own emotions.

This is how I spent my afternoon in the Sahara, lounging on a sandy rug and gazing out over sand dunes at vast amounts of space in every direction. When I slipped too far into the world of emotionality and lost touch with physicality, the flies brought me back. The discomfort the flies provoked regrounded me in a more concrete reality. I tossed and turned and fidgeted and swatted. I lost my train of thought and didn't bother to chase it back down. Instead, I rolled over to focus my attention on what was happening within the tent. Usually, not much had changed in the time it took me to check back in. The one Berber guide who stayed behind to chaperone us, Yasin, was still sleeping. After spending so much time in the desert, Yasin had apparently developed a special type of mind control that enabled him to tune out the incessant buzzing of the flies. Neither Nate nor Liam appeared to have moved at all, although Nate must have gotten up at some point to grab the guitar. He picked away at a few chords and sang quietly to himself, which told me that he was playing a song he had written and was still too self-conscious to want us to hear. Liam held a book open in one hand but stared off in the opposite direction. Liam's face was a closed door that my eyes scavenged like thieves looking for a way to break inside. Before long, I gave up trying to guess what was on his mind. I started counting each of the new freckles that had appeared on his face since our desert adventure that morning. I did this mainly just to give myself an excuse to keep looking at him.

I got only to the number seventeen before Liam caught me watching him and turned to face me. I blushed and was inclined to look away, but something in his gaze tethered me to him, pinned me to the spot. I searched his eyes for the tenderness I had come to expect from him. Instead I was met with a gaze that was hard and uncompromising. All at once, I felt the heat of the desert air around me as if it had its own weight. The heat came at me from all sides and pressed itself into my skin. It trickled in through my pores and permeated my bloodstream. With each beat of my heart, a languid, helpless sort of longing surged through my body. I felt as if the private space of my body was being invaded. I wanted to close my eyes, to flee to darkness as a refuge, a space in which I could be left alone with myself again. I summoned all my strength to resist this urge.

In the end, Liam was the first to turn away, as if he had found the answers he was looking for. I could not be satisfied so easily. I swatted at the flies but could not dismiss the buzzing of the questions that spun around my mind in circles. How did I get here? Or better yet, why did I bring myself here? How could I leave and go anywhere else? I feared that I would never be as free again as I was there in the sprawling vastness and dizzying emptiness of the desert. Yet I wondered if it was possible to experience so much freedom as to become trapped by it. I imagined the open blue sky unfurling all around me as a giant, inescapable net in which I had somehow become entangled. The fabric of this net was woven with a truth that I'd long been avoiding and from which I could no longer run or hide. This truth rode on the wings of the desert wind. I heard it as a faint murmur that I had to strain my ears to understand.

To be totally free is to be totally alone. This is the sound of the desert wind sighing. One day, this freedom will catch up to us all. I knew then that I was not ready. So I prayed for the possibility of a compromise. Putting pen to paper, I asked— you, the one I came here for, will you meet me in this strange and terrifying new place? Can we learn again to speak the truth openly between each other? Or am I condemned to whisper my truth quietly within the confines of my mind?

chapter one

THE ONSET OF BLINDNESS

OUR SENSE OF CONTROL is intimately connected with our sense of sight. It is our sense of sight that gives us the ability to see what lies ahead of us, which in turn allows us to make predictions about the future. Without clear sight, we must learn how to use and trust our other senses. With time, it is possible to develop a new type of intuition, a sight into the unseen. Yet, in order to move forward, we must first overcome our fear of blindness.

The onset of blindness is usually sudden. It is not something you can prepare for but something you must react to in the moment. It is like driving home at night down a familiar road and getting caught in an unexpected snowstorm. Normally, you would be confident enough of where you are going that you would hardly be paying attention to the road, tuned instead into the juicy beats pumping out of your car stereo. On this particular night, you turn the music off. The snowfall is so thick and relentless that you can see no more than a few feet in front of you. The painted lines on the road are no longer visible. You no longer have any idea where you are going. Any moment now, you fear you will take a wrong turn and send your car careening off the road. For although the world outside your car may no longer be visible to you, you are in fact still moving, driving onward into the great whiteness.

The day I lost my vision was June 19, 2017. At the time, I was still living in Durango, a small city in the mountains of southwestern Colorado. On this day, in the span of two phone calls, my life went careening off the road I had laid out in front of me. The morning of June 19, I woke up outside, the first of many mornings to come when this would be the case. Blinking the sleep away, my freshly opened eyes were greeted by another pair of eyes. I wondered how long these eyes had been staring at me, waiting for my eyes to open.

"Good morning," Liam smiled at me.

Dazed, it took me a moment before I remembered to reply, "Good morning, Liam."

I peered into the face that was so close to mine. This face was so familiar. It had been on the periphery of my vision for years, but this was the first time I'd studied it up close. Liam's skin was adorned with more freckles than I previously realized, small brown stars spattered across a milky white sky. As I took in the constellations on the face in front of me, my mind flashed back to a vision of the starry sky from the night before. The stars were so beautiful that we never bothered to pitch a tent. We made love out in the open of a forest meadow with the stars shining down on us, illuminating our bodies with a pale, otherworldly glow.

Although Liam and I had been dating for over a month, this was only our second night sleeping together. This was also the first significant amount of time that we'd spent alone with one another. I met Liam almost six years before because my best friend, Evelyn, was dating his freshman-year roommate, Tyler. However, I'd never spent any real time with Liam until this winter, when I started dating another one of Liam's best friends and roommates, Nate. From the beginning, Nate and I knew we weren't right for each other. Neither of us was ready to seriously date anyone. Yet, without meaning to, we fell into an accidental kind of relationship. Toward the end of winter, after a few rocky, tumultuous months together, Nate and I walked away from each other equally confused and heartbroken. For most of the spring, Evelyn and I hid out in our cabin in the woods outside of town. I didn't see or talk to Nate or Liam or any of their friends.

Out of the blue, toward the beginning of May, I received an unexpected phone call from Liam. Liam's pretext for calling was that he hadn't seen me in a while and wanted to catch up. I believed him the first few times he called. When Liam continued to call me every single day, the phone calls became increasingly hard to explain. I found out only later that Nate had moved away from Durango at the end of April, a week before I got Liam's first call. Knowing how close Liam and Nate are, it took me far too long to realize that Liam's sudden interest in becoming closer friends with me might not be purely platonic. Right around the time that I connected the dots, Liam invited me to go see one of our favorite local bands play a show that Saturday night. The first time Liam kissed me was between songs on the dusty, peanut-covered floor of our town's old-time saloon.

The day after the concert, Liam called Nate to confess the feelings that he'd developed for me. Nate took the news with a surprising amount of grace. Despite Nate not having been the best boyfriend, I will give him credit for being a very good friend. As strange as it felt for me to go back to the house where I'd spent so much time with Nate the past winter, none of my mixed feelings proved strong enough to keep me away from Liam. After our first date, he continued to call me every single day until we were hanging out so often that he didn't need to call me anymore. Ever since we first started dating, Liam and I had been talking about wanting to go camping together. Finally, we'd managed to escape from our work-saturated routines and well-meaning friends to go camp out for a night in the woods.

Together we drove down a dirt road deep into the San Juan National Forest. For just one night, we left civilization and all of its accompanying worries behind us. After finding a suitable spot to set up camp, we spent what was left of the sunlight wandering around the woods, talking and laughing the whole time. Dusting the silence off our long-held secrets, we talked late into the night. We shared the kind of stories that you have to muster up the courage to tell, the kind of stories whose telling is met with a sense of relieved liberation. We got so absorbed in talking that neither of us bothered to cook any of the food we brought for dinner. Instead, we finished off a whole carton of strawberries between the two of us. By the time we ran out of strawberries, Liam and I had also run out of words. Having reached the limits of what is possible to express out loud, we continued our conversation in a different language—the language that bodies speak to each other through the skin.

The next morning, the language that my body was speaking to me was hunger. Its not-so-subtle cues included the angry grumbles emanating from my stomach and the vague sense of wooziness making my head spin. I forced myself to sit up and drink some water. In the time it took me to do this, Liam was already on his feet, rifling through the contents of our cooler.

"Lie back down," Liam insisted. "I'll cook us breakfast. We can pretend I'm making you breakfast in bed."

I was too tired and hungry to put up a fight. I just sort of fell back onto Liam's large sleeping pad. For a while, I watched the clouds drift by in the sky above me and the trees in the meadow around us sway in the wind. The soft creaking of the swaying pine trees lulled me back to sleep. I woke up an unknown amount of time later to the smell of eggs and bacon. I rolled over to find Liam sitting on the pad beside me with two plates of breakfast tacos and a full french press of coffee. Liam beamed down at me, proud of himself. After thanking Liam with a kiss, my first instinct was to reach for the coffee.

Pushing my plate of food toward me, Liam reminded me, "Eat up, babe. We're going to need all the fuel we can get for the long day ahead of us, especially since neither of us has climbed in a while."

At the mention of climbing, I felt my stomach tighten. My nerves overpowering my hunger, all I could do was pick at my breakfast between large gulps of scalding coffee. I hadn't been climbing in over a year and was terrified of embarrassing myself in front of Liam. Climbing was still too terrifying for me to consider it a fun or casual sport. Normally, I would have agreed to go only with a select few trusted friends, but Liam was so excited about the idea of us climbing together that I didn't want to let him down.

As I sat imagining all the possible worst-case scenarios for how this day could go, the sound of Liam's voice snapped me back into the present moment.

"I've never seen someone drink coffee as fast as you do."

"I don't like my coffee to get cold," I justified myself.

Liam nodded. Nonetheless, I could tell by the smirk on his face that bringing up coffee was just an excuse to break the silence, a way to bring me back to him.

Finally coming out with what he really wanted to say, Liam reassured me, "We can take it easy today."

It would take me a long time to get used to Liam's uncanny knack of reading my mind. I borrowed one of Liam's most frequent habits and raised my eyebrows at him, wanting but not quite daring to buy into his reassurances.

"I'm here to hang out with you," Liam assured me. "Climbing is just a bonus."

Staring back into Liam's eyes, I was met with a gaze of pure softness, a gaze that reached out a hand and lightly stroked my face. I relaxed enough to set down my cup of coffee and offer Liam a grateful, albeit tentative, smile. After changing into stretchy pants and my favorite flannel, I began the process of pulling my long, blond hair back into a braid, a sure sign that I meant business. Finishing off the rest of my coffee, I stood up and began to pack the rest of our things into Liam's car. This was the moment that I decided to give Liam a chance, to risk trusting him.

The first of the two phone calls came on our drive back home after a satisfying and only mildly petrifying day of climbing. Liam drove slower than usual with the windows rolled down, in no hurry to get home or bring the day any closer to an end. With every hip-hop song he played on the stereo, I fell a little bit more in love with him. Good rap, and anyone who listens to it, are two of my weaknesses. It was in between songs that I remembered to turn my phone back on, having turned it off the night before to unplug from the outside world. As soon as it came back on, my phone made that annoying bing to let me know I had a new voicemail. I was half-tempted to turn the music up louder and ignore the bing, but I noticed that the voicemail was from Evelyn. I turned the music down instead.

"Heyyyyy, Skye," Evelyn's voice drawled on voicemail. "I guess I'll just get out with it. My alarm didn't go off this morning, and then I couldn't find my keys ... so I showed up late to work again. According to Chris, this was *my third strike* or some bullshit. So, yeah, Chris fired me from the café this morning."

As patient as I tried to be with Evie, my shoulders slumped in an instant of irrepressible exasperation. For the past year, I'd worked at Chris' café as a means of earning some extra income on top of my main job as a counselor at Durango's detox center. Since graduating from college two years ago with a questionably useful degree in international affairs, I'd been searching for my own way to make a positive impact on the world. The field of mental health, and becoming an addiction counselor, fit that bill. It was the first job I landed out of college—a job I loved, but it barely paid the bills. When I quit working at the café, it was only to transition to another part-time job working for my second summer season as a rafting guide on the Animas River. Since Evelyn had been out of work all winter, I recommended her to take my place at the café. I made this recommendation in spite of my concerns about whether Evie would be able to handle Chris's anal-retentive tendencies. More than being exasperated at Evelyn for being fired, I was irritated at myself for not having seen this coming. Moving past my own frustration, I concentrated on listening to the rest of Evie's message.

I caught Evie in the middle of saying, "... since we're planning on leaving town in a few months anyway. If we don't renew, our lease technically ends in, like, two weeks. This means that we'd have to move out a little ... um, sooner than planned, so I was calling to warn you about that. I wish things weren't this way, but I can't seem to keep my shit together right now. Just call me back when you get this. OK?"

This was Evelyn's final, frantic request before the message cut off. Out of the rubble of my confusion, the words *two weeks* and *move out* emerged. Not wanting to give these words the time to connect and form a complete sentence, I turned the music back up to drown out the noise of my own thoughts.

"Everything OK?" Liam shouted out over the Anderson .Paak blasting from his radio.

Unsure of how else to answer this question, I shook my head.

"Was that Evie? What's going on with her?" Liam yelled a little louder.

Reluctantly, I turned down the music a notch.

Unable to stay upset with Evie even if I wanted to, I sighed, "Evie got fired from the café. Add that to everything else she's going through, and it sounds like she's ready to get out of town ... which means we have to move out a lot sooner than I was expecting. And by sooner, I mean in, like, two weeks."

Checking to make sure he'd heard me correctly, Liam turned off the music.

"Two weeks? I thought you were sticking around until September!"

"Yeah. I need to work a few more months to save up enough money for my move to Denver. But it's OK. I just have to find a place to crash for the next two months. That shouldn't be too hard, right?"

Liam fell silent for a moment, his face closed and unreadable. I would later come to recognize this as a sign that Liam was mentally working his way through some sort of problem.

A beat later, his voice only slightly unsteady, Liam offered, "You can always stay with me. I'm here only for the next six weeks, so you'd still have to figure out something for August. But I could talk to some friends about that and maybe ..."

I cut Liam off before he could go on any further. "Thanks. I just don't know if ..."

The truth was that spending the next six weeks living with Liam sounded like a dream. This was precisely what worried me. Liam had only six weeks left in Durango before he left for three months to hike the Camino de Santiago in Spain and travel around Europe and North Africa. By the time Liam came back to the States, I would have already moved to Denver with my sister, Alice. Neither Liam nor I knew if we could expect to see each other again after this summer, a fact that neither of us were keen to talk about.

Sensing my uncertainty, Liam stepped in. "Just think about it. Either way, we'll figure something out."

Little did either of us know that we would have almost no choice in the matter. Six days later, a wildfire erupted in the forest surrounding my neighborhood, and all 170 homes in my neighborhood were evacuated. Sure enough, the first place I ended up after the evacuation was on Liam's doorstep, carrying nothing but my wallet, phone, and the clothes on my back. By then, I'd spent every night at Liam's place anyway. The biggest change in my circumstances was not where I was staying but my lack of personal possessions. When the fire was contained and our homes were no longer in imminent danger of burning down, it took me less than a day to pack all my belongings into my car and drive straight back to Liam's house. Yet, as we drove back from our camping trip on this seemingly mundane Sunday afternoon, neither of us had an inkling of all that was to come. When Liam pulled up in front of his house, I couldn't imagine that I would, even for a short period of time, call this house my home.

Tired from our long, physical day, we left unpacking Liam's car for the next day and moseyed over to the couch on Liam's back patio. In the backyard, we were greeted by Liam's new roommate and a few of his friends who were lounging out on the grass, drinking beer and swapping stories of their weekend adventures. Cracking open our own PBRs, we half-listened to the conversations unfolding around us and slowly sank deeper into the folds of the couch. With Liam's arms around me, I was so comfortable that I couldn't imagine being anywhere or doing anything else. Yet, in the back of my mind, Evie's voicemail nagged at me. I unconsciously reached for the phone in my pocket, knowing that I needed to get over myself and call her back. I got as far as actually removing my phone from my pocket when Alice's name flashed across the screen. Signaling for Liam to release his hold on me, I got up to take my sister's call.

"What's up, Alice?"

Alice paused for a second longer than usual before answering, "Hey, Skye. All's good here, I'm just calling because … well, I don't exactly know where to start with this."

"Please don't tell me you have more bad news."

I was met with silence on the other end of the line.

"OK," I sighed, "if it is bad news, you might as well just get it over with."

"I don't mean for this to be bad news," Alice hesitated, "but I've been thinking a lot about our move to Denver in a few months, and … this is the part that I don't know how to say."

"Just say it!"

"All right, all right! I'm sorry, Skye, but I just don't feel right about moving to Denver right now. Don't get me wrong; I love the idea of us living together. I'm just not ready to leave Fort Collins and my friends here. I kept hoping these feelings would change, but the closer I get to my move-out date, the more I've been second-guessing this."

Then it was my turn to be at a loss for words.

Alice asked quietly, "Are you mad at me?"

Drawing in a shaky breath, I composed myself enough to be able to reassure her.

"No, I'm not mad—just confused. We've been planning this move for over a year. Why didn't you bring this up earlier?"

When she replied, Alice sounded more disappointed in herself than I could ever be.

"I didn't want to admit that I wasn't ready. I still really want to live with you. Would you ever consider moving to Fort Collins instead?"

Answering honestly, I told Alice, "I don't think that's the right move for me either. I was really excited about the idea of living in a bigger city. As much as I would love to live with you, I'm ready for something totally outside of the small Colorado college town lifestyle, you know?"

Watching my dream of living in Denver with my sister crumble before me, I let my head fall into my hands. Trying to come up with a new game plan for what I wanted to do in September felt pointless when I didn't even know where I would be living in two weeks.

Fighting the urge to cry, I told Alice, "Now's not the best time for me to talk. But I'll call you back tomorrow, OK? I love you."

I waited just long enough to hear Alice say that she loved

me back before hanging up. Slinking back over to join Liam on the couch, I resisted the urge to throw my phone across the yard. Picking up on the distress written all over my face, Liam pulled me closer and nuzzled his face into my neck.

"You've got that look on your face again ... What happened?" Liam whispered in my ear so no one else could hear.

"My sister doesn't want to move to Denver with me anymore," I whispered back.

Liam's mouth froze on my ear.

"Fuck."

I tried and failed to fight back a fresh wave of tears. Hoping that Liam wouldn't notice the silent teardrops leaking out from my closed eyelids, I held myself as still as possible, squeezing my eyes shut. When I felt his hand on my chin, turning my face toward him, I knew my flimsy cover had been blown. Brushing away my tears, I blinked my eyes open. For the second time that day, my newly opened eyes were greeted by another pair of wide-open eyes—eyes that had been waiting for me to find them. The longer I held Liam's gaze, the more I felt my sense of control slipping away. I felt as if I were stuck behind the steering wheel of a car that would no longer obey my commands. This car was my life, and I was supposedly the one driving it, but I no longer had any clue about where I was headed. I was lost in my own inner storm, and the whole world around me had gone white. Yet, when I turned toward the passenger seat,

I found Liam sitting right there beside me. He smiled up at me as if all of this was one big joke, as if none of the chaos around us mattered because there we both were, lucky enough to be sitting next to each other in the same car.

chapter two

A PROPOSITION

IT WAS TUESDAY MORNING, so I woke up early to mow the campground lawns before driving to the hospital for my afternoon shift in detox. We'd enjoyed a spell of warm, dry days, so it was easier than usual this morning to wriggle out of my sleeping bag and leave the warmth of my tent. Although rain brought up the water level of the river and prolonged our rafting season, it also threatened to wash my home away, so I privately appreciated our lack of rain. Slipping into the sandals I wore every day that summer, I ambled over to my car, which had also come to serve as my closet, to pick through my boxes of clothes in search of a decent outfit. My next step was to walk down the hill to where all the campground's paying guests parked their RVs so I could use the campground's shared bathroom. After washing my hands and face, I walked back up the hill, past my tent, and a little farther up the road toward the spot where Kaden had set up his camp for the summer.

Since he'd been living in the campground all summer, Kaden's camp was far more developed than my own. He had two tents set up, one that he slept in and one for all his gear, with three tarps hung overhead to keep his space dry when it rained. In between the two tents, Kaden set up a small kitchen area with a Coleman stove, rickety table, and three camping chairs. Lounging in his favorite chair, Kaden looked up from rolling a cigarette to greet me.

"You ready to mow some lawns for these bastards?" Kaden mumbled, lighting up the cigarette hanging loosely between his lips.

I knew Kaden well enough by then to expect him to be a little extra ornery whenever Tuesday morning rolled around. In exchange for a free place to camp, Kaden and I did yard work around the campground every Tuesday and Wednesday to help keep the grounds looking nice. I was so thrilled about not having to pay rent that I would have happily worked every day of the week if needed. However, I had only been living in the campground for the past two weeks. Kaden had been living and working there for over three months. Unfazed by his grouchiness, I shone Kaden my most winning smile.

"I will be as soon as I get some caffeine into my system. Do you want coffee this morning?"

Kaden nodded, so I added a little more water to my pot and lit the Coleman stove.

Settling into one of the camp chairs as I waited for the water to boil, I asked Kaden, "What trips are you running on the river today?"

Kaden grumbled back, "Two half-days so far, so I've got a long day ahead of me. How about you? You sitting in with the crazies for ten hours today?"

I gave up a long time ago on reminding my friends that I worked in detox, not the psych ward. Admittedly, detox resembled an insane asylum more days than not. Along with being a safe place to detoxify from drugs and alcohol, detox also functioned as a homeless shelter, a holding cell for suicidal patients, and an overflow space when the town jail was full.

"Yep," I replied, "I won't get back here until, like, midnight. But don't worry, I'll be up tomorrow to help you mow some more lawns. After that, it's Thursday, thank God, and I'll be back on the river again."

Having overcommitted to both of my jobs, I'd hardly had a day off all summer. The first three days of the week, I worked three ten-hour shifts in detox, and then I finished out the week guiding four days on the lower Animas River. Since Liam had left for Europe, I stopped complaining about how busy I was. On top of all the extra money I was making from working such long weeks, I also no longer had to pay rent or utilities. The figure in my savings account was higher than it had been in years. For this and other reasons, I hadn't minded working so much.

It had been sixteen days since Liam left, not that I was counting. The last night Liam and I slept together was also the last night I slept with a roof over my head. Since the beginning of the summer, Kaden had been bugging me to come pitch a tent next to his spot in the campground. Although I had several friends who invited me to stay on their couches for as long as I needed, I took Kaden up on his offer. While living in a tent may have been the less comfortable option, it provided me with a space of my own without having to feel like I owed anyone anything. With each glorious, rainless day that went by, I questioned why I ever bothered to pay rent for a house in the summertime. Whenever I managed to squeeze in a little free time, I set out my camp chair in the wildflower-adorned field near my tent. Between reading pages of my book, I snuck glances up at the snow-capped spires of the La Plata Mountain Range. If I were still living in a house, I probably would have been sitting on a couch inside, staring at a TV or a computer screen instead. I was grateful for my new home's lack of roof and walls.

Besides all the additional time I got to spend outside,

the best part about my new setup was getting to share a space with Kaden. Although Kaden was a large, intimidating man, I recognized him for the teddy bear that he was on my first day of working with him. Despite his grumblings and general tendency toward moodiness, Kaden was one of those rare beings who operated in a mode of instinctual generosity. Of the many raft guides I worked with, Kaden was the guide who took his job the most seriously. He was the guide who would do your work for you if the work needed to be done, the one you could count on to react swiftly in a dangerous situation, and usually the one to walk away from the day with the biggest tip in his pocket. Many nights, after getting off the river, the two of us would drive back to the campground and spend all night together philosophizing over cans of cheap bear, so absorbed in our conversation that we forgot to notice the cold of the night setting in. Mornings with Kaden were a time of silence and recovery. More often than not, we ate our breakfast and drank our coffee without saying much.

This morning was no different. Before I knew it, half an hour had flown by. Besides me getting up to pour the coffee and Kaden rolling another cigarette, we'd barely moved. Glancing up at the sun to gauge how far it had moved in the sky, Kaden reluctantly put out his cigarette.

"What do you say? Time to make it look like we're busy?"

After finishing off my coffee, I followed Kaden down the

hill to the entrance of the campground. I ducked behind him into the large storage shed.

"I get to mow the lawns today!" I insisted.

"I don't know how you still get so excited about cutting grass," Kaden groused, but he obliged me by picking up the hedge trimmer.

Equipment in hand, we got to work on mowing the large lawn at the front entrance of the campground. As the morning hours trickled by and the sun's rays increased in intensity, the temperature steadily rose. Wishing I'd remembered to put on sunscreen, I stopped to wipe the sweat off my face and breathe in the smell of the freshly cut grass. Right when I stopped to take a break, Greta, the middle-aged German woman who ran the campground, strolled by on the other side of the road. She gave Kaden a sly wink and shot me a dirty look before sauntering back toward her air-conditioned office at the campground's front entrance.

Taking a few steps closer to me, Kaden hissed in my ear, "Every time I see that woman she strokes my arm and asks how my girlfriend is doing. I don't even have a fucking girlfriend."

"Well, that explains the death glare she gives me every time I see her. At least Greta talks to you. She's never graced me with more than a 'hello.'"

"Believe me, you're lucky. All Greta sees in me is the chance to live out her repressed Filipino pool boy fantasy. All I am to her, and every other middle-aged woman in this camp-ground, is some weird sort of fetish," Kaden spat out with audible disgust.

As Kaden flipped his straight black hair out of his face, muscles bared and dark skin glistening in a loose tank-top, I couldn't refrain from giving him a casual once-over.

"Maybe you should start wearing a shirt with sleeves," I suggested, struggling to keep a straight face.

Crossing his arms over his chest, Kaden shot me an even dirtier look than the one I'd received from Greta.

"Do you realize that, if I was a woman, the equivalent of what you just told me would be that it's my fault the creepy guy at the bar pinched my ass because my jeans are too tight? Speaking of having my ass pinched, Greta isn't the only one here who's guilty of that. Let me tell you something, Skye ..." Kaden began.

Sensing that Kaden was about to deliver another one of his impromptu sermons, I chuckled, "Please, enlighten me."

Ignoring me, Kaden continued, "There ain't nothing in life that's free. You may not be paying with money, but all that means is that you're paying with something else. It may seem like we're getting to stay here for free, but all these old cougars here sure are getting something out of it."

Twenty days had gone by since Liam left to go hike the Camino de Santiago in Spain with Nate and their friend Stephen. I still hadn't heard a single word from him. Since I didn't use social media, the only clue I'd gotten as to why Liam dropped off the face of the earth was a Facebook post Kaden showed me saying Liam lost his phone. Before he left, Liam told me he wanted to find a way for us to be together again when he got back from Europe. He mentioned the possibility of us trimming weed together in the fall since a few of his friends had offered him work on their farms. So our looming goodbye turned into a hopeful but poorly planned see-you-later. While neither of us was willing to commit to a long-distance relationship, we both committed to finding our way back together again somewhere, somehow.

Having made this commitment, Liam's three-week silence was particularly flabbergasting. The lack of any concrete knowledge about how Liam was doing or where he was created a dangerous vacuum in my mind that served as a breeding ground for the worst kind of imaginings. The same sickening doubts and anxieties replayed themselves so many times inside my head that I felt as if I'd been trapped for the past twenty days riding a high-speed merry-go-round. What started as a slight sense of unease grew into an unremitting nausea. Seeking out any means of distraction available, I continued working long hours every day, letting my last summer in Durango slowly pass me by.

The only problem with being as busy as I was came when I finally received the phone call I'd been waiting for but missed it because I was out guiding a river trip. When I got off the river, I replayed the garbled, unintelligible voicemail Liam left so many times that I felt as if I were attempting to decode a strange cipher left by aliens. The same international number called me again the next day, and then again the next. On the fourth day Liam called, I finally managed to get to the phone in time to answer.

"Liam?"

"Skye?" Liam echoed back to me.

"It's been three weeks, Liam. How the hell have you been?"

"I've been good, really good."

A small, terrible part of me was heartbroken to hear these words. This part of me wished Liam had spent the past three weeks feeling as devastated as I had. Banishing these petty thoughts, I tuned back in to what he was saying.

"Every day that goes by on the Camino feels like a short lifetime. I can't believe how much I'm learning every day and how many amazing people we've met. There's one woman especially I wish you could have met. She's a nun, but she's not at all what I pictured a nun would be like. For one thing, she ..."

Liam launched into the story of his blossoming friendship with the nun. One story quickly turned into another. Having spent the past three weeks living in an information vacuum, I ate up every little detail. The trouble came when Liam turned the conversation around to ask me how I'd been doing.

Unsure of where to start, I stuttered, "Um, well, I've been really busy. Living in a tent hasn't been so bad. I've just been working a lot, and ... I couldn't help worrying that ..."

I heard a shuffling and the hum of other voices on the other end of the line.

"Skye?" Liam cut in, "The crew is calling me out to dinner. I've got to go. But I'll call you back soon, OK?"

Shocked at this abrupt end to our conversation, I didn't know what to say. Finally, I said the only thing of which I was capable—the truth.

"I didn't know if I would ever hear from you again ..."

I whispered my confession into the phone so quietly that I couldn't be sure if Liam even heard me. In way of reply, Liam exhaled my name in one long breath.

"Skye ... I'm sorry."

After taking some time to piece his thoughts together, Liam explained himself.

"I lost my phone on the first day of the trip, which has honestly helped me be more present and enjoy my time here more. Being present has been ... harder for me than I would like.

You've already seen so much of the world, but this trip is a first for me. I've been planning it for years, and I'm finally here now."

At the mention of the word *planning*, I sighed. Planning, particularly the ability to follow through with a pre-established plan, was one way in which Liam and I were different. As long as we'd been friends, I had always known Liam as a man with a plan. Since I sometimes felt like I had a disability when it came to making plans, I greatly admired Liam for this. On one hand, I yearned more than anything for a home and a community, a place to call my own. I yearned for the fulfillment that comes with committing to one place, one path, one person. Yet there was another part of me that feared stagnancy above all else. This part of me found the comfortable dull and repellant. This part of me dreamed of living in a far-away country. This part of me longed to get lost and never be found. Taking into consideration how much these two sides of me clashed, it made a lot more sense why I had such a hard time making and executing plans. As good at Liam was at making plans, the issue for us was that I never neatly fit into Liam's plan.

Although I may have been a disruption in Liam's grand plan, he admitted to me, "As much as I try to be present, I can't help thinking about you. I've been dreaming about you almost every night. That's how I knew that I needed to call."

I fell silent, taking in Liam's apology and explanation as if I'd been given a handful of mismatched puzzle pieces that I had to hurriedly try to fit together.

Eventually, I murmured, "I'm just glad to know you're doing OK."

This was my way of accepting Liam's apology. It was the best I could do in the moment.

Taking this in stride, Liam replied, "I want to know more about how you've been. The next time I call, I'm the one who gets to listen to you talk. Deal?"

The next time ... With no small amount of bitterness, I wondered when I could expect this to be.

In response to my unvoiced question, Liam promised me, "If you'll talk to me, I'll call you back tomorrow."

"I work every day, Liam. Plus, there's the eight-hour time difference ..."

All these words were excuses to hide the fact that I was terrified to risk trusting Liam again. Liam saw straight through them.

"If I can't get ahold of you tomorrow, I'll try again the next day. And the day after that. Or, if you want, I could just go back to leaving you alone?"

"No!"

The word slipped off my tongue before I could do anything to stop it.

Settling for a compromise, I acquiesced, "I guess we can try again in the next few days."

After working every day for most of the summer, I was inclined to spend my first day off in weeks lounging around camp with Kaden. But when my friend Hayley called to ask why she hadn't seen me in so long, I found myself accepting her invitation to drive up to the nearby town of Silverton to go on a long hike with her. Even with Evie being gone, I still had quite a few friends in Durango who I'd barely seen all summer. My lack of a future plan turned my impending move-out date into more of an abstract concept than a concrete reality. It took Hayley's phone call to wake me up to the fact that I had less than a month left in Durango, a town that was the closest to a home that I'd found anywhere. I could no longer afford to waste my remaining days there working myself to distraction.

An hour after her call, Hayley and I met up in the parking lot of our local grocery store, where I parked my car and hopped into her truck. Taking in the sight of Hayley's warm brown eyes, her luxuriously messy bob of dark brown hair, and the dimples that appeared in her cheeks whenever she smiled, I relaxed in a way that felt almost foreign to me. We took advantage of the hour-long drive up to Silverton to catch up on all that had happened since we'd last seen each other. When we arrived at our designated trail, it was early enough that the trailhead parking lot was mostly empty. The trail

Hayley chose was a popular local hike up to three lakes carved into a mountain valley at 12,000 feet of elevation. The trail was steep enough that it took us almost two hours to hike the four miles up to the first lake. The lake was above tree line, so we were surrounded on all sides by wide-open vistas of gorgeous high alpine tundra and towering mountain peaks. Taking in big gulps of the crisp mountain air, we soaked in the stunning three-hundred-and-sixty-degree panorama. The clear, open expanse of land imbued my mind with a mental clarity that I hadn't experienced in weeks. The still, blue waters of the lake reflected the clouds gathering in the sky above us—clouds that threatened a thunderstorm within the next hour or so. I couldn't help but feel a little resentful toward these clouds, wishing that we had the luxury of spending all afternoon lost among the awe-inspiring San Juan Mountains.

Before beginning our descent back down the mountain, Hayley worked up the nerve to ask me the question that she'd been biting back all morning long.

"A hell of a lot's changed in the past few weeks, and things with Liam have been ... rocky. Are you still leaving town in a month?"

I stared out past Hayley at the crystal blue lake in front of us, envying the stillness of its waters.

"I have no idea where I'm going or what I'll be doing, but yes, I'm still leaving. I want to experience city life for awhile, or at least live some place less isolated. That's not to say that I won't end up back in Durango eventually. I love this place. But right now, staying here would mean staying in my comfort zone."

Hayley nodded.

"I get that. As much as I'll miss you, you're brave to go."

I snorted, "Brave or crazy?"

I switched the conversation away from me before Hayley had the chance to answer.

"What about you? Do you know what you want to do between rafting and ski season this year?"

"I wouldn't mind lying on a beach somewhere for a few weeks. But I haven't gotten far enough past my ocean waves and palm trees fantasy to actually plan anything."

"I'm digging this ocean wave and palm tree fantasy! I could use some time to slow down again," I chuckled. "What if we planned a beach getaway together this fall?"

Hayley's big brown eyes widened in excitement.

"Are you kidding? I'd love that! Even just a quick trip down to Mexico sounds rad. Anything to hang out more with you, dude."

Hayley and I would have been content spending the next few hours scheming if it weren't for the increasing number of raindrops splashing onto our bare skin. In our excitement, we practically floated our way back down the mountain. We barely got to Hayley's truck in time to beat the thunderstorm crackling over our heads. The rain was coming down thick, so we paused our conversation for Hayley to concentrate on getting us safely down the winding mountain road. I stared at the rain splattering onto Hayley's windshield, marveling at how it blurred the scenery outside her car to make it appear as if we were driving through a watercolor painting of the mountains. Lost in this watercolor daydream, my mind became as hazy as the world around us. As we re-entered civilization and cell phone service range, my buzzing phone woke me from my daydream. When I saw that it was the same international number calling me as before, I hastened to pick up the call.

"Liam, is that you?"

"Sure is, babe. You free to talk?"

"Yeah, Hayley and I finished our hike early because of the rain, so you called at the perfect time. How are you? Where are you today?"

Liam told me the name of some small town in Spain that I immediately forgot in my elation at hearing his voice. To give us some privacy, Hayley pulled over to wait for me at Silverton's one and only coffee shop. Just as I was about to launch into my next series of questions, Liam stopped me mid-interrogation.

"I'm the one who gets to ask the questions this time, remember? For starters, did you finally get a day off?"

Our usual roles reversed, I transitioned quickly from short, self-conscious answers to longer, more detailed ramblings. I'd forgotten how good a listener Liam was—so good that I talked much longer than I intended. It was only after I'd been talking for a good half hour that Liam interjected with a proposition.

"I've been turning an idea around in my head. We talked about this once, but it never got brought up again ..."

Liam let out the breath he was holding as I prepared to hold mine.

"We've got a few more weeks left in Spain to finish out the Camino, and then we'll take a boat south and go to Morocco for a month. Since you finish work at the end of August, would you want to meet up with us in Morocco? Stephen will have left by then, so I don't want you to feel weird traveling with just me and Nate. I asked Nate about it, though, and it's not a problem for him. So depending on how you feel about it ..."

The only word that I managed to choke out was, "Morocco?"

Liam laughed the booming chuckle that I loved.

"Yes, you and me in Morocco. Plus, Nate, I guess. What do you think?"

I barely knew what I was saying when I blurted out, "Can Hayley come?"

Liam agreed without hesitation. "Why not?"

"Oh my God! Are you sure?"

"Sure as I've ever been. I miss you. I want to share at least part of this experience with you. So ... do I take it you want to come?"

By this point in the conversation, I was practically yelling in my excitement.

"Of course I want to come! Hayley and I were just talking about escaping to a beach somewhere this fall. I never could have imagined that I'd be on the same beach as you!"

When Liam spoke again, his voice exuded tenderness.

"I can hear your smile through the phone. I wish I was there to see it in person."

I was smiling so hard that I could hardly get my mouth to move to form words. Pulling myself together, I clarified a few of the rudimentary details concerning dates and meet-up locations for the trip. I decided to save the rest of the conversation for when I was able to think more coherently. Hanging up the phone, I didn't take the time to question this new plan or wonder how rational it was. I didn't take the time to consider what it would be like traveling with Nate after having seen him only a handful of times since our breakup. I didn't take the time to estimate costs or come up with even the most basic plan for what I would do when we got back from Morocco. I didn't take the time to question if I should trust Liam enough to fly overseas for him after not hearing from him for three weeks. While most people consider *carpe diem* a nice idea to aspire to, it was my instinctive way of being.

Bolting out of the car, I ran through the rain to find Hayley reading in the coffee shop. Out of breath, I struggled to get out the only question on my mind, the only unknown factor that still mattered to me.

"Do you want to travel to Morocco with me to meet up with Liam and Nate?"

Glancing up at my wet hair, sparkling eyes, and face-splitting smile, Hayley didn't take the time to think this all over either.

"There's good surfing in Morocco, right? Either way, fuck yeah. Count me in."

We bought our plane tickets the next day.

chapter three

DESERT DA(Y)ZE: COLORADO PLATEAU – MOAB, UTAH

I GLANCED IN MY REARVIEW MIRROR for one last peek at Durango before I rounded the bend and the town receded out of view for good. I was headed west toward the desert of southern Utah, where I planned on hiding out from the world for a few days to recover from the stress of the past few months. After this, my plan was to drive back east and spend the two remaining weeks visiting friends and family in Denver before my flight to Morocco. My flight to Marrakesh didn't leave until September 17, which felt agonizingly far out in the future. Once I got to Morocco, I would meet up with Liam and Nate and travel with them for two weeks before Hayley came to join us for the last ten days of our trip. Per Hayley's request, we would devote these last ten days to surfing in southern Morocco. Before flying back to Denver, Hayley and I would then spend five days together exploring Paris, my favorite city in the world. After working the entire summer to save up for a still unknown future, I finally felt that all my hard work had purpose. I didn't stop to consider what I would do when I got back from my adventures and had turned all my savings into spendings. All that I could think about was seeing Liam again.

That afternoon, I experienced a rare moment in which my looming departure date occupied little space in my mind. I was consumed instead with the task of processing the fact that I'd just said goodbye to the town I'd called home for the past two years. As I drove away, I was surprised at the sense of elation I felt in place of the sadness that I was expecting. My eyes ate up the glorious sight of the long, open road in front of me, a sight I instinctively equated with freedom. As I crossed the border between Colorado and Utah, the scene outside my car window transformed from my familiar Rocky Mountain landscape into the almost extraterrestrial terrain of southern Utah's desert. My heart soared to be reunited with the impressive sandstone rock formations, the rich red soil, and the unfurling blue sky of my most beloved outdoor wonderland. Out of everywhere I'd been in the world, southern Utah had claimed my heart. Nowhere else did I feel the same effortless bliss. Nowhere else did I feel as alive.

Turning off the main highway toward Canyonlands National Park, I drove several miles down a bumpy dirt road that took me over a series of steep hills and through a gate that I stopped to open. I headed deep into the high desert of the Colorado Plateau toward one of my favorite campsites. I had Nate to thank for showing me how to get to this remote campsite, as he was the first person to take me there. However, when I arrived at the spot Nate showed me, I was greeted by the angry buzz of ravenous flies picking away at a rotting cow carcass strewn across the center of the trail. The stench of decay overpowered me, even as I covered my mouth and nose with my hands. The vacant sockets of the dead cow glared up at me as if in warning.

Skin prickling, I took this carcass as an omen and retreated back to the safety of my car. After putting a few miles between me and the dead cow, I stopped high up on a hill at a place where I had never camped before. My position at the top of the canyon provided me with an even better view of the desert wash below me. More than satisfied with my new campsite, I got to work setting up camp. I pitched my tent, found a flat spot for my stove, and set out my camping chair to face west, the direction of the setting sun. In a few minutes, I'd built myself a new, temporary home. This left me wondering what the hell to do with my remaining hours of sunlight. I cracked open my book, but I couldn't quiet my mind enough to focus on the words in front of me. I didn't know whether the sight of the dead cow had unsettled me or if I was restless because I had become unaccustomed to this amount of free time. The heaviness of my newfound aloneness slammed its full weight down onto my chest, and I struggled to take in a full breath.

I came to the desert running away from one life and toward another, but I found myself stuck in the space in between. This space was filled with questions that I couldn't answer. Left unattended, these festering questions morphed into nagging doubts. *What am I doing here?* Even harder to answer, *what am I doing with my life?* I knew less about my future than ever before. I had just turned twenty-four and was coming up on my second year out of college, but I had no career path or life direction that I was headed toward. Nor did I particularly want a career—at least not the traditional nine-to-five. That being said, I missed having a sense of direction. I'd just quit both my jobs and moved away from the place I called home, which made me homeless and jobless. I would have felt totally lost and completely uprooted if it weren't for the person for whom I chose to uproot myself. This person was halfway across the world, which was why my only solid plan at the moment was to fly across the ocean separating us and meet him in Morocco.

By the time Liam and I were reunited, we would have been apart from each other for two months—the same amount of time we had dated before he left. So much happened to both of us in the span of those two months that I couldn't be sure that the Liam with whom I was reuniting was the same Liam I fell in love with at the beginning of the summer. Taking a risk this big, there was so much that could go wrong. When I allowed myself to consider all the possibilities, fear rose up in me like a multi-headed serpent. In an attempt to escape these nagging fears hissing in the back of my mind, I stood up in haste from my camp chair. Having nothing better to do, I started walking.

Picking a direction at random, I loped down the hill I was camped on and headed toward the long desert wash that extended for miles across the valley. When I reached the mouth of the ravine, I picked my way over large piles of fallen boulders and carefully lowered myself down into the wash. Once in the wash, I became so absorbed in studying the ancient rock formations and bizarre plant life around me that I lost all sense of time. The steady rhythm of my feet against the sand lulled me into a sort of trance. All the same anxious thoughts continued firing off in my mind, but the pressure to pay attention to these thoughts lessened. The longer I walked, the less distinct each individual thought became. The underlying pattern connecting these thoughts became apparent. I caught my mind recycling through the same set of thoughts. My mind dressed up these thoughts in different guises, playing all its tricks on me to see which expression of a thought would succeed in recapturing my attention.

The world outside my mind was so much more riveting that I effortlessly jumped over all the snares that my mind set for me. Surrounded by so much life and beauty, I no longer felt trapped in my aloneness. What I found the most beautiful about the Utah desert was not its ancient, imposing rock walls or the delicate plant life that speckled the earth below, but the space between these things. The tremendous amount of open space around me first magnified, but ultimately cured, the pain and anxiety I was feeling. I appreciated the honesty this space forced upon me. In such a stark, austere environment, I had nothing left to hide behind. I had no choice but to face up to whatever feelings I'd been avoiding. Confronted with the desert's boundless emptiness, my sense of loneliness shrank down to the point of irrelevance. My sense of self shrank down to the point of irrelevance. To comprehend one's own smallness may for most people be a terrifying experience, but I found it comforting.

Plodding through the wash, the cadence of my thoughts decelerated to match the even pace of my stride. I realized how long I'd been walking only when I noticed how much lower the sun sat on the horizon. When I stopped to take a drink of water, my aching feet told me it was time to turn around. To pass the time on the trek back to my campsite, I sang quietly to myself, making up my own words whenever I forgot the lyrics to a song. I made it most of the way back to my campsite with the sun still hanging a few inches above the horizon. When I noticed I had about fifteen minutes before the sun set, I scanned my environs and picked out the tallest rock nearby. It took me only a few minutes to clamber up to the top of the rock. As far as my eyes could see, I spotted no other human or car on the horizon. My only companions were the colossal, burnt red rock spires that jutted out of the earth like fingers reaching up toward the sky. The golden haze of the setting sun painted these rocks with an orange hue, melding the earth and sky together and setting the whole world aflame.

Without giving myself time to fully consider what I was about to do, I snuck another peek around me to double-check that the coast was clear. With nothing in sight besides my little green tent on top of the hill, I pulled my shirt over my head. Throwing my shirt to the ground at my feet, I reached back to unclip my bra, giggling with giddiness. I hastily slipped out of my pants and underwear. Before I knew it, I ran out of clothing items to remove. I found myself standing completely naked on top of the tallest rock around. Reveling in my uninhibited nakedness, I imagined looking down on my body as a bird in the sky would. From this perspective, I no longer picked my body apart or judged each of its individual parts. For once, I was able to appreciate my body as a whole, both for its functionality and its beauty.

As soon as the sun dropped below the horizon, the temperature dropped with it. Although I would have been happy to dance around naked on top of my rock tower for much longer, it didn't take long for goose bumps to cover the surface of my skin. Looking forward to the additional layers of clothing waiting for me back at my campsite, I lowered myself down from my perch and scampered back up the hill toward my tent. After cooking an easy dinner of mac and cheese, I cracked open a beer and settled back into my camp chair. The day was a long one, but I'd finally reclaimed enough of a sense of peace to enjoy the stillness at the end of it. Content to do nothing but sit and sip at my beer, I watched as the blue of the night sky deepened to black. However, I wasn't left to sit alone in the dark for long. Bright and almost full, the moon rose steadily on the other horizon, taking the sun's place in the sky.

chapter four

REUNITED

SCANNING THE THRONG OF PEOPLE waiting outside the glass airport doors, my eyes stopped when they found the face they were looking for. In the few seconds I was given before Liam noticed me, I took in all the little ways in which Liam had changed since I last saw him. For starters, he was noticeably tanner. He'd also added a few new freckles to the collection on his face that I'd spent so much time studying. Although Liam had buzzed the hair shorter on the sides of his head, the mane of golden brown on top had grown long enough to fall down over his forehead. As Liam brushed his hair back, our eyes connected across the remaining distance that separated us.

Without breaking eye contact, Liam reached back to grab something from the top of his backpack. He pulled out the leather-bound journal I gave him as a going-away present before he left and opened the notebook to a page in the middle. The words *WELCOME TO MOROCCO, SKYE!* filled two full pages of his notebook. Unable to hold myself back any longer, I ran to embrace him. I had imagined this moment so many times that I giggled at how much more awkward it was in reality. Liam and I tried to hug each other but were blocked by our huge backpacks. Shrugging off our backpacks, we let them fall to the ground with a thud and came together for a real hug. Liam leaned in for a kiss, but I pulled away after a few seconds, unsure about whether kissing in public was acceptable in Morocco.

Laughing as he pulled away, Liam exclaimed, "You're taller than I remembered!"

"You're so much tanner!"

"We've been surfing every day for the past two weeks. I can't wait to show you Taghazout, the surfing town we were staying at. You're gonna love it! But before I get ahead of myself, let's check into our hostel and get rid of these damn backpacks."

Slinging his backpack over one shoulder and mine over the other, Liam strutted forward into the oncoming traffic of the nearby street, holding one arm up high. When a taxi pulled up to the curb, Liam launched into a series of negotiations. I stood to the side, accustomed from my previous travels to doing all the negotiating myself. Although my more passive role in this situation made me slightly uncomfortable, I admired the skill with which Liam talked the taxi driver down from his original price. After a minute of the two men bantering back and forth, Liam opened the taxi door for me to get inside. As we drove through the streets of Marrakech, I took in the palm trees, cream-colored buildings, budding pink flowers, and sand-colored mountain ranges encircling the city. When I left Colorado, winter was just setting in, but the heat in Marrakech made it feel like I'd traveled back in time to the middle of summer.

After driving through the city for a half hour, our taxi driver pulled off in front of a dark alleyway. He motioned to us that this was our stop. Still carrying both of our backpacks, Liam loped off ahead of me. We turned left, then right, then left again before stopping in front of a nondescript metal gate in a remarkably narrow alleyway. Liam pressed a button that I hadn't noticed, and a doorbell rang. The metal gate swung open, and a young Moroccan with dreads and noticeably bloodshot eyes ushered us inside.

"Welcome!" the man crooned in an almost Rastafarian cadence.

The man greeted Liam with a friendly pat on the back and me with a polite nod of the head.

"Good to see you back so soon, man! And you brought your wife with you this time!"

Chuckling at the word wife, Liam raised his eyebrows at me without bothering to correct the man.

"It's good to be back, Aamir," Liam said. "My friend Nate will be joining us tomorrow, too."

Feeling guilty for hardly noticing Nate's absence, I asked, "Speaking of Nate, where is he?"

"He's staying in Taghazout another night to give us a little alone time," Liam smiled.

Rubbing his temples as if this would somehow aid his memory, Aamir ruminated out loud.

"Nate? Hmm ... let me see ... Ah, yes, your friend with the mustache! I remember him now. He smoked all my hash the last time you were here. I have never seen a man who could ..."

Gazing past Liam, Aamir's eyes briefly landed on me before he glanced back down to the ground. Trailing off without finishing this last sentence, Aamir apologized, his apology clearly directed at me.

"Never mind about those things. Let me take both of you to your room. I have good news for you, man! We ran out of beds in the common room, so tonight you and your wife get a room all your own. No extra charge. I promise! It is a very nice room. Come see."

Aamir led us a through the hotel lobby and a few flights up a spiral staircase. For the remainder of our conversation, Aamir never again looked me in the eye. It would take me only a few days in Morocco to get used to the fact that the men never addressed me directly in group conversations. I would come to understand that they meant this as a sign of respect rather than condescension. In contrast to many of the other countries I'd traveled to, I appreciated not being stared at all the time. Plus, the men acknowledged me and responded openly whenever I added something to the conversation. They simply refrained from speaking to me before I spoke to them. Although I could appreciate this cultural norm, I still got irritated whenever Aamir tried to stop me from leaving the hostel alone. Warning me about how the world we live in is a dangerous place, Aamir would stand in the doorway to physically block me from leaving the hostel until enough time went by that I eventually gave up. Over the few days we spent in Marrakech, Liam and I went almost everywhere together anyway, so I didn't have to deal with all this fuss very often.

The private suite Aamir showed us to was much more luxurious than anything we would normally be able to afford. It came with a queen bed, its own bathroom, and a small lounge area with a comfortable couch and a few chairs. After spending over forty-eight hours in transit to get to Liam, my first inclination was to collapse onto the bed and not move for a while. As enticing as the queen bed looked to me, Liam had something else in mind. As soon as we set down our stuff, Liam stood back up again, unable to sit still for long. I practically expected him to start pacing back and forth, but he contained this impulse and merely hovered in place over the bed. Although he was standing upright, I could feel him energetically leaning toward the door.

"How about I show you the main square? There's a nice café that overlooks the square where we can sit for a cup of tea."

At the time, I didn't think much of the noticeable uneasiness hiding behind Liam's outward enthusiasm to show me the city. If I hadn't been so tired from the long journey, I would have been uneasy myself. Hoping this excursion would help calm Liam's nerves and bring us back to a sense of togetherness, I gave the bed one last look of longing before following him out of the room and locking the door behind us. Taking me by the hand, Liam led me through a succession of narrow, twisting alleyways. After taking enough turns for me to completely lose my sense of direction, we emerged in a pedestrian passageway crowded with small shops and hordes of tourists. However, the maze didn't end there. It didn't appear to end anywhere. Liam marched forward, leading me past candy stores, leather stores, lamp stores, metal-work stores, hookah stores, rug stores, jewelry stores, wedding gown stores, shoe stores ... so many different types of stores that they all started to look the same. There was so much to buy within even a small section of this marketplace that I lost the desire to buy anything at all. Squeezing my hand tight to make sure he didn't lose me, Liam waved his free hand at the chaos all around us.

"This is the medina," Liam informed me. "It's an ancient marketplace protected on all sides by thick mud walls. Nowadays, the medina is mostly just a big tourist trap, but something about it still feels like stepping into a different world. What do you think?"

Glancing around me, I couldn't tell if we had already passed this particular scarf store on our right or if we'd just passed twenty other scarf stores that looked exactly the same. I had no idea how far we'd ventured from our hostel. Although some light slipped in through the medina's slatted roof, I couldn't see enough of the sky to tell what time of day it was.

"I think that I've never felt this lost in my life! Do you know where we are?"

"I may not know where we are, but I know where we're going," Liam reassured me.

I shot Liam a skeptical look.

Smirking a little, Liam continued, "Don't worry. This may feel like a huge maze, but all these passageways feed into one big square at the center of the medina. That's where we're headed."

Relieved to know we weren't just walking around in circles, I relaxed enough to find the chaos thrilling. No longer caring if we got lost, I trailed behind Liam at an easy pace. Every once in a while, I made Liam stop to admire a particularly unique stall among the multitude. I almost forgot where we were going until we emerged in plain daylight in the center of Jemaa el-Fnaa, the bustling medina square. We walked into the section of the square that was crowded with open-air restaurants, food stalls, and juice shacks. In front of every food stall, one or two men stood waiting to pounce on any tourist who walked by. Most of the stalls offered the same general fare: couscous, kebabs, tajines, various types of soups and stews ...

Too overwhelmed to contemplate eating, we pushed past the stalls and the men promoting them and continued on toward the more open section of the square. This part of the medina felt like a large outdoor theater. There were musicians playing instruments that I'd never seen before, henna artists grabbing me by the hand and attempting to pull me toward their stalls, magicians, snake charmers, and acrobats twisting their bodies in unthinkable ways. When we almost walked into a long, narrow patch of Astroturf that was set up in the center of the square as a mini golf course, I had to laugh. Undeterred by even the wildest of spectacles, Liam plowed through the madness, pointing up to a rooftop at the other end of the square.

Sensing my hesitancy to leave the square so soon, Liam promised me, "Don't worry. We'll come back through here again. You'll have plenty of opportunities to take it all in."

"You don't feel like playing a game of mini golf?" I joked.

"Whatever you want, babe."

Slowing down, Liam made a show of pulling me back toward the narrow strip of Astroturf. I laughed, pulling him back in the opposite direction.

"That rooftop café isn't sounding so bad anymore," I conceded.

I happily followed Liam into the restaurant he chose, away from all the noise. Almost all the tables and chairs on the bottom three floors were empty. This made more sense when we arrived on the fourth floor and had to scan the entire room to find an open table. Everyone in the restaurant was there for the same reason—to enjoy the good view and a little peace and quiet. Once we were seated, Liam ordered us a large pot of mint tea without bothering to look at any of the other items on the menu. Our waiter poured us the first of many cups to come, and Liam visibly relaxed in his chair. I was so preoccupied with drinking in the sight of Liam, golden and smiling and sitting right next to me, that I had to remind myself to keep sipping my tea.

"We made it back to the same place again ... I can hardly believe it."

Echoing my sentiment, Liam declared, "I missed you. We met so many cool people here and along the Camino. But let me tell you, babe, nobody came anywhere close to being as cool as you. Whenever I did meet someone amazing, I just wished you were there to meet them. Now you are."

Unsure how to respond, the easiest thing to do was simply dismiss Liam's compliment. However, I couldn't so easily dismiss the flush of red that spread across my cheeks.

"Why don't you tell me more about some of these amazing people you met?"

"I told you about our *familia*, the group we hiked with on the Camino, right? Did I tell you about Ruolan, the Chinese girl who hiked with us? What about Kuan-yu from Taiwan? We didn't realize until the end of the Camino that Kuan-yu barely spoke a word of English and probably didn't understand what we were saying half the time ..."

I leaned in to hear the rest of Liam's story, as if physical proximity could somehow transport me back to the time and place he was describing. Taking in as many details as I could, I couldn't help but notice the way Liam's voice caught every time he mentioned the name Claudia. I learned that Claudia was one of the women they'd traveled with, another twenty-something-year-old from Italy. As if he could read my mind, Liam paused the next time Claudia's name came up.

"Claudia is someone I've been meaning to talk to you about," Liam confessed, eyes downcast. "I just haven't known how."

Fear snaked its way back into my consciousness. The same doubts that consumed me before leaving for this trip flooded my mind all over again. As I drowned in my pool of liquid anxiety, Liam found within himself the courage he needed to continue.

"Being honest with you matters to me. That's why I'm bringing this up. So bear with me on this. I think you'll feel better once I've had the chance to explain everything."

Steeling myself for whatever was to come, I clutched the teacup in front of me, hoping to absorb some reassurance from its warmth.

Taking my silence as a cue to begin, Liam explained, "I've been planning this hike along the Camino de Santiago for years. Way back when I first started planning this trip, Darian gave me all this advice about the Camino. He told me about this concept of a *way girl*, which is basically a woman you meet while walking on the trail—someone you share your experience with on the Camino. Chances are that this woman lives on the other side of the world, so all you have is this moment in time together. That's what's so beautiful about it, at least according to Darian. Darian talked to me so much about his experiences with his own way girl that, whenever I pictured what hiking the Camino would be like, I always imagined I would meet someone along the way."

This first part of Liam's explanation hit me like a punch in the stomach, although this certainly explained some things. When I first brought up the question of what would happen to our relationship after we'd both left Durango, Liam closed down. He talked about practicalities and what was realistic for us and how hard it would be for us to find a way to see each other again. Not only had he been planning this trip for years, but Liam had also planned in detail what he wanted to do for the year following this trip. Now I knew that Liam had purposefully left space in his plan to meet someone else besides me.

Not giving me the time to mull this over, Liam carried on. "A few days into the Camino, we met the people I now call our familia—the group we hiked with the rest of the way. One of those people was Claudia. Claudia and I hit it off right away. We walked and talked for hours together. She's Italian and super Catholic, which made her very sweet and pretty naïve. A significant part of our conversations involved her asking me a lot of questions. Eventually, Claudia started asking me questions about love and my past relationships ... not that I didn't see this coming. By that point, I knew Claudia liked me. Some of the time that we walked together, we would hold hands. And yes, I kissed her. But we never slept together."

Most of this conversation, Liam's eyes roved around the room, staring at the tea set in front of us or drifting down toward his lap—anywhere to avoid looking at me directly. Perhaps involuntarily, Liam glanced up then, searching my face for the reaction I refused to give him. He held my gaze for long enough that I was the one to look away. I was afraid my heartache would betray itself if I looked at him an instant longer.

When he continued speaking, I could tell by Liam's tone of voice that I'd looked away too late. He spoke less defensively and more softly now. His voice held me the way one would hold a fragile, injured bird, enveloping me with its warmth but not daring to squeeze too hard.

"When Claudia started asking me all these questions, you came up. I talked a lot about our time together. After everything I said about you, Claudia asked me why I hadn't committed to being with you during the time I was away. I had no answer. In all my time talking with Claudia, I'd started to ask myself the same thing. No matter how hard I tried to be present, my thoughts kept circling back to you. Even if I managed to shut you out of my head during the day, I would dream about you at night. By the time Claudia and I had this conversation, I'd dreamt about you every night for a week straight. That's when I called."

Speaking even more softly than before, Liam said, "The day after Claudia and I had this conversation, I told Claudia that we needed to just be friends. I felt like I'd betrayed you and led her on. Starting the next morning, I asked Nate and Stephen if we could walk separately from Claudia and her friends. They were so bummed that I knew this wasn't the right thing to do either. I didn't want to make my problem everyone else's problem, so we ended up walking together the rest of the way. At first, Claudia and I just ignored each other and walked separately. Eventually, we were able to spend time together in a more casual, detached way. Since all this happened, I haven't been with, or wanted to be with, anyone else."

Liam paused as if about to say something else. Thinking better of this, he fell silent again. I took Liam's pause as a chance to compose myself and try to understand my own feelings. Looking within, I found myself torn between the bitter wish that Liam had never told me any of this and a reluctant appreciation for the fact that Liam's story was nowhere nearly as terrible as some of the things I'd imagined. On one level, I was grateful to have heard the whole story from Liam himself so that, had it all come out later, I wouldn't have to wonder about it and question my trust in him. While my rational mind could appreciate Liam's honesty, the tired, cranky side of me simmered in an exasperation that I reluctantly recognized as anger. I was angry at Liam for bringing all this messiness into our first moments of being back together. I was angry at him for tainting this precious time. In an attempt to restore balance within myself, I took another sip of my tea, followed by a long exhale.

"I need some time to process this. I think we both made a lot of assumptions about what would happen in the time we were apart. One of mine was that, if either of us did meet someone else, we wouldn't tell each other. It's not something I wanted to know about. But now I know, and I think you were probably right to tell me. With the intention of full disclosure, I should tell you that I have also kissed, but not slept with, someone else."

My memory transported me back to the end-of-summer party at our rafting company's boatyard. After a lot of drunken philosophizing and reminiscing about past river trips together, I let one of our head rafting guides, Trey, kiss me. This wasn't the first time Trey had tried to kiss me, but it was the only time I let him. The kiss was nice, thrilling even, but it meant nothing to me. Despite Trey's insistences, I left the party afterward. When we saw each other in the boatyard after that, both of us pretended nothing had happened. To me, it felt like nothing did. I was pulled out of this memory and back to the present when Liam withdrew his hand from mine. Brushing his hair out of his eyes, Liam cursed under his breath.

"Fuck."

"It didn't mean anything to me," I said truthfully. "I never would have brought it up if we weren't having this conversation. I was drunk at a party. That's all I have to say about it."

With visible effort, Liam conceded, "I should have expected as much since we hadn't committed to being in a long-distance relationship with each other."

Rubbing my eyes as if I could rub my tiredness away, I was again filled with an overwhelming longing for the comfort of our hostel's queen bed. Sensing my exhaustion, Liam paid for our tea and led the way back to our hostel. I felt so dazed by the events of the day that I could hardly take in my new surroundings. The long trudge back through the crowded square and winding streets of the medina turned into one long blur of indistinguishable colors, smells, and sounds. When Aamir ushered us back inside the hostel door, I was about ready to collapse on him in gratitude. Once we reached our room, it was all I could do to brush my teeth and throw my clothes in a heap on the floor.

Despite my exhaustion and general misgivings, Liam and I somehow still scraped up enough energy to make love this first night. Our bodies came together in a way that was so inevitable as to feel almost involuntary. While we were having sex, I did my best, and failed, not to think of Claudia. I could only hope that Liam wasn't thinking about her, too. Despite the conflicting emotions I felt while we were making love, I found serenity in the silence we shared afterward. Liam and I lay facing each other, arms wrapped around each other, leaving as little space as possible between our bodies. As I had before, and would again many times, I reminded myself that this moment and the miracle of us being together were the only things that mattered to me.

The rooftop terrace I stood on was just as I dreamed it would be. Mountains circled all sides of the city, but they were so far in the distance as to appear almost ghostlike. The other rooftop terraces I looked down on were covered in pink and white flowers and green vines. Most of the buildings were painted some variation of the color of sand. The sun hung low on the horizon and emitted a soft, yellow light that bathed everything it touched in a silky hue. It painted my insides a little softer, too. My eyes opened wide like those of a child as I marveled at the wonder of this calm, quiet world that existed on the rooftops above Marrakech's busy streets. As tranquil as this rooftop patio was, fear and hope mixed in my blood with every heartbeat. Even as I told myself that it wasn't too late, that I could still walk away and emerge from this unscathed, the desert wind blew down my self-constructed walls. My house of cards collapsed.

My heart reached out a hand in the direction of the evening sun as if to ask the question, "Is it safe for me to blossom here?"

I'd felt many things since my arrival in Marrakech, but safe was not among these feelings. Although I'd flown halfway across the world to be with Liam again, I still felt an ocean of distance between us. Treading water, it was all I could do to keep my head above the rising sea level of my own anxiety.

Every once in a while, Liam and I would share a glance or a touch, a moment of clandestine intimacy, and I would imagine his head popping out on the crest of a wave beside me. The next moment, Nate would walk up on us holding each other, or Liam would look away, and another wave of loneliness would come crashing down.

Nate came to join us the day after my flight landed. We'd been so busy exploring Marrakech that I scarcely had a moment to myself since then. Without any alone time to process and unpack my own emotions, I couldn't even be sure if the isolation I felt was real or self-imposed. This time alone up on our hostel's rooftop felt precious in the way that only stolen goods do. The only reason I managed to sneak away was because I had nowhere near as much tolerance for smoking hashish as Liam or Nate did. Sitting around the dining table in the lobby with Aamir and our new Australian friend, Red, I excused myself when Liam started to roll yet another joint. Since Nate joined us, I noticed Liam used hash as a social lubricant to ease the tension between all of us. Hanging out with Red helped with this, too. Any time that Liam, Nate, and I ended up alone, Nate picked apart everything Liam said. Eventually, Liam just went quiet. Then it became my job to keep a conversation going with Nate to avoid falling into long, awkward silences. When Liam offered to roll another joint and it went around the circle a few times, conversation played out much smoother between us.

A small, gray head poked out from the bed of pink flowers on the other end of our hostel rooftop, distracting me from these thoughts. After the head surfaced, out popped a furry white paw that batted at a bee buzzing around in the air above it. Eventually, the entire cat emerged. Bored with this particular insect-tormenting session, the hostel cat slunk away toward its subsequent diversion. My gaze rose above the bougainvillea bush from which the cat emerged, landing upon a woman on the rooftop across from me. I watched mesmerized as she retied her hijab, twisting her silk, lilac-colored scarf so it fell in careful folds around her head. For once, I envied her this form of protection. I had nothing there to cover myself with besides sunglasses and a smile. Even then, I knew my time hiding up on the rooftop was almost up. The sun had set, which meant it was time to head to the main square for dinner at one of the street stalls. Savoring one more stolen moment, I watched as the color in the sky faded from gold to pink to purple.

By the time the purple in the sky faded, I found myself missing Liam. It was without regret that I headed back downstairs. Passing by the door to the luxurious queen suite, I reluctantly trudged onward until I arrived at our cluster of bunks in the common room that Aamir demoted us to after the first night. Liam's bunk was directly below mine, and Nate's was across from us. Sleeping in a separate bed from Liam while knowing I was close enough to reach out and touch him was its own form of torture. On top of sleeping in separate beds, Liam and I hadn't had the chance to speak privately since our first conversation over mint tea when Liam had told me about Claudia. While I hadn't been able to stop myself from thinking about Claudia, the idea of her became less threatening to me in the few days that Liam and I spent together. Although this was only my third day in Marrakech, every day there felt like a lifetime. Every night, I was sentenced to my own form of purgatory. Thankfully, after this night, we had the Sahara to look forward to. The next morning, we left Marrakech and the new friends we'd made there. At long last, we were making our way out toward the desert.

chapter five

DESERT DA(Y)ZE: SAHARA DESERT – MERZOUGA, MOROCCO

THE NIGHT WAS STILL BLACK and the morning air bitterly cold when I heard the first sounds of the Berber guides rustling around outside our tents. They shouted unintelligible words at each other and clamored noisily about camp, waking up their foreign guests with the same brusque efficiency with which they outfitted the camels for the morning's journey. The race against the rising of the morning sun had begun. When all was in place for the company to vacate camp, the head guide lingered a moment longer than usual, unable to shake the feeling that he was forgetting something. And he *was* forgetting something: three things, or to be precise, three people. This negligence was not accidental or careless. It was demanded of him and paid for with coveted American dollars. Nonetheless, he couldn't resist making one last stop outside our tent. He poked his head inside and stared at our unmoving figures.

"We leave now. You come with us?"

Liam rolled over, away from me, and sleepily began to mumble his way through another explanation of how we'd already paid to spend an extra day out in the desert. The guide shrugged his shoulders and turned to leave. Nonetheless, he couldn't resist muttering one last word under his breath before he left.

"Americans!"

This wasn't the first time we'd heard this word used against us as a curse in Morocco, so it was all too easy to pay the guide no mind. In a few minutes, Liam and I fell back asleep. Nate continued to snore a few feet away from us, never having woken up in the first place. Thick camel-wool blankets shrouded us from the cold, and Liam and I cuddled a little closer together for warmth. None of us were inclined to move until many hours after the first light of dawn spread its golden tentacles across the sky. When we woke up, the camp was eerily quiet. The night before, the camp was bursting with the barely contained exuberance of more than twenty Nigerians. The Nigerians came out to the desert with a single purpose, as evidenced by the fact that they brought almost no water with them but multiple coolers full of booze. They also brought their own speakers, out of which they blared a raucous set of West African dance songs all night long. Our guides built us a large fire but mostly stayed out of the way after that, content to hang back in the shadows and survey the large dance circle taking place around the fire. The dancing went on until at least two in the morning, so I could only imagine how challenging it was for our guides to rouse the whole troop before sunrise.

Grateful for the extra hours of sleep, I soaked in the pristine tranquility of a fresh new morning. As the first of our little group of three to wake up, I grabbed my journal and headed over to the main dining tent. Upon noticing me, Yasin, the youngest of the Berber guides and the one who was elected to stay behind and guard the camp, jumped to his feet and loped off to the kitchen tent. When he came back, Yasin bore a tray loaded up with a pot of mint tea, a basket of stale bread, and a sticky jar of honey. This was breakfast, the only food we would have access to until the rest of the Berber guides returned for dinner with a new set of tourists coming to stay the night. Mostly just licking off the honey, I nibbled at the bread and waited for the tea to cool down. Although it couldn't be past eight in the morning, the heat of the morning sun had already begun to beat down on us. The second one to wake up, Liam made his way toward the dining tent and sat down beside me. Nate wasn't far behind him, still groggy but smiling at the sight of tea.

"Good morning," I greeted them both.

In turn, they each wished me good morning. Settling into silence, we sipped our cups of tea and forced ourselves to swallow as much of the stale bread as we could stomach. As I drank the tea, I made a mental count of the number of water bottles we had left between the three of us. I felt a surge of gratitude toward our Berber guide for sharing his water with us to make tea, as I could only hope we had enough water to last us through the next day.

Liam interrupted my calculations to ask, "What should we do today?"

Again, silence reigned. My gaze drifted away with my focus, and I found myself staring up at the mountain of sand closest to us. My eyes traveled from its base to the highest peak I could see. My feet itched to cover this same distance.

Pointing up at this sand dune, I suggested, "Climbing to the top of that sand dune sounds fun."

Since no one could come up with a better idea, we thanked Yasin for breakfast and headed back to our tent to prepare for the upcoming trek. I'd brought only my large backpack, packed to the brim with clothing, shoes, and books, so I transformed the scarf I had been using to hide my hair into a sash in which to store my water. Gleefully, I stripped down to shorts, a sports bra, and my most lightweight T-shirt. Since getting to Morocco, I'd worn long sleeves and pants to hide my skin out of respect, so my relative lack of clothing felt scandalous. I debated for a while over my sandals and ultimately decided not to wear them, as they'd given me a few new blisters already. I figured we wouldn't be gone too long. Nate threw his water bottle into Liam's daypack and tied an old T-shirt around his head for protection from the sun and sand. Liam was the only one of us who brought a real pack, inside which he stashed two water bottles, sunglasses, and a pair of flip-flops. As we were getting ready to leave, Liam went back to the tent one more time and slipped on a pair of socks.

When we told Yasin we were leaving to go for a walk, he gestured up to the sun to remind us of the fact that it was still rising.

"We'll be back soon," Liam reassured both Yasin and himself.

In my impatience to get moving, I started walking before Liam had time to finish his sentence. I drew an imaginary line straight up to the peak of the dune. This line was the path I took. Nate zigzagged his way up behind me while Liam hiked up along the dune's ridge. Despite Liam and Nate having chosen far more efficient paths, I floated up the dune on a high that allowed me to forget the burning of the muscles in my legs. Out of breath, I reached the highest point I could see, only to discover that this first peak was a false summit behind which the true summit of the dune was concealed. Allowing myself no time to rest, I pushed forward. All that existed was me and the tip of that sand dune, a diamond-shaped ridge whose edges the wind had smoothed over with time. When I made it to the peak of the diamond, I collapsed onto the sand, hovering above my own body on the wings of my adrenaline. The beauty of this place was so surreal that I wondered if I'd traveled to a different planet. The wind whipped up millions of minute sand particles that hung midair and colored the sky a grayish-yellow. Gleaming the same golden yellow, the sun, air, and sand melted into one another. Only the rise and fall of the dunes distinguished earth from heaven.

By the time Nate and Liam made their way to the summit, we were all sweating profusely and out of breath.

"This place is fucking crazy," Nate exclaimed, voicing the thought on all our minds.

"You know what's really crazy?" Liam interjected. "I was talking to the head camel guide yesterday, and he said if we got up high enough and looked east, we'd be able to see Algeria from here."

We squinted in the direction of the rising sun. I tried to imagine the sand dunes in front of me expanding out to cover most of Algeria, Tunisia, Libya, and Egypt, stopping only when they met the Red Sea, almost three thousand miles from where we sat. We were on the edge of a desert that spanned an area almost as large as the country we came from.

His brow furrowing, Liam continued, "The guide warned me that the whole border is littered with land mines, so let's steer clear of anything east of us. What do you guys think? Should we head back to camp?"

Not yet ready to call it a day, I turned my back to the sun to study the dunes to the west of us. Although everything looked the same at first glance, two features of the landscape caught my eye upon closer scrutiny. Directly to the northwest of us was another sand dune that rose noticeably higher than all those around it, the peak of all peaks to conquer. As alluring as this peak was, I focused my gaze back on our more immediate surroundings, narrowing my eyes on a green patch on the other side of the dune we just climbed.

Pointing down at the small fleck of green decorating the sea of yellow, I asked, "Do you think that could be an oasis? And if so, do you wanna go check it out? Or if you guys have enough energy, that giant sand dune to the north of us looks cool to climb. Either way, I'm down to keep walking."

"I'm down to check out the oasis, or whatever it is. Then we can reassess from there," Nate offered.

Squinting at the sun, then back in the direction of the

green patch, as if trying to make up his mind, Liam finally agreed, "There's no point sitting around camp all day. But let's get moving before it gets too much hotter."

Liam stood up to remove his shirt and tie it around his head like Nate had. I stripped off my T-shirt and stuffed it into my scarf sash, feeling practically naked in just shorts and sports bra. We passed around one of the water bottles, each taking a long swig. Once we were all set to go, I set off running down the ridge of the sand dune, letting gravity have its way with me. I sailed up and over hills of sand, sliding on the downhill sections to give my stinging calves a break. When I reached a hill that gave me a better view of the green patch, I paused to catch my breath. While I was hoping for palm trees and shade, I saw from closer up that most of the greenery consisted of tall grasses, stout shrubs, and prickly-looking bushes. This oasis was no refuge. It appeared as unfriendly toward humans as the rest of the desert.

By the time we reached the outskirts of the green patch, the sun was almost halfway up the sky. Every direction I turned, I was blinded by its brightness. I pictured us as actors on a stage, trying to peer out beyond the unforgiving stage lights at the audience watching us, but seeing only white. However, our stage spanned almost four million square miles, and, as far as I knew, no one was watching us.

Watching my step, I ventured into the tall grasses, running

my fingers along their tips. I made a game of counting how many different types of plants I ran into. Along with the grass, I counted six different types of plants, including various forms of cacti and a few different types of shrubs. Almost every plant came with a built-in self-defense system in the form of thorns or spines. The plant life in our make-believe oasis was so uninviting that Liam and Nate hung around the outside of the green patch, ducking behind taller mounds of grass in pursuit of small slivers of shade. Having grown accustomed to the desert's omnipresent silence, all three of us jumped in unison at the sound of a car motor cutting through the quiet. Lurching their way across a sand dune, we glimpsed two Jeep 4x4s in the distance. Hidden among the tall grasses, we stood unnoticed as the Jeeps and their passengers careened past us, the hum of their engines fading into a memory that we may as well have imagined. With the return of silence, I breathed a little deeper.

The cost of our seclusion was feeling trapped in an overheated oven. I waded through the desert grass to reconvene with Nate and Liam and decide on our next move. Liam greeted me with an outstretched hand, holding out the second of his water bottles to offer me the last few gulps. As far as I knew, the water bottle in my sash, a little over half full, was the last of the water we brought along for the hike. Although reason would tell us to head back to camp, the oasis we hiked so long to reach was unsatisfying enough that ending our adventure there felt anticlimactic. I cast my vote before doubt could change my mind.

"I don't know about you guys, but I still want to climb to the top of that big sand dune. Now that we're all the way over here, the peak looks so much closer."

Nate and Liam's eyes moved to size up the distance to the peak. Our little green patch was situated right at its southern base, so we could clearly see the peak from where we stood. Nate processed his thoughts on the matter out loud.

"On one hand, this is probably the hottest that I've ever been. On the other hand, it's not like we have anything better to do today."

Liam caved.

"You know what, why the fuck not?"

We made it about a third of the way up the dune before we ran into trouble. All morning long, the desert sand had been baking under the growing heat of the sun. Liam's socks offered his feet some protection, but my feet and Nate's were starting to suffer. We learned to hike along the back side of the dune's ridge, as the temperature of the sand was bearable on the side of the ridge not facing the sun. Since he didn't have to be as careful where he stepped, Liam took the lead. Neither Nate nor I complained, but we both knew it would make the most sense to turn around before the sand got any hotter. We were just beginning to appreciate how unprepared we were for this journey, how much we'd underestimated the desert we'd set out to explore. Realizing that we had been careless did not keep us from engaging in further carelessness. We were so close to reaching the highest point of the highest dune around that we couldn't bring ourselves to relinquish the peak's conquest. We were intoxicated on a strange cocktail of heat, dehydration, and adrenaline, too weak to resist the rush of the risk we were taking.

Despite being the one loping up and over sand dunes all morning, I was the last to arrive at the dune's summit. I dug out a cooler patch of sand below the baked layer on the surface and fell back, not caring if sand got in my hair or covered my body. Oddly enough, the sand already covering my skin served as a surprisingly effective layer of sunscreen. Liam and Nate stretched out next to me, and Liam reached over to take my hand in his. We'd sacrificed precious sweat for this view, and this loss of water left us so depleted that all we wanted to do was lie down and look up at the sky. For the first time today, a fairly large patch of blue sky was visible through the sand haze. I drank in this blue, relishing the turquoise for being different than the desert's all-pervading yellow. With all of us lying together like this, Liam laughed, not at anyone in particular, but at the absurdity of the situation in which we'd landed ourselves. His laugh took responsibility for his own recklessness. His laugh was the sound of release. Its boldness was imbued with the magical power of reassurance, removing us from the immediacy of our predicament.

"This whole time we've been walking, I was imagining that we were marooned on a deserted island," Liam said.

"If you look at it from the perspective of the ocean, every land mass on this planet is an island," Nate responded.

Liam placated Nate through acquiescence.

"You're right. What I'm trying to say is that, if I had to be marooned on a deserted island, I'd want it to be with you two. I love you guys."

Nate softened, "Love you too, man."

With less than a second to make up my mind, I was left wondering what on earth to reply. My relationship with Liam was new enough that we hadn't yet spoken these three words directly to each other. I wasn't ready yet, and certainly not in this context.

I stammered, "I ... love you guys, too."

Relieved that the moment was over, I sat up with a new nervous energy. Staring out at the endless miles of sand all around us, I was reminded of how far we had to go before we made it back to camp. Once we descended from our current dune, there was still a large sand dune separating us from our tents—the same sand dune we climbed earlier that morning. From where we were, circling around that dune looked a lot less grueling than trying to climb back up and over it.

"Speaking of being marooned, I'm a little nervous for what happens when we try to leave our current patch of sand. We should probably head back to camp," I said.

Liam dug into his backpack and pulled out his pair of flip-flops.

"One of you should seriously put on these flip-flops. I'm doing OK with just socks on."

Nate's hand flinched in the direction of the sandals. While the bottoms of my feet burned a little, Nate's looked swollen and almost purple.

"It's OK, Nate," I said. "You should totally wear them. I'm doing OK for now."

Nate opened his mouth to protest, but I waved him off. After Nate slipped the sandals onto his grateful feet, we each allowed ourselves another gulp of water from our dwindling supply and set off on our way. Although I could never explain this to Nate or Liam, the truth was that I didn't want to wear the sandals unless I had to. Feeling the raw power of the desert sun under my feet made me feel more connected to this power, more in tune with the desert somehow. I learned to move slower, to dig my feet in deeper to touch the cooler sand beneath the surface. When I couldn't find a cooler patch of sand or take the burning any longer, I fell to my knees. As absurd as this appeared, this method was remarkably efficient in providing my feet with enough of a break to continue moving.

By the time I made it to the bottom of the dune, my eyes were so focused on the ground beneath my feet that I almost walked right into Nate and Liam crouched in a darker patch of sand. It took me a moment to realize that this darker patch of sand was shade. The source of the shade was an abandoned, collapsed white tent. Smiling in disbelief, I settled down to join Liam and Nate in the shade.

"What a fucking miracle, huh?" Nate remarked. "Just don't look inside the tent. There's a bunch of broken vases and trash and stuff in there. I don't know why, but it kind of creeps me out."

Unwilling to invest the energy to investigate myself, I shrugged. I was perfectly content curling up into a ball and not moving for a while, at least until the throbbing in my feet lessened to a more manageable level of discomfort. Resolute in my dedication to immobility, my whole body slackened, shoulders falling back and eyelids growing heavy. Just as I was about to drift off, my vision started to blur. I wondered if I was hallucinating. Standing on top of the nearest sand dune, I could swear that I saw a man dressed all in blue with a large turban wrapped around his head, staring straight at us. I blinked once, then twice, trying to clear the fog from my vision. No matter how many times I blinked, the apparition lingered, unmoving. Liam nudged me with his elbow, assuming I had fallen asleep.

"We should go. There's a strange man standing on that hill

glaring at us. I don't know how property laws work out here, but maybe we're trespassing on his land or something."

Nate and Liam rose to their feet, and Liam pulled me up with him. As soon as we moved, it was as if a spell had been broken. The man in blue jerked into action, descending from his hilltop in one smooth sliding motion that made it look as if his feet were barely moving. Liam and Nate were nervous, tugging at my arm to get me moving. They were intent on pretending that we'd never seen the man in the first place.

I pulled my arm out of Liam's grasp. "You're being ridiculous."

Liam and Nate's strategy throughout this trip had been one of avoidance. Ignore something long enough, and it would go away. As far as I was concerned, all this avoidance felt a hell of a lot like running away. I was done running. My aching feet wouldn't let me run even if I wanted to. Instead, I put on my biggest smile and waved at the man in blue, opting for the tactic of diplomacy. As far as we knew, this man had no ill will against us. He probably just wanted to know what we were doing out there. Realizing I had no intention of budging, Liam sighed in resignation, motioning to Nate to stay put. The man in blue continued his graceful descent down the dune, gliding to a stop a few feet in front of us. The man was younger than he looked from a distance, most likely only a few years older than us, and rather dashing. He was dressed as our camel guides were, wearing a long-sleeved tunic, lightweight linen pants, shoes that looked like slippers, and a large scarf wrapped around his head. All his clothing was the same deep shade of royal blue. Observing the man from closer up, I relaxed immediately. Although he kept his facial expression neutral, his eyes twinkled in amusement.

"It is ..." the man broke off to choose his words carefully, "very hot."

Giving us a sly up-and-down, the man's eyes stopped at our feet long enough to give away his judgment. When he looked up at us again, his brows were furrowed. He appeared genuinely concerned.

"You have shoes? Water?" The man asked.

Our silence was the only answer we had to offer. Squinting at us, the man in blue asked us one final question, the question to answer all other questions.

"Where are you from?"

We all knew where this was going, but we had no choice but to answer. Liam was the brave one to step forward.

"We're from the U.S."

Mortified though we may have been, the man in blue reacted as if he'd never heard anything funnier in his life.

"Americans!" He chortled, clapping one hand on his thigh.

In an effort to rehumanize us, and also as a means of diverting the man from his laughing fit, I introduced the three of us.

"My name is Skye. This is Liam, and that's Nate. What's your name?"

Softened by my friendliness, the man made an effort to contain himself.

"My name is Omar. I work at a camp nearby."

Omar pointed up and over the hill he came from.

"There are some Germans staying in my camp. They are doing yoga."

Just thinking of the Germans, Omar looked like he was about to break out into another laughing fit. I wasn't quite sure what was so hilarious about the idea of a camp full of Germans doing yoga in the middle of the desert, but whatever it was had Liam and Nate bent over double. Omar chimed in with a hearty laugh of his own. I waited for the hilarity to die down, thinking to myself that doing yoga in the desert with a bunch of Germans sounded rather nice. Having shared a good laugh with us, Omar regarded us with a new warmth. He stared at our feet again and shook his head.

"Let me get you some water," Omar insisted. "And shoes? You need shoes?"

"Thanks, man. We're fine. Don't worry about it," Nate objected gruffly.

Scowling at Nate, I replaced the smile on my face before turning back to Omar.

"You have water? We will most definitely take some water!"

Omar nodded, and his face assumed the somber expression of a man on a mission.

"You wait here. OK? Camp is not far."

The three of us sidled back over to our patch of shade, resuming our former crouched positions.

Nate exclaimed, "I thought this tent was a miracle. This guy Omar is a saint!"

Fetching our last water bottle from my sash, I held it up, revealing the bottle to be less than a third full. When Omar returned with two full water bottles, the three of us thanked him with the fervor of people whose lives had just been saved. Among the three of us, we finished the first bottle in a few hungry gulps. I felt my internal body temperature lower a degree. Omar gestured for us to take the second water bottle with us, stealing one last glance down at our feet. He reiterated his opening line.

"It is hot. Very hot."

Again, we nodded. I waited for him to crack another joke about our country of origin.

Instead, all Omar said was, "Do you need anything else? Shoes maybe?"

Although shoes weren't sounding so bad anymore, we declined out of politeness. Ready to resume our journey, we bowed in gratitude to Omar.

Holding back a smirk, Omar repeated one more time for

good measure, "It is very hot."

For the first part of the way back, the boys distracted themselves from the heat through various retellings of the joke about the Germans doing yoga in their desert camp. I was so absorbed in trying to locate the cooler splotches of sand amid what felt like a trail of burning coals that I barely heard a word they were saying. Noticing me falling behind, Liam stopped midstep. Staring at my feet with a pained expression, Liam unwound the shirt he had wrapped around his head. Before I had time to protest, he ripped the shirt clean in half. Walking back to where I was kneeling, Liam squatted down beside me. He took the foot I was massaging out of my hands and wrapped one half of his T-shirt around this foot, tying a knot on top to secure it in place. He did the same with my other foot. Before I knew it, I had myself a new pair of shoes.

"You may just be able to turn this into a new style," Liam murmured to me, kissing my second foot before he set it down.

"You didn't have to rip up your T-shirt," I protested.

"We're just giving it new life," Liam winked at me.

As distant as I may have felt from Liam throughout most of this trip, Liam looked closely at me then. His eyes melted into mine, pouring out a warmth that rivaled the heat of the desert sun. Feeling dangerously close to crying, I glanced back down at my feet. From where he waited, Nate cleared his throat, and the intimacy of our moment was broken.

With even just this thin layer of cloth shielding my feet from the sand, I floated over the sand, invincible. Moving faster, we rounded the corner of the sand dune we were circling. Instead of seeing our camp, we almost marched into another one. The camp was quiet besides the subtle droning of the flies and the sound of empty tents flapping in the wind. Although there were no humans at this camp, a different species greeted us upon arrival. Resting in a small grassy area behind the tents, a flock of about a dozen camels paused midbite, grass hanging from their jaws, to gape at us. To be more specific, these were not camels but dromedaries. As our guides had corrected us many times, dromedaries have only one hump. Studied from up close, dromedaries were truly outlandish-looking creatures. With their lower jaws jutting out, their mouths moved in slow circles as they batted their massive eyelashes at us. Returning to the more important task at hand, they lowered their heads to inhale another mouthful of grass. Suspended in wonder, the three of us studied the strange behavior of these exotic creatures.

"One thing's for sure," Liam speculated, "these animals belong out here way more than we do."

After passing around our water bottle one more time, we trudged onward past the dromedaries. The herd no longer cared enough about our presence to lift their heads in note of our departure. Circling farther around the giant sand mountain, we finally spied the white of our tents on the horizon. Our journey was almost over. Besides the missing layer of skin on the bottom of my feet, we'd made it out unscathed. However, our return to camp was no triumph. Yasin found us sunburnt, flushed, and covered in sand, sprawling out like fallen soldiers on the large rug in the dining tent. Unsure of what to say at first, Yasin chose his words wisely.

"It is very ..." he commenced.

The three of us shouted in unison, "We know! It's hot!"

"Do you want to take shower?"

The question was so absurd that I assumed Yasin must have mistranslated the word shower. While I wasn't inclined to take Yasin's offer seriously, Nate jumped on it.

"Shower?" Nate repeated.

When Yasin nodded, I could only assume that he was pulling some kind of prank on us. We scarcely had enough water to make it until the end of the day, so fantasizing about showers felt masochistic.

Despite my skepticism, Yasin insisted, "Yes, yes, Berber shower! I will show you. Come see!"

Yasin motioned for us to follow his lead, intending to prove to us the validity of his outrageous claim. He steered us over to a hole in the ground that I hadn't noticed before and lowered a bucket into the hole. When Yasin pulled up the bucket filled to the brim with water, our eyes widened in disbelief. Nate stepped forward, begging to be the first recipient of the bucket's magic contents. Yasin poured the water over Nate's head and shoulders, then filled another and repeated this process. Nate's head fell back and his arms hung wide at his side in a gesture of open surrender. With each bucket of water that crashed over his head, Nate moaned in an almost spiritual ecstasy. The soberness of Yasin's facial expression and Nate's stance of humble submission made me feel as if I were witnessing a baptism.

Liam patiently waited his turn to be baptized, stepping forward only when Nate moved back from the well. Yasin had to stand on his toes to be able to pour the water over Liam's head, so eventually Liam bowed down to him. I recognized the expression on Liam's face but was not used to seeing it displayed so publicly. Hardly daring to move, I realized that I'd been holding my breath throughout this whole spectacle. Exhaling, I swallowed my fear and strode forward. I, too, wished to be reborn. I no longer cared enough about cultural norms or appropriateness to curb my desire. As I moved forward, the men fell back. When I reached the well, we all froze in an instant of uncertainty about how to proceed. Yasin looked like he'd swallowed a frog. He croaked out strange sounds as if his knowledge of the English language had deserted him.

"It's OK," I assured Yasin as gently as I could, "I can do it myself."

Moving backward but unable to make himself turn around, Yasin retreated to join Liam and Nate standing underneath the kitchen tent. The three of them pretended to look away, and I could no longer bring myself to care whether they were watching. Stooping down, I lowered the bucket into the well, surprised at how much effort it took to pull the full bucket back up. I raised the bucket above my head and dumped it over myself in one swift gesture. The water soaked into my hair and trickled down my face. It washed away all my doubt and uncertainty, along with the sand. I repeated this process a second time, and then a third. For my fourth and final bucket, I forced myself to pour the water out more slowly, savoring every last droplet of water as it hit my skin.

Dripping wet and barely clothed, I spun around to face the men. Yasin gave me a wild look, the look of a boy who'd never seen a woman this close to naked before. I returned his stare with a wild laugh, the kind of laugh that made no sound and came out through my eyes. Moving to relieve Yasin of his discomfort, I slipped my T-shirt back over my head, ignoring the fact that I was still soaking wet. All eyes were on me, but not a single word was spoken among us. Nor would we ever use words to speak of this.

Try though we may to pretend this moment never

happened, it made an impression on all our subsequent relations with one another. After our showers, Yasin fixed us another pot of mint tea to stave off our hunger until the rest of the company returned with dinner. We sat cross-legged in a circle around the teapot. Nate seemed lost in thought, Yasin refused to look me in the eye, and Liam's jaw had locked itself into a clenched position. I sipped my tea and rolled my eyes at all of them. After we sat like that for long enough, I felt something shift in Yasin. He swallowed loudly before voicing what was on his mind.

"There is something about her, about the Sahara, that is very ..."

Yasin paused here, almost losing the courage to continue. I almost expected him to repeat the word hot. Finally, Yasin came out with it.

"... very sensual. Don't you think?"

Yasin stared straight at Nate as he said this. Nate looked uncomfortable and didn't reply. Liam and I glanced between the two of them, unsure what to make of Yasin's comment. Later that night when we retired to our tent, Nate admitted to us that Yasin invited him to go on a star-gazing walk together. Nate almost agreed to go on the walk before the full implication of Yasin's offer sunk in. Liam and I giggled at this underneath our camel-hair blanket, but Nate didn't find the episode quite as amusing.

Nonetheless, I had to agree with Yasin's description of the desert. Something about the intensity of the Sahara provoked an equally intense desire in its visitors. The heat of the desert stoked this desire at the same time that it smothered it. Although we were lying next to one another, our bodies touching, Liam felt miles away from me. Since the Berber shower experience, I'd felt Liam withdraw his affection. Whenever we caught each other's eyes, Liam either looked away immediately or refused to look away at all. I didn't know what to make of his sudden coolness toward me, especially when contrasted with the warmth radiating from his eyes when he looked up at me after kissing the foot that he'd wrapped with his mangled T-shirt. It's funny how, in a single instant, you can go from feeling totally connected to feeling totally alone.

chapter six

SECRET SEX

"DAMN. I FORGOT HOW UNCOMFORTABLE this is,"
Liam griped, trying in vain to adjust his position in the camel
saddle to find a more pleasant arrangement.

"I'm still sore from when we rode in. How long is this ride
again?" Nate chimed in.

Although I was nowhere near comfortable in my own
saddle, I had to laugh at how much had changed in Nate and
Liam's attitudes since we rode in two days ago. When we first
arrived in the Sahara, I'd never seen anyone more excited than
Liam was to ride a camel. Liam named his camel Samantha,
and he talked lovingly to Samantha throughout the entire

three-hour ride. This time, Liam didn't bother giving his new camel a name. Neither Nate nor Liam looked back once to say goodbye to the desert camp. I, on the other hand, couldn't stop looking back. Remembering the way the desert heat made the air glitter, how it transformed the great dune mountains into hazily painted apparitions, I couldn't help but wish we had at least one more day to spend there. With better shoes, sunscreen, and a lot more food and water, I could have happily spent a week out there, exploring and conquering new sand dunes every day.

More absorbed with looking behind us than ahead, I was taken aback when I turned around to see the speck of a human-made structure appear in the distance.

Exhaling a groan of gratitude, Nate muttered, "Thank God. I was about ready to jump off this damn camel and walk the rest of the way."

We had to endure only another twenty minutes of riding in our uncomfortable saddles before our guides dropped us off at the hotel at the desert's edge. When Yasin told us there was water and breakfast waiting for us in the hotel, all our soreness and discomfort were forgotten. Instant coffee would never again taste as good as it did that morning. After we finished breakfast and a second round of coffee, we headed to the front desk to check in on the bus that we'd paid for to take us up north to the city of Fes. Other tour groups started to arrive from different desert camps and were descending from their own camel caravans to mob the lobby. Everyone arrived all at once and wanted to leave all at once. For every other group, this process went relatively smoothly. Before we knew it, there was only one small bus and a tour van left in the parking lot, and all the seats were occupied in both vehicles.

The drivers of the vehicles kept asking us, "Where is your group? You cannot leave without the whole group!"

Calmly at first, Liam explained, "Our group is gone. We paid to stay an extra day out in the desert after everyone left. We also paid for a bus ride to Fes."

None of this got through to either of the drivers except for the fact that we'd lost our group. Both drivers whispered between each other, shaking their heads and glancing over at us with visible skepticism. Instead of trying to explain our predicament all over again, Liam attempted a different tactic altogether.

"Where do we go to call a taxi?"

The expressions on the drivers' faces morphed from skeptical to appalled. At that point, they assumed we were attempting to abandon our group out in the desert.

"Tell me one thing, young man. Where are you from?" the bus driver interrogated Liam.

Struggling to keep his voice level, Liam snapped, "It doesn't matter where we're from. What matters is where we're going. Do either of you have a phone we can use to call a taxi?"

Scowling at Liam, the men resumed what had started to sound like an argument. I heard them exchange the word *Amriika* a few times. Luckily, it was around this time that we heard a car start up at the other end of the hotel parking lot. Nate sprinted over in time to catch one of the hotel employees on his way to town to run an errand. After a little bargaining, the man agreed to squeeze the three of us and our bags into his car in exchange for twenty dirhams each. Despite knowing that we'd been ripped off by our tour company, we had no choice but to accept his offer.

When the man dropped us off at the bus station in the nearest town, we discovered that we'd missed the last daily bus to Fes. We had no choice but to dish out more money to hire a private taxi to drive the three of us up north. By that point, we were so discouraged that we barely bothered to haggle with the taxi driver over a reasonably priced fare. Liam refused to talk, and had Nate do the haggling this time. Along with refusing to talk, Liam would barely look at me. His face was even more impenetrable than it had been after our Berber shower experience. As distant as Liam felt from me, he wasn't the only one who'd been closed off during our time together in Morocco. I'd kept an emotional distance from him since our first conversation over mint tea. It was if I'd constructed an imaginary mud-walled fortress around myself for protection. I'd trapped myself in my own inner medina and was left starving for affection. Over the many hours we were stuck in this taxi, I felt a deeper longing for Liam than ever before. Never mind that he was sitting right next to me.

Still uneasy when we arrived in Fes seven hours later, I was itching to get out and explore Morocco's most highly esteemed and cultural ancient city. The medina in Fes is the world's largest urban, car-free area. The medina streets were so convoluted, twisting, and narrow that they made Marrakesh's medina seem organized. As thrilling as wandering through this maze sounded to me, the only thing Liam and Nate were interested in was food. After checking into our hostel, the only place they agreed to go was the nearest restaurant, at which point they refused to walk any further. Then I was the one sulking in silence. I was disappointed in what I perceived as a lack of a sense of adventure on the boys' part. Liam didn't say much throughout the dinner either, which left Nate to the task of keeping a conversation going all by himself. Nate told a few long-winded stories before giving up and eating the rest of his meal in silence.

As soon as we finished eating, we paid the bill and got up to leave. Although no one was willing to explore Fes that late at night, none of us were quite ready to go to bed just yet. After all, we'd spent the better part of our day dozing on and off in a taxi. Nate proposed a card game, a social activity that didn't require much dialogue. Fortunately for Nate, the second-story rooftop patio tables were filled with other hostel guests, many of whom also wanted to join in, to make for a larger, more competitive game. Unsure of what I wanted to do, the only thing I knew was that I wasn't up for another large group activity. Instead, I did the only thing I felt I could.

Pulling Liam aside, I asked, "Can we talk?"

For one of the first times that day, Liam looked me in the eye.

"I was just about to ask you the same thing."

In search of a little privacy, we climbed the stairs to the third-floor rooftop patio. We made it up just as the strand of hanging outdoor lights flickered on above us. From our elevated perch, we gazed down on the rooftop patios below us, marveling at the way their lights shimmered to form a second sea of stars below the sea of stars above us. For once, we were blessed to have the whole patio to ourselves. We sat facing each other on one of the outdoor couches, not quite touching. The few inches of space separating my body from Liam's buzzed with an electricity that reverberated in the air between us. As small as this space between us may have appeared, I had no idea how to bridge this gap. My arms hung useless and limp, bound to my sides by the straightjacket of my anxiety.

Not knowing where else to start, I asked, "What's going on with us?"

Liam's eyebrows moved in the opposite direction that I was used to, furrowing downward. He started to say something, only to change his mind. Just as the strain of waiting was about to snap my nerves in half, Liam began to speak.

"As far as today goes, I'm sorry for being in such a bad mood. I'm still recovering from everything that happened in the desert yesterday. When we got ripped off by the tour company and were almost left stranded at that hotel, I'd just about had it with this place. Then, I noticed your mood change when we got here, and I didn't know if it was my fault from being so grumpy ... or what was going on."

This is when I realized that Liam was at just as much of a loss to understand what was happening between the two of us as I was.

Hoping to ease some of the confusion, I clarified, "I was upset that neither you nor Nate wanted to explore Fes. I know I was being childish. I've just been feeling ... frustrated. We haven't had a moment alone since my first day here. I have no idea what's going on with Nate, let alone between you and me. And I agree, our time in the desert was ... weird. I loved being there, but the whole time I felt so disconnected from you."

Looking more disappointed in himself than anything else, Liam sighed.

"To be honest, I don't really know how to handle any of this. I don't know how to handle Nate being so defensive all the time. I'm getting really sick of having him correct me every time I speak, especially when you ask me a question. Sometimes it feels less awkward when we're in a bigger group, but then I notice you withdraw. Seeing you on edge makes me question everything that I'm doing, so I sort of just ... check out."

Hearing Liam bring up my tendency to withdraw in group settings, I acknowledged the truth behind his words.

Doing the best I could to explain my behavior, I reminded Liam, "I didn't come to Morocco to collect new people and new experiences. I came here to be with you."

The sternness of Liam's face softened a little.

Under his breath, Liam muttered, "God, you're so fucking cool."

Hoping that my cheeks weren't as red as they felt hot, I asked, "What does that have to do with anything?"

Half-smiling, Liam replied, "You always keep it real. I get distracted by who we're with and what's going on around us. When I get off track, you remind me of what matters. It makes me wish that it was just the two of us traveling together ..."

Swallowing my unease, I forced myself to bring up the elephant in the room.

"I wish that we at least had a room to ourselves every once in a while. That's been one of the hardest things. All I can think about since coming here is sex ... or the lack of it. Like what are we now? Friends who hold hands? I want more than that, Liam. I want so many things. I want ..."

Embarrassed at my own boldness, I cut myself off. Liam let out a soft, bitter-sounding chuckle.

"Friends who hold hands ... Damn. That's not what I want."

I looked up, surprised to see how upset Liam looked. Eyebrows drawn back together, Liam stared off into the space behind me. The distance separating us felt larger than ever. When he turned back to face me, Liam's face had closed down again. I could no longer read what was behind the eyes staring into mine. Feeling myself drowning in all this space and silence, I broke the silence before it could break me.

"It sounds like we want the same thing, but neither of us can have it, not right now at least. So I guess we're at an impasse?"

Liam hadn't taken his eyes off me. I sensed that he was challenging me again in a way I couldn't fully grasp. I felt him waiting for something. A shiver rolled down my spine, and I was brought back to the Sahara. I saw both of us sitting in the kitchen tent, hiding from the sun and trying not to think about the heat or the flies. I remembered catching Liam's gaze and being shocked by the hardness behind it. I remembered being locked into this hardness, feeling fear and a slight sense of aversion but being unable to look away. Then, something fell into place and I came to a new understanding. I realized that this hardness was at the root of our problems.

When I spoke again, my voice came out in a hoarse whisper.

"What about tenderness? I can get used to not having sex. But what about sensuality? And softness? I miss that …"

I stopped myself there, closing my eyes, waiting for this new wave of longing to pass. The yearning that tore at my stomach was so strong that I repeated myself again, even quieter this time.

"How do we get back to tenderness?"

When I opened my eyes, Liam's whole demeanor had changed. He was giving me that look—the look I'd been waiting for, the look where Liam's eyes went soft and melted into mine. Unable to hold back any longer, Liam reached out to take my hands between his own. I pulled away, not ready yet, but the gesture softened me a little. Liam appeared unfazed. He touched me with his eyes in the way that he couldn't with his hands. I suspected that, for Liam, our conversation could have ended there. The space separating us no longer existed for him. Yet whatever new peace we'd found still felt too tentative for me to trust it yet. To me, we'd only touched upon all there was to say.

Still uncertain of where to start, I started from the beginning. Together, out loud, we processed each day we'd spent together in Morocco up until that point. We talked about our first tea and what Liam had told me about his time on the Camino with Claudia. Never breaking eye contact, Liam told me again how sorry he was for having hurt me, for any sense of betrayal I felt. When Liam picked up my hand, I didn't pull away this time. His touch helped reassure me enough that we were able to carry on. We were even able to laugh about how ridiculous our dynamic was traveling as a trio with Nate. For the first time, we openly poked fun at the twisted history that connected Nate, Liam, and me and at the turn of fate that had brought us there together. With every moment of awkwardness that we were addressing out loud, I felt us coming together again.

One by one, each little truth that we'd brushed over and refused to acknowledge came bubbling up to the surface. The final image my mind rested upon was the Berber shower. Again, I saw the scene replay with the men taking their turns at the well as I watched, half-hidden and waiting for them to finish. I saw myself take a step forward and the men fall back. I watched myself kneel down to lower the bucket into the well. I could almost feel the relief as the cool water washed over my head and down my body. I saw myself turn around, dripping wet and barely clothed. I caught Yasin staring at me as if I were a peculiar, perhaps even dangerous, wild animal. All eyes were on me, but not a word was spoken among us. Disconcerted, I shook my head to come back to the present.

"Liam, about our time in the Sahara..."

Before I could say anything else, Liam's lips were on mine. He pulled me to him, closing the remaining distance between us. As his lips traveled from my mouth down to the skin of my neck, Liam's hand found my inner thighs. So much energy had built up behind my inner medina walls, but Liam found his way past these gates. All he needed to do was kiss my neck in just the right way, his lips soft enough to tickle just a little. Eyes closed, I smiled my truce, and my body folded open. Not a care in the world, I fell back onto the cushions of the rooftop couch. Liam fell with me, on top of me. Together we fell back through space and time, finding our way back to each other. Never mind all the people on the rooftop patio on the floor beneath us. Never mind that a flimsy, straw fence was the only thing blocking us from the view of all the surrounding rooftop patios. My hands trembling, I fumbled with Liam's belt as Liam's hands, noticeably steadier and more confident than mine, moved from my thighs down to the hem of my dress, pulling it up above my hips in one swift motion.

My vision blurred by the adrenaline pumping through my veins, everything happened so fast that all I clearly remember is the weight of Liam's body pressing into me and the blue of his eyes piercing through my mental haze, pinning me down with a gravity of its own. Yet the more hurriedly we moved, the more time slowed down, like being trapped inside one of those time-warp dreams where, try as you may, all you can do is run in slow motion. For a moment that could have lasted a lifetime, or perhaps just the blink of an eye, I couldn't move or breathe or think or do anything. And then, all at once, I felt Liam slide inside of me, filling up my whole body, blocking out all other sights, sounds, and sensations. Slowly at first, Liam began to move inside of me, and time resumed its normal flow. I wouldn't call the sex that followed tender—the desire that had built up between us was too strong for this to be possible. As charged as the air between us still felt, Liam's eyes held me softly throughout, and the warmth behind his gaze helped me relax into the rawness of the moment. Despite the protests of my still hesitant mind, I felt my heart bloom open. I had found the answer to the question that my heart asked the sun when I first arrived.

By the time Liam and I descended from our third-floor rooftop haven and joined Nate at his table on the floor below, the energy between us had noticeably changed. Liam was much more talkative, and I finally felt comfortable enough to settle into silence. Nate studied me and Liam each in turn, marveling at the sense of peace that had replaced the impending conflict brewing between us. True to his usual style, Nate refrained from making any comment about whatever changes he noticed. He was also much less inclined to counter everything Liam said, as if he somehow sensed that Liam had become less vulnerable to attack. As I watched Nate watching us, I felt a new compassion for him. Not only was Nate having to deal with traveling abroad with his ex-girlfriend, but he was also stuck trying to navigate the tumultuous waters of this ex-girlfriend's new relationship with his best friend. Throughout all of this, I knew that Nate was missing the girlfriend he'd left back home—the same woman he'd left me for back in the winter, the woman he now called his true love.

Exhausted from the effort of trying to figure out what was going on, Nate called it a night after finishing the next round of cards. Liam and I were soon to follow, slinking back down the stairs toward our shared hostel dorm room. I had started climbing up the ladder to my top bunk when Liam tugged at my nightgown.

"If we squeeze, this bed should be big enough for two."

Giggling a little, I conceded, "OK, let's try."

As long as we both slept on our sides, sharing the twin bed was feasible. It was definitely preferable to suffering through the almost painful separation that came with sleeping in two separate bunk beds. Neither of us was willing to suffer through that again, so we spent the remainder of our nights in Morocco squeezing into twin beds together. After kissing each other good night, we were usually so tired that we simply fell asleep curled up in each other's arms.

Although we had little-to-no privacy at night, we managed

to sneak in some alone time during the day. The next time we were able to steal away was in Chefchaouen, Morocco's beloved blue pearl. On top of being famous for the striking blue color of its buildings, Chefchaouen had earned itself the reputation as the hash capital of Morocco. While most people pay for a tour of the surrounding hashish farms, other backpackers encouraged us to venture out into the hills above town on our own. Taking their advice, we made our way up a staircase leading beyond the medina walls and into the mountains encircling the town. When the stairs came to an end, we continued our climb upward. We scuttled up steep terrain and scrambled over large boulders until the beautiful, blue-washed town below us receded out of view. Undeterred by any obstacles, we kept climbing straight up the mountain until eventually we stumbled onto a dirt mountain road. It didn't take us more than ten minutes of walking up this road to find what we were looking for. All around us as far as we could see, marijuana grew as freely as grass. Both Nate's and Liam's faces lit up as if we'd walked straight into Eden.

As enthusiastic as Nate was at the beginning, he lagged behind the farther that we walked up the road. By the time that we rounded the next curve in the road, Nate slowed to a stop.

Bending over to catch his breath, Nate called out, "Hey guys, I'm not feeling so hot. Those bus station kebabs I had for lunch are hitting me the wrong way. Feel free to keep trekking, but I'm turning back."

I saw the uncertainty flash across Liam's face as he glanced longingly up the road.

With reluctance, Liam offered, "We can head back down if you want."

Nate waved him off.

"Nah, dude. It's all good. I'm just gonna take the road back to town."

As Nate began his trek back down the road, Liam turned to me. His eyes were lit up with a joy that made him look much younger than his twenty-five years.

"You up for walking a little farther?"

Seeing Liam this carefree and excited, there was no way I could say no. As we continued farther up the windy mountain road, I watched entranced as Liam's smile grew to envelop his entire being.

Taking a deep breath followed by an even deeper sigh, Liam declared, "It feels so good to be back in the mountains again. I've spent so much of these past few months in cities surrounded by tons of people. Not that I'm complaining, but I missed this. And being here with you ... I can hardly believe it's real."

"It's a lovely dream we're in, isn't it?" I mused.

"You're a dream," Liam replied, never missing the chance to embarrass me with a compliment.

Utterly absorbed in each other and this stolen moment together, Liam and I almost walked into a herd of sheep as we circled the next bend in the road. In no time at all, three huge white sheep dogs flocking the herd doubled back toward us to protect their herd from these two unexpected aggressors. With the dogs snapping at our heels, Liam jumped up onto the brick wall bordering the edge of the road. Just as one of the dogs prepared to lunge, Liam pulled me up behind him, shielding me with his body. Luckily, the dogs remained at the edge of the wall, snarling at us but not daring to jump up. Holding his hands open in a gesture of peace, Liam nudged me to back up slowly. As focused as we were on backing away from the dogs, we didn't notice their owners approaching us from the other side of the wall. We were so startled to hear human voices that we almost fell off the wall.

"Hey, you! Amriika! What time is it? We need to see your phones!" The taller bearded man shouted, waving his gnarled wooden walking stick up at us.

For a second, we were so confused as to why we were being asked the time, or how cell phones fit into any of this, that we failed to connect the dots.

"Didn't you hear?" piped in the second man, "We want to see your cell phone!"

I was surprised at how calm and level Liam kept his voice as he replied, "We don't have our cell phones on us. All we brought is water. We're sorry for walking up your road. We're going to turn around now."

"No, no! We know you Americans ... " the tall man started in again, "You always carry cell phone. I want to see the time. Show me the time!"

"Just keep backing up, OK?" Liam muttered, his voice barely audible over the din of the barking dogs.

Never turning my back to the men or their dogs, I carefully walked backward on the narrow brick wall. As I backed up, Liam backed up as well, only a little more slowly. He opened his backpack to show the men its meager contents, insisting all that we came with was water and sunscreen. Unable to hide their disappointment as they peeked into his backpack, the sheepherders quarreled among each other in an indiscernible language.

Taking advantage of their indecision, Liam asserted, "We're leaving now. If there is any more trouble, I will report you to the police."

The smaller, rounder man frowned at the word police, fed up enough with the unsatisfactory results of this situation to turn his attention back to managing his flock of sheep. The taller man and three dogs didn't take their eyes off us as we proceeded with our careful retreat. It wasn't until we'd dipped over the next hill and dropped out of sight that Liam and I felt comfortable enough to turn around and face back down the road.

Alternating between glancing behind us and trying to read the expression on my face, Liam asked, "Are you OK?"

More stunned than anything else, I replied, "I think so. You?"

"I think so. I'll feel better the more distance we put between us and them. What do you say we go for a little jog?" Liam suggested, clearly still on edge.

Nodding my agreement, I hopped off the wall, and Liam jumped after me. Hand-in-hand, we set off running down the road. At first, we ran silently, holding tightly onto each other's hands and glancing behind us every few yards. It was only after we'd been running for a good ten minutes that I dared to let out a nervous laugh. When we'd run far enough for the blue speckle of Chefchaouen to be plainly visible below us, we slackened our pace to a brisk walk. After turning another bend in the road, we relaxed back into what could almost be called a stroll. The closer we got to the town's medina walls, the less inclined Liam seemed to push forward. As we were about to exit the wooded part of the mountain and descend into flatter, grassier terrain, Liam slowed our progress to a halt. Scanning around us, his eyes stopped to rest on a nearby pile of rocks. When Liam refocused his gaze on me, his eyes sparkled with the adrenaline kicking in from our long, drawn-out flight down the mountain.

"Can we take a second to just be here together ... without having to worry about any angry men or their dogs?"

Liam asked so sweetly that I would have consented to even

the most outrageous request. I scampered up behind Liam onto a nearby pile of rocks and took a seat beside him. Basking in gratitude for our escape from the sheepherders and their dogs, Liam pulled me in closer. He leaned in to kiss my neck in that special way he had, where it tickled just a little. I reached up to thread my fingers through Liam's hair, melting into him in a moment of pure pleasure.

"I think we may actually be alone for once ..." I whispered, "unless we're in for another surprise."

Liam peeked up from my neck in time for me to catch his eyebrow shoot up as he grinned. His eyes fixed on mine as if to test my reaction, Liam began to unbutton my light cotton blouse. Liam's hands shook slightly as he went. He had to stop midway to close his eyes and take a deep breath. By the time Liam reopened his eyes, his hands were steady again. They moved gently between my breasts and the skin at my stomach. I could tell they were itching to carry on their downward investigation. My mouth opened as if to protest, but no words came out. Losing myself to the softness of Liam's touch, I forgot about the hardness of the rock beneath me or the exposure of our surroundings. Liam's eyes were so focused on mine that I doubted he was taking in the rock, the trees, or much of anything going on around us. Called out of myself by the intimacy of this gaze, I felt my own eyes melting out into Liam's as if I were leaving my body. I reached a point when I could no longer distinguish between his body and my own. Suspended in space and time, I imagined us hovering above the rock below us, floating among the trees. Soon, even the rock and the trees faded away. My whole world was painted the same light blue as Liam's eyes.

By far, the most beautiful place that Liam and I made love in Morocco was underneath God's Bridge. This was only a few days after our trek up to the ganja farms surrounding Chefchaouen. In order to reach God's Bridge, Nate, Liam, and I set off hiking along a different trail through more marijuana fields. Eventually, the trail turned and descended steeply down a cliff into a narrow, lush green canyon. From there, we made our way up the canyon toward God's Bridge by following the stream that descended through the gorge. For miles up the canyon, we rock-hopped, scrambled, climbed, and occasionally waded through the pools formed by the valley stream. Finally, we looked up to see the red rock of God's Bridge arching over our heads, joining both sides of the valley together a few hundred feet above us.

By this point, we'd been hiking for hours. Although Liam must have been just as tired as Nate and I were, he was the most willing of us to ignore his exhaustion in order to keep going.

Content at having arrived at the bridge, Nate refused to go any farther. He settled in to sunbathe on a rock while Liam continued his explorations. Liam dove into the cold pool without hesitation, yelling and splashing his way across the pool until he made it to the other side. Reminding myself that I would probably come there only once, I dove in after him and swam as fast as I could to the rocks on the other side of the pool. From there, we rock-hopped and swam our way up the valley until we could barely see God's Bridge behind us. Once we put a good distance between ourselves and the bridge, we peeled off our wet clothes and left them to dry on a rock in the sun. We proceeded the rest of the way up the canyon naked, which made both swimming and drying after our swims much easier. I stuck to the side of the valley where the sun shone down, using the warmth of the sunshine to warm my body after our many cold swims. Being naked outside together in such a beautiful place felt so wonderfully natural that I could hardly be bothered to mind the cold. Yet when he noticed me shivering, Liam stopped. He hopped back to the rock I was standing on and pulled me in close to warm me with his body heat.

Wrapped up in each other, we sat down on a nearby rock in the sun, laughing to find ourselves naked on top of another large rock together.

"How long do you think Nate's been waiting for us? Think we have time to ...?" Liam trailed off, grinning suggestively.

In reply, I lifted myself on top of Liam until I was straddling him with my arms woven around his neck.

"Time to what?" I asked him with feigned innocence, all the while sliding one hand down from his neck to help guide him inside of me.

I moved slowly on top of Liam, holding myself as lightly as possible above him.

Craning his head up to nibble at my ear, Liam murmured, "This is by far the most beautiful place I've ever made love … but all I want to do is close my eyes and get lost in you."

Just as we were about to slip into each other and out of reality, a large rock came flying down off one of the cliff sides and landed in the pool next to us. Unsure about whether the rock fell or if some unseen person above had thrown it down at us, we peeled apart from each other. It took us only ten minutes to find our clothes and rejoin Nate sunbathing on the same rock where we'd left him. Both of us were a little shaken, anxious about who may have been watching us from above. From the way Nate stared at us, I could tell that he sensed our nervous energy. However, Nate's reluctance to ask too many questions saved us from having to explain why we'd been gone so long. We focused instead on rock-hopping our way back out of the valley.

After our scare at God's Bridge, Liam and I stuck to making love in showers and empty hostel bedrooms. The three of us spent one more day in Chefchaouen before traveling back down south to meet Hayley in Marrakech. We stayed in Marrakech only long enough to drink mint tea with Hayley before taking another bus farther south to a little surf town called Taghazout. We spent our remaining week in Morocco surfing every day in Taghazout. Having a friend along to break up some of the tension between me, Nate, and Liam helped relieve a lot of the stress surrounding this trip. It didn't take long for the four of us to settle into the comfort of a new routine. This routine mostly consisted of surfing, eating, and sleeping. Sometime between our morning and evening surfing sessions, Liam and I found time to disappear for a few stolen moments alone together. As passionate and highly charged as our illicit lovemaking was, I longed for the day when we could make love behind a door that locked and lie naked together for as long as we wanted to afterward. As it was, we limited our time together and were always on the alert to avoid a potential intrusion. Despite a few close calls, we were never caught alone together. We always made sure to resurface in time to go check out the waves before sunset. If the waves looked good enough, we wriggled back into our wetsuits and headed back out into the ocean to watch the sunset on our boards. After sunset, the four of us cooked dinner and hung out on the rooftop patio with the other guests and hostel staff. We stayed up late into the night playing card games and sipping on our illegal and absurdly expensive beer.

This precious time spent together in Taghazout slipped through my hands like sand through an hourglass. Before I knew it, Liam and I snuggled up together for one last night of cramped sleep in a twin bunk bed. All four of us had booked separate flights to Paris for the following day. Although we'd all meet in Paris eventually, we each arrived at different times on different days. This would be the first taste of separation that Liam and I had experienced in weeks. After a few precious days together in Paris, Liam and I had come up with only vague, undefined plans for what we would do when we got back to the States. We'd left our plans vague because neither of us wanted to go back, so we'd been reluctant to talk about it. However, if we'd learned anything throughout our time in Morocco, it was that ignoring something difficult doesn't make it go away.

chapter seven

LA NUIT BLANCHE

I FOUND MYSELF ALONE in my favorite city in the world, Paris. The moon, a full one that night, had taken the place of the sun. Its light bounced off the faces of the people walking by and shimmered on the dark water of a nearby canal, tingeing everything it touched with a silver hue. The city streets pulsed with anticipation for all the night held in store. The people strolling by my window leaned in toward each other and spoke in low, feverish whispers interrupted by the occasional burst of laughter. I'd been staring out the window of the little café in the lobby of my hostel for hours. I yearned to be on the other side of the window, to be outside and moving as one of many in the throngs of passersby. I forced myself to sit still a little while longer, carefully scrutinizing the faces of those walking by my window in search of a pair of dark brown eyes I recognized.

My friends were strewn across Europe, slowly making their way there to join me. Making the best of his twelve-hour layover in Barcelona, Liam was out wandering the streets and soaking in the culture of a different city. Nate was visiting a distant aunt in a coastal Spanish town. Hayley was somewhere between the Paris airport and our hostel. It was her brown eyes I sought out among the many. Since neither of us had working phones, I couldn't help but worry that Hayley had gotten lost in transit somehow. It didn't help that I was the only one in our group who spoke French.

As a means of distracting myself while I waited for Hayley, I scribbled down the experiences of my past few weeks in my journal. Besides its usefulness as a diversion, my initial purpose in opening up my journal was to try to come up with some sort of plan for the rest of the year. While we were waiting to board our flights in the Marrakech airport, Liam shared some of his goals, of which he had many, for the following year with me. He then asked me what my goals were for the next year. This simple question left me speechless. I realized I had no clearly definable goals. Since Alice had told me she no longer wanted to move to Denver with me, I'd been floating haphazardly from one opportunity to the next. I had no vision of where any of this floating would take me. I had no certainty that my floating would take me anywhere at all.

The closing of this day marked the end of day one out of my five precious days in Paris, after which I would fly back to the States and back to reality. My entire future after October 11 was a blank slate. I had no home to return to and no job or reliable source of income I could count on. My return to the U.S. would also mark the commencement of a new period of uncertainty with Liam. As of a few days ago, Liam's friends had offered him a spot as a trimmer on their small ganja farm. The farm owner had made it clear that he wouldn't be needing any additional help. The closest thing I had to a job was a few loose connections to people who worked on marijuana farms in California, but none of these friends had been able to make me any guarantees.

Perhaps the most shocking part of my predicament was that this was the first time I'd actually worried about any of this. Up until that point, I'd clung to the faith that everything would somehow magically work itself out. Now, suddenly, everything worried me. I worried about the fact that I hadn't been worried. Worry as I may, I came no closer to having a clearer vision of what my future held. Attempting to come up with any sort of concrete plan felt like walking over and over again into a brick wall. I felt blind, unable to see anything beyond my immediate reality. Thinking like this, I felt the walls of the hostel's shabby café press in on me. I stepped outside for some fresh air, leaning against the same window out of which I'd been staring. Taking in the sights, sounds, and smells of my most beloved city, I felt my fear morph into an uneasy sense of exhilaration. Regardless of how undecided I was about what came next in my life, I was grateful to have found my way back to Paris.

And so it went, time and time again. Whenever I got overwhelmed by the volatility of the future, I sought refuge by losing myself in the immediacy of the present. This made any later attempt to return to future planning more overwhelming, as I then had to deal with guilt over the time I'd wasted that I could have used toward actually planning out my future. As much as I struggled with a sense of blindness regarding my own future, I had a certain responsibility in creating this blindness.

As I stood outside that evening on the sidewalk of a busy Parisian street, I let the brisk autumn air waft over me, scattering all worries, all thoughts, all guilt to the wind. Breathing in this cool air, absorbing its freshness, I relinquished the desire to do, plan, or control anything. I simply waited. On the brink of forgetting what I was even waiting for, the sound of my name being called jolted me back into alertness. Turning in the direction of this voice, my favorite pair of honey-brown eyes greeted me, reflecting back to me the same sense of relief that I felt flooding over me.

Finding Nate and Liam the following day proved even more difficult than reuniting with Hayley. Nate never showed up at the meeting place we agreed on. Liam was the last one to arrive in Paris and was the only one who knew the precise address of our Airbnb. Not knowing what else to do, Hayley and I headed to the metro station closest to our Airbnb, since we knew this much at least. Once we got off the metro, we happened to spot a man with a thick mustache and a head of jet black hair crossing the street a block down from us. Recognizing this particular mustache, we chased him down the street, our large backpacks bouncing on our backs. Sure enough, the mustache belonged to Nate, who took us both in for a big bear hug. Although Nate never managed to find the café where we were supposed to meet, he'd succeeded in finding an internet café and messaging Liam to get the address of our apartment. We walked over together to wait outside the apartment building, not knowing exactly when Liam would arrive.

About an hour later, a taxi pulled up with the most delightful delivery inside, a bleary-eyed but equally relieved Liam. After climbing the seven flights of stairs up to the apartment, we threw our stuff down and collapsed onto any horizontal surface. True to Parisian style, the apartment was a small one. Liam and I stretched across the only bed in the apartment, which was tucked into a corner of the living room. Nate dozed off on the nearby futon, and Hayley lounged on her belly with a book on the rug on the living room floor.

Eventually, we got hungry enough to pick ourselves up and head back out into the streets. Since I'd lived in Paris for a year in middle school and had since visited many times, I knew the city well. I knew from experience that it was worth dressing up a little to avoid sticking out like a sore thumb among the throngs of immaculately dressed Parisians parading the streets. I threw on my tightest black pants, my favorite leather jacket, and a pair of black ankle boots, which I complimented with black eye liner, mascara, and a touch of red lipstick. I finished off the look by tying my long blonde hair into a knotted bun at the top of my head. Not having thought to bring a nicer change of clothes, Nate, Liam, and Hayley were all stuck wearing hiking sandals or flip-flops, jeans, and hoodies.

Leading the way for the rest of the group, I directed us toward what I remembered being a trendy neighborhood near the famous Sacré-Cœur Basilica. After getting off the metro, we squeezed our way into a packed, dimly lit French bistro. Once seated, we ordered the first of what would turn into many bottles of wine and scarfed down the bread on our table. Liam and Nate each ordered some kind of steak entrée, while Hayley and I split a smorgasbord of my favorite French appetizers: escargot, foie gras, and a charcuterie board with a variety of meats and cheeses. In no time at all, the four of us found ourselves seated around a table of empty plates and red-stained wine glasses. Propelled onward by the energy from the food and a slight buzz from the wine, we drifted back out into the streets. Our first stop was a grocery store to buy another bottle of wine. We passed the bottle back and forth among the four of us as we walked down the hill from Sacré-Cœur toward the Seine River.

As we walked the streets, Nate spewed Hemingway quotes about what Paris used to be like in its glory days, totally missing the gloriousness of the night unfolding in front of us. Hayley was mostly quiet and wide-eyed. Stuck wearing flip-flops, Liam did his best to keep up with me and to maintain a positive attitude toward a city that even I admit can be daunting upon first impression. I was in rapture, hardly daring to blink for fear of missing out on even a second of the beauty surrounding us. Witnessing the majesty of Paris's moonlit streets, I may as well have been the twelve-year-old girl who used to live here. Everything I'd learned—all of the heartache and change I'd been through since then—none of it could convince this little girl to stop believing in magic. All the proof I needed that magic was real was there in front of me. There I was, walking hand-in-hand with the man I loved through a street that looked like an oil painting. As beautiful as all of the old buildings, parks, and canals surrounding us were, the most beautiful thing to watch was the people, who sailed through the city streets as living, breathing pieces of art.

As delighted as I was, I forced myself to slow down my pace enough for the rest of the group to catch up and to give everyone's feet a break.

Motioning to a quiet alleyway off the street we were walking down, I asked, "Wanna take a break to drink some of our wine? I don't know if we're supposed to be carrying an open bottle around like this anyway."

In clear agreement, Nate slumped down onto the closest curb and took a large swig from our already half-empty bottle. Taking our seats beside him, we each took our turn chugging from our undisguisedly terrible bottle of wine. As we sat in the alleyway passing the bottle back and forth among us, two people dressed up as zombies approached us to ask for a cigarette. I translated the question, and Nate reached into his jeans pocket to offer them one of his. After lighting up the cigarette, our new zombie friends relaxed enough to start up a conversation, which I translated back and forth for the rest of the group. Initially, the zombies asked me all the questions, wanting to know where we were from and how long we were visiting. The most obvious question hung in the air between us, waiting to be asked. Unable to hold back any longer, I interrupted their questioning with a gesture toward their costumes.

"What's the occasion?"

They shot back in rapid-fire French, "You don't know? Tonight is *la Nuit Blanche*!"

While I was able to understand that *la Nuit Blanche* translated to *the White Night* in English, I had no idea what this meant. Registering our cluelessness, the two zombies jumped over each other to fill me in.

"La Nuit Blanche is Paris's biggest party of the year! Everything is open late, and everything is free. All the museums and cathedrals turn into dance halls. The metro never stops running. The whole city becomes one large art exhibit. Don't tell me that you seriously had no idea this is happening?"

I could barely keep up with what they were saying to translate for Liam, Nate, and Hayley, who looked more daunted by the news than enthusiastic. Before I could finish my translation, our zombie friends were pulling us to our feet and ushering us onward. We followed them to their next destination, which was a nondescript blue door that opened into a poorly lit staircase. This staircase led downward toward a dark, crowded club. The first thing we noticed about this club was how terrible the music was, a mix of all my least favorite hits from the eighties and nineties. The next thing we noticed was how almost none of the men on the dance floor had their shirts on. Both men and women swung energetically around the stripper poles scattered around the middle of the dance floor. The majority of the crowd was noticeably younger than us, in their early twenties or late teens. I couldn't tell if the intensity of energy in the room came from how young everyone was or if everyone there was rolling on ecstasy. We made it through only a few songs before squeezing our way off the dance floor and hurrying back up the stairs toward the refreshingly quiet street above.

From there, we made another pit stop at the closest grocery store to purchase our third bottle of wine for the evening. Nate had offered up the theory that our problem at the last bar could have simply been that we weren't drunk enough. Determined to test this theory, we winced our way through another bottle of cheap wine. From the alleyway we chose, we noticed a line forming across the street in front of what looked like an old cathedral. When we weren't able to stomach any more wine, we set the bottle down and made our way to the back of the line. None of us had any idea what we were waiting for. What we were in for next was unlike anything we could have imagined anyway. Ushered inside, the crowd that we'd become a part of pressed forward until we all stood lining the walls of the cathedral. The cathedral had a passageway cleared in the center. The passageway was filled with fog, off of which pink laser light beams bounced. In the pink fog, a girl danced with a hula hoop swinging around her waist. The pink lasers and the girl dancing in them moved in sync with a set of sounds that couldn't quite be called music.

Alternative electronic is what I later learned this sound was called. I'd heard talk of this type of sound production from one of my more hipster friends in college. From what this friend explained to me, alternative electronic is the production of a series of sounds aimed at creating a certain experience with the listener. Trying to process all the bizarre sounds echoing off the old church walls, I was utterly entranced by the outlandishness of this scene. This was probably the moment when my friends lost their momentum. After all, this old cathedral was no club. There was no sweaty dance floor or pumping bass line to keep them awake and interested. By the time the light show came to an end, Liam, Nate, and Hayley were already on their way out the door. Nonetheless, I stalled our exit long enough to ask someone what we had just witnessed. I chose the right person to ask and found myself listening to a far lengthier description of alternative electronic sound than I asked for.

Noticing me glance back toward my friends, the man I was talking to cut himself off before I had to.

Introducing himself with a kiss on my cheek, the man said, "My name is Hamish. You and your friends are visiting, right? What do you say you come to the next venue with me? I'm very familiar with this scene and would be happy to show you around if you'd like."

Hamish had a mustache even longer than Nate's and was wearing tight pants and a sparkling unicorn shirt. It was the unicorn shirt that made me inclined to trust him. I pitched the idea, and my friends half-heartedly agreed to follow Hamish at least as far as the next venue. Enthused at the opportunity to show a group of Americans around his city, Hamish insisted that we make a stop along the way at one of his favorite bars, a feminist bar near the Modern Art Museum. Once at the bar, Hamish ordered some kind of fruity cocktail, but we all cut straight to the chase and ordered a round of tequila shots. Hayley was the only one who didn't partake. She'd stopped even pretending she was having fun and had mostly stopped talking altogether. Nate wasn't so crazy about the alternative electronic scene and would rather have gone clubbing instead, and Liam wasn't crazy about our new friend Hamish. I made the mistake of leaving the three of them alone together when I went to the bathroom. By the time I came back, they'd made up their minds to go home.

"We realize this is a special night and all," Liam explained as gently as possible, "but it's past midnight. We've been drinking shitty wine for hours. Not trying to sound like an old man here, but my feet hurt. My head hurts. I'm ready to call it a night."

Looking out for me as usual, Hayley offered, "Just because we want to go home doesn't mean you have to. As far as I'm concerned, this Hamish guy seems trustworthy. You could always go with him to check out this next venue and catch the metro home after that? I don't want to rain on your parade."

I was unable to hide the sparkle that returned to my eyes as soon as Hayley brought up this idea. While Nate chimed in with his concurrence, Liam said nothing. He simply looked away, refusing to meet my eyes.

Vacillating in a state of indecisiveness, I mumbled, "I feel bad leaving you guys to fend for yourselves getting home."

Unable to mask his growing impatience, Nate was the one to give me the last little nudge I needed.

"We can find our way back by ourselves. Don't feel like you have to babysit us. Hell, if I had more energy, I would stay out, too!"

I couldn't stop the smile that spread across my cheeks upon hearing Nate say this. I may have never heard of la Nuit Blanche before this, but if it happened only one night a year and it was a night I happened to be in Paris, then I sure as hell wanted to stay out for it. Nate and Hayley hugged me goodbye with a certain respect evident on their faces. Liam's face had that look of a book that has just been shut. As much as his silence stung, Liam's disappointment that I wouldn't go home with him still wasn't enough for me to call it a night. After leaving the feminist bar, Hamish and I forged ahead into the throngs of people encircling Paris's ultra-modern, architecturally bizarre Modern Art Museum.

After walking around the large complex multiple times and failing to find where the line even started, Hamish and I gave up on getting into the Modern Art Museum. Changing plans, we hopped back on the metro all the way back to the Notre Dame to meet a group of his friends. While we'd hoped to check out what was going on inside the Notre Dame, Hamish's friends refused to entertain any plan that didn't involve stopping for food somewhere first. We followed them to a large square filled with late-night food stands and smoky barbeque stalls. Unable to stomach the kebabs that Hamish's friends ordered, I sipped halfheartedly at the beer Hamish and I got to share. Hamish tried to keep a conversation going between the two of us. There was so much going on around us that I had a hard time focusing on what he was saying. I was starting to wonder if this could be where my night ended. Noticing my waning energy level, Hamish stood up in an attempt to recapture the group's attention.

Waving his hands in the air rather dramatically, Hamish declared, "Listen, friends! I came here tonight to listen to alternative electronic, and that is what I am going to do! Come with me if you wish. If not, this is where our paths split ways."

Hamish's speech was motivating enough to get the majority of his friends to their feet, me included. We headed back to the metro for another jaunt across the city. I no longer had any idea of where we were going. It was almost 3:00 a.m. by the time we made it to the next venue. The space where we ended up was a large, open-air music venue that looked like it could have been a train station in the past. Now the space was filled with trees, plants, and flowers. Something about the wildness of the green vines snaking around the old gray structure reminded me of a post-apocalyptic scene where nature had recolonized man's former industrial spaces. In a cleared space in the middle of all of the plants, a DJ spun an alternative electronic set. His sounds flowed over us as we walked among the plants, transporting us to a time and space where reality was no longer as fixed or as solid as we imagine it to be. As we wandered around the complex, Hamish and I stumbled upon a set of stairs that we climbed up to a second level. We walked along the balcony of this second story, admiring the scene from above. Few people were visible through the leaves of all of the plants except the DJ spinning away in the center of the room.

Hamish's friends, who left to explore on their own, found us leaning over the railing and peering down at the show below.

They prodded us, "Come, come you two! We discovered a whole other room! It's a totally different vibe in there. You've gotta check it out."

Somewhat reluctantly, we followed them through the second nondescript door that I'd walked through that evening.

Just as when I'd walked through the first door, I found myself suddenly thrust into a bumping club scene. Thankfully, the music playing in this club was much more up to date, the dancers were less sweaty, and everyone had their shirts on. Hamish grumbled under his breath that he would rather listen to the alternative electronic set, but he agreed to stay long enough to grab another beer with his friends. We fought our way up to the bar, shouted out an order for five beers, and then fought our way over to a table. The only space we found where we could sit down was at a long community table next to a couple voraciously making out and practically lying on top of the table. Hamish and I did our best to ignore them and carry on a conversation until the man took a break from his make-out session. He reached over to rehydrate himself with a sip of Hamish's beer.

Hamish snatched back his beer just in time, yelling, "Have you no shame?"

The couple at least had enough shame to pick themselves up and move their make-out session farther down the bar. Calming down after a few minutes, Hamish shook his head in disbelief.

"I can appreciate passion," Hamish complained, "but have enough respect to buy your own fucking beer!"

Having successfully held myself back up to this point, a giggle snuck out from my pursed lips.

"Is that passion or just being wasted and sloppy?"

"Don't tell me you and your boyfriend have never been *that* couple before! Combine being in love with the right amount of alcohol, and it's easy to lose one's composure," Hamish said.

I shrugged, trying not to blush as a few memories bubbled up of times when Liam and I had gotten embarrassingly close to crossing this line. Taking in my discomfort, it was Hamish's turn to laugh out loud.

"So you are in love then!" Hamish groused. "How disappointing..."

I did a double take upon hearing this last word. I'd been caught in my own assumptions, having pegged Hamish as being gay because of his eclectic style and effeminate mannerisms. Reading my face as if he could read my mind, Hamish grinned.

"*Ça va ma chérie.* I'm in love, too. I've been in love my whole life, usually with more than one person. I don't discriminate between sexes. Far more interesting to me than any discussion about pre-assigned genders is a discussion about the multifaceted nature of love and the trending experiment that is polyamory. Have you ever experimented with it for yourself?"

"Not really. As exciting as polyamory sounds, I might be a little too ... simple for it."

"I don't think you're simple at all. I'm more worried that you're overthinking this," Hamish chuckled, raising his eyebrows.

I'd seen a similar facial expression on Liam's face so many times that Hamish's face washed away for a second. His dark, almond eyes were replaced by Liam's speckled blue ones— sky-blue eyes that penetrated to my core, pinned me to the spot, and wiped away all other thoughts or realities. I shivered. This unconscious movement brought me back to the present, back to the set of inquisitive brown eyes in front of me. Hamish sat patiently in front of me, waiting for a reply.

"Well, I do tend to ruminate on things, I guess..."

This was the only halfway adequate response I could come up with on the spot. However, Hamish took my admitting this the wrong way. In his next gesture, I sensed Hamish thought he was doing me a favor. Perhaps he believed he was saving me from myself. Before I knew it, Hamish had one hand on the back of my neck and was pulling my face in to plant his lips on mine. Unable to process the speed at which all of this happened, my first reaction to Hamish kissing me was to freeze. Snapping out of it, I gently pried Hamish's hand off my neck and pulled away. Hamish stared at me with fear in his eyes, recognizing that he'd made an error in judgment. Nonetheless, I wasn't angry at Hamish. I understood the mostly benevolent motivation behind his rashness. All I felt in that instant was how tired I was.

After a long exhale, I pronounced, "I'm ready to go home, but I have no idea where we are. Could you help me?"

Happy that I'd given him a chance to redeem himself, Hamish jumped to his feet.

Glancing down at his watch, he muttered, "Somehow, it's almost five already. The metro shuts down for a few hours at five. But if we walk about twenty minutes from here, we'll be at my apartment. I have two folding bikes there, mine and another one you can use. From there, we can bike to wherever you're staying."

Not having any better options, Hamish and I set off for the first stretch of our next adventure, which turned out to be far longer than a twenty-minute walk. Just when I was starting to doubt that we would ever arrive at Hamish's apartment, he pointed to a building across the street. Letting me know that he'd be right back, Hamish bounded away before I could offer to help. When he came back a few minutes later, Hamish was carrying one bike over each shoulder and had two helmets piled on top of his head.

Setting both bikes down and tossing me a helmet, Hamish exclaimed, "All right, *ma belle Americaine*. Are you ready to see Paris as you have never seen her before?"

With me pedaling as fast as I could to keep up with him, we raced off on our bikes, zipping over bridges and around corners. It was so early that we had the road to ourselves. Clearly used to biking this distance and longer, Hamish zigzagged from one side of the street to the other while I panted some distance behind him. We biked without slowing down or stopping for almost an hour.

At one point, Hamish shouted back to me, "What do you think of her, naked and unadorned in the soft morning sunlight? Have you ever seen a Paris so serene, so intimate?"

Hamish's words reminded me to let go of my agenda for a bit, to stop daydreaming of Liam and the full-sized bed that awaited me with him sleeping in it. I looked around me and watched as the color of the rising sun leaked out from the horizon, spilling across the still-starry sky. Hamish was right. To watch the city wake up like this was a rare privilege. To feel the pale morning sunlight dance across my skin and to watch this same light glistening off the buildings and the trees around me made this whole sleepless night worth it.

By the time we finally made it to my Airbnb, I thanked Hamish sincerely and promised him, "I won't forget this."

Hamish, who had been folding up my bike to strap onto the rack on the back of his, glanced up at me.

"You better not," Hamish admonished me, "but go now. Your lover is waiting."

Struggling through a nasty wine hangover, Nate somehow managed to get to the airport in time to catch his flight back to the States the next afternoon. With that, we lost one member of our little tribe of four. Liam's flight was booked for the following day, which gave us only one full day together in Paris before we faced yet another daunting goodbye. All three of us woke up around noon, heads pounding and throats crying out for water. Already, we'd lost half of the day to the previous night. Even though I'd slept the least, I was the only one who showed any genuine enthusiasm at getting out of the apartment to explore the city. As I played tour guide and led Liam and Hayley around the city to more of my favorite places, I watched as their energy levels waned and their feet dragged. I saw in their faces that they weren't able to appreciate the beauty of the city or its inhabitants because it alienated them.

"All of these old buildings are really impressive," Hayley conceded eventually. "I'm just not that big a fan of buildings in general. I prefer open spaces."

Hearing Hayley's confession, I felt the combined weight of my lingering hangover, lack of sleep, and my friends' negative attitudes hit me all at once. While I could hardly contain my joy at being back there, Liam had barely said a word all day. Most of the words Hayley had spoken were some form of complaint. After trying so hard for so long to make this day better or different than it was, I was exhausted. I could no longer hold back the tears collecting in the corners of my eyes. Liam, who'd been wrestling with something akin to jealousy since I'd ditched him the night before, melted the moment he witnessed my first teardrop fall. He stepped forward and took me in his arms.

"I'm sorry, babe. I'll try harder," Liam murmured into my ear.

Burying my head into Liam's chest, I took the time I needed to forget the rest of the world for a while. I forgot time and place and circumstance. My world shrunk down to the size of two people holding each other tightly in an embrace. By the time I re-emerged from my Liam cocoon, I was surprised to find that we were still standing in the middle of the sidewalk, people streaming by us on both sides. The way that I imagined it, we were standing together on a rock in the middle of a flowing river, and the level of the water was rising. Soon enough, we would have to let go of each other and allow the current to carry us away. Standing unmoving in the middle of our urban river, I spotted Hayley sitting on a bench across the sidewalk. When I caught her eye, Hayley got up and crossed the length of sidewalk. I imagined her swimming across the river to join us. We moved to make space for her on our small island in the river. We wrapped our arms around her, and she wrapped her arms around us.

Hayley apologized, "I'm sorry, Skye. I can't promise you that I'll ever love this city, but I can respect the fact that you do."

The word *city* brought me back. Just like that, the remaining surface of our rock was submerged under water. I, too, found myself submerged, plunged suddenly into a body of fiercely cold, raging water. Surrendering to a force bigger than me, I allowed time's unstoppable tide to carry us away, away and back to where we were all at once. Sensing the shift in energy, Hayley released her grip on us. Reluctantly, Liam and I released our grip on each other. Yet Liam managed to grab my hand before we lost contact with each other. He held on tightly to my hand and to my gaze.

In an effort to keep spirits high, Hayley chimed in, "Is anyone else as hungry as I am? The one thing you'll never hear me say a bad word about is the food in this city. Someday, I'll come back here just for that."

With Liam smiling in concurrence, we set off to wander the streets of an unfamiliar neighborhood, waiting for the right restaurant to catch our eye. We ended up squeezing our way into the back corner of a run-down but undeniably authentic Chinese restaurant. Just a few minutes after ordering, every inch of our table was covered in steaming plates of dumplings, fried rice, stir-fry vegetables, seafood, lo mein … We ate until the only thing we were capable of doing was catching the metro back to our apartment. Once back at the apartment, we abandoned all aspirations of doing anything besides going to bed. The lack of sleep from the night before had caught up to me. Giving in to my exhaustion, I curled up with Liam on the living room bed, limbs intertwined in one last attempt to fight the force that would pull us apart the next day.

Our goodbye the next morning was more rushed than either of us would have liked. Underestimating the amount of time it would take Liam to get to the airport, the only thing we had time to do before Liam left was stop at a nearby bakery for breakfast on the go. I was pouty over the fact that Liam had to leave and that we hadn't enjoyed a true moment to ourselves in this city. Liam was distracted and stressed about the potential of missing his flight. We ended up bickering over something silly, and I ended up crying again. Seeing fresh tears rolling down my cheeks, Liam didn't melt this time. He deflated, collapsing inward on himself.

"I'm afraid that I'm always going to disappoint you," Liam confessed.

Not wanting to give the implication behind these words the time to sink in, I protested, "I'll never be disappointed in you! I may be disappointed by something that you *do*, but that doesn't mean I am disappointed in *you*."

Liam stepped in close to me then, nuzzling my nose with his. My mouth reopened as I prepared to admit out loud to Liam that I loved him, but the words got caught in my throat. Although I loved Liam, and I knew he loved me, those three terrifyingly concrete words hung unspoken in the air between us. Unable to dislodge these words from my throat, I said the closest thing I could.

"To me, you are a miracle. This whole trip with you was a miracle."

Trying to make this moment lighter, Liam did his best to smile for me. I could see in his eyes that he was the one trying not to cry.

"I miss you already," Liam told me, leaning in to kiss me one last time.

The moment Liam stepped away, Hayley came over to put an arm around me. The weight of Hayley's arm resting on my shoulder served as a physical reminder that I wasn't alone. Hayley's presence and the fact that we had two more days together in Paris before we had to leave were the only things that made this goodbye bearable. For no matter who I loved, Paris would always be like a second lover to me. Whenever I was away from her for too long, she haunted my dreams at night. Now that I'd found her again, my life felt like a dream. In two days, I would have to wake up again. For the moment, I let myself dream just a little while longer.

chapter eight

FUCK REASONABLE

IN THE TWELVE PLUS HOURS I spent floating in limbo inside an airplane, I still didn't manage to come up with any concrete goals. Ten hours into my flight and many journal pages later, I at least managed to make a plan for the next few weeks. In the days Hayley and I spent tooling around Paris, Liam started working on his friend's marijuana farm near Durango. My heartbreak over Liam's decision to accept the job on this farm without me was part of what allowed me to adopt the *fuck it* attitude I needed to commit wholeheartedly to my next plan of action. I also felt drawn to the allure of working on a marijuana farm because of its promise of making quick money without being tied down anywhere for long. I decided to take the fork in the road that offered the greatest potential reward at the highest potential risk. While it would have been easy to find a more stable, reliable job somewhere in Colorado, I wasn't ready to settle back into a stable or easy life. I decided to take a chance on the connections I had out in California and look for a trimming job with one of my friends out there.

Still hurt at Liam forging ahead in his own plans without me, my first inclination was to blow him off completely and drive straight out to California after arriving back in the U.S. Without any solid idea of when or how we would see each other again, I felt that Liam's decision to accept this job basically amounted to him giving up on our relationship. As hurt as I was, this didn't mean I was ready to give up on our relationship, at least not without giving us one more chance at figuring things out. Despite all my mixed feelings, I couldn't bring myself to leave Colorado without seeing Liam one last time before I went. Along with all my attempts at future planning, I spent the last few hours of my flight from Paris to Denver filling up multiple pages of my journal with everything I wanted to say to Liam. After my breakdown in the middle of a busy sidewalk on Liam's last day in Paris, we'd gone to bed too exhausted that night to attempt another conversation. This had left me to continue my own conversations with an imaginary Liam in my head. No matter how good an argument I made on our behalf, this imaginary Liam remained frustratingly silent. However, his face reflected the words he couldn't bring himself to say.

Even as I reasoned and pleaded with him, all I could see was the way Liam's face had collapsed in on itself as he warned me, "I'm afraid that I'm always going to disappoint you."

Preparing myself for the disappointment of heartbreak, my arrival back in Colorado filled me with no warm sense of homecoming. The only thing I could do to fight my sense of foreboding was to keep moving. After landing back in Denver, I drove straight up to my mom's house in Breckenridge to empty my car of all superfluous possessions. After packing my car with as many potentially useful things as I could think to bring, I hopped back in the car to begin the five-hour drive down south to Durango. Staying awake for the drive proved to be a struggle, as I was still fighting jet lag and in desperate need of a good night's rest. Upon arriving back in Durango, I opted for the best substitute for sleep at my disposal—caffeine. Since Liam got off work around the same time I was arriving in Durango, we agreed to meet at the Durango Coffee Company. This was the only coffee shop in town that was open past dark. The coffee shop was mostly empty when I showed up, and Liam wasn't there yet. Given my choice of open tables, I settled down to wait for Liam at the table closest to the window. A few sips into my cappuccino, I noticed a tall, broad-shouldered figure approaching on the other side of the street from me, his face obscured in darkness. I didn't need to see the man's face to recognize that it was Liam.

Liam must have spotted me, too, as his pace noticeably quickened. Hurrying to cross the street, his body was momentarily illuminated in the headlights of an oncoming car. My breath caught in my throat at the sight of him. I was so used to seeing Liam wearing the same clothes throughout our time traveling together that I was astonished at how handsome he looked in a black, long-sleeved button-down shirt, gray pants, and a backwards snapback hat. He crossed the remaining distance separating us in fewer steps than I would have thought possible. As much as I'd been dreading this meeting, Liam was beaming like a kid on Christmas morning. Pushing through the coffee shop door, he took me in his arms and spun me in a full circle before setting me back down. All it took was this one spin for my mind to empty of all previous thought or concern. I was glad to have written out my thoughts beforehand.

"Skye, baby, we made it back! I missed being here with you ..."

Then, it was my mind that was set spinning as I thought about how much we'd experienced, both together and alone, since the last time that Liam and I were in Durango together. If only I could afford to stay longer than the two days I'd allotted for this visit. If only I wasn't running out of money. If only there was another spot for me to work on Liam's farm.

With a sigh, I admitted, "I missed you, too ... way more than it's reasonable to miss a person you've seen less than a week ago."

Smiling still, Liam leaned in to kiss me.

His lips brushing up against my own, Liam said, "Fuck reasonable."

Even after Liam ordered a drink and we sat back down, he didn't stop smiling. Playful at first, he pulled my chair closer to him, twirling a strand of my hair between his fingers, kissing any inch of exposed skin that was accessible to him. Trying to bring some sense of purpose back to this meeting, I did my best to rein in Liam's focus.

"Liam ..." I called out, practically pleading at this point.

Liam leaned back and made a valiant effort at pulling his facial features into a more serious expression.

"I know. We need to talk."

"Do you want to start? I don't think I can say one thing without saying everything. I'm afraid I'll end up talking for a while."

Just contemplating the idea of having to speak first, Liam's smile was wiped right off his face.

"I like listening to you talk. You're always so thoughtful and well-spoken."

"I'm only this thoughtful because I spend so much time thinking about you."

I murmured this so quietly that, even while leaning into me, Liam missed my confession.

"What was that, baby?" he asked.

Steeling myself to make a far greater confession, I mumbled, "Oh, nothing. I'll start then. I'm going to start from the beginning, so bear with me here."

Saying these words, my mind flashed back to the memory of Liam and me sitting at the rooftop café in Marrakesh and Liam telling me the same thing. Shaking my head to shake off this memory, I forged on.

"When we first started hanging out, neither of us were at a place in our lives where we wanted a relationship. We both had other plans. But despite those plans, we decided to find a way to stay together, even after your travels. Then, you went off to Europe, and I didn't hear from you for three weeks, so I guessed you changed your mind about that. From what I could tell, you'd made up your mind to drop me. What you told me in Morocco about Claudia and your *way girl* fantasy confirmed this for me. But without realizing what she was doing, Claudia screwed herself over by asking you all these questions that forced you to think about me. Next thing I know, you're calling me up and inviting me to join you in Morocco."

Liam struggled to meet my eyes as I said this. Like so many times, I thought back on our day in the Sahara. This time, it was my turn to pin Liam to the spot with the penetrating beam of my own green-blue eyes. Sensing my challenge, Liam smiled a little. His smile was a white flag waving his truce. I smiled a little back, but I refused to lose the focus I needed to continue.

"Even though our communication in Morocco was really bad at first and we were sexually frustrated as fuck, Morocco was still absolutely magical for me. Getting to spend so much time with you in such a different context only made me appreciate you more. I wasn't even anxious about our future at that stage in the trip because you told me that you wanted to find a way to be together after Morocco. In my head, I kept thinking we had more time. Then, your friend offered you this job on his farm. You told me that you had to take the job because it would allow you to *get your foot in the door of the marijuana industry*."

I made air quotations with my hands around this last part, just barely holding back an eye roll.

Trying to keep my bitterness in check, I continued, "When it comes to us and our future, all you've offered me is a vague proposal to meet up when the trimming season is over. After all this flip-flopping back and forth, I'm afraid to take that offer seriously."

In the heat of Liam's stare, I felt a flash of shame. This was no longer a game. Liam glanced away from me, looking about ready to give up. My aim wasn't to make Liam feel anything close to shame, so I softened my voice as much as possible before continuing on.

"I'm not trying to bring this up as some sort of list of complaints that I've been holding against you. I've just noticed this wishy-washiness when it comes to how committed you are to me. I get that it's hard. You'd already made all these plans when we started dating, and all your plans are so noble. All I want to know is if there's room for me anywhere in those plans."

Not ready to hear Liam's answer, terrified that the answer would be no, I carried on.

"On my end, I'm not tied down to much of anything. I'm free to go wherever I want. Where I want to be is with you. For now, this fall is what it is. We're both going to be in different places for a few months. But beyond this fall, I don't mind moving somewhere new if it means we get to be together again. As long as you're still meeting me halfway, that doesn't feel like a sacrifice to me. The one thing that I won't do, that I can't do, is sit around and wait for you to make up your mind about whether you want to be with me. I'm too much of an anxious wreck to be able to handle that."

Pausing, I took a deep breath to soothe the anxiety that was stirring up in my stomach even just talking about this. Now that I'd explained to Liam what I needed and why, there was only one thing left that I wanted to tell him. Or rather, it wasn't so much that I wanted to tell Liam this, but that I felt I had to. In a day or two, I would be driving away from Liam without knowing if or when we would be seeing each other again. If

I couldn't find the courage within me to say these words, I would be driving away with regrets. These three unspoken words circled my mind like little birds, hovering on the edge of my tongue, hovering on the edge of expression. By the time I opened my mouth and forced myself to actually speak these words out loud, I practically felt like I was regurgitating one of these little birds, like a dense clump of flesh and feathers had lodged itself in my throat.

Doing my best not to choke on my own fear, I whispered, "I'm here right now telling you all this because ... I love you, Liam."

The worst part being over, I took another breath, a sigh of relief that came out in the form of a shudder. Eyes widening, not one but both of Liam's eyebrows shot up this time. He opened his mouth as if to say something. In my dread, I cut him off again.

"I'm not telling you this just to hear you say it back. I'd rather that you don't say anything right now. I'm not sure I would believe you if you did. I just want you to know how much you mean to me. That's all."

Hardly having allowed myself to take a breath this whole time, I stopped myself there. I let go of the stale air in my lungs and inhaled a large gulp of fresh air to replace it. For a moment that felt like forever, a heavy silence hung between us. By the time Liam finally said something, I'd stopped expecting much in the way of a reply.

"Next time, could you start with the *I love you* part?"

I covered my mouth with my hand in a failed attempt to keep in the half-laugh, half-sob that escaped my throat.

"I just got so nervous ..."

Liam silenced my apology by reaching out to gently cover my mouth with his fingertips. Caressing the skin of my face, Liam moved his hand from my mouth to cheek.

"It's OK. I like your long-winded speeches. They always have a nice structure to them. It's part of what I ..."

This time, it was Liam who cut himself off.

"Oh, I forgot," Liam teased me, "I'm not supposed to tell you that right now."

I laughed even as I pushed Liam away.

"So you were listening?" I joked back, hesitant to take Liam's jest seriously.

For a moment, Liam's face was overtaken by the same look of shame I'd caught earlier in our conversation. In the split second it took me to identify this expression, the look was gone. It was replaced with the most familiar expression of them all. One eyebrow raised, the corner of Liam's mouth lifted up to hint at a smile.

"To every word," Liam promised me.

Over the course of my next day in Durango, Liam and I cycled back to various points in the previous evening's conversation. Little did I know that this would turn into a conversation we had many times, in many forms, over the course of the next few months. During the last day I spent in Durango, talking didn't really get us anywhere. We circled back, stalled, deliberated, and repeated again with little progress in any direction.

At one point, Liam directly asked me, "Can you give me just a little more time?"

Considering the amount of mental fortitude it would take for me to acquiesce to this request, I felt about ready to give up. My own anxiety and the inner paralysis that it caused terrified me. I didn't know how to communicate the extent of this anxiety to Liam because even thinking about it numbed my mind into a state of vacant wordlessness. On Liam's end, I knew his request wasn't intended to be cruel. I saw in his face that he hated having to ask me in the first place.

Doing his best to explain himself, Liam told me, "In some ways, I have my shit together. In other ways, I have no idea what I'm doing. In those ways, you're different than me. You're different than most people. Whenever you talk about what you think or the way you feel, you always seem so sure of yourself. You know what you want. When it comes to that kind of thing, it takes me longer to find the right words. I have a hard time figuring out what feelings I'm trying to find the words for. With time, I'll get there. I just can't give you the clear-cut answer you're looking for right now."

In my mind, I yelled silently, "But *how much* time?"

Here was yet another question to which there was no defined answer. Every question I asked seemed to produce only more questions. By this point in the conversation, I'd stopped even asking the questions. Sensing my withdrawal, Liam paused, his blue eyes clouding over with a milky-colored fear. Forcing himself to continue, Liam spat out each of the following words as if the words themselves were shameful.

"I'm sorry, Skye. I just don't know if I have my shit together enough to be able to commit to you in the way you deserve. If I'm being completely honest, a part of me was hoping that you'd be OK waiting for me. I know that's not fair to ask of you. It's just where I'm at right now. I'm confused as fuck and just as scared as you are."

No longer able to meet my eyes, Liam dropped his head into his hands. Seeing Liam this vulnerable, I felt a piece of my own protective armor crack. A door I'd closed within me reopened. For once, I was snapped out of my own perspective and able to distance myself from my own fears, hopes, and desires. Instead, I fell into Liam's, into the mess of all his uncertainty and insecurity. While my own anxiety manifested in my stomach as an all-consuming, sickening nausea, I felt Liam's as a dull sort of panic, the kind of panic that makes your heart beat like a drum in your chest, a shuddering thud that resounds throughout your body and echoes in your eardrums, throwing your whole world off balance. Feeling this panic as if it were my own, I saw how all of Liam's elaborately designed plans were simply a means of holding this panic at bay. For Liam, leaving Durango to travel around Europe was just the first step on his own hero's journey. This journey had much more to do with him, and a lot less to do with me or with us, than I was previously willing to acknowledge.

At some point during one of our many conversations, I distinctly remember Liam telling me about his desire to write a book about this time in his life. Leading into this, I'd casually mentioned to Liam the idea of one day turning my journal entries into a book. At the time I brought this up, I had no serious intentions of following through with this proposal. Nonetheless, Liam took me more seriously than I took myself.

"That's a great idea, babe. I'd like to get this all down on paper someday, too," Liam said.

Hearing this declaration, a missing link in my relationship with Liam clicked into place. I saw how, for Liam, this wasn't about what was happening in *our* story, but what was happening in *his* story. No matter what Liam did, the backbeat that drove the entire narrative remained constant.

"Tumtum … tumtum … tumtum … tumtum …"

On and on and on again, the same shuddering thud resounded. At times, this sound was dim enough to be dismissible; at other times, loud enough to be deafening. Loud or quiet, I saw how easily this panic turned into a form of mania, a mania that pushed Liam to do more, strive harder, fight dirtier. I felt this mania as Liam's fight to assert his right to exist, his fight to prove his existence has value. All at once, I felt the full weight of how much Liam believed that he had to prove to the world. Even though this struggle had been happening in front of my face since I'd known him, I'd had a hard time seeing it because Liam's value was always so undeniably apparent to me. However, it didn't matter what my perception of Liam's worth was. What mattered was Liam's own sense of worth.

In light of this new understanding, I accepted that I may not get the clarity I was looking for in the timeline I was hoping for. It took me until my second and last night with Liam to accept this. Laying naked together on a mattress in one of Liam's friend's sheds, I fell into an uneasy, restless sleep, a sleep haunted by a dull pounding in my eardrums. When I woke up the next morning, I reached up to touch my own face, surprised to find that my cheeks were damp with tears. I'd never woken up crying before. I didn't fully understand what was happening. Had I been crying in a dream? As I lay puzzling over this, Liam stirred in his sleep, awakening from his own dream world.

Taking in the sight of fresh tears on my face, Liam's hazy, sleep-clouded eyes widened and refocused. Still confused and now somewhat embarrassed, I tried to turn away, not wanting to have to explain myself. Interpreting my desire for space as an attempt to disconnect from him, Liam pulled me closer and took my face in between his hands.

In a voice that was both quiet and strong, Liam murmured, "Would you please look at me?"

Liam wiped the tears off my cheeks, and I blinked a few times, trying to stop a new wave of tears from falling. I felt totally out of control of my own body, at the mercy of an intense wave of emotion that I wasn't sure even belonged to me. With time, the gentle, steady pressure of Liam's hands on my face helped reground me, and I was eventually able to look up at him. Liam's eyes reached out to hold my eyes with the same gentle presence with which his hands held my face. Neither of us moved or said anything for quite some time. Held in this space of quiet stillness, all the anxiety and panic I'd been holding onto from the past few days subsided. For a moment, I experienced peace in the form of a deep silence and a stillness within my belly. Finally, it was Liam who spoke first.

"I love you, too, Skye," Liam told me.

Just like that, the silence was broken. Time started back up again, carrying us away, away and back to where we were all at once.

When I arrived in Los Angeles at 11:00 p.m. on October 16, I was simply grateful that my 1997 Toyota RAV4 had enough life in it to get me to California without breaking down. I'd left Liam earlier that morning after the two of us stopped again by the Durango Coffee Company for coffee and breakfast burritos to go. The only thing that I recalled about our time together in the coffee shop was that the song "The Lengths" by the Black Keys was playing. Then, all of a sudden it seemed, Liam was kissing me goodbye and wishing me a safe drive. Just as suddenly, I found myself sitting alone in my car, surprised to see that my car was moving and that I was the one driving it. I drove for thirteen hours, speeding the whole way. I flew past the Four Corners, the Grand Canyon, Flagstaff, Las Vegas, so much of Arizona and California, so many places where I would have stopped if I had the time. I ended up in the least likely of places: Long Beach, Los Angeles. As absurd as it felt to have landed in Los Angeles, there was also a certain sense of inevitability to it. Unable to shake the feeling of having lost control over my own life, mind, and body, I believed in destiny more than I ever had.

For the next two days at least, my friend Jake relieved me of the need to be in control of anything. Jake was another friend I'd met working as a rafting guide in Durango, and he just so happened to be from Los Angeles. When I told him that I was looking for work in northern California that fall, Jake insisted that I stop to see him before continuing up north. He was one of those friends with whom I could talk about everything, but he was also a good enough friend to sense when I wasn't in a talking kind of mood. As he heated up a late night dinner for us of frozen dumplings, rice, and stir-fried vegetables, Jake did most of the talking. He also had the foresight to make sure his fridge was fully stocked with a twelve-pack of hazy IPAs and a few bottles of California wine.

During the two days I spent with Jake in Los Angeles, we barely left his house. We spent our time together drinking beer, watching Disney movies, and writing in our separate journals. Both nights, Jake gave me his bed to sleep on and took the couch without complaint. We both knew this could be the last time for a long time that I had a mattress to sleep on. More than just enjoying his mattress, I soaked in every minute I got with Jake. I found relief in the sense of safety he provided me.

As I was getting ready for bed on my last night there, Jake offered, "You can always stay longer, you know."

I sighed, trying not to crumple onto the floor right there in front of him. I used up the last ounce of my willpower to turn down his offer.

"I'm broke, Jake. I need to be making money right now, not

spending it. I know you mean well, but I wouldn't feel right crashing here for free."

Jake knew me well enough not to try to change my mind. The next day, I was propelled forward blindly once again. By then, the sight of a long, open road in front of me had become familiar enough to be almost comforting. While I was on the road, I found some relief in knowing I was at least moving in some direction. While I didn't know where the road ahead of me led, a part of me didn't need the road to lead anywhere at all. When you wander long enough, the road itself can start to feel like home.

chapter nine

MIRACLES AND MARIGOLDS

THE BRIGHT, UNFILTERED MORNING SUNLIGHT
awakened me to a brand new world. I was alone out in the
woods, woods unlike any place I'd ever seen. Late the night
before, I'd driven through Nevada City and pulled off the side
of the road onto Tahoe National Forest land. In my exhaustion, I chose to cowboy camp, throwing my sleeping pad and
bag down on a flat surface and calling it good enough for the
night. The sunshine the next morning revealed the hidden
glory of the spot that I'd haphazardly chosen. There I was,
surrounded by sugar pines, the tallest trees I'd ever seen, with

the autumn sun shining down on me and painting the forest scene an orange-gold hue.

As picturesque as my new campsite was, I didn't dare rest for long. The first thing I did that morning was call the three friends who'd brought up the possibility of helping me find work in California. No one answered. I left three separate voice mails and sent three texts for good measure. The friend who'd brought up the most promising offer of working on his brother's farm never got back to me. The second friend called me back later that day and gave me the phone number of the farm owner that he'd worked under the year before. I called this number a few times, but no one picked up. The third friend told me she would be back in town in about a month and could try to get me a job on the farm she worked on then.

"No guarantees, though. Sorry, Skye," this friend warned me.

Having already hit three dead ends, it was time for me to get more creative if I was going to make this work, especially considering that I had only a few hundred dollars left in my bank account. The two friends I managed to get ahold of promised that the work was out here if I looked hard enough. I decided to give myself a one-week deadline to find a job. If I failed to find anything, I would use the remaining money in my bank account to buy enough gas to get me back to Colorado. Not allowing myself enough time to mull over the very real possibility of failure, I packed my things up, hopped into my car, and drove back down the forest road toward town. Turning back onto the main highway, I drove past a sign that said *Nevada City – 15 miles*. I took the next fifteen miles to make the energetic switch toward extroversion. Despite being more of an introvert, introversion was a luxury that I could no longer afford. My survival there depended on me being able to very quickly gain the trust of a stranger—enough trust that they were willing to take the risk of inviting me to work on their land. Since most of the farms in this area still operated illegally, this entailed taking a significant risk. Nevertheless, I'd taken my own risks in coming out there. I refused to be deterred by the first challenge that came my way.

If anything, it was sheer stubbornness driving me forward at this point. I couldn't fully justify to myself why I'd taken such a huge risk in coming out to California, outside of a blind faith that somehow everything would work itself out. This blind faith was the driving force moving my life forward, propelling me onward into the great unknown, onward down the never-ending road. I had no idea where this road was leading me, but I had an unspoken, intuitive understanding of what it was taking me away from. Looking out upon this road, all I could see was darkness and uncertainty. Yet this darkness held within it a certain mystery, the allure of infinite possibility. Looking back down this road in the direction of home, I could all too easily imagine what my life would be like if I were to return. I could see how easy it would be to fall back into a comfortable routine, to trade in freedom and growth for stability and ease. Over and over again, I'd seen in the lives of my family and friends the power that comfort held to lull people into the trance of complacency. I feared complacency far more than I feared the unknown. My aversion toward anything that felt like settling dictated most of my major life choices. Yet I never paused long enough to question how much my fear of losing my freedom was actually limiting and constraining my choices. By the time I made it out to California, I was in full-on survival mode. I didn't have the time or space to question much of anything. I just kept moving.

Pulling into Nevada City, I parked near the first coffee shop I saw. I could hardly afford to buy anything at a coffee shop, but I also had no idea how I would meet anyone without spending any money. For the rest of my time in Nevada City, I made a rule of spending money only on food, gas, and one cup of coffee each morning. The only way I could justify purchasing a four-dollar latte every morning was by using my time in the coffee shop to network. Walking through this first coffee shop's front door, I put on my most charming smile. I could only hope it would prove enough to hide the desperation in my eyes. Despite my fear, I struck gold with the first stranger I approached. Or perhaps the more appropriate idiom for this situation would be to say I struck green. For while Nevada City owed its existence to the Gold Rush, a new rush was taking place there. Green had replaced gold as the new currency. Since I myself had come as part of this green rush, I started by introducing myself to the man sitting at the table next to me.

"Hey, sorry to bother you. My name is Skye, and I'm new to town. Do you know this area well? Or maybe have any suggestions for things to do around here?"

I wasn't sure how to bring up the real question I was getting at, which was where I could go to find work. However, my more indirect approach paid off well.

Extending his hand out to me, the man replied, "Nice to meet ya, Skye! Welcome to town. My name's Moon."

Moon appeared to be somewhere in his midthirties. He had a soft, young face, but his hair was graying at the temples. A rather tall, lanky man, there was something gentle and almost feminine about the way that Moon moved. I chose him to approach out of everyone else in the coffee shop for this softness that he exuded.

"I've lived in Nevada City for six years," Moon said. "I'm proud to call this place my home. I used to work as a mechanic fixing wind turbines, but I hurt my back in a bad fall. I got a pretty generous workers' comp. It's what allowed me to move here and buy my little piece of land. Since I can't really work right now, I've got a lot of free time on my hands. If you're not doing anything today, I'd love to show you around."

Before responding, I scanned Moon's body language and energy one more time. Unable to detect anything other than openness and good intentions, I accepted Moon's offer.

"I'd love that!"

A few minutes later, I found myself stepping into the passenger seat of Moon's car. The presence of Moon's dog, Sadie, waiting for him in the back of his car helped put me at ease. Sadie was a beautiful golden, long-legged dingo. Sadie and I bonded the first instant we met. As I reached back to scratch behind her ears, Sadie whined at me in a way that made it sound as if she was humming.

"She's talking to you," Moon explained. "For a dog, Sadie has a lot to say."

"I wish I could understand what she's saying."

"Give it a little more time. You just might."

As we drove off in an unknown direction, Moon shared with me the story of how Sadie had *found* him.

"I was camping out in the forest around Lake Tahoe, and I woke up one morning to the sound of howling. I stuck my head out of my RV to see what the hell was going on. Off in the distance, I spotted five furry little heads poking up over a hill. I thought I was looking at coyotes until they got close enough for me to see that it was a pack of five stray dogs. Sadie was the alpha of the pack; that much was clear from the start. She walked right through the open door of my RV and sat her butt down in my kitchen. Any time another dog got too close, she came back out to teach them a lesson. So I didn't have much choice in the matter. Sadie walked into my life one day and settled down to stay."

As if to confirm this story with Sadie herself, I glanced back at Sadie stretched out along the whole length of the backseat. Sadie occupied this space as if this was her car and she was the one doing Moon a favor by letting him drive it.

"The day after Sadie found me, a big bus pulled into to the campground," Moon continued. "Mind you, I was camped out in a pretty secluded spot. I'd banked on having the whole place to myself for a week. Then this bus rolls in that's all painted with flowers and vines and stuff, and a bunch of hippies are living in it. When the hippies discovered the pack of stray dogs living at the campsite, it was love at first sight for all of them. A few days later, they rolled out on their bus and took the other dogs with them, all four of them. All five dogs got homes that weekend. It's like the pack of dogs called all of us out there. Now, that's what I call a miracle."

While Moon talked to me about miracles, we drove down the steepest, windiest road that I'd ever been on. I was so absorbed in taking in the view out my car window that I couldn't come up with a decent response to Moon's story. To my relief, we reached the bottom of the valley a few minutes later. We parked near an old metal bridge that crossed over a raging river at least forty feet below us. A nearby sign welcomed us to the Yuba River Recreational Area. Sadie, Moon, and I hopped out of the car and crossed the bridge, looking down at the white rapids churning underneath us.

Sadie led the way as we set off down a steep trail following the banks of the river. Moon followed behind her, moving noticeably more slowly, and I followed a few steps behind him. The farther we got from the bridge, the calmer the water became. In the eddies along the shores of the river, the still water was an almost turquoise blue. The banks of the river were lined with smooth black stones peppered with large chunks of milky-white quartz. I almost stumbled over one of these large quartz stones on the trail, which was how I happened to notice a yellow marigold lying in the middle of my path. Had the rock not been there, I would have probably stepped on the flower without even realizing it. My curiosity piqued, I paid a little less attention to the water and a little more attention to the path I was walking down. Sure enough, I needed only take a few more steps forward before running into another marigold, a red one this time.

"Are you seeing these, Moon?"

Carefully picking his way over a large pile of boulders in the middle of the trail, Moon looked back at me with a wild grin on his face.

"You just wait! It gets better!"

By the time I clambered over the next boulder pile and caught up with Moon, I found him standing in front of a small creek that meandered down to join the Yuba. The marigolds were everywhere. Moon ushered me on. We pushed our way through the brush lining the creek and waded over to the other side. Moon led me down to the junction of the small creek and the mighty Yuba. The creek water had carved a smooth tunnel into the black rock that it ran down. The tunnel ended in a small waterfall where the creek water cascaded down to join the rushing waters below. Sitting on each side of this perfect little waterfall were two women with large baskets of marigolds by their sides. Both women were wearing flowing, white dresses and appeared to be performing of some kind of ceremony. Wordlessly, they tossed handfuls of marigolds down the stream, watching the flowers brave the long drop down the waterfall before floating away down the Yuba.

Not wanting to ruin the moment, I whispered, "Where are we?"

"Talk about miracles enough, and eventually you'll get one," was all that Moon offered in way of reply.

Following Sadie's lead, we climbed farther down the rocks and found a comfortable seat below the waterfall. From this vantage point, the marigolds cascading down the waterfall appeared like flowers woven into the braid of a woman's long, watery hair. We watched the flowers weave their way through the liquid locks of the waterfall all the way until the last flower fell. Even then, we continued watching, entranced by the movement of the water itself.

"This river is the reason I live here," Moon murmured in reverence.

Moon and I became so lost in the waterfall that Sadie was the one who signaled when it was time to leave. Doing my best to keep up with her, I stumbled back up the trail in a daze. Our whole drive back up the steep, winding road, I kept asking myself—Have I died and come back again? How did I get here? Moon must have been wondering the same thing.

After we successfully made it to the top of the hill, Moon asked, "I'm not trying to be nosy, but how did you end up here in Nevada City, of all places?"

It took me a second longer than I would have liked to come up with an answer to this question. I was afraid that bringing up the reason I was there would somehow taint the time Moon and I had spent together. That being said, I didn't have the luxury of wasting any opportunity that could potentially lead to work. So I told it to Moon straight.

"I came out here to trim. I had a few leads for work out here, but none of them seem to be working out. So I have to ask, do you know anyone who needs extra help?"

Moon took a moment to mull this all over. He drummed his hand on the steering wheel, humming to a song under his breath. I almost wondered if he had forgotten my question when he shook his head and snapped back out of his trance.

Speaking slowly, Moon said, "I like you, Skye. Sadie likes you, too. If I can help you, I will. But here's the thing. All of my friends' farms are full right now. If I hear anything different, I'll let you know. What I can offer you, though, is a place to stay. I own some land a little way out of town. It's just me and Sadie posted up in my RV out there, so there's plenty of room for you to pitch a tent. I understand if you don't feel comfortable with that idea. Just know that I'm not expecting anything from you out of this. I've got the space, and I don't mind sharing it for a while, as long as it takes for you to get settled somewhere. And don't worry—you will find work. There's plenty of it out here."

Unable to believe the generosity of Moon's offer, I thanked him wholeheartedly.

"I can't tell you how much that means to me. I'm in a tough spot right now. I could use a safe place to lay my head."

When we got back into town, Moon dropped me off at my car, and I followed him the rest of the way out to his property. The drive out to Moon's place took us only about ten minutes, although I noticed right away that there was no cell phone reception on his land. After we both pulled through his front gate, Moon walked back over to the gate and latched it shut with a padlock.

"I'm not locking this to scare you or anything. This is just the way things work out here. Everyone locks their front gate, because almost everyone has got a little something to hide. I've got a few little somethings that I'm hiding myself. Not much compared to most of the people out here, but enough to keep me stocked until next season."

Moon motioned for me to follow him over to a large shed. This was the only structure on his property besides his parked RV. Inside the shed, ten marijuana plants grew tall under fluorescent lights. The whole shed smelled dank with their aroma. Carefully surveying each plant, Moon looked out over his growing plants like a proud father. Once we completed the tour of his personal grow room, Moon reluctantly closed and locked the door of the shed behind us. From there, he proceeded to give me another tour of the property at large. Moon's property was far bigger than he'd originally let on. When I asked him where the property ended, Moon admitted that he owned the whole mountain at the base of which his RV was parked.

Struggling to believe what Moon had so casually mentioned, I repeated, "You own a mountain?"

"Just a small one," Moon qualified. "The locals call it Red Mountain because it glows red at sunset. Hopefully, you'll get to see that tonight. It's quite the show."

For the rest of our walk around the property, Moon expounded upon his plans and projects for the land, detailing the buildings he wanted to construct, the water lines he wanted to put in, and the gardens he wanted to plant. Moon told me he would eventually like to use some of the land higher up on the mountain to start a marijuana grow-op of his own. On this first tour of the property, neither of us had enough energy to make it all the way up the mountain to see what he was talking about. We made it only a short distance up the hill before Moon stopped at a large, majestic tree with glossy green leaves and smooth, cinnamon brown bark.

"This is Mama Madrone," Moon waved toward her branches, introducing me to the tree. "She looks over this place for us."

In awe, I stepped forward and placed both my hands on Mama Madrone's smooth, brown-red bark. I felt a deep sense of connection with the quiet power of this tree. Not inclined to move much farther, I asked Moon if I could pitch my tent underneath Mama Madrone's branches. It took me less than ten minutes to hang my large tarp high up from the branches of the surrounding trees and to pitch my tent on a smaller tarp I laid out below it. After playing around with the tarps, I set up my mini camp kitchen with my cooler, large box of kitchen-ware, and Coleman stove. I faced my camp chair toward Mama Madrone and Red Mountain rising behind her, and I hung my solar light from one of her branches. From there, it was just a matter of moving my sleeping stuff into my tent.

After setting up camp, I headed back down the hill to check in with Moon. I found him lying on the couch in his RV, vaping casually, and flipping through an article in an old history magazine. Sadie sprawled at his feet. Moon offered me a hit from his vape, but I refused.

Intrigued, Moon commented, "You're a trimmer who doesn't smoke, huh?"

Blushing, I admitted, "I can handle a little bit now and then, but most of the time, weed just makes me anxious."

In a gesture of reassurance, Moon reached out to rest his hand gently on top of mine.

"I respect that. For me, smoking weed is mostly about pain management. It helps me forget that my whole body is aching all the time."

I squeezed his hand in sympathy.

"I'm sorry to hear you're in so much pain. I hope our hike today didn't make it worse."

"Don't worry yourself over me. Honestly, it's hard to tell what makes it better or worse. I just do my best to live around the pain. Like anyone, I've got my coping mechanisms and my distractions. But enough about my shit. Did you want to ask me something?"

"I was just about to run a few errands in town. Do you need anything?"

Pulling in another hit from his vape, Moon shook his head.

"I'm good at the moment. I'll open the front gate for you, though. Then, I can give you the combo so you can get back in whenever you want."

After Moon unlocked the front gate, I tested my memory of Moon's directions and managed to make it back into town without taking any wrong turns. The first place I stopped in town was at the local hardware store, where I bought a good pair of trimming scissors. My next stop was the grocery store, where I stocked up on the bare minimum amount of food I needed to survive for the next week. Once I finished these more essential errands, I spent some time walking around the downtown areas of both Nevada City and Grass Valley, the bigger town next to Nevada City. It took me no time at all to realize how much more I liked Nevada City than Grass Valley. Despite being smaller than Grass Valley, there seemed to be more going on in Nevada City, at least more of what I was looking for, and the main thing I was looking for was opportunities to meet new people.

During my time exploring both downtown areas, I forced myself to approach new people and start up a conversation whenever the opportunity presented itself. The easiest way for me to start up these conversations was by asking people questions about Nevada City and the surrounding area. I did my best to mentally catalog all the information these strangers gave me, even if it didn't seem useful at the moment. With a few people who seemed especially open, or some of the people who just looked like they smoked a lot of weed, I worked up the courage to ask more specific questions about the trim scene and possibilities for work.

On that first afternoon, none of these questions led to much in the way of a response besides banal encouragements like, "You'll find something!"

One guy my age told me, "You're a girl, and you're alone, right? Don't be afraid to use that shit to your advantage. Just be careful of some of the sketchier offers for work that you'll get by openly admitting that fact to certain people. You don't want to end up on one of those farms where they make all the women trim shirtless."

Upon receiving this warning, I decided to take a break before approaching anyone else. After speeding through the drive back to Moon's house, I practically ran up the hill to find Mama Madrone. I took some much needed time alone to recharge. The easiest meal I had on hand was lentil soup, so I warmed this up over my Coleman stove. Although the soup helped to warm my insides a little, the woods around my campsite were dark and cold enough to feel ominous. The air hung heavy with the expectation of rain. Sitting in the dark by myself, it didn't take long for me to wish I had some company after all. The only choices available to me in that moment were continuing to sit by myself in the dark or going back into town and forcing myself to approach a countless number of new strangers. Thinking of all of the people I would have to talk to before I met one person who had real work to offer me, I lost any drop of energy I had left. It was hardly past seven o'clock, but I was so discouraged that all I wanted to do was curl up in my sleeping bag.

Sitting there by myself, I reached a point of such hopelessness that the only thing I could do without giving up entirely was laugh. Laughing at my fear gave me the ability to see through it, to see through to the tricks my mind was playing on me. I reminded myself that none of my fears were real—not yet at least. Coming back to what was real, I reassessed my situation. Truth number one—I was sitting alone in the dark on some strange piece of land, close to broke, and totally dependent on strangers' kindness to get by. Truth number two—it was only my first day. In that first day alone, I'd found a place to stay and had already made myself two new friends, never mind that only one of them was human. As if to confirm that this distinction didn't matter, I heard the crunch of footsteps approaching my camp. Sadie scampered over to nestle her head into my lap. She, too, wanted to let me know that everything was going to be OK.

Not long after Sadie joined me, Moon called out, "Hey, Skye! I'm heading into town for this event called the Human Experience. Wanna come?"

Glancing back longingly toward my tent, I swallowed any remaining trepidation and replied, "Sure thing!"

Since I didn't have enough energy to put on makeup or change into nicer clothes, I threw on a warmer sweater and called it good. Wearing my coziest oversized sweater as my armor, I ran back down the hill to find Moon waiting for me in his car with loud electronic music bumping from his car speakers.

Sliding into Moon's passenger seat, I asked him, "This song is cool. Who's it by?"

Moon waved a hand in the air dismissively.

"I can't keep track of their names. I just have this psytrance playlist saved on SoundCloud that I listen to on repeat. Are you a psytrance fan?"

"Psytrance?" I repeated, making sure I got the word right. "Never heard of it.

"Psytrance is an umbrella term for a wide variety of multi-cultural electronic beats. Usually, psytrance is pretty chill, but it can be hyphy, too. High or low energy, its aim is to transcend. You'll know what I'm talking about after the Human Experience tonight."

Even more confused than before, I gave Moon a dubious smile.

"Wow," was all that I could think to reply.

"Don't worry," Moon continued as I made a mental tally of how many times I'd heard that today, "We'll warm up before jumping right into it. I like to start my nights out at this place called Elixart. Elixart is kind of like a bar, but they don't serve any alcohol—more like tonics and healing potions. It's their open mic night tonight, so we'll get to hear a little music to get us going."

After we parked on Nevada City's Main Street, I followed Moon into a space that was a mix between an art gallery and a tea room. There was a constant flow of people spilling in and out the front door. Just as many people stood on the sidewalk outside the bar as did inside. The people standing on the sidewalk huddled in clusters around glowing red dots that were passed around. From their loud voices and uninhibited laughter, it was clear these people had come outside to let loose a little. Inside Elixart, a respectful hush reigned across the packed room. Everyone was straining to hear the dreaded man at the back of the room, crooning a song in what sounded like Portuguese as he strummed a beat-up guitar. Squeezing our way inside, one of the first things I noticed was the Bitcoin currency converter ATM just inside the front door.

Even crazier than the Bitcoin ATM or the sacred geometric art covering Elixart's walls was the way everyone in the bar was dressed. The eccentricity of the outfits put the art on the walls to shame. All around me, I saw fairies and elves decked out in the most sensual, extravagant garb. One woman was wearing a skin-tight leopard-print body suit. Another floated by me in a floor-length, completely see-through white dress. The woman following her appeared to be wearing nothing at all besides gold body paint. The men in the bar were decked out in just as much jewelry, tattoos, body paint, and flamboyant accessories as the women. Glancing down at my simple black wool sweater and faded blue jeans, I felt like the most boring person in town. Sensing my intimidation, Moon dragged me farther inside until at last we stood before Elixart's crowded bar. He ordered two cups of something called kava and handed me a cup before I could ask what it was.

"Here's to drinking the Kool-Aid," I chuckled to myself.

Taking my first sip, I was surprised by how bitter and earthy the drink was. It was certainly not something that I would have ordered for the taste alone.

"What is this?"

I could tell how much Moon was enjoying blowing my innocent little mind in the effort that he put into holding back a smile.

"Kava is a Polynesian root that induces a calming, sedative effect. Drink enough of it, and you should feel a nice little buzz. Just don't stress yourself out too much about it. I ordered you one to help you relax!"

Relax, I did. The first effect I noticed from the kava was a tingling in my tongue. This tingling slowly expanded downward to the rest of my body. It was almost as if I could trace the path the kava took from my mouth, down my throat, and into my stomach in the way that it made everything it touched quiver a little. Besides the tingling, the next thing I noticed was how much more inclined I was to talk than usual. I watched myself talking Moon's ear off as if watching another person engaged in some sort of strange performance. Moon sat and listened with a knowing smile. I talked long enough to remember that Moon wasn't the person I should be spending all of this extra energy talking to. I figured that I might as well ride this kava high in the hope it would help smooth out my awkwardness around meeting new people. I excused myself from my conversation with Moon with the pretext of getting some fresh air.

Once outside, I picked a circle of people to approach at random. Using the joint they were passing around as a lead-in, I asked a few questions about where everyone was from and how long they'd been in town. The common answer was that most people had been in town only for about a month or two. Locals were few and far between. Even more interesting was the variety of accents I detected. I learned that people traveled from all over the world to come to this little town in the mountains of northern California. Not only that, everyone was there for the same reason that I was. The majority of the travelers were from countries like Israel, Italy, Spain, and France. Almost everyone at this particular venue seemed to be a trimmer like me, or looking for work like me. When I asked people if they knew of any job openings, they glanced among each other as if holding back some kind of shared secret. The most information the other trimmers were willing to give me was pointers as to the best locations to go to in search of work. The two most popular job-hunting spots they named were the co-op in Grass Valley and *the café on the Ridge,* whatever that meant.

Just as I was starting to get frustrated by the imprecision of the information, one of the friendlier trimmers pulled me aside. She was a French woman about my same age. She looked like a nymph who had emerged from the woods to rejoin human civilization for the evening. Her wavy brown hair fell past her hips, and her eyes glowed a brown that almost looked orange. She was wearing a red dress that was the same deep rich red as the color of clay, and a silver-wrapped tiger eye pendant hung at her neck. While I gaped at her like a dumbstruck idiot, this French forest nymph smiled up at me as if we'd known each other a long time.

Acknowledging the boldness of my approach, she proclaimed, "You are friendly, and you are not afraid. You will do well here, I think. Welcome to the trimmigrant family."

I repeated the word silently in my head. *Trimmigrant.* Before I had the chance to reply, the French forest nymph disappeared. Feeling disoriented, I spun around until I caught sight of Moon making his way through the throng of people hanging around the front door. Taking me by the arm, Moon towed me off to our next destination.

"I can't listen to music anymore if I'm not dancing to it," Moon declared.

We sauntered a few blocks down Main Street before Moon stopped at a staircase that led downstairs to the one and only club in Nevada City, the Haven. We waited our turn in line until we got close enough for me to hear that there was a twenty-dollar cover charge. Dismayed, I turned to Moon to tell him that I had to leave. Before I could excuse myself, Moon cut in with his magical mind-reading powers.

"Did I tell you that it's my birthday this weekend? As a birthday present to myself, I insist on treating both of us to this show."

All I could do was throw my arms around Moon and utter another heartfelt, embarrassed thank-you. Without thinking twice about it, Moon handed over forty dollars to the woman guarding the front door. After strapping wristbands onto both our wrists, she motioned for us to remove our shoes and place them into a large pile by the front door. Proceeding into the club barefoot, I glided into the world of psytrance.

The people there were even more extravagantly dressed than those at Elixart. There was not a hint of grunge to be found on this dance floor—just an overwhelming amount of glitter, skin-tight clothing, and bare skin. As visually enticing as everyone in the room appeared, what was sexier than their clothes was the way they moved in them. Eyes closed so as to more fully lose themselves in the music, the people on the dance floor looked almost like puppets being yanked on invisible, perfectly rhythmic strings. The music coming from the DJ stand was so powerful that it took over the bodies of its listeners, transforming these bodies into mere instruments for its physical expression.

Moon winked at me, "Pretty wavy, huh?"

Although this word was so heady that I hardly felt comfortable using it, there was no better word to describe this style of dancing. I couldn't peel my eyes away from the way the couples in the room moved with each other. Moon later described this particular style of dance as *contact improvisation*. Sometimes contact improv was intimate enough to make it appear as if the partners were making love to each other on the dance floor. Sometimes it looked more like martial arts or wrestling. Whatever form contact partner dancing takes, the key is not to lose physical contact with one's partner. Never having seen an act so publicly intimate, I took many breaks from dancing just to stop and take in the beauty of it all.

As enthralling as this scene was, a nagging voice in the back of my head reminded me that I couldn't waste this opportunity, and the twenty bucks Moon paid, to meet more people. Steeling myself to face rejection all over again, I began my rounds along the outskirts of the dance floor. Similar to my attempts at Elixart, most of the people whom I approached were reluctant to give away too many of their own secrets. After talking to a few people, I met one Israeli man who identified himself as a farm owner. This man made an ambiguous reference to possibly needing more help in the upcoming week. When he invited me outside to smoke a joint with him, I followed him up the stairs. I should have predicted the attempt he made to corner me in the alleyway and grab my ass. An image flashed before my eyes of this man watching me and a line of other women trim weed without our shirts on. Disgusted, I pushed the man away and ran back downstairs, losing myself in the crowd on the dance floor.

I had a hard time making myself approach many more people after that. I'd given my phone number to over ten people by now, but I had little expectation that I would ever hear back from most of them. Out of the hundreds of no's or maybe's I would hear during this job quest, all I needed to get by was one honest yes. This yes would justify all the no's that came before it. In the meantime, I relinquished my immediate need for a solid answer. Finding Moon again, I let the music loosen up my tense limbs and mind. While I'd come there searching for solidity, the nature of this human experience was something much more *wavy*.

chapter ten

TRIALS OF A TRIMMIGRANT

THE NEXT FIVE DAYS WERE A LESSON in mastering the art of rejection. I talked to so many strangers and was turned down so many times that the word "no" stopped meaning much to me. Even more frustrating than all the no's I heard were the maybe's. There was something I could appreciate about the honesty of someone rejecting me to my face. What became harder to deal with were the sugar-coated promises that people churned out to avoid making me feel bad. Inevitably, these promises got my hopes up, and I started to relax into a relief that wasn't yet mine to enjoy. When I called the number the person had given me, the phone usually rang through to voice mail. I lost count of how many voice mails I sent out into the ether, voice mails to people whose names I could hardly remember and would probably never see again. The most heart-crushing maybe's were the ones delivered by the farm owners, the people who had the real power to do something to change my situation. In my few days there, I became better than I would like to admit at finding these people, the ones with power. The sense of authority they emanated drew me to them like a moth to a flame. In my drive for survival, my entire field of vision became narrower. The people I met were reduced to opportunities. The amount of time and effort I was willing to put into each person depended on my gauge of the person's potential benefit to me. I could only wonder if I appeared as two-dimensional and unreal to everyone around me as they appeared to me.

In my fight for survival, I couldn't afford to shirk away from fighting dirty. I used whatever means at my disposal to get by. Along with desensitizing myself to rejection, I also dabbled in some of the darker arts. I learned how to use persuasion, and at times even manipulation, to create a certain feeling in each person I addressed. The primary feeling I was trying to create was trust. If I couldn't manage to evoke a feeling of trust, then my next move was to try for pity. Being young, female, and blond, I was disappointed, but not surprised, to learn that one of the most effective techniques in soliciting the help of strangers was pretending to be more stupid than I am. While I may have been alone and desperate, I was not nearly as helpless or vulnerable as people assumed. It would be impossible to do something as irresponsible as coming all the way out there if I didn't have an extremely high tolerance for stress and uncertainty. Avoiding succumbing to this stress became a far bigger challenge for me than dealing with rejection. I was not only fighting odds that seemed stacked against me; I was fighting my own mind.

I owed what was left of my sanity to a few precious things and people who kept me going. During my time there, I was reminded of how nothing great or daring is possible without the help of other people. One of the people I came to depend on the most was my sister, Alice. Alice was the only person from back home with whom I was somewhat honest about my current struggles. When things got bad enough, I eventually called Evelyn, but I tried to spare her from worrying about me for as long as possible. Along with Alice and Evie, the most helpful person in renewing my faith was Moon. I was beyond grateful for the miracle that I somehow managed to pick the sweetest, most generous person as my first stranger to approach. Spending time in Moon's presence helped me tap back into my own softness. When we weren't out exploring the wonders of Nevada County together, Moon and I sat in the small kitchen of his trailer with Sadie lying at our feet. Moon puffed away at his vape and spouted out ludicrous conspiracy theories while I mostly just spaced out to the soothing sound of his voice. This obsession with conspiracy theories was the one odd thing about Moon. He preached to me about the dangers of corporate infiltration in politics, clogged pineal glands, cloned babies, brain-cell-killing pesticides, and underground stockpiles of bombs and deadly weapons, among other things.

Realizing that he'd lost me after one particularly long tirade, Moon joked, "This is what you get when you a give a man his own mountain and nobody to share it with besides his dog."

Both of us got such a good laugh out of that one that Sadie got up from her resting spot on the mat by the front door to investigate the cause of all of the noise we were making. She pushed her nose onto Moon's lap and made her whining noise that sounded like humming. Moon ruffled Sadie's ears and gave her a reassuring pat on the head.

"Don't you worry, girl," Moon clucked at her. "I'm not complaining. I'd rather your company than most humans'. You're an exception, Skye."

I tried and failed to convey to Moon how grateful I was for the gift of being able to stay on his land. Coming back to Red Mountain after my long days out job-hunting felt like taking my first deep breath after holding my breath underwater for a long time. I set aside some time every day to soak in this relief as a means of recovering from the almost constant state of panic I felt whenever I left Moon's land. During this precious time off, I would sit under Mama Madrone with my headphones on and play Chance the Rapper's album *Coloring Book* on repeat. I listened to Chance's song "Blessings" almost as a form of meditation, using this song as an exercise to come up with a list of all the blessings in my life right now. I always surprised myself with how long this list was. Even in this time when it felt like I had nothing, I realized just how many blessings were keeping me alive, safe, and well.

Whenever I could tear myself away from the sense of safety Red Mountain afforded me, I was in town trying to meet as many new people as possible. The first thing I did in the morning was head to one of Nevada City's many coffee shops, my favorite being an espresso bar called the Curly Wolf. After buying the one cup of coffee I allotted for myself each day, I picked the most crowded part of the coffee shop to sit in for a couple of hours. Every conversation I initiated became a part of the numbers game I was playing in my head. The more people I talked to, the more likely my chance was of meeting the one person who could truly help me.

Once I hit a social wall in the coffee shop scene, I alternated between going to the co-op in Grass Valley or the elusive *café on the ridge*. The co-op was a local, organic grocery store with a nice patio and seating area out front. Although I refrained from purchasing any of the countless delicious-looking items within the store, I spent more hours than were reasonable sitting at the tables outside it. I wasn't the only wannabe trimmer who'd been told to come to the co-op. In my time sitting outside the co-op, I not only met other potential job leads, but also a lot of other trimmers who'd come here from all over the world looking for work. Relieved to meet other people who understood what I was going through, I spent a day roaming around the co-op with a band of fellow wannabes. Although this made approaching new people a lot easier, it took me only a few hours to understand how roaming in a group lowered my personal chances at finding work. I decided I could no longer allow myself this indulgence.

The hardest part of making the decision to go solo was telling one particularly clingy trimmer from Spain, Jaime, that it was in both of our best interests if he didn't follow me around anymore. Jaime didn't even try to hide his disappointment in hearing this and went so far as to fight me on it. I met Jaime when he bought me a beer on my second night out on the town. Unlike Moon, Jaime believed I still owed him something for that first beer he bought me. Or perhaps he was just hoping those five dollars would go a lot further than they did. In an effort to avoid running into Jaime for a few days, I decided to replace my time at the co-op with a visit up to the ridge. Like the co-op, the *café on the ridge* was recommended to me as a destination farm owners visited on trips into town to restock supplies. I pestered one of the trimmers at the co-op into finally sharing with me which ridge everyone was alluding to. Glancing around to make sure no one else was listening, the trimmer gave me directions to the ridge.

In hushed tones, the trimmer explained to me, "When they need extra help, farm owners drive over to the ridge in pickup trucks. They pick up as many people as they can fit in the bed of their truck. If you're not there early holding your spot in line, you'll never have a chance at getting picked up."

The morning after I received this beta, I woke up at six and drove straight up to the ridge. The scene I landed on pushed me further out of my comfort zone than any of my previous experiences in Nevada City. What I discovered could most crudely be described as a large camp of homeless people living in the woods. Although the town on the ridge had a small main street with a few buildings, the only building that looked open was the café. The main gathering spot in the town was not the café but the parking lot across the street. This parking lot served as base camp for everyone there. Tents were strewn wherever there was space among the cars and RVs. While I picked out a few faces that belonged to people about my age, the overwhelming majority of the population was men in their forties or older. Most of the men who I walked by looked down when I passed. The eyes I did catch were red with strain. I ran into more than one old man talking to himself as if he were addressing an invisible crowd. The overall atmosphere on the ridge was one of paranoia.

I couldn't help but wonder how I'd ended up among this collection of crusty, tripped out homeless dudes. While I may have received a fancy college degree in international affairs, traveled all around the world, and learned to speak multiple languages, none of these assets did me much good. As hard as it was to admit to myself, I was just as desperate as most of these homeless men. The main difference was that I had been desperate for a lot less time than they had. From the looks of it, I had also smoked a lot less weed. While I guessed my mental faculties were in better working condition, I was in no place to judge. Sitting down on the curb outside the café, I joined the ranks of men waiting their turn for a promising pickup truck to pass by.

By the time I'd spent over two hours roving around the co-op or hanging out at the ridge, I no longer had the energy to mask how exhausted I was with another forced smile. Around lunchtime, I headed back to Red Mountain to see what Moon was up to. Most days, Moon invited me to venture off the property in his jeep. We drove for hours down unnamed, irretraceable forest roads. Moon showed me the view from the top of Red Mountain. He took me to the best place in Nevada County to watch the sunset. He shared with me a secret spot he found where water had carved a natural bath-tub into an outcropping of smooth, black stone. As seemed to be the way with us, Moon did most of the talking on these outings. I relaxed into a less bubbly but far more natural version of myself. Since Moon couldn't hike too far before his back started hurting, our outings didn't take up more than two or three hours. This gave me enough time back at camp to recharge under Mama Madrone before cooking my one hot meal of the day on my Coleman stove.

With or without Moon, I drove myself back into town to take advantage of Nevada City's thriving nightlife. Almost every night of the week, there was music playing somewhere or some type of event going on at Elixart. I attended every event I caught wind of, although I made sure to stick to my no-spend rule. Very sadly, this meant forgoing beer. On these nights out, I sometimes wondered if I should have allowed myself the purchase of one alcoholic drink per night instead of one cup of coffee every morning, if anything just for the social lubricant alcohol provides. Regrettably, I am too much of a coffee freak for this to have been a viable option.

Walletless, I hopped among bars as perhaps the most sober, boringly dressed person in town. I didn't trouble myself to compete with the other women there in terms of sexual appeal or extravagance in costume. For better or worse, the vibe I exuded was simple and forthright. Since I had no access to a washing machine or regular use of a shower, simple but respectably put-together was about the only look I could pull off. I was also cautious not to seem to be overtly selling myself or my body. Most of the clothes that I chose did a better job of hiding my curves than highlighting them. Although I was a lot less beguiling than my competition, my straightforwardness won me favors when it came to gaining people's trust. Most everyone I talked to tried to help me in whatever way they could, even just by offering me advice. Then, there were the countless phone numbers I was given—phone numbers that almost always rang through to voice mail whenever I tried calling them the next day.

Day five found me back at the co-op, sitting at the table outside closest to the front entrance. I'd been here for at least two hours, and I was about ready to pack up my stuff and leave. That day marked a new low point. I hadn't found the energy to approach a single new person at the Curly Wolf Espresso House that morning. The only way that I internally justified the four dollars I spent on my cappuccino was by researching blogs from other trimmers with their recommendations for how they managed to find work. Following the advice from one of these blogs, I'd resorted to my most desperate and self-abasing tactic yet. Ripping out one of the pages of my journal, I made myself a sign. The only thing on the sign was a pair of trimming scissors that I'd drawn in, followed by a large question mark. I'd been sitting behind this sign for a few hours now, half-waiting for someone from the co-op to come outside and kick me out.

The sign drew a few people over to me, but not the kind of people I was looking to meet. Most of the people who approached me were seedy-looking men with leering smiles who talked down to me in a manner meant to remind me I was below them. Then, there was Jaime, who'd learned my routine well enough to show up at most of the places I frequented around the same time I got there. Every time he appeared, Jaime put on a show of it being a big, pleasant surprise to see me again. He did his best to sell me on all the opportunities he'd heard of and make the same empty proposals he was receiving sound more promising than they actually were. When Jaime discovered my newest strategy, I could no longer feign the self-assuredness that I wore like a protective cloak whenever I was around him.

Jaime admonished me, "Skye! Why do you do this to yourself? I tell you so many times how much easier it is if you work with a partner. Every day, I tell you about all the people I am talking to. Every day, you tell me, 'No, no, Jaime. I'm fine by myself!' You put yourself at risk like this. Don't you see? Without someone strong to protect you, anything can happen."

Glaring up at Jaime, I folded my paper sign in half and stuck it inside my journal for safe-keeping. Realizing that I was getting up to leave, Jaime tried one last time to stop me.

"Did you hear what I said? You should think about my offer. With me, you do not have to worry. No signs, no worries, no danger."

What infuriated me so much about Jaime's proposition was that his premise wasn't entirely wrong. Exposing myself like that *did* put me at risk. Nonetheless, I resented the idea that just because I was alone and female, this automatically implied that I needed a stronger, male protector to defend me. Jaime was yet another person who had confused my vulner-ability with helplessness. As I was about to walk away, I spun around to face him one last time.

"Listen. I know how to ask for help when I need it. Until then, you disrespect me by continuing to offer help I have not asked for and do not want. So please, back off."

Jaime let out an exasperated sigh, shaking his head at me.

"You are a very stubborn girl. You know that, don't you?" Jaime shouted after me.

I didn't bother turning around. Once I reached my car, I slid into the only safe space I could call my own. I glanced around me one more time to make sure Jaime was out of sight before collapsing onto my steering wheel. My sobs were like birds pushing their way through the bars of my ribcage. They ripped my chest open. As hard as I cried, no sound escaped my mouth. I'd used up the last of my voice standing up for myself to Jaime. The mental strain was causing my nerves to fray and snap in places. I didn't know how much longer I could hold myself together. That day was only day five of my allotted seven, but so much had happened on each of these days that they felt more like five lifetimes.

When the flow of my tears reduced to the point that I could at least clearly see in front of me, I drove myself back to Red Mountain. Once through the gate, I ran out of my car and up the hill to Mama Madrone. Sliding my back down her smooth trunk, I came to a seat at the base of the tree, my legs splayed out on the ground alongside her roots. I didn't bother listening to music or trying to come up with a list of the things for which I was grateful. I simply zoned out and turned my brain off for a while. I was jolted out of my zombie-like state by a wet tongue lapping at my fingers. Sadie had come to make sure I was OK. She wagged her tail and looked up at me with big, inquisitive eyes, humming at me in that way she had. By the time Moon caught up with Sadie, I was hugging her close to me in a full-on embrace, my face buried into her neck. Moon knelt down near where I was sitting and pulled both me and Sadie in for a big hug.

"Is everything all right?" Moon probed cautiously.

Moon had come to understand and respect me as a mostly

private person. With all the time we'd spent together, Moon had picked up on my preference to listen more than talk. I was hesitant to share how hard a time I'd been having. I was afraid that admitting the truth to someone else would somehow make it all more real. Before I wrote all this down, Evie was the only person I told about the hours I spent sitting behind a paper sign. This sign was a white flag of surrender I put up in one last effort to avoid drowning along with my sinking ship. Of course, it was once I'd stowed my flag that a genuine offer for help finally came. Now that a real friend was there, I didn't know how to accept the help he was offering me.

All I could get out at first was, "I don't know if I can keep going like this …"

Moon looked down at the ground, giving me the space and time to collect myself.

A few breaths later, I continued, "I'm trying really hard to stay positive, but I have so many doubts. Whenever I let my guard down, these doubts eat me alive. I'm starting to wonder if any job I find is even worth all this stress in the first place."

Moon sighed, sinking down from his kneeling position to take a seat beside me.

"The work is out there, Skye. You're going to find it. Or, if you can relax a little, the work is going to find you."

"I hope you're right," I muttered back, sounding unconvinced.

Moon reached over to squeeze my shoulder.

Speaking in a firmer tone than I was used to from him, Moon insisted, "What you need is to take your mind off all of this for a bit. I have a proposal that could help with that. The original reason I came up here was to invite you to a tea party my friends are hosting tonight. These friends have some pretty powerful potions and tonics that they share with the group after the tea ceremony—really healing stuff. If you're up for it, I feel like coming tonight could do you some good."

My first reaction upon Moon mentioning the word *party* was exhaustion. I imagined a whole new house full of strangers with whom I would be forced to introduce myself. Picking up on my mood change, Moon jumped in to assuage this anxiety.

"Maybe this time, you could take it easy on yourself. You don't have to force yourself to talk to so many new people. You could just go to have a good time."

"You may not believe this," I told Moon, "but under normal circumstances, I love a good house party. I'm not always this ... wound-up."

"Why not take this as a chance to come back to that part of yourself? You deserve a break."

Sensing the pureness of Moon's intentions, I relented.

"OK, OK. I'll come. Just give me some time to put the pieces of myself back together again."

"Don't worry, hon'. I won't be leaving for the next few

hours. I also have some good news for you. I fixed my water heater, which means I can officially take hot showers in the RV again! I filled up my water tank, so I was going to ask if you wanted to take one. I can step out and take Sadie for a walk around the neighborhood while you're in there."

The closest I'd come to showering since staying with Jake in LA was jumping in the Yuba River. My skin itched for a good scrub. The idea of hot water cascading down onto my skin from a magical source above me was such a luxury that I almost started crying all over again.

"Moon, you're an angel," I said, pulling Moon and Sadie in for another hug.

~⌀

I walked into the party wearing a new protective armor, the *fuck everything, I don't care anymore* shield. Lingering around the table with the food, I nibbled on healthy vegan snacks and casually chitchatted with the people standing around me. Out of the corner of my eye, I spotted Moon at the other end of the backyard. Lost in conversation with one of his friends, Moon was waving his hands to accentuate whatever point he was making. I chuckled to myself a little, wondering if his friend was getting to hear one of Moon's infamous political spiels. Neither of us had made it into the house yet where the tea ceremony was taking place. The house was so packed that I had little motivation to squeeze my way inside. Everyone inside appeared to be engaged in some kind of group meditation, a pretty unappealing activity to me at the moment. I was too scattered and unfocused to be able to reach any kind of meditative mind state right then.

Half an hour later, a ripple of movement spread throughout the house. Everyone in the group meditation stood up and began to move around the room. I hadn't moved much in this time, although I had talked to three or four different people standing around the food table. Interestingly, the people I was talking to were actually from Nevada City. Although I caught wind of a few different accents floating around the backyard, most of the people I met from overseas had been living in the area for a few years. Besides me, the other new arrival to town was Jaime, who showed up at the party shortly after Moon and I arrived. After acknowledging my presence with a curt nod of the head, Jaime knew well enough to leave me alone.

As more people flowed from inside the house out to the backyard for fresh air, I was relieved to lose sight of Jaime in the crowd. Everyone coming out of the house seemed to be on some kind of elevated level. They moved through the backyard as if they were swimming through water. I caught a few of them nod and smile at each other knowingly. I felt like I'd been left out of some kind of shared group secret. I needed to wait only a few minutes before discovering the liquid nature of this secret. A white-haired man with a pointy beard, a bright yellow scarf, and the biggest smile of anyone at the party ambled around with a pitcher of liquid in one hand and a stack of plastic cups in the other. The man offered everyone he passed a cup of the murky green liquid. By the time he reached me, I was intrigued enough to accept.

"Thanks for sharing. What's in the pitcher?" I asked, trying not to seem overly suspicious.

"Kratom, sister. Do I take it that this is your first experience with the herb?"

The man beamed at me benevolently to indicate the lack of judgment behind this question. Staring down at my cup uneasily, I nodded. Rather than be offended at my open show of distrust, the man appeared genuinely delighted at the opportunity to educate me. Setting down the pitcher and cups, he brought his hands together as if he were about to deliver a sermon.

"Going back to its origins, kratom is a tropical evergreen tree native to South Asia that's part of the coffee family. What's remarkable about this herbal extract is that the plant acts as both a stimulant and a sedative. From my energetic reading of you, you seem to be in remarkable physical health. Nonetheless, kratom has much more to offer besides its pain-numbing abilities. This powerful potion also helps dull unpleasant mental sensations. One of the most powerful mental sensations that it numbs is fear. As both a sedative and a stimulant, kratom doesn't numb its drinker to the point of dopiness. It simply clears the space that fear once occupied in the mind and allows for a fresh, unburdened sense of euphoria to take its place."

My mind flashed to an image of me sitting under Mama Madrone with my eyes closed and Chance the Rapper playing in the background. I thought of all the hours I'd spent meditating under this great tree, pulling out each fear-consumed thought like a gardener extracting weeds from her secret garden. Then there came this smiling, bearded man telling me that I needed to work no more. He offered a magical fertilizer. He promised me that all I needed to do was sprinkle a little bit of this fertilizer onto my tongue and all the invasive, fear-bound thoughts would disappear from my internal garden. Accepting the kratom felt like cheating, but I was too weary to concern myself with playing by a set of made-up rules. I'd been forcing my way forward for too long, fighting to regain some elusive sense of control. I'd bought into the idea that, if I pushed hard enough and fought long enough, I could bend my life to my will. In reality, life was bending me to its own will, and I was the one on the verge of breaking. The only thing I could do without breaking was let go.

Peering down at the green-brown liquid in my cup, I downed its contents in one swift gulp.

Taking another sip out of his own cup, the man saluted me, "May kratom bring you the peace that you are seeking."

Then, the man moved on to serve the next eager party guest in line. It took no more than a few minutes for the potion to work its effects on me. I felt a little dizzy at first, nauseated from all the food that I'd eaten. However, the dizziness cleared away like a dust storm swirling across the field of my mind, gathering up and removing all the debris in its path. Once the dizziness subsided, I was overcome with a desire to laugh for no particular reason. I surveyed the backyard scene in a whole new light, marveling as all the unfamiliar faces around me lost their intimidating effect. As I took in all the shining faces of the party-goers around me, I found myself drawn to one face in particular. Or perhaps I should say I was drawn to one particular head of hair. The hair belonged to a young woman about my same age. It was bright copper, almost orange in color, and was pulled up into a messy top bun to highlight the side of the woman's head, which was shaved. The woman had a soft-looking face with remarkably pale skin, although the skin on her cheeks was pockmarked and covered with tiny, red scars. Noticing me watching her, the woman locked eyes with me from across the backyard. Her eyes were the color of pale blue glacial ice. Although she was staring directly at me, there was a hazy, distant quality to her stare that made me feel as if I were peering through an opaque glass window.

Unable to restrain myself, I walked up to the small group of people standing around her and introduced myself.

"Hey. I don't think I've met any of you yet. I'm Skye," I murmured in a daze, surprised at the effort I had to put into not slurring my words.

Everyone in the circle went around and said their names. The copper-haired girl was the last to speak. She greeted me in a drawl that sounded at once lazy and intimate.

"Hi, Skye. I'm Lulu, Lulu Chimera. You new around here?"

Clearly Lulu was not new to this scene, for she recognized me as a strange face.

"Yeah, I am. I came here with Moon, if you know who he is. What about you? Are you from around here?"

Intuitively, I sensed to share as little about myself with Lulu Chimera as possible. I deflected any questions Lulu asked me back to her. This strategy worked remarkably well. Similar to Moon, Lulu was another person who loved to talk. Having already listened to Lulu talk for a while, the people standing in the circle used my arrival as an excuse to slip away. Before I knew it, Lulu and I found ourselves talking alone on the outskirts of the backyard. In the five or so minutes since I'd introduced myself, Lulu had already divulged to me intimate details about the three lovers revolving in out of the rotating door of her life. The name of the lover that came up the most was Pavos.

Her eyes clouding over with an indescribable emotion, Lulu asked me, "Have you ever felt like you've given away a part of yourself to someone that you can never get back? That's how it is with Pavos. All my other lovers are just distractions I use to bide my time until Pavos comes back to me. He always comes back, usually around the time that I start to forget about him. Whenever Pavos and I are together, all the time we spent apart doesn't seem real anymore. Sometimes, our love feels like the only real thing I've ever experienced. Have you ever felt anything like that?"

I was stuck for a moment, uncertain of how to reply. I sensed that what Lulu really wanted in that moment was someone to tell her that they understood. Although Lulu didn't really care about the details of my story, I couldn't evade her question entirely. This meant that I couldn't dodge the emotional blow that would come with bringing up Liam's name. Since leaving Durango, I'd avoided thinking about this name, or the person attached to it, whenever possible. Yet there I was, being asked to talk about my experiences with love. To not bring up Liam up would be like lying. My intuition told me that Lulu Chimera was not a person to whom I should lie.

"Something like that ..." I replied after a long pause.

Lulu's icy blue eyes narrowed in on my own, prompting me to continue.

"To be honest, it's hard for me to talk about him. I'm trying not to even think about him, but he's always there, hovering on the margin of my thoughts."

The icy distance in Lulu's eyes melted, and her shoulders relaxed a little farther away from her ears.

"Your lover, where is he now? Did you leave him to come here?"

Again, I was aware of the fact that I had to be selective with the information I shared. I also felt a gentle sort of prodding that poked at my side like a nagging reminder of some forgotten piece of advice that could be useful to me then. Exploring the source of this prodding, I received a flash of insight that pointed me to the potential opportunity laced into this exchange. This was the third time that my intuition had spoken to me in the course of this conversation alone. For weeks, months even, my intuition had lain dormant, frustratingly inaccessible. Or perhaps my intuition had been there all along, whispering its guidance to me, but the incessant anxious chatter in my mind had been too loud for me to hear it. Finally, I'd been given a reprieve from all the noise in my own head. The kratom had turned down the volume on my anxiety, raising the volume of my instinct. Thanks to the kratom, I glided through this conversation effortlessly, following each gentle intuitive prodding, trusting that my instinct would take me where I needed to go.

Seizing the opportunity that had presented itself, I replied, "Yeah, I did. Tell you the truth, I'm not sure it was worth it.

I'm in a tough place right now. I don't know how much longer I can get by out here."

Reaching out to touch my hand, Lulu asked, "Are you safe? You mentioned that you came with someone to this party. Moon, was it? Is he someone you can trust?"

Jumping in to defend Moon, I assured her, "So far, Moon is the only person here who I can trust. He's letting me camp on his land while I look for work. I don't know what I would do without him."

Lulu raised and lowered her head in a slow nod that indicated her understanding of my situation.

"I see. You're a trimmer then. So am I. I've been trimming every season for the past five years. What about you? Do you have experience trimming?"

Again, I selected my words carefully to highlight the information I wanted Lulu to pick up on. As carefully as I'd chosen my words, I still had to focus so as not to slur them.

"Yeah, I've trimmed before, mainly back in Colorado to help out my friends. You wouldn't happen to have any friends out here who need help on their farms, would you?"

It didn't take Lulu more than a second to respond, "Of course. Give me your number, and I'll hook you up. But here's the thing. If I'm going to help you out, I need to know I can trust you. Maybe we can get together outside of this party and grab coffee sometime?"

I did my best to appear nonchalant as I gave Lulu my number, unable to believe the ease with which this opportunity fell into my lap. Lulu was the first person who had told me a solid yes instead of a retractable maybe. My elation at finally hear the word yes, mixed in with the kratom swirling through my bloodstream, lifted my spirits so high that I looked down at my feet to make sure they were still connected to the ground. In the time it took me to look back up and meet Lulu's eyes again, I took in a deep breath and composed my face into a more neutral expression. I didn't want Lulu to know how desperate I was. I sensed that my neediness would estrange me rather than endear me to her. After I put my number into her phone, I changed the subject, circling the conversation back around to the lovers and friends Lulu had met throughout her own travels. We talked for a few minutes longer until we heard the sound of music floating over to us from inside the house. Drawn to the high-tempo psytrance beat, Lulu became sidetracked enough that we could no longer continue our conversation. She excused herself to go join the dance collective that was forming inside.

I floated my way over to the circle that Moon was a part of. Eventually, his group of friends also decided to make their way inside toward the source of the music. I trailed behind Moon and stepped into the house for my first time that evening. A live DJ had set up a small booth in the hallway between the living room and kitchen. The once full pitcher of kratom now sat empty on the kitchen counter. In contrast with the fast-paced tempo of the beat, the people on the dance floor moved at the same languid tempo that made it appear as if they were swimming through water. I jumped into the imaginary pool and swam a few laps around the dance floor myself. Just when I felt about ready to drown in my kratom-induced languor, Moon came to the rescue yet again. With Moon holding my arm, we floated out of the house, into his car, and back up the road that took us home to Red Mountain.

The next morning, I lingered an extra hour or so at the Curly Wolf Espresso House, still trying to recover from my kratom hangover. I could feel the anxiety snaking its way back into the internal garden of my mind. Looking back, the events of the past night were hazy. I couldn't shake the fear that I'd made a fool of myself. Just as I was contemplating splurging on an extra shot of espresso, my phone vibrated in my pocket. A number I didn't recognize flashed across the screen. Sifting through my hazy memory, I tried to recall who all I'd given my number to. The only thing I clearly remembered was the color orange.

In a voice as sluggish as my thoughts that morning, I answered, "Hello?"

"Skye? It's Lulu, Lulu Chimera."

Thank goodness for the uniqueness of Lulu's name. Hearing it unlocked the door to my memory. Our whole conversation from the previous night, or at least most of it, replayed itself in my head. Even in my memory, I found myself fixated on the icy blue color of Lulu's eyes. I wondered at their opaqueness, at what lay hidden behind this glass façade. Musing on this, I heard myself exclaim something appropriately enthusiastic in reply to Lulu.

The next thing I knew, Lulu was asking me, "Are you free right now?"

Lulu invited me to come meet her at her favorite coffee shop in Grass Valley. This provided me with the perfect excuse to purchase the second cup of coffee I'd been craving. Fewer than fifteen minutes later, Lulu and I met at a small coffee shop in Grass Valley that doubled as a local florist and plant store. I was the first to arrive by a few minutes. Hoping to smooth out the jitteriness of my nerves, I pulled out the book I was reading, *Désert* by J.M.G. Le Clézio. I bought *Désert* while traveling around Morocco as a means of practicing my French. It turned out to be one of my favorite books I'd ever read. Reading it brought me so much joy that I took the book with me almost everywhere I went. In no time, I got so lost in the world Le Clézio created that Lulu's arrival a couple of minutes later startled me.

Setting her coffee down on the table, Lulu grabbed *Désert* right out of my hands.

"Tu parles français aussi?" Lulu quizzed me with a noticeably rusty French accent.

I couldn't help the smile that spread across my face. Lulu and I threw a few French phrases back and forth with each other. I overlooked the occasional grammatical mistake that slipped into her sentences. As easy as I went on her, Lulu tired of speaking in French after a few minutes.

Rolling her eyes, Lulu proclaimed, "French is hard. I only learned it because I was married to a Moroccan man, Rafiq, who spoke French. Technically, I'm still married to him. Moroccans can be very jealous men. Neither of us loves each other anymore, but Rafiq doesn't want to relinquish possession of me to someone else. So I just pretend we're not married and wait for the day that he agrees to sign the divorce papers."

Lulu broke off there, studying me again with narrowed eyes.

"Did you say he's Moroccan?"

"Yeah, Moroccan. You know, like from Africa," Lulu dismissed my question with a wave of the hand.

"I was just there! And *Désert*, the book you're holding, that takes place in Morocco!"

Lulu glanced at the book she was about to set down with new interest.

"Really? I was honestly just looking at the picture on the front cover. But fuck the book. Did you say you were just in Morocco?"

"Yeah! I went there to meet the lover I was telling you about, Liam. Along with an ex-lover of mine who was traveling with him, but that's a long story."

Lulu drawled, "Wow, we must be some kind of synchronized, honey. Most of my friends have never even heard of Morocco."

Taking full advantage of this lucky coincidence, I shifted the conversation back to Lulu and her husband, Rafiq. The longer we talked about her marriage with Rafiq, the harder time I had holding back the burning question on my mind. Finally, I could no longer help myself.

"I have to ask, Lulu—how old are you? You look so young. But you've already been married, and you've been out here on your own trimming for so many years ..."

Lulu giggled in a way that made her seem younger than ever.

"I'm twenty-two. I left home when I was fourteen. I've been drifting since then. As you know, I've spent five years trimming weed out here. Finding my first trimming job saved my life. The first farm owner who took me under his wing is one of the lovers I told you about, Boss. And, yes, Boss is his real name. The door to my legs will always be open for Boss after all he's done for me."

So many lovers, so many experiences, so few years. As wild as my life seemed at the moment, Lulu had a thing or two to teach me about recklessness. Looking so directly at Lulu that she couldn't avoid my gaze, I perceived a new beauty in the icy coolness of her stare. To survive a life as difficult as hers hardens a person. No longer able to dismiss her as the tripped-out hippie that I originally took her for, I regarded Lulu Chimera with a newfound respect.

In honor of the frail sense of respect that had been built between us, Lulu promised me, "If I can help someone out in the same way that Boss helped me, I'll feel like I'm finally free of the debt I owe him. So I'll do what I can to help you. Do you have a piece of paper I could use? It helps me to sketch things out as I speak."

I ripped out an empty page at the back of my journal and slid it over to Lulu along with my pen. What she drew on the paper at first appeared to be nothing more than a few half-assed daisies and lazily drawn butterflies. Without picking the pen up off the paper, Lulu looped the stems of the flowers into one another until the haphazard shapes she was drawing began to form a name. The first name that she wrote out was *Genji*, followed by *Boss* a little farther down the page. Squeezed into the very bottom of the paper was a third name, *John*.

"These are a few of the options I have for work this season. I know a lot of people, but these names belong to the people I owe something to. Genji lives here, much closer to town than the rest of them. The main reason I need to work for Genji is to repay him for this tattoo."

Lulu moved her right leg out from underneath the table and pulled up her long skirt to reveal a tattoo that swirled up the whole length of her leg from her ankle to her hip. The part of the tattoo I could see depicted a forest scene in which real-life animals were intermingled with fantastical ones. The tattoo was a bold and elegant piece of art.

"Anyway," Lulu carried on, "I owe Genji big time for this. I could always ask if he needs another hand. Don't worry, you'd be paid in cash. Then, there's Boss. There's always Boss. Boss lives on the coast near Humboldt. I would be there trimming for him already, but Boss's ex-girlfriend threatened to shoot me the last time I was there. So we just have to go out there and kill her first. Then, you're guaranteed a job."

My eyes widened as I waited for Lulu to laugh or indicate in some way that she was joking. An instant later than acceptable, her mouth fell open to release a lolling, lukewarm chortle.

"Don't worry. I'm a lover, not a killer," Lulu assured me with that same dismissive wave of the hand.

I said very little, sensing that Lulu was on a roll and not wanting to disrupt the fragile momentum she'd gained.

"The thing is, Boss pays so well, and he has a huge house right on the ocean. I'm his best trimmer, too, and he knows it.

I'm sure he's missing my hands for more than one reason right now. If you're up for the risk, we could drive out there and see what happens. But I don't really know you or have any idea of how you would handle all of that. So I put John's name down just in case. John is a friend of a friend, and he really needs help right now. I just don't know where John's farm is exactly."

Presented with these three mostly underwhelming options, I was unsure how to reply. Smiling, Lulu continued her casual doodling as if lost in some kind of daydream. This time, it took Lulu only a minute or so to snap out of her stupor. She set my pen down and folded up the piece of paper.

"Keep this, why don't you?"

I agreed, with the intention of holding onto Lulu's drawing as more of a keepsake than anything of potential use to me. As I tried to process the many turns our conversation had taken, Lulu stood up and gathered her belongings to leave. She'd barely touched her coffee. She gave me no explanation of where she was going. Feeling dazed, I packed up my own stuff to leave, unsure as to where I would head next. Trying to come up with any sort of a game plan, I sat for a moment longer. Fidgeting anxiously with my hands, I opened and closed the piece of paper that Lulu had given me. Opening the paper one more time, I scanned the three names Lulu had written as if they held some sort of secret code that would tell me what to do. My eyes came to rest on the final name Lulu had written, *John*. Besides this name, hidden among all the haphazardly drawn flowers, I noticed a new pattern that wasn't there before, a pattern that upon careful scrutiny looked a lot like a phone number.

chapter eleven

BLESSINGS

I CALLED THE PHONE NUMBER written next to John's name immediately upon leaving the coffee shop.

"Hello? Is this John?"

A surprisingly young-sounding voice on the other end of the line replied, "Who's calling?"

"My name is Skye. Lulu gave me this number. She said you're a friend of hers and that you may need some extra help right now?"

For a moment, there was silence.

"Lulu?"

"Yeah, Lulu Chimera," I elaborated, praying that this

phone number wouldn't turn into another dead end.

"Oh, Lulu!" the still-unnamed voice repeated, "The redhead. Gotcha. Most people call me Aukai these days, so you threw me off guard. But you're right, we could use some help right now."

"Great! And you said it was ... Akai, then?"

"Aukai," he corrected me, "but John's fine if you can't remember that. And you're Skye? Are you interested in working for us then, Skye?"

I toned down the enthusiasm in my voice to an acceptable level before chiming in, "Definitely! I would ... um ... just love to know a little bit more about your farm and what you're looking for right now."

"Well, we're hurting for trimmers. We've got about fifteen trimmers onsite, but our max capacity is closer to thirty. Anyway, you'll have plenty of space on the property to set up your camp. Camping on the farm is free, and we provide breakfast, snacks, and dinner. That's on top of your wage, which is $125 per pound. We'll pay you all your wages at the end of the season, unless something happens and you need to leave earlier."

John paused here as if expecting me to object or react in some way. As little as five years ago, farms paid around $300 or even $400 per pound of trimmed marijuana. Everyone I'd met on my job hunt had warned me how much the industry had changed in recent years. The upcoming legalization of marijuana in California brought the statewide prices of marijuana way down, which in turn caused trimming wages to plummet. Aware of these recent changes, I'd been optimistically hoping to make somewhere around $150 per pound. While John's farm fell below the average going wage, the free food and lodging helped make up for some of that difference.

After doing some quick math in my head, I agreed, "I can work with that. When's the soonest I can start?"

"The sooner the better, as far as we're concerned."

"OK, awesome! I'm in Nevada City right now. Depending on how far you are from here, I should be able to get to the property sometime tomorrow."

"We're a few hours south of you. And just to warn you, we're pretty far out here. The closest decent-sized town is called Jackson. There's not too much going on in Jackson, so take the time to get whatever supplies you need before coming down."

"Got it. And ... um, what's your address?"

I held my breath, hardly daring to believe the conversation had come this far already. I didn't dare exhale until John gave me the address and I had him repeat it a second time. Along with the address, John gave me the gate code to get into the property.

Paying close attention, I listened as John explained, "You'll pull up to a dark green gate. The code I gave you will open the padlock on that gate. Once you're through, drive up the hill and go left at the split in the road. You'll see everyone's cars and tents a little farther down the hill. After you've parked, walk the rest of the way down the hill. You'll find me with my nose stuck in one of the big sheds. Sound good?"

I took a second to go over the details in my head and make sure that I hadn't missed anything in my excitement. I'd been given an address in the middle of nowhere and a gate code to let myself into a locked property. The property was locked because the operation underway on its land was illegal. I'd agreed to join in on this illegal operation and work as a trimmer with a band of strangers led by a man whose name had undergone a radical, unexplained transformation from John to Aukai. This man vaguely knew Lulu Chimera, who I also vaguely knew as one of the trippiest people I'd met in the trippiest town I'd ever been in.

"Yeah, I think we're good! I'll see you tomorrow."

The only thing that came close to dampening my spirits on this long-awaited day was having to break the news to Moon that I was leaving. After I'd packed everything except for my tent into my car, I walked back down the hill and sat inside Moon's trailer with Moon and Sadie one last time. The first thing that Moon did after I told him about John's job offer was pull me in for a big hug.

Pulling back from our hug to ruffle my hair playfully, Moon teased, "What did I tell you? Sometimes, it's not about finding the right opportunity. It's about relaxing enough to let the right opportunity find you."

Laughing, I let myself fall back onto the little couch in Moon's trailer. Moon hovered around the kitchen, flitting from one cupboard to the next as he prepared to make us both some tea, this time the herbal and not the hallucinogenic kind. The lankiness of Moon's limbs and the erraticism of his movements made it appear as if he were flailing midair. Sensing the excitement and nervous energy between us, Sadie picked up her head to whine at us intermittently throughout the conversation. Moon did his best to act unfazed at the news of my upcoming departure, but he talked even more than usual and made less sense than he normally did. I was too distracted to pretend I could follow what he was saying. I simply nodded my head at what I hoped were appropriate points in the conversation. Moon carried on like this for some time while I sat silently, savoring the sound of his voice, even if the contents of its message were beyond me. Finally, Moon tired himself out with his own rambling and slouched down onto the couch next to me. He took a few deep puffs from his vape and joined me in my silence. There was so much I wanted to say to him, so much that I wanted to thank him for, that I found myself unable to say anything at all. Moon ended up being the one to break the silence.

"It'll sure feel lonely on Red Mountain without you here," he admitted. "What's Sadie going to do with only me to whine at all day?"

"What am I going to do without Sadie whining to wake me up in the morning?" I joked back in a sorry attempt to duck around the sadness that hung heavy in the air.

Unable to keep up this false sense of light-heartedness, I sighed. The only peace of mind that I'd glimpsed in the past week, or really in the past few weeks, came from the time that I'd spent hanging out with Moon. Moon's kindness felt like the glue holding my life together, and it took all my energy not to fall apart at the thought of saying goodbye to him.

Rather than say goodbye, I conceded, "I'm gonna miss you, Moon."

Taking another pull from his vape, Moon sighed out a cloud of smoke.

"It won't be the same without you here ... so don't be a stranger. You've finally got the code to open up a stranger's gate, but don't forget who first opened his gate to you, OK? For you, my gate's always open."

Not only did I find my way to the mystical green gate that John described to me over the phone, but I succeeded in unlocking this gate and letting myself through it. Driving up the hill beyond the gate, I passed a painted wooden sign that said *Ganesha Wellness Community* in flowery green letters. Ever more curious, I continued onward toward a vacant dirt lot filled with fully packed, similarly grimy cars. God bless my RAV4 and the collection of beat-up cars parked around it, vehicles that served as homes on wheels for the roving, nomadic dirt bags who owned them. After parking my car in the first open space I saw, I sauntered down the hill toward a cluster of sheds and small wooden buildings around which several small groups of people sat outside working. I walked past rows upon rows of ten-plus-feet-tall marijuana plants growing on both sides of the road. I heard shuffling sounds in the field of plants to the right of me and picked out two people standing amid the plants on ladders, which gave them the extra height they needed to cut down the buds at the top of the giant plants. I was impressed enough by the size and quantity of the plants to understand why having only fifteen trimmers constituted a problem for this farm. I walked over to a group of five trimmers working outside around a large folding table that had been set up under a picnic tent canopy. Greeting the group, I introduced myself with a wave and a nervous smile.

Going around the circle, the trimmers introduced themselves in turn. The first woman was from Spain and didn't speak much English. She had short dark hair and was covered in tattoos and piercings. She was wearing so many rings that I wondered how she managed to trim effectively. The woman sitting next to her was a friend of hers from the U.S. Although I couldn't for the life of me remember the name of the Spanish woman, the American woman went by Penelope. Penelope was remarkably pretty and emanated a casual, effortless sensuality. As visually appealing as she was, Penelope's body language and facial expression were not altogether friendly. As if to make up for Penelope's lack of friendliness, the man next to her hurried to introduce himself. This man was middle-aged, Greek, and introduced himself as Delias. Delias had a full head of curls and a smile that made him hard to forget. Delias had come to the farm with his best friend Vasili, another middle-aged but quite handsome Greek man. While Delias exuded the energy of a much younger man, Vasili was much calmer and more soft-spoken. Sitting next to Vasili was a woman about my age with long blond hair and Germanic features. This woman was Hungarian and had come with her Polish boyfriend, who was also blond with the same kind of bland, symmetrical facial features.

Throughout this entire round of introductions, no one in the group set their scissors down once. Everyone sat in front of their own large yellow bin filled to the brim with bud. It was clear to me that some people were working through their bins faster than others. Even the slower moving hands in the group amazed me with their fluidity and grace. Instilled with a new sense of urgency, I excused myself from the group to head farther down the hill toward the collection of wooden buildings and sheds in a clearing at the bottom of the road. On my way, I ran into two women standing in front of a car that was filled with bags and boxes of food and had all its doors wide open. The two women were speaking to each other in hushed tones. One of them smiled and waved her hands to accentuate whatever point she was making. The other woman was doing her best to maintain a neutral expression but looked like she was about to cry. I slowed down my canter as I neared them, sensing that this wasn't a conversation I wanted to interrupt. However, both women had noticed me. It was too late for me to retreat.

"Hey, I'm Skye!" I introduced myself again. "Do you know where I can find John?"

The woman who looked upset used the distraction that my arrival provided as a means of stepping away. This woman appeared to be about my age and was beautiful in a simple, clean-cut way. She had shoulder-length, straight, dirty blond hair and was wearing a V-neck T-shirt and Carhartt overalls. The other woman was also in her midtwenties, and she looked vaguely South American. Brushing her bangs out of her eyes, this woman raised her eyebrows at me before putting one hand over her mouth to suppress a giggle. Her full breasts, barely contained in her earth-colored crop top, jiggled with the slight shake of her shoulders. I could tell from the mockery flashing in her eyes that she was laughing at me and not with me.

She parroted, "John? You mean Aukai? He's probably somewhere in the back of that big shed. I can hardly keep track of him myself these days."

A voice that I recognized shouted out from within the dark recesses of the shed.

"Maya, baby, I'm right here!"

"Oh, Snookums! Do come say goodbye! Calista and I are heading out for the hot springs, and I miss you already, baby," Maya cooed back toward the shed, waiting expectantly with her hands on her hips.

The man who emerged from the shed was young, as I'd predicted—thirty at most. He definitely looked more like a John than an Aukai, but I stuck with calling him Aukai to avoid further ridicule. Aukai was a little taller than me with sparkling blue eyes, light brown hair, and a surprisingly well-maintained beard. He held his arms open to sweep up Maya for a goodbye kiss. I pretended to be busy and wandered off to explore the nearest building, an open-aired kitchen with a large outdoor table covered in trays of utensils, stacks of plates, and two large tubs that served as the dishwashing station. A little outside of the covered kitchen area was a fire pit surrounded by logs, a few folding chairs, and two car seats that had somehow found their way into this circle. The woman wearing the overalls had walked over to sit down on one of the logs. I plopped down on one of the car seats across from her. Lost in thought, the woman looked as if she was trying to work out some kind of troubling idea in her head. When she noticed me sitting across from her at the fire ring, her face softened. Casting aside whatever had been bothering her, she beamed me a smile whose warmth instantly put me at ease.

"Skye, right? Welcome. My name is Sierra."

Staring at me with startlingly large brown eyes, Sierra observed me with a disconcerting focus. She made no attempt to hide the fact that she was studying me, but I detected no judgment in her gaze, just curiosity.

Putting aside my feelings of self-consciousness, I replied, "Thanks. Have you been here for a while?"

"Three months. I'm working with the harvesting crew out in the fields."

I could tell by the sigh that followed this proclamation that, for Sierra, three months was a long time.

As if reading my mind, Sierra continued, "Three months is nothing compared to how long management's been here. And just so you know what's up, management includes Bill, Aukai, Maya, Luke, and Pedro. They've all been here for six months to a year. I will say, though, you're coming at an interesting time ..."

Just as I was about to ask what Sierra meant by interesting, Aukai walked over to the fire circle. I peeked over my shoulder to see Maya hopping into her packed car with a dark-haired, bronze-skinned woman I presumed to be Calista. As the car backed up and took off up the dirt road, I turned back to face Aukai. I was taken aback by the size of the smile on his face. Despite Aukai's public show of affection toward Maya, this smile was noticeably bigger than the one he wore in her presence.

"You must be Skye?" Aukai greeted me, walking over to offer me a warm handshake.

Again, Sierra used Aukai's arrival as an opportunity to make herself scarce. Head down and both hands shoved into the pockets of her overalls, she slunk away, disappearing among the towering stalks of marijuana growing in the fields. Aukai gave me a short tour of the fields and the rest of the property before concluding the tour right back where we started, showing me around the kitchen and to the outdoor shower behind it. Finally, we came back to the shed from which Aukai had emerged. Squinting into the darkness of the shed, the smile that had been on Aukai's face throughout his tour faded into a look of resignation.

"It's about time for me to go back into my hole … This is where we keep all the marijuana, trimmed and untrimmed. I'm in charge of processing all of it. I'm also in charge of giving everyone new bins of bud, so come back and find me when you've set up camp and are ready to work."

I wasted no time in hiking back up the hill toward my car. I picked a spot to camp away from most of the other tents, close enough to two trees for me to be able to put up my large over-head tarp. It took me no more than ten minutes to set up my camp, and then another ten minutes to call Alice and inform her that I was safe and had found a job. I gave her the address of the farm as a backup safety measure, figuring that at least one other person should know where I was. After my conversation with Alice, I hurried back down the hill and found Aukai right where he promised he would be. He handed me my first yellow bin with a strain of weed I would later come to appreciate as remarkably high in quality compared to many of the rest.

"Have you trimmed much before?" Aukai asked me, just as I was about to walk away with the new bin.

After hesitating a second, I admitted, "A little, mostly for friends."

"Well, if you need any help, talking to the other trimmers is your best bet. Delias and Vasili are good workers. I'm sure they'd be glad to help you out with a few pointers."

"Sounds good," I told Aukai with as much conviction as I could muster.

While I knew the basics of how to trim, what worried me was being able to trim at the pace that was expected of me. I'd set the personal goal of trimming two pounds per day. At my current pace, even trimming one pound would be an accomplishment. Part of my problem had to do with my tendency toward perfectionism. I liked to produce a finished bud that looked prettier and more polished than it needed to be. Realizing that I could use the advice, I set down my bin in an open space between Delias and Vasili. I took a few minutes to set up my station, placing the full bin of marijuana next to an empty bin I would use to store all my trimmed marijuana. Delias helped me find a grated tray to sift through the untrimmed bud. He pushed a handful of marijuana across the grates of the tray to exfoliate the larger leaves. The last thing I did before grabbing my scissors was fill a red solo cup with isopropyl rubbing alcohol, which I would use to clean my scissors of the sticky resin they would soon accumulate. Once I was ready to go, Delias picked up a large bud to demonstrate the technique that he preferred.

"Before you start trimming, spin each bud between your fingers. Your fingers spinning over the bud creates friction, which removes the bigger leaves. You should need to cut only one to two times—at most three times. After this, move onto the next bud. Stick to small cuts. Big movements are wasted movements. Eventually, your hands will learn how to do this all by themselves, like you are on autopilot. For now, don't let yourself spend too much time on one bud. Remember, snip, snip, done."

In the minute that he'd spent explaining this, Delias had already worked his way through a handful of the buds on his tray. I did my best to mimic Delias's movements, but my hands felt too large and clumsy to produce the micromovements being asked of them. I was nowhere near being able to trim on autopilot yet. While my hands weren't trained to move in this particular manner, the one thing I had going for me was concentration. I sat down to trim around 3:00 p.m. and didn't stop working until the dinner bell rang four hours later. Even at dinner, I didn't spend much time hanging around the fire circle after eating. I gulped down the bean stew and toast that had been set out for us before moving my trimming station into the indoor, brightly lit trimming shed. I worked until Aukai came into the shed around 10:00 p.m. with another manager, a man named Pedro from Mexico. One by one, Aukai and Pedro called up everyone working in the trimming shed to weigh their product.

Along with the group of trimmers I first met outside, there were three trimmers from Argentina who sat across from me in the shed, a couple from England, and two other Americans. The American woman was good friends with the last trimmer I met, a man named Rudy from Uruguay. Rudy exuded a machismo that was justified by the fact that he trimmed almost a pound more per day than everyone else on the farm, producing an average of three pounds of trimmed marijuana every day. As if I needed another reason to dread my turn at being weighed, my name was called right after Rudy's.

My hands were sweating so much by this point that I was no longer able to effectively hold my scissors anyway. Jotting numbers down in a large notebook, Aukai was as friendly as ever in greeting me. Pedro, on the other hand, wasted no time scrutinizing the trimmed bud that I'd brought up. He picked through my finished bin and pointed out a few buds whose stems were too long.

"When the stems are too long, they rip through the plastic bags we sell them in. Plus, it just doesn't look as pretty," Pedro explained.

Although quick to critique my work, Pedro was just as quick to help me sift through my finished bin one more time in search of these longer stems. Together, Pedro and I snipped away at the imperfect buds. While we worked, Aukai and Pedro bantered back and forth about business on the farm, units produced and units sold, potential buyers ... a lot of inside business talk that went over my head. The main thing I took away from this conversation was that Aukai and Pedro were good friends. Although they never broke from their work, Pedro and Aukai were so much at ease with each other that I eased up around the two of them, as well.

When Pedro and I finished sorting through my weed, Aukai weighed me in. The number on the scale was 222 grams. There are 453.6 grams in a pound. I'd managed to produce almost half a pound of trimmed weed in less than half a day's work. In order to earn my stay, I knew I had to trim a minimum of one pound per day. I could only hope that my ability to work for hours without interruption would save me until my fingers caught up in speed with the other trimmers on the farm.

chapter twelve

THE GANESHA WELLNESS COMMUNITY

ALTHOUGH THE NIGHTS WERE COLD and we were often hit by a drizzling of rain, the sun shone down powerfully on the farm during most of my days there. I loved that it was late October and I got to spend the majority of my day outside wearing a tank top, shorts, and sandals. The only part of my body that still felt cold and stiff in the morning were my fingers. It pained me to watch how much slower my hands moved in these first few morning hours. To reduce the unpleasantness of my mornings, I made myself a full french press of coffee and listened to a podcast on my iPod. By the time I finished my coffee and my podcast, my hands were moving a lot faster. Instead of having to consciously direct the movement of my hands, I focused on studying the particular strain of bud I was trimming. Each strain asked something a little bit different of me. Some strains were hardy enough to be treated with more force and could be sifted through my grate to remove most of the leaves before I even began trimming. With other strains, the easiest way to remove the larger leaves was by hand, so I spent more time spinning the bud in my fingers than actually snipping with my scissors.

This time spent learning and observing the secrets of each strain of marijuana turned into a sort of meditation for me. When I reached this state, the plant itself seemed to guide the movement of my fingers. My mind relaxed enough to think of other things, firing out all sorts of random, half-baked ideas. The inspiration that struck was of the ephemeral kind. Most of my ideas were hard to verbalize and slipped away if I tried to grasp at them. After my past few weeks of high stress and forced extroversion, half-thinking about life felt like a healthy change for me. While being in a safe environment helped slow down my thoughts and reduce their intensity, it had the opposite effect on my emotions. Up until that point, the only emotion I was in touch with on a daily basis was fear. Suddenly, I was hit by an onslaught of emotion demanding to be felt all at once. I didn't know what to do about all these conflicting emotions that threatened to contaminate the happiness I'd worked so hard to reclaim.

The hardest emotion for me to handle was anger. I didn't know how to handle anger because I was so unused to feeling it. The anger originated from one thought in particular, or rather one name. This was the name that I'd made taboo to pronounce even in my own mind—Liam, of course. Spending my entire day doing one monotonous activity on repeat, I had so much time to think that I couldn't evade this name any longer. The more days that passed between our last time together in Durango, the more bitter toward Liam I became. Where was Liam when I needed him? I hadn't heard a single word from him, not even a phone call to check that I made it to California OK. After a few days of letting this bitterness build, my hurt toward Liam escalated to a point that it started affecting my concentration at work.

On one of my lunch breaks a few days after I arrived at the farm, I worked up the courage to call him. When he didn't answer, I tried the number Liam had given me for one of his other friends working on the farm. This friend had a different cell phone carrier that sometimes got better reception out on their farm. Sure enough, the friend answered within a few rings. As soon as I identified myself, I heard shuffling and the sound of this friend shouting out Liam's name.

It took only a few seconds for Liam to take over the phone from his friend.

"Skye?" Liam asked, sounding like he didn't know whether to believe it was me on the other end of the line. "Is everything OK? Where are you?"

I tackled his second question first, because this was the easier one.

"The middle of the nowhere. The closest town to where I am is called Jackson, but it's not much of a town. I'm only out here because this is where I found work."

Liam released the breath that he'd been holding. He coughed a few times at the bottom of his exhale. It took Liam a moment after this bout of coughing to regain his breath again.

"I'm glad you found something. Who ended up being your hook-up for the job?"

Chuckling under my breath, I sighed, "This woman I met in Nevada City named Lulu Chimera. Lulu's the last person that I would have imagined saving my ass, but save my ass she did."

Liam remained silent, waiting for me to continue. I did my best to consolidate the events of my past week into one cohesive narrative, but I didn't dare tell Liam about the homeless camp up on the ridge or sitting behind a paper sign in front of the co-op. After I'd finished telling him even just half the truth, Liam was left momentarily speechless.

Finally, Liam pronounced, "Damn, Skye. You're a bona fide hustler."

A confused laugh punctuated by an unspoken question mark escaped my lips.

Half-serious, half-teasing, Liam repeated, "You're a hustler—someone who makes something out of nothing. You met some tripped-out hippie named after a mythological creature at a kratom tea party and turned that into a job opportunity. Now, that is the work of a hustler."

This time, my laughter was genuine and unrestrained. Liam laughed right along with me, and it took both of us a minute to quiet down enough to be able to speak again.

I could still hear the smile in Liam's voice as he told me, "I missed hearing your laugh."

Liam's words reminded me of my original intention in making this call, which also reminded me that I was the one who had called Liam in the first place.

Old feelings of betrayal bubbled up inside of me. I point-blank asked Liam, "Why didn't you call?"

Liam apologized and confessed all at once, "I'm sorry, Skye. Our last conversation hit me pretty hard. I needed some time to think ... and I don't have anybody to talk to about this. I didn't know what to do."

Unsure whether I was begging him, accusing him, or professing a weakness of my own, I admitted, "I needed you, Liam ... and you weren't there."

Coughing again, Liam's voice came out in a raspy whisper.

"Here I go disappointing you again ..."

Hearing these words, I traveled back through time until I landed back on the sidewalk in Paris with Liam standing in front of me, confessing this fear to me for the first time. In protest against the untruth of this statement, my love for Liam roared out like a battle cry within me. I repeated something very similar to what I'd told him in Paris, but with more conviction, desperately hoping to make him believe me this time.

"You've never disappointed me. You never will. Yes, I'm hurt that you didn't call. Yes, I want to know that I can count on you. But that doesn't change the way that I feel about you."

For a long moment, Liam said nothing, perhaps wrestling with the question of whether or not to trust me. In the end, all that Liam managed to reply was a softly spoken incantation of my name.

"Oh, Skye ..."

Again, Liam sighed. Again, this sigh was accompanied by a cough. This time, it took Liam a good minute to stop coughing.

Once the coughing fit subsided, Liam explained, "You won't believe this, but I think I'm allergic to dry weed. I have to trim with a mask on, and I still cough all the time. It's bad enough that I'm starting to wonder if I have bronchitis. I'm taking the strongest cough medicine I can get my hands on, and I use my inhaler throughout the day. Sometimes, I cough so hard that I can barely breathe."

Perturbed by this confession, I said, "Please don't stay someplace where you feel like you can't breathe."

Liam exhaled, coughing again at the bottom of the exhale.

Liam conceded, "Yeah, I may have to leave here before too long..."

The confusing part of this proclamation was that Liam didn't sound at all disappointed.

Trying to understand his unexpected nonchalance, I said, "Well, I'm glad to hear you're taking care of yourself. Where will you go if you leave?"

Without skipping a beat, Liam replied, "Well, there's this woman I love, but she's all the way out in California. This woman, she's a badass. If I didn't know her so well, I would think that she isn't afraid of anything. She flew across a whole ocean to meet me once. After that, driving across a few states doesn't seem like such a big deal. So I've been thinking about leaving here in the next week or so to join her in California..."

The doubt in my voice made plain, I asked, "Are you being serious with me, Liam?"

I started to bring up my list of questions and objectives, the number one concern being that Liam take care of his health before anything else. Liam cut me off midlist.

"I'll figure it out. You've had enough to worry about these past few weeks. Don't worry yourself over me now. For me, the most important thing is hearing that you still want me there."

I told Liam that I could at least start by asking Aukai if it would be all right for Liam to come join me. Maybe Liam could help with some of the other work on the farm besides trimming, which would give him some space away from the trimming shed and all the marijuana resin hanging in the air. Before I got too ahead of myself, Liam brought me back.

"Just remember, I don't want you worrying yourself over this. Promise?"

All I could grant Liam was, "I promise that I'll try."

The tentative peace that fell over the farm in Maya's absence dissipated immediately upon her return a few days later from the hot springs with Calista. At first, I didn't know Maya well enough to attribute the change in the farm's atmosphere to her personally. However, I soon noticed the wake of stress that Maya created wherever she went. For reasons I couldn't yet ascertain, Maya picked on me more than most of the other trimmers. She rarely called me by my name, referring to me instead as *the new girl*. When she was trying to sound nicer, Maya called me *the newest member of our community*. With both names, my newness there was the fact that she wished to highlight. Another example of Maya's fondness for renaming things could be seen in the title she made up for the farm, *the*

Ganesha Wellness Community. Maya was the painter of the sign that I noticed at the front entrance. She was the only one who called the farm by this name, although everyone on the farm placated her by using the title whenever she was in earshot. I had no idea what the Hindu deity Ganesha had to do with our work there, and I would hardly call the random collection of people working on the farm a community.

Although she picked on me especially, I wasn't the only subject of Maya's random assailments. Technically, Maya's job as manager of the trimmers was quality control over the product we trimmed. However, a lot of Maya's objections seemed to undermine our productivity rather than bolster it. For example, Maya would decide that she didn't like where we were sitting and would have all of us get up, move our chairs, and rearrange our stations. This took away precious time from our work trimming. The pretext that Maya came up with to justify this hassle was something along the lines of making our working space more feng shui. My hunch was that Maya didn't like certain trimmers working too close to each other.

My growing wariness of Maya solidified on the second night that she, rather than Pedro and Aukai, weighed all of us out. She had done so the night before, but I didn't notice anything bothersome or unusual about her weighing methods. I just noticed that she weighed our weed differently than Aukai and Pedro did. Maya weighed our weed while it was still in the bag and then subtracted the weight of the plastic bag from the tally of the total grams we'd trimmed. On the second night Maya weighed us out like this, I'd moved my trimming station from the larger trimming shed into a smaller, more insulated, shed nearby. Rudy was the one who'd invited me to trim in the shed, which I later recognized as a privilege. Having realized that Rudy was by far the best trimmer on the farm, I'd set up my trimming station close to his while I worked outside during the day. Sometimes, I asked Rudy questions or solicited his advice. Other times, I just watched the way his hands moved and did my best to simulate their agility. For at least a few hours a day, I unplugged my headphones and put the energy into being more social with him.

Most of what Rudy and I talked about was the places we'd traveled to. Rudy was one of those backpackers who had unlocked the secret of how to travel forever. So far, Rudy's favorite place he'd visited in the whole world was India. Although I let Rudy do the majority of the talking, I shared with him a few of my own adventures from having spent four months traveling around India. Rudy was a man who moved quickly in everything he did. His attention jumped swiftly from one thing to the next, his hands were always moving, and his whole body was wound up like a tight spring, leaving you with the impression that you could look away for a moment and then look back to find him gone. But when I spoke to Rudy about India, his quick, sharp, brown eyes paused and came to rest on me with an unex-pected softness. After our conversation about India, Rudy was noticeably more open with me. As we worked, Rudy would tell me stories about all the different women he loved in different parts of the world. Each story inevitably ended in heartbreak. No matter how much Rudy loved a woman or how much a part of him wished he could stay with her, Rudy's wandering ways always called him back out onto the road again. After learning how often Rudy had to leave his friends and lovers behind, his guardedness, and even his show of machismo, became a lot more understandable to me.

Rudy's machismo and Maya's floweriness didn't mesh well together. Having felt the tension brewing between the two of them, I was already nervous when Maya stepped into our shed to weigh us out at the end of the day. Although Rudy contained himself for as long as Maya was in the shed, I could tell by the way his face flinched when Maya weighed him out that something had deeply upset him. A few minutes after Maya left, Rudy motioned for everyone in the group to lean in so we all could hear him.

"I cannot hold my tongue when I see myself and others being cheated!" Rudy exclaimed in his thick Uruguayan accent. "You see how Maya weighs the marijuana without taking it out of the bag? When she does this, there are parts of the bag that spill out over the scale. Since the whole bag does not fit on the scale, the whole bag is not being weighed. This is why Pedro and Aukai take the weed out of the bag and weigh it in batches. But no, no, Maya keeps the weed in the bag. I see what she is doing. Maya knows that this little trick saves Maya and the farm money."

Once Rudy explained this to us, everyone in the small shed cried out in outrage. Every gram we trimmed represented precious time that we'd given to sitting in one place and cutting for hours. As shocked as I was, I was even more surprised when Rudy turned around to directly address me. His keen brown eyes, which had been gleaming like newly sharpened swords, softened ever so slightly.

"Skye, you must know that writing your totals down each day in your journal is not enough. Every single night after you get weighed, you must take a picture of the manager's trimming log. I have heard stories of trimming logs *disappearing* on farms. If you have a picture, your work doesn't disappear if the log does."

As Rudy's warning sunk in, I realized that I was not nearly as safe on this farm as I'd imagined myself to be.

Accentuating his point with sweeping hand gestures, Rudy proclaimed, "On big farms like this, you must always watch your back. Pay attention to everything going on around you, and then no one can pull tricks on you. Do you understand?"

I nodded solemnly, grateful that Rudy had stepped in to

help me when he could have very well kept his mouth shut. After that night, my entire perspective on working at the Ganesha Wellness Community changed. Not only did I take pictures of my trim log at the end of every night, but I no longer dared work alone throughout the day. Isolating myself socially made me too easy a prey for Maya's assaults. I also made myself switch it up and work with other people besides Rudy. While Rudy's status as the best trimmer on the farm made him relatively untouchable, I sensed that my alliance with him could be damaging to me. In order to forge stronger alliances, I moved my station back to trim alongside Delias, Vasili, Penelope, her Spanish friend, Calista, and the Polish-Hungarian couple. As socially depleted as I still felt, I pushed myself to talk more in an effort to build rapport with the others trimmers. Delias was by far the most talkative member of this circle. He was the glue that kept our group together.

The work I put into building these relationships was rewarded when Delias invited me to a small, private barbecue their group was having back at our campsite. Vasili and Delias took a night off of trimming to prepare a large Greek feast for the group of us. They grilled chicken and beef, whipped up their own Tzatziki sauce, and chopped up an assortment of fresh vegetables for us. After hanging out with our little group for a quasi-family dinner, I felt a sense of peace, albeit a still somewhat fragmented peace, return to me. We spent a lot of that night complaining about the management on the farm, Maya in particular. Apart from complaining, we also brainstormed ways to advocate for our rights, even as illegal workers there. We realized that our only real chance at producing any kind of positive change on the farm would come from sticking together. Engaging in this kind of conversation made me feel as if I was part of a team. This was a welcome relief after forging my way solo for so long. For better or for worse, I'd earned my place in this community, the Ganesha Wellness Community that didn't feel much like a community at all.

chapter thirteen

THE GANESHA
WELLNESS CIRCUS

MAYA'S RETURN TO THE FARM was only the first wave of change to come crashing down on Ganesha Wellness Community. After Maya's takeover of the farm, many, many more waves of change hit the farm in quick succession. The biggest change came in the form of the many new trimmers who arrived on the farm daily. As if summoned by the sounding of an inaudible trumpet, these trimmers appeared out of nowhere. In the span of less than a week, twenty-three new people showed up on the property. Some of these new trimmers were friends of people currently working on the farm. Others' stories as to how they got there were as vague and implausible as my own. With the arrival of each new trimmer, I felt my heart constrict as if caught in a net that tightened and shrank as it was being reeled in. I hadn't found the right opportunity, or maybe just the courage, to ask management if Liam could come join me on the farm. I was terrified that Aukai or Maya would say that we'd reached, or even exceeded, the maximum number of trimmers allowed on this farm. Almost overnight, I watched as the once spacious field in which I'd set up my tent filled up with other tents, tarps, and hammocks. With the parking lot overflowing and so many new tents popping up everywhere, the farm started to feel a lot more like a marijuana-related music festival than any sort of productive work space.

Despite Maya's insistence on calling me "the new girl" for the first week I was on the farm, I suddenly found myself part of the "OG Crew." Outside my little crew, the two people I found myself the most drawn to on the farm were Sierra and Luke, both of whom worked out in the fields as farmhands. With her easy smile and tendency to blurt out whatever was on her mind, Sierra was irresistibly fun to be around. She wore the same thing almost every day: Carhartt overalls, a neutral-colored T-shirt, and sneakers. She was simple, unadorned, and unfailingly real. Whenever I needed a break from the farm's bullshit power dynamics and hierarchies, I would scrape together the energy to stay up a little later after trimming and sit next to her at the fire circle. As was typical for me, I wouldn't always say much. I just listened to her laugh and talk openly about whatever she was thinking or feeling that day.

Sierra almost always sat next to Luke, and most of what she laughed about was goofy stuff he said. Like me, Luke listened more than he talked, but he had a special gift for one-liners. While Sierra sat, Luke would almost always stand, and he was tall enough to tower over everyone. The long, blond dreads that Luke wrapped in a large bun on top of his head only added to his height. Whenever I looked up at Luke standing on one end of the fire circle towering over us like this, I imagined him as a sort of guardian standing watch to protect us. Luke was a gentle, soft-spoken man with everyone, but he was especially sweet with Sierra. Just based on how much time they spent together and the chemistry they exuded, I assumed they were probably together. They never touched each other in public, but this could have been because of the death glares Maya gave them whenever Sierra laughed too loud or drew any attention to herself. Whatever Maya's problem was, she kept her distance whenever Sierra was around.

Although I would have been more than happy spending all my free time trying to unlock the mysteries that Luke and Sierra represented, I also pushed myself to talk to some of the newer trimmers on the farm. I started by approaching the group of eight people who had pitched a huge, circus-style tent next to mine. One of the only people whose names I remember was an American guy named Arrow. Arrow had long, brown dreads, which was not unusual in this neck of the woods, and frequently sported T-shirts emblazoned with the anarchy logo. He and most of his friends in their traveling group of eight had worked multiple seasons trimming marijuana in California. They told me all kinds of stories of their previous experiences on other farms, including multiple accounts of having to escape from farms that got raided by the police in the middle of the night. His eyes wide and red from all the weed he'd smoked that day, Arrow urged me to come up with my own escape plan in case of a police raid at Ganesha Wellness Community. I was so focused on understanding all the complex and ever-changing social dynamics on the farm that I didn't have much energy to think about what I would do if I were forced to leave it.

Just when I thought that nothing else could surprise me, two new people arrived on the farm whom I will never forget, Chumani and her son, Zaire, or Z for short. When Chumani and Z first arrived, they were accompanied by Chumani's partner and Zaire's dad, a burly Hawaiian man with only one eye, a booming voice, and an unexplained limp. Z's dad worked full time on another farm nearby, a smaller farm that was run exclusively by Hawaiians. While Z's dad left the evening of their arrival, Chumani and Z settled down to stay. Chumani was a member of the Sioux tribe from South Dakota. She openly displayed her pride in this affiliation. Her entire face, neck, and both of her arms were covered in tribal tattoos. As distinct a first impression as Chumani made, even more remarkable was her son Z. The most remarkable fact about Z was his age, three. At first, I didn't know how to feel about a mother bringing such a young child to work on an illegal marijuana farm. But Z was almost so young that his innocence was still incorruptible. I doubted that he understood the nature of the business taking place on the farm.

Although Chumani took frequent breaks throughout the day to attend to Z's needs, Z was happy playing by himself most of the time. He built structures out of leaves, rocks, and other random objects that he found on the farm. Z took just as much pleasure from knocking these structures down as he did from building them. Hearing his high-pitched giggle and watching him play like this, it was impossible not to fall in love with Z. Within a matter of days, everyone on the farm did. At first, Z didn't know what to make of all of these strangers coming up to play with him. When approached, Z would get scared and run to find Chumani. As he began to recognize some of our faces, Z became much more willing to engage with us. It turned out that Z wasn't the shy boy we first mistook him to be. Basking in the warmth of so much love and attention, Z blossomed open like a flower. Before we knew it, Z was the one coming up to us demanding that we take breaks to play with him. Chumani gently reprimanded Z for bothering us while we worked, but no one really minded his intrusion.

The only time that Z caused any real trouble was on the day he stole his mom's phone and took a series of blurry, unfocused pictures of us trimming. Once Chumani realized her phone was gone, she found Z and deleted all the pictures. For most everyone on the farm, this took care of the matter. Arrow, the American guy traveling with the band of eight, was the only one who took this seriously. Babbling on about incriminating evidence and jail time, Arrow asked to see Chumani's phone to make sure all the pictures had been deleted. After Arrow double-checked this, he quieted down and focused his attention back on the large joint he was rolling. Arrow passed this joint around our circle as a peace-making gesture, making sure that Chumani was the first person who hit the joint. Once the joint made a few rounds of the room, peace was restored. After a few days, Arrow became one of Z's favorite people to play with, and Arrow and Chumani became good friends. Arrow actually moved his trimming station to set up next to Chumani and Z's corner. Chumani, Arrow, and Z laughed and talked together all night long, or at least until Z started yawning and asking his mom to go to bed. On the nights when Chumani wanted to work later, she set up a napping station for Z by her feet. Shrouded in warm blankets and surrounded by pillows, Z curled up in a ball on the ground until Chumani carried him up to sleep in their tent.

One of these nights as Z lay nestled in his cocoon of blankets, he peered up at Chumani one last time before closing his eyes.

So quietly that I could barely hear him, Z whispered, "Mommy? How long do we get to stay here this time? I like it here."

Setting down her scissors, Chumani reached down to brush Z's hair out of his eyes.

"I don't know, baby. All we can do is enjoy the time we're here."

Little did Z know, he'd asked the question that everyone on the farm was dying to have answered. In the past week alone, the number of trimmers on the farm had risen from fifteen to almost forty. No one knew how much longer our work there would last.

Looking back now, I see how my entire journey was made possible through the help of others and, more often than not, the kindness of strangers. Rudy was one of those angels; never mind that he left my life as quickly as he'd entered it. One day on our lunch break, Rudy pulled me aside to tell me that he was, "done dealing with this shit." He said that one of his lady friends in the area knew of a farm that paid $160 per pound.

In the thick Uruguayan accent that I'd come to love, Rudy admitted, "Now, there is a chance that this friend of mine stretches the truth to get me back with her. But it is worth taking this chance. I lose my mind if I stay here."

I was afraid that I was losing my mind, too, but I didn't have the same courage to get up and leave. The process of finding this job took so much out of me that I'd lost the willpower to risk starting all over again someplace new. Rudy, on the other hand, had more practice leaving a place than staying. Knowing that there was nothing I could do to change his mind, I hugged Rudy and thanked him for all he'd done for me. Clearly embarrassed, Rudy was quick to dismiss my show of gratitude.

"Just remember what I told you. Not everyone is as trustworthy as you are, so you must learn to watch your back. Stay awake and be careful, my friend."

After issuing this last warning, a warning that felt more like an omen, Rudy headed back up the hill toward the campground to pack up his belongings. He never walked back down that hill again.

The way I like to imagine it, Rudy called up to his other angel friends on the day he left and sent word that there was a woman stranded by herself on this crazy farm who could use some help. The same day Rudy left, a relatively new white Toyota Tacoma pulled up and parked in front of Aukai's big shed. The man who stepped out of it was yet another person I'd never met—an older man with tousled, gray hair wearing dad jeans and a strand of prayer beads around his neck. As clueless as I may have been, all of the OG Crew recognized the truck as soon as it pulled up. Recognizing our crew as well, the man waved at my friends before disappearing into the shed to talk to Aukai. By the time the man re-emerged from the shed, I had largely forgotten about him, so I jumped a little when he approached our trimming circle. The man took his time going around and greeting everyone in the circle by name. He walked over to clap Delias on the back, and the two men bantered back and forth for a few minutes, swapping jokes and anecdotes about their kids. Finally, the man turned in my direction with a sheepish, almost apologetic grin on his face.

"Sorry for not introducing myself earlier. I always get a little carried away with Delias around ... but I see you've made yourself a good group of friends here. What's your name?"

"It's easy to get carried away with Delias," I chuckled. "I'm Skye. Nice to meet you ...?"

Filling in the blank for me, the man introduced himself, "Bill. I know we've never met, but I'm actually the head manager for this farm. One of my kids got sick, and I had to leave the farm for a few weeks to help out my wife. I'm glad to say that my son is doing better now, so I should be back to stay. Anyway, I promise I didn't come back just to lay a bunch of new rules on you. Just know that I'm here if you need anything. I'll probably be in the kitchen most of the time helping our boy Pedro out."

With that, Bill left us to our work. I didn't see Bill too much over the next few days, and I sometimes forgot that he was there at all. Since Bill was the head manager, I'd rather hoped that his return to the farm would bring more change than it did. One change that appeared was an overall improvement in the quality of our meals. As Bill had announced on his first day back, he spent most of his time helping Pedro in the kitchen. I'd walk into the kitchen in the morning to find Bill meditating on one of the kitchen chairs, fingering the prayer beads around his neck and whispering an inaudible mantra under his breath. During the workday, he made his rounds from the fields to the trimming shed to Aukai's larger processing shed, hopping from one casual conversation to the next with the same benevolent smile on his face throughout. As much as everyone liked Bill, no one took him very seriously, least of all Maya. Even when she rolled her eyes at him or talked back to him, Bill just looked at Maya the way a father would look at his moody, unpredictable teenage daughter, with some mixture of affection and disappointment.

Without Bill stepping in to check her power, Maya's position as the tyrant ruling over the farm solidified. She played with our minds like a cat plays with a mouse. She'd let us relax long enough to grow comfortable before pouncing on one of us again for some new thing that we'd done wrong. A few days after Bill's arrival, Maya came up with a new game. The purpose of this game was to create a thief, real or imagined. Two nights before Halloween, Maya ordered everyone working in the trimming shed to stop working so she could make an announcement.

"Hello, all of you lovely people!"

Brushing her bangs out of her eyes, Maya flashed us her most winning, seductive smile, a sure sign that there was trouble ahead.

"As you are all aware, our little community here isn't so little anymore. Working on a project of this scale ... well, let's just say that things can't go on exactly as they were. We're in a new cycle of change and expansion, and we have to collectively honor that. Y'all feel me?"

As usual with Maya's rants, no one knew what to say because no one was ever fully sure what Maya was talking about. We waited in awkward silence for Maya to come to her real point, whatever that was.

Oblivious to the blank stares she was receiving, Maya carried on with her characteristic zeal. "Glad y'all are with me so far. I think we can also agree that there's no such thing as being too safe, right? We're all still getting to know each other, which is really exciting, but also a time when we need to take extra precautions. Now, I've worked for years as a trimmer on marijuana farms that were as big, or bigger, than this one. On projects of this size, internal theft can be a huge issue. There are some simple steps we can take to prevent that, as long as we're all working together on this. On all the other farms I worked at, management would have periodic inspections of all the cars, RVs, tents, and living arrangements on site … but I'm sure we'll never find anything in any of your cars or tents, of course."

At the thought of Maya rifling through my personal possessions, my insides crawled a little. The only thing I really had to hide from Maya was my journal, which admittedly included multiple entries that mentioned her name in a not-so-positive light. I could only imagine how strongly Rudy would be reacting to this if he were still there.

Maya hastened to finish her announcement before any of us could object. "As scary as this may sound, it really won't change much in the daily routine around here. All we're asking is that you keep your cars unlocked during the day in case we end up carrying out a random inspection. If you'd like to be there when we're doing the inspection, that's also an option. Just let us know what makes you feel more comfortable, and we'll see what we can do to work with that."

For once, no one maintained the restraint necessary to hold their tongues. All at the same time, people raised their hands to ask questions, shouted out in protest, or whispered angrily among each other. The din of noise reverberating around the trimming shed became so overwhelming that Maya had to raise her hand to signal for everyone to quiet down.

In an attempt to pacify us, Maya proclaimed, "Peace y'all! This is just a way for us to strengthen our trust in one another. *I trust* that none of you here have anything to hide. In which case, I don't see what the big deal is ... *unless* someone is trying to hide something from me. If so, now's your time to speak up."

Hands on her hips, Maya looked out over us like a sheep-herder appraising her flock of sheep. Her intimidation technique worked remarkably well, as the whole shed fell silent. The next few days on the farm were uneasy ones. We had so little privacy and time to ourselves as it was. Whatever privacy we'd had was suddenly under threat of invasion. Dreading the time when all our belongings would be searched, I held my breath along with everyone else. I failed to foresee the eventual outcome of all of Maya's big talk—nothing. As far as any of us knew, Maya never ended up searching our tents or cars. After a few days, I wondered if the real intent behind Maya's proposition was to test us, to see if there were any members of our group brave enough to challenge her in front of everyone else. I didn't have the courage. Then again, neither did anyone else.

By remaining silent, I couldn't tell if we'd failed or passed Maya's test. What I knew was how much having all these empty threats dangling over our heads put us on edge. Even the strength of the OG Crew's alliance weakened under the pressure of so much looming tension. The greatest difference I noticed was in how much less we talked to each other as a group. Maya must have perceived these new changes, as well. She no longer forced us to rearrange our stations as frequently as before. At last, Maya had effectively managed to dissolve the strength we once had in numbers. This left me, the one member of the group who came to the farm alone, especially vulnerable to attack. Maya made sure I was well-aware of this fact.

Two nights after her announcement, on the night of Halloween, I finally slipped up and made the mistake that Maya had been waiting for. It was past nine by then. Maya had just called my name to weigh me out. With it being as late as it was, my plan was to trim another hour, hang out by the fire for a bit, and then go to bed. Although a part of me was disappointed that I wasn't doing more to celebrate Halloween, I didn't have a costume to wear even if I were to celebrate. Plus, Luke and Sierra were the only people on the farm planning to leave the premises to celebrate. They'd invited whoever wanted to come to go with them to this big bash at a local, supposedly haunted hotel. One by one, everyone bailed. Almost everyone was planning on sticking around camp and having a big party around our own bonfire. This is what most people did every night after work anyway, but I'd heard rumors that, this night, LSD and mushrooms would be passed around for the taking.

This is what I was thinking about in the time that it took

Maya to weigh me out. Distracted, I handed Maya my bag of trimmed marijuana without double-checking that I had labeled the bag with the correct date and name of the strain. It was only after Maya placed my bag in the processed marijuana bin that I remembered to double-check the label. Wanting to make sure that I'd written everything down, I reached over the table to grab the bag. When Maya turned back to face me, she saw me holding the bag that she'd just set down in the processed marijuana bin.

Eyes narrowing, Maya questioned me, "What are you doing with that bag?"

Stumbling over my words, I mumbled, "I was just making sure that I wrote down the name of the right strain. I forgot to check when I handed the bag to you."

Maya's eyebrows drew even closer together.

"Why didn't you ask me to grab the bag for you? Your story seems a little fishy, don't you think?"

"I didn't want waste any more of your time. I'm sorry. I'll make sure to ask next time."

"There isn't going to be a next time. Under no circumstances are you allowed to touch a single bag of the marijuana that I have processed. Do you understand?"

This is when I realized what deep shit I was in. After all Maya's talk about needing to make sure that no one was stealing the farm's marijuana, Maya had caught me with a bag of processed, trimmed marijuana in my hands. This was exactly the opportunity that Maya had been waiting for to demolish me. Demolish me, she did. Pushing her chair away from her, Maya stood up in one big huff. Holding the bag of marijuana that I'd taken over her head, Maya threw her other arm up in the air to signal that she needed to make an announcement. In front of everyone, Maya explained what I'd done.

Only after railing on me for a good minute or two did Maya concede, "Maybe Skye didn't mean anything by grabbing the bag from the bin. Either way, she provided me with a great opportunity to re-establish some firm boundaries here. This time, the type of boundaries that I am talking about are physical ones. You see this table that I stand behind? No one comes behind this table without my permission. In fact, I would appreciate it if no one even touched this table or any of the equipment on it. I'm going to let Skye off with a warning this time. Whoever disrespects my space again will not get off so easily next time."

Head hung between my shoulders, I was about to slink back to my trimming station to work out some of my anger and shame, but Maya stopped, addressing me directly this time.

"I hope you don't feel I was being too harsh on you there. Can you understand why this matters to me?"

All I wanted to do was leave. I could barely stifle my frustration at having to stand in front of Maya for even another minute.

Nonetheless, I gritted my teeth and repeated, "Yes, I understand. I'm sorry for what I did, and it won't happen again."

Although I naively hoped this answer would appease her, Maya was no longer willing to be appeased. Nothing I said would placate Maya because she was wrestling with her own sense of guilt over the public humiliation she'd just put me through. Without apologizing, Maya babbled on interminably, justifying her actions to me in many different ways with many different arguments. The conversation circled back over itself so many times that eventually Maya ran out of things to say. When she finally excused me from her table, I no longer had the energy to walk back into the shed and keep trimming. My desire to escape was so strong that I had to force myself to walk out of the shed instead of run. Instinctively, I headed up the hill toward my tent. My intention was to spend the rest of the night hiding away in my little cave. My plan was thwarted when I practically ran into Luke and Sierra, who were in just as much of a rush as I was to get off the property and head over to the party at the nearby hotel. Noticing my sense of urgency, Sierra assumed that I was running for the same reason they were.

More excited than I'd ever seen her, Sierra exclaimed, "Oh my god! Did you change your mind about coming out with us?"

I wrestled with how to tell Sierra the real place I was rushing to, which was my tent. Before I could come up with the right words, a long-dormant part of my brain took over my conscious mind. This was the part of my brain that didn't care about anything, the part of my brain that said *fuck yes* to just about any opportunity presented to me.

This was the part of my brain that spoke when I answered, "You know what? Why not? Can you give me a few minutes to come up with a costume?"

chapter fourteen

HALLOWEEN REVELATIONS

THE LAST-MINUTE COSTUME I came up with was courtesy of Evelyn, whom I called to solicit some much-needed advice. Per Evie's instructions, I slipped into my sexiest black dress, a pair of holey black tights, and black combat boots. Then, I drew a thick line of black eyeliner across my eyes to make a mask. Evie's last instruction was to fill a pillowcase with some socks, write the word *BOOTY* on the pillowcase in all caps, draw some dollar signs on the pillowcase, and voila! I had myself a robber costume. Proud of my hasty work, I sauntered back down the hill toward the fire, where I found Sierra and

Luke in the middle of a conversation with Aukai. Still feeling on edge, I glanced around the fire circle in search of Maya. The coast was clear, so I trotted over to join Aukai, Sierra, and Luke. Luke, Aukai, and a few of the other men around the circle raised their eyebrows in appreciation of my costume.

After making me do a little twirl, Sierra commended me, "Nice work! I have a black beanie you could borrow if you want. It would totally complete the costume."

"That'd be great!" I thanked Sierra before hastening to say, "Also, sorry for making you wait so long. I'm ready to leave whenever you are."

Aukai held up a hand to protest, which was when I noticed how dilated his pupils were.

"No need to rush off so fast. I just offered Sierra and Luke a droplet of my, um …" Aukai cleared his throat and then went so far as to actually wink at me before continuing, "… magic potion. You interested?"

Taking in the somewhat alarmed expression on my face, Luke spoke up to shed some light on Aukai's mysterious offer.

"It's concentrated LSD. Sierra and I just took a drop of it."

Something about the fact that my manager was dosing everybody at our worksite with liquid acid was so ludicrous that I couldn't pass up the chance to participate in the fun. When I felt the smallest of droplets land on my tongue, I closed my mouth with a smile.

At this point, Luke stepped back in to say, "Now that we're all on the same page, let's hit the road. I want to get to the Avery Hotel before this stuff kicks into full gear."

After hugging Aukai in thanks and shouting out a general farewell to the rest of the crew, the three of us set off toward Luke's old Chevy truck parked at the top of the hill. Conceding the passenger seat to Sierra, I slid into the back seat of the truck. Watching Sierra take her seat beside Luke, I couldn't help but think to myself how much more she belonged there anyway. The pair of them exuded such undeniable chemistry that I hoped for their sakes they were together. When Sierra placed her hand on the arm Luke was using to shift his truck into gear, I took this as confirmation of my suspicions. I was so excited to be getting off the farm that I couldn't be bothered by the fact that I was effectively their third wheel.

We drove for over half an hour down roads that were supposedly highways but looked a lot more like beat-up driveways. The roads were windy and narrow—so narrow that I was terrified of what would happen if another car drove down the road coming from the opposite direction. I held onto my car seat with every sharp turn we made, waiting for Luke's truck to go careening into one of the ditches on the side of the road. Before this venture, I'd always thought of California as modern, bustling, and over-crowded. The only thing that seemed to be going on in this part of the state was farming, although who knew how many of the farms surrounding us had converted into marijuana-growing operations. Nonetheless, I was having just as hard a time imagining a raging party happening anywhere in this vicinity as I was believing that I'd finally managed to get away from the farm for a night. It felt as if I'd spent the past few weeks trapped inside some sort of dark, leafy green tunnel. The only thing I could think about was the money waiting for me at the far end of the tunnel. Now that I'd escaped the constrictions of my own tunnel vision, the whole world opened back up to me.

In my elation, I declared out loud, "I'm not even high yet, but it feels so good to be off the farm that I might as well be. Thanks for inviting me to come out with you tonight. I needed this."

Eager to shed the heaviness I was still carrying inside me, I told Luke and Sierra about Maya's explosion earlier that night. Since Luke and Maya worked in the fields, they were some of the only people on the farm who hadn't witnessed my humiliation. Once I finished recounting the whole episode, I held my breath, nervous that Luke and Sierra would judge me, at the very least for having done something stupid, and at the worst for being a thief. Instead of being disappointed or judgmental, Sierra and Luke were outraged.

"That's fucked up," Luke muttered.

"No one in their right mind would think that you're capable of stealing!" Sierra said. "You're one of the most innocent people I've ever met. I mean, as innocent as you can be when you're working on an illegal marijuana farm. But that's the thing; Maya isn't in her right mind."

Shaking his head, Luke agreed, "Her irrationality is like a virus that contaminates everything it comes into contact with. Hell, it's fucked with my head plenty. It almost ruined our friendship. Penelope won't look me in the eye anymore, and Calista thinks I'm some cold-hearted fuckboy."

Clearly shocked, Sierra leaned away from Luke as if unable to believe what she was hearing.

"Oh, so we're going into that story now, are we? If we're really doing this, I'm going to need a swig of your tequila. Sorry, Luke, you'll have to wait until we get to the hotel to partake. Help yourself, Skye. You'll probably need something to wash this down, too."

Sierra reached under the truck seat to retrieve a half-empty bottle of tequila. She took a long pull from the bottle before handing it back to me. I took a bigger swig than I intended to, grimacing as the tequila burned a passage from my throat down to my stomach.

After giving me a moment to recover, Luke explained, "I've been on the farm for over six months now. For the first few months, it was just me, Aukai, Maya, and Pedro. Bill wasn't around much. Then, Calista flew in from Brazil to join Maya, and I invited Penelope up from LA. Skye, you'd never guess this because we don't speak to each other anymore, but Penelope and I used to date before this. We were together for almost two years before Penelope broke up with me to be with another guy down in Los Angeles."

Even this early into Luke's story, my mouth dropped. This whole time that I'd worked alongside her, Penelope had barely been on my radar. The main thing that had stood out to me about Penelope was how beautiful she was. Luke must have seen past Penelope's beautiful face to an even more beautiful interior.

He admitted to me, "Before she broke my heart, I really loved Penelope. As hurt as I was when she left me, I wanted to stay friends. When things didn't work out for her in LA, I invited Penelope to come work on the farm with me. She needed an escape route, so I did what I could to help her out. By that point, I was just offering this as help from one friend to another. There was no way in hell that I was going to get back together with her. Penelope had a different idea in mind. According to her version of this story, she'd realized that I was the one for her or some shit like that. The truth is that Penelope just isn't good at being alone. I knew this, so I kept my distance. The whole situation got worse when Bill invited Sierra onto the farm, because Sierra and I hit it off right away. Because, let's be real here, who could help themselves from loving Sierra?"

Giving Luke an affectionate squeeze on the shoulder, Sierra seconded, "I love you, too, Luke ... But not in the way you might think, Skye. Let me guess, you thought we were a couple, right?"

"So ... you're not together?"

Giving each other an intimate, knowing look, Luke and Sierra laughed. This was when I would have expected them to lean in toward each other for a kiss and confess that they'd been playing a joke on me all along.

Getting serious again, Sierra answered, "I love Luke, but only as a friend. You see, I'm in love with another man, who ironically is also named Luke. The other Luke, my lover, lives in Washington. He works on another farm, a fruit farm actually. Before meeting him, I didn't believe humans were wired for monogamy. But as attracted as I am to this Luke, the deepest part of me just doesn't want to be with anyone else."

Even doing my best to curb my disbelief, I couldn't help but ask, "How is this whole arrangement working out for you guys?"

The silence that fell over the car wiped the disbelieving smirk right off of my face.

Sounding more beat down than I'd ever heard him, Luke confessed, "It's fucking hard. The hardest part is that everyone on the farm thinks we're together when we're not. We have to deal with all the complications of being in a relationship without the benefits. That being said, I value Sierra way too much to let this get in the way of our friendship. So, for the most part, I'm hanging in there. At this point, I mostly feel bad for Sierra. The way the other women on the farm treat her is awful."

Laying her hand back down on its favorite resting spot on Luke's arm, Sierra assured him, "I'm fine, Luke. Maya has her own set of issues she's dealing with. Things aren't good between her and Aukai right now. They haven't been good for a while. Skye, I'm only telling you this to help you understand why Maya acts the way she does. You can never breathe a word of this to anyone else on the farm, but ..."

Despite all my conflicting feelings toward Maya, the next part of Sierra's story was hard to swallow. Before Maya had taken up her vendetta against Sierra, the two of them had started off as friends. As Luke had said, Sierra was hard not to love. She was open in the way that usually only children are, almost genuine to a fault. By the end of telling Maya's story, Sierra was waving Luke's tequila bottle around in one hand and wiping away tears with the other, unabashedly crying for the woman who had bullied her. To avoid turning this into an unproductive gossip session, Sierra stuck to telling the bare essentials of the story.

"Here's the thing ..." Sierra continued, "Aukai wanted to break up with Maya a long time ago, way back at the beginning of their relationship. But someone messed up somewhere, and Maya got pregnant. Maya was determined to keep the baby. You know how obsessed Maya is with femininity and motherhood. Her biggest dream in life has always been to raise a family. Being the good guy that he is, Aukai committed to sticking with Maya through the pregnancy and coming up with a plan for how to raise their child together. But about halfway through the pregnancy, Maya lost the baby in a miscarriage. This all happened right at the start of trim season, so Maya and Aukai were thrust into the task of running an entire farm with no time to grieve. As much as this sucks, Aukai has been unhappy in their relationship for so long that he's just waiting for the trim season to end to break up with her. Although she may not know this explicitly, Maya has strong enough intuition to know something is deeply wrong with their relationship."

Having seen for myself how much Maya doted on Aukai, my heart ached for her. What started as an improbable, almost comical, story turned into an unexpectedly complicated and heartbreaking one. Sierra and I were pulled out of the swirling whirlwind of our gloominess when Luke jerked the steering wheel sharply to the left, just barely avoiding the deep ditch to the right side of the road. Concerned about Sierra and barely paying attention to the road, Luke had almost missed the next turn.

Brushing away any residual tears, Sierra made light of the situation by teasing Luke. "Are you tripping already?"

With a sigh, Luke conceded, "A little bit. But don't worry. We're almost at the hotel."

Luke's admission helped explain why the trees lining the road looked like they were reaching out to grab our car. I could only assume that Sierra was feeling the onset of the acid too, because she wrapped up the rest of the story real fast. None of us were looking to start our trip off on a bad note.

"We don't need to talk about that anymore. It's not really my story to tell. I only became involved in this mess when Maya, Penelope, and Calista teamed up against me for *stealing* Luke from Penelope. I'd sensed Maya's aggression toward me for a while, but she never said anything to my face until ... well, actually, the day you arrived on the farm. Remember the argument that you walked up on me and Maya having? She made me out to be some kind of heartless monster who intentionally broke Penelope's heart for my own sense of validation. She never bothered to get to know me well enough to realize that I have a boyfriend, too. So there you have it. Most of this drama boils down to petty jealousy. All of this could have easily been cleared up by now, but Maya made it taboo to talk about it. As long as our forced silence stands, all of us will keep acting like children toward each other. Sooner or later, innocent bystanders like you were bound to get caught up in our mess. I'm sorry for that."

Sierra's story shed a new light on Maya's crusade against me. All that I was to Maya was another young, supposedly single woman who randomly showed up on her farm alone. To Maya, I was a threat that she had to do everything in her power to neutralize—hence, the public shaming.

Heaving a sigh, I asked myself, "What the hell did I get myself caught up in?"

My head spinning, it took me a moment to realize that Luke's truck was no longer moving. We'd pulled up in front of a gold rush-era hotel that was crawling with people dressed in the most outlandish costumes. As long as this night felt already, the party had just begun.

Once we made it inside the hotel front doors, we found ourselves in an old-school dive bar that connected to the hotel lobby. The hotel décor looked a little worse for the wear. The combination of antiquated bar stools, animal heads mounted on the walls, and heavy red velvet curtains hanging over the windows made me feel like I'd stumbled into some kind of creepy hunters' den. I didn't imagine that any of the guest rooms had been used in a long time, although the hotel bar was certainly popular. The rest of the building had such a spooky feel to it that I, for one, would not have paid to spend the night under its roof. Not wanting to spend more time inside than necessary, we pushed our way through the lobby's back doors and stumbled onto the hotel's back lawn.

The hotel lawn was set up like a mini music festival, complete with four separate stages, although two of the stages had already closed down for the night. It was, after all, past midnight. The first stage we approached was the smaller of the two still in use. The DJ at this stage was playing a mix of hip-hop beats and world music. His beats were so danceable that I couldn't imagine why the whole party wasn't revolving around his stage. It was only when Sierra, Luke, and I took a break from dancing to check out the second stage that I understood why this first stage was relatively deserted. The music going on at the bigger stage was good, even if it wasn't quite as much to my taste. The beats bumping from these speakers were more traditional psytrance beats with a house influence. However, the real reason people were drawn to this stage was the giant bonfire raging in front of it. The night was a cold, damp one—a hard night to be dressed in a skimpy outfit like the one I was wearing. As much as I appreciated the first DJ's set, there was almost nothing that could convince me to leave the warmth of this fire.

Sometime after I discovered the miraculous warmth of the bonfire, the acid really kicked in. Sierra and Luke stood nearby, but they were absorbed in their own conversation and in flirting around the sexual tension hanging in the air between them. For a while, I stood silent and big-eyed, content to sway to the music and people-watch. The scene at this party reminded me of a more diverse version of the party scene in Nevada City. There were other groups of people here besides hippies, even though hippies made up the majority of the crowd. Just as in Nevada City, all the hippies were scantily dressed, many of them dreaded, and most of them covered in tattoos and jewelry. Along with the hippies, I noticed a sizeable punk scene; a more simply dressed, woodsy crew; and a collection of fashionably dressed hipsters, most of whom were from Europe.

As the girl who was dressed all in black and dancing by herself, I wasn't sure where I belonged in this scene, or if I belonged at all. However, I wasn't left to dance alone for long. Out of the hundreds of strangers at this party, the first stranger to approach me was a tall man wearing a mushroom hat and oversized, bug-eyed sunglasses.

The mushroom man saluted me with an enthusiastic, "Hello, my beautiful and mysterious robber friend! Tell me, sister, what is it that you love?"

Confused, I did my best to come up with an answer on the spot.

"Um ... I love my sister, Alice, and ... coffee and books and hip-hop and the desert and ..."

Throwing his hands up in the air, the mushroom man interrupted me, "Wonderful, wonderful! Now, I am not a very serious person, obviously. But let us get serious for a moment. What is it that you love *the most*?"

Befitting the mood of this party, I had to laugh at the fact that the first question I was asked wasn't what my name was or how I was doing but what I loved more than anything else. It took me a minute to come up with an adequate response.

Finally, I replied, "Can I use your question as my answer? So far, the most amazing thing that I've experienced in life *is* love."

Beaming his most encouraging smile, the mushroom man prompted me to continue with a wave of his hand.

Unsure what this man wanted from me, I stammered, "Listen, if you're looking for some kind of answer to life, you're talking to the wrong person. I have no idea what I'm doing. I'm lost as hell right now."

"And definitely not sober," I thought to myself, trying to stay focused on what I was saying as the mushroom man's face morphed from a human one into that of a cross-eyed, alien-beetle creature.

Carrying on in an effort to at least finish my point, I explained, "I've been all over the place these past few months, and I battle with anxiety almost every day. That being said, I've met so many amazing people, strangers even, who went out of their way to help me. I've ended up in all of these magical places, places so beautiful that I can't tell if I'm awake or dreaming. It makes me wonder if, on some deep level, this is what we're secretly longing for—not to find ourselves, but to lose ourselves. Love does that."

Clapping his hands, the mushroom man appeared genuinely moved. His face softened back into a more human-like form, although his huge eyes continued to dominate most of his face, and his relatively tiny mouth and nose kept resituating themselves and changing positions.

Not one to shy away from theatrics, the man roared, "Lovely, darling! My heart is overflowing with the truth of your words! If I may be so bold, I would love to share some of this overflow with you. What stirs the deepest love in my heart is song. Sister, would you mind if I sing you a song?"

I was too dazed to answer, but the mushroom man started singing anyway. All it took was hearing the first note off the mushroom man's tongue to melt away any of my lingering uneasiness. For the rest of this night, my heart stayed at an almost-dangerous level of open, a state of being for which I also had the acid to thank. Bringing my trip to a whole new level, the mushroom man sang to me in a language I didn't recognize—a Slavic language, perhaps. Although I doubt that anyone else could understand what he was saying, the purity of the mushroom man's voice attracted a small assembly of awe-struck listeners, Luke and Sierra included. Luke was so taken by the mushroom man's song that he came forward to compliment the man at the end of his performance. The two of them became absorbed in their own conversation, which, from what I could hear, involved a lot more talk about mushrooms and those kind of substances than it did about love.

Moved by the emotion this man's performance inspired and by the strength of the acid flowing through our bloodstreams, Sierra's whole body looked like it was vibrating. After Luke and the mushroom man stepped away, Sierra turned around to face me. Staring straight at me with her big doe eyes, her face split into a wide Cheshire cat grin. The freckles on her nose and cheeks danced around her face in circular patterns.

"Tell me," Sierra laughed, "how do you do it—get people to open up to you like that? Luke doesn't usually say much, but suddenly he's telling you everything, and I'm spilling secrets that aren't even mine to spill. You show up at all these places alone but make new friends right away. I mean, look, we're here for ten minutes and you have strangers singing to you! I can't quite put my finger on it, but it's like you have this special type of magnetism. Not only do you draw people to you, but you draw them out of themselves."

Sierra paused midsentence, taking a breath to collect herself.

No longer laughing but still staring at me just as intently, Sierra asked me again, "How do you do it?"

"Why does tonight have to be the night I get asked all the hard questions?" I thought to myself, yet again at a loss for words.

When I did finally reply, I had no concrete grasp on what I was going to say ahead of time. I just let myself express whatever idea arose within me. Nonetheless, the words felt true to me as they rolled off my tongue.

"If I have any of this magnetism you're talking about, then I wouldn't say it's drawing other people to me as much it's drawing me to them. I was trying to explain this to the mushroom man earlier, but, for months now, it feels like I'm being pulled around by all these forces outside of my control. The only thing I can really say I chose is not to do something just because it feels comfortable. Even when things get really hard, I keep moving forward. No matter what I see or feel, I try my best to stay with it. I don't look away."

Eyes wide with some mixture of fear and admiration, Sierra's jaw dropped ever so slightly. Written all over her face was the surprise she felt at realizing that I wasn't the meek, obedient person I presented myself to be on the farm. Although Sierra flaunted her audaciousness more publicly, that same boldness lived within me. It simply took on a quieter form. My version of courage would never be about reaching some kind of mystical state in which I transcended fear once and for all. My fear traveled alongside me as an almost constant companion. It caused me to doubt myself all the time, to hesitate, to second-guess my decisions. Every day, I waged war against my mind and the fear that plagued it. I fought to live a life of my own choosing rather than a life dictated by fear and comfort. I fought the impulse to close, to numb, or to seek some form of escape. Every day, over and over, I chose to see, to stay, to remain open.

These were thoughts I rarely shared with anyone. I doubt most people had any idea of the internal struggles that I'd gone through when I walked away from a comfortable, relatable life into a life that, multiple years and an entire book later, I still struggle to explain to myself. However, I wasn't there to prove myself to anyone other than myself, so I felt almost embarrassed by the vehemence of the proclamation I'd made to Sierra. Knowing Sierra as one of the most bold and radically honest people I'd ever met, I should have known better than to feel self-conscious.

Drawing back slightly, Sierra grinned her wild, wide-open Cheshire grin, eyes sparkling with that special glint that signifies mutual understanding.

"You know, Skye," she proclaimed, "you're not nearly as innocent as I thought you were."

Totally absorbed in our little two-person world, Sierra and I would have been content to spend the rest of the night talking if it weren't for our realization that we'd lost track of Luke.

Berating herself for having forgotten about him, Sierra offered, "I'll go find Luke. Feel free to stay by the fire. I'll come right back here when I find him."

Just like that, I found myself dancing alone in a circle of strangers again. The DJ onstage was still pumping out high-tempo house beats with little care in the world as to what time it was. No one else dancing around the stage cared either. After all, this was one of the only occasions of the season that brought all the marijuana trimmers, harvesters, managers, and farm owners out from their holes. Almost everyone at this party had been working twelve-hour days, six days per week, for months now. This was the one night we got to loosen our grip on the self-control we'd worked so hard to cultivate.

All inhibitions put aside, I danced my way around the fire circle, striking up a conversation with anyone who struck my fancy. I was so absorbed in meeting new people that I lost track of Sierra and Luke for a long time. I completely forgot that I was supposed to stay in one place so that Sierra could find me again. I talked to people who had come there from all over the world, many of whom had been coming to California to trim for years. I got to practice my French and Spanish and even pick up some vocabulary in a few new languages. After switching back and forth between languages so many times, my brain started to mix them all up. At a certain point, I barely felt capable of speaking in English anymore. Talking in so many languages about so many abstract subjects, I felt myself untether from the physical world. I pictured my feet detaching from the ground beneath me as my body began its slow ascent into the realms of the metaphysical. Everything felt so temporary, so subject to change, that I couldn't trust that any of what I was experiencing was real. I very seriously questioned whether I'd lost my mind and made all of this up.

Doubting everything, I studied the strange faces around me, many of them covered in masks, face paint, and grotesque makeup. For a moment, I actually felt afraid. I scanned the crowd for Luke's and Sierra's faces to provide me with some sense of security. Finally, I spotted them sitting on a log a little way away from the dancing circle. Luke's eyes were half-closed, and he was swaying even while sitting down. Her arm around his shoulder, Sierra was doing her best to prop Luke up.

Pointing to Luke, I mouthed to Sierra, "Is he OK?"

Looking doubtful, Sierra whispered back, "I don't know. He hasn't been talking for a while now. The last thing I understood was that he took some mushrooms from that guy who sang to us earlier."

Conscious enough to understand we were talking about him, Luke warbled back, "I want to lie down."

Rubbing his back, Sierra reassured Luke, "I understand. We just need to get back to the farm before you can do that. I feel sober enough to drive us home now. It's four in the morning, and I haven't taken anything since we left the farm. But if we're doing this, you have to stand up for me, Luke."

Doing what I could to help, I rushed over to the other side of Luke and wrapped his free arm around my shoulder. Supporting Luke as best we could, the three of us swerved and zigzagged the whole long walk back to Luke's truck. After dropping his keys multiple times, Luke managed to open the driver's door. Sierra had to remind Luke that he wasn't the one driving, after which he slid resignedly into the passenger's seat. Sierra drove slowly, so it was past five by the time we made it back to the farm. In a few short hours, the sun would rise to herald the arrival of a new day. Luke, Sierra, and I closed out our night together by chugging as much water as we could stomach. From there, Luke crawled into the bed in the back of his truck, too tired to make the trek down the hill to sleep in his far more spacious RV. As I walked away toward my tent, I heard Luke issue Sierra a quiet plea for her to stay and keep him company, after which I heard Sierra's quiet sigh of consent. Free of all obligation toward anyone, I stumbled over to my tent and collapsed onto my sleeping pad.

chapter fifteen

DIVING INTO THE INNER OCEAN

GIVEN HOW MUCH HAD HAPPENED since my arrival, it was almost unfathomable to me that I'd only been at the Ganesha Wellness Community for ten days. After all I'd learned on Halloween, nothing much changed on the surface at least. None of the drama or conflict magically resolved itself or disappeared. Yet having some sense of the root causes behind these issues made it so I no longer felt as blindsided by the aggression or pettiness that I saw playing out around me. I still avoided Maya whenever possible, knowing that the power she wielded over me made her dangerous. However, she no longer held the same power over my emotions as she did before. In the times when we were forced to interact, like when she weighed us out at the end of the day, I tried to just hold space for her. I said little and listened more, doing my best not to judge or even really react to what she had to say.

In general, I felt more secure in my place on the farm and more confident in the value I had to offer, as I was now easily trimming over two pounds per day. After putting in many long hours of work during the day, I got to look forward to hanging out with Luke and Sierra by the fire circle in the evenings. By becoming closer friends with the two of them, I made myself another new friend—someone who I hadn't expected to get as close to—Bill. Most of my interactions with Bill had nothing to do with work or marijuana. Bill had been in the marijuana industry for so many years that he was understandably burnt out. Searching for topics that were more interesting to both of us, I discovered that one of Bill's primary passions was the study of dreams. During the early morning hours as Bill cooked breakfast and I made my coffee, we recounted to each other our previous night's dreams and interpreted them out loud together.

One morning, I scraped up the courage to have a more real-world-oriented conversation with Bill and asked him what he thought about Liam coming to join me on the farm. Bill promised that he would put in a good word for Liam with the rest of the management team, but we both knew the matter wasn't entirely in his hands. When I approached Aukai regarding this same matter, Aukai was as sweet and supportive as expected, despite his concerns about how many trimmers were already working on the farm. Swallowing my aversion toward interacting with Maya for any reason outside of absolute necessity, I approached her next. A few days after Halloween, I walked up to Maya and Calista chit-chatting around the weighing station at the end of a long day. Throughout the first five minutes of our conversation, Maya maintained a skeptical stance with her hands on her hips, her lips pursed, and eyebrows raised. To my surprise, Calista, Maya's best friend, was the one to jump in to defend my case. Calista had a husband back in Brazil who had been unable to join her for the season because of issues with his visa.

Perhaps missing her own husband, Calista implored Maya, "Come now, Mayita. We have let so many strangers onto this land. Surely we can make enough room for Skye to reunite with her boyfriend, no?"

I swallowed, slightly self-conscious by Calista's use of the word *boyfriend*, as Liam and I hadn't yet gone so far as to use those titles with each other. Nevertheless, Calista was on a roll, and I wasn't going to be the person to stop her.

Calista and Maya went at it back and forth with each other for a few times until Calista finally interjected, "Mayita, hermana mía ... please remember, we are talking about two lovers who have been separated and are trying to find their way back together again. What matters more than this?"

Once Calista removed me from the story and turned my request into a bigger issue about making sacrifices for love, Maya softened. Almost as if she was consoling me for some kind of loss, Maya reached out to touch my shoulder. For the first and only time that I can clearly remember, she looked me directly in the eyes. It was as if her eyes were trying to speak to me, but they were telling me so many things at once that it was hard to get a clear message.

In the end, all Maya said was, "I'll see what I can do."

This was, perhaps, the shortest proclamation I'd ever heard her make.

To signal that our conversation was over, Maya simply turned back toward Calista and stated, "Well now, it's time for me to find my own partner. I haven't seen him all day."

Without so much as another glance in my direction, she spun on her heels and walked out of the shed.

During the days following my request to Maya, she no longer picked on me in the same way that she used to. If anything, she ignored me. This change in attitude came to me as a relief. I would far rather have Maya look straight through me instead of glare at me with daggers shooting from her eyes. Without intending to, I'd neutralized myself as a threat to Maya. All that I had to do was identify myself as being in love with another man. As relieved as I was at the newfound tranquility I'd been granted, I didn't know what Maya's silence meant regarding Liam's potential arrival. All I could do was warn Liam about how precarious the situation was on the farm. I kept waiting for Liam to change his mind about coming.

Contrary to my expectations, Liam insisted, "I'm coming to California for *you*. It doesn't matter to me where we are or what we're doing."

Knowing how much Liam liked his well-laid-out plans, I didn't know what to make of this carefree ambivalence. He had so much faith that all would be well as soon as we were back together again that I eventually succumbed to the contagion of his optimism. I spent most of my trimming time fantasizing about what it would be like to see him again. Riding on the wings of the most powerful drug of them all, I floated through my days untouched by the stress of my life's unanswered questions. Once I was able to let go of my worries over the future, certain ambiguities about my future resolved themselves of their own accord. The morning before Liam was supposed to arrive, Aukai pulled me aside from the breakfast table. He whispered into my ear a four-digit code, patted me on the back, and retreated back into his shed without further explanation.

It took me a minute to realize that these numbers were the new code to open the farm gate, a code Aukai had changed to prevent any unexpected arrivals from letting themselves onto the land. I repeated these four numbers over and over again in my head like a mantra.

After being granted unofficial approval for Liam to come, the next set of numbers I had to deal with was the thirty-six or so hours until I got to use the code Aukai had given me. Since Liam still didn't have reliable service, I only managed to get ahold of him on the morning that he left to start his long drive out west. Although Liam told me to expect him by ten, he didn't arrive at the farm until well past midnight. The last hour of his sixteen-hour-long drive was spent driving in circles in a five-mile radius around the farm, trying to locate the mystical green gate that marked the entrance to the property. Not only was it dark out, but there were also very few street signs in this area to guide Liam in the right direction. To make matters worse, there was little-to-no cell phone service in the area except at the top of the highest hills. I spent over an hour sitting on top of the front gate to the farm, doing my best to guide Liam over the phone whenever he managed to find a spot with service. With every pair of headlights that passed me by, my heart jumped a little. Just when the cold was really starting to set in, I recognized the headlights that belonged to Liam's Subaru.

Liam pulled up to park behind the gate. He opened the

door and bridged the distance between us in a few quick strides. He took me in his arms and kissed my neck, face, hair, and ears. Liam was exhausted but nowhere nearly as grumpy as I would have been after such a long day of driving. Offering no reproach against my rather misguided driving directions, Liam moved and spoke in a manner that was as calm as it was patient. Caught in the bright beam of Liam's headlights, we stood unmoving in front of the farm gate, holding each other. Something about the bright lights shining on us and the total stillness of the moment made me feel as if we'd temporarily been caught inside a photograph. For just a moment, time paused in the way that it does only in pictures.

"Holding you again ... It's even better than I imagined," Liam murmured at last, burying his face in my neck.

As reluctant as we were to let go of each other, I eventually pulled away to open the gate for Liam. Being as late and dark as it was, I promised to give him a tour of the farm the next day. By the time we were zipping ourselves up into my tent, I had to laugh at how crowded my formerly spacious two-person tent suddenly felt. Exhausted as we were, we did our best to stay awake a little while longer. Whispering incoherent banalities to each other, we slipped in and out of the dream world. Liam traced his hand along the curve of my back and the nape of my neck, stroking me so slowly and deliberately that I was practically purring with pleasure. Our minds numbed into silence, we let our bodies take over. Lips locked and limbs intertwined, Liam rolled on top of me, easing himself inside of me. We moved together with a smoothness that felt both careful and effortless, familiar and new. When we curled up together afterward, I couldn't be sure whether I'd just woken up from the most fantastic of nightmares or entered the most wonderful of dreams.

I woke up from my reverie the next morning to the sound of Liam coughing. By the time I rolled over to check on how he was doing, he was already sitting up, taking deep pulls from his inhaler.

Wrapping myself around him, I asked, "Are you OK? You didn't tell me your cough was still this bad."

Stowing away his inhaler, Liam bent down to kiss me good morning.

"Don't worry, it's always the worst when I first wake up. All I need is some fresh air. What do you say, babe? How about that tour of the farm you promised me?"

Reluctantly, I unwound my limbs from around Liam's body. As worried as I was about the condition of his lungs, I could tell by his tone of voice that the topic was closed for discussion. By the time I turned back around from getting dressed, he was already one step ahead of me. Sticking his feet out through the open flap of our tent, he laced up his shoes.

Bursting with excitement, Liam exclaimed, "I finally get to meet all the characters from the Ganesha Wellness madhouse! You'll have to remind me of everyone's names. And nudge me or something if I'm talking to one of the really crazy ones ... Like what's that one manager's name ... Mandy?"

Giggling and shushing Liam all at the same time, I whispered, "Maya! But be careful what you say. You never know who's listening around here. Thank God you're here now. It's so nice to have someone here who I know from the outside."

Poking his head back into the tent, Liam objected, "Oh, so I'm just someone you know from the outside now, huh?"

Laughing despite myself, I assured him, "You're only my favorite someone from the outside. Plus, you're on the inside with me now. That makes you the newest member of this so-called madhouse."

"Whatever weird shit you're into, sign me up," Liam winked at me.

Rolling my eyes at Liam, I focused on putting my shoes on as a means of hiding the blush spreading across my cheeks. When I finished, Liam offered a hand to help pull me up to my feet.

Slipping his fingers between mine, he proclaimed, "I missed you rolling your eyes at me."

We bickered and teased each other all the way from our tent through the parking lot until we reached the top of the hill. Looking out from this viewpoint over the rest of the farm, Liam stopped in his tracks at the sight of the towering stalks of marijuana sprouting up in tight rows along both sides of the road.

"Damn," Liam swore, "this is a serious operation. Those are some nice-looking plants they've got growing down there. As nice as you can get with an outdoor crop, anyway."

The rest of our way down the hill, Liam picked my brain for information about how the marijuana on this farm was grown, harvested, trimmed, and sold. We compared trimming techniques from each of our farms. When we reached the kitchen, we put this more technical conversation on hold so I could introduce Liam to all the workers in our immediate vicinity. As we stood in the kitchen talking to Bill and Pedro, Aukai walked up to join our conversation. Despite Liam's struggle to pronounce Aukai's name, the two of them hit it off right away. They launched into marijuana-related business talk and comparisons of the industries across different states, most of which went over my head. As I set the water for my coffee on the stove to boil, Aukai took off with Liam to give him a more professional lay of the land. The tour ended with Aukai giving Liam his first bin of marijuana to trim.

Full marijuana bins and french press of coffee in hand, we

made our way toward the large trimming shed. As autumn yielded to winter, the cold and the rain made it harder to work outside during the day. Most of the trimmers on site spent their whole days and evenings rimming inside the shed to avoid having to move all their stuff whenever it rained. I'd resigned myself to hunkering down with the OG Crew in the back of the shed. Nonetheless, I still grumbled about spending so many hours inside the claustrophobic trimming shed. The trimming shed had little-to-no ventilation, so all the smoke produced by the wood-burning stove hung over our heads like a heavy, gray cloud. Under normal circumstances, working in an indoor area with such poor air quality would probably be illegal. But of course, nothing we were doing there was legal.

Just walking into the smoky shed was enough to make Liam start coughing all over again. Taking in my scowl of concern, Liam pulled a heavy-duty respirator mask out of his backpack.

"It's OK. I came prepared."

Peering longingly back outside the shed, I muttered, "Let's just hope that we get a few more sunny days when we can work outside again. That would help a bit at least."

For the time being, we squeezed our way through the narrow passageway to the back of the shed. After finding a small space for Liam to set down his bin, I introduced him to all the OG Crew members. Per usual, Delias was the most boisterous of the bunch.

Throwing his hands up in the air, Delias proclaimed, "Ah, the infamous American boyfriend has at last come to join our friend Skye! With how much Skye has traveled and all the languages she speaks, I've been telling her that she would be much better-suited dating a European—a Greek man perhaps. I have plenty of cousins and nephews I could set her up with, but Skye was never so crazy about this idea."

"If you pretend like you can't hear him, he will eventually stop talking," Vasili advised Liam with a wry chuckle.

Unintimidated by the nonexistent threat of his Greek competition, Liam joked right back, "You better watch out. Not only am I American, but I am also a born-and-bred Texas boy. As far as most Texans are concerned, we don't even belong in the same country."

Delias threw up his hands in feigned uproar while Vasili and I rolled our eyes at the two of them. All fun and games aside, it was time to get to work. Because Liam had to wear the respirator while trimming, he wasn't able to talk while working. While I'm quieter by nature, I had a hard time seeing Liam forced into silence like this. The mask stifled all his natural fluidity in social settings. It prevented him from being able to banter back and forth with the people around him like he usually would. If Liam had been capable of replying to Delias's jokes, Delias and Liam would have become great friends. That being said, ever since Maya indirectly accused all the trimmers of stealing the farm's marijuana, even Delias joked around less than usual. It made me sad that Liam never got to see the OG Crew as the tight-knit, indestructible unit we once were. Missing this sense of group safety, I was even more grateful to have an ally by my side.

Not only was Liam there to stick up for me, but I also ended up having to stick up for Liam. I had no idea what to make of Maya's constantly changing attitude toward the both of us. All of a sudden, Maya was so amicable toward me that Liam had a hard time believing I was ever a primary target for her aggressions. When Liam and I went up together to be weighed out at the end of the night, Maya actually complimented me on the quality of my work. In contrast to this newfound warmth toward me, Maya showed nothing but skepticism toward Liam. It felt almost as if Maya had decided to strike up a vendetta against men in general. The most overt attack that Maya made against Liam happened on the second night after his arrival. Speaking loudly enough for everyone to hear, Maya criticized Liam for leaving too many leaves on the bud. She completely ignored the fact that he had been given one of the leafiest, most difficult strains of marijuana to trim.

"Maybe double-check the quality of your boyfriend's work before you come up next time. Who knows what kind of standards he got used to back in Colorado," Maya admonished the both of us.

"Maya, everyone's been complaining about how ..." I wisely refrained from using the word *shitty* and replaced it with "*difficult* the B12 strain of marijuana is to trim. Liam did the best he could with what he was given."

"Are you complaining about the quality of our marijuana? You're a good worker, but watch yourself. I'm sick of hearing people talk poorly about the marijuana that Aukai, Bill, Pedro, Luke, and I spent a whole year growing."

Sensing that I was treading on dangerous ground, all I could do in way of remonstration was saunter off in sullen silence. It was one thing for Maya to humiliate me, but I had no tolerance for her pulling the same tricks on Liam.

Heading back to our stations, Liam leaned in to whisper, "I see what you mean about her. That woman is very intimidating. I've got to say, though, I don't mind this whole *boyfriend* development."

Internally, I hit myself on the forehead for not having warned Liam about this earlier.

"Oh, about that ... I'm sorry, I meant to warn you earlier. I had to call you my boyfriend because there's no way they would have let you onto the land otherwise. It doesn't have to mean anything, though."

Without skipping a beat, Liam teased back, "Wait, so I don't get to be your boyfriend?"

Caught off guard, I stuttered, "We haven't really talked

about that, so I don't want to push anything on you. I just ..."

Taking pity on me, Liam interjected, "It's OK. I like being your boyfriend. That also means I get to call you my girlfriend, right?"

Hearing the world girlfriend come out of Liam's mouth in reference to me, the most delightful combination of nervousness and joy tumbled in somersault-like motions inside my stomach.

"Um, sure. I mean, yeah ... that would be nice."

The last thing Liam said before slipping his respirator back on was, "Time for me to focus, babe. As your newly official boyfriend, it looks like I'm going to have to work harder to be able to stay here with you."

Over the next few days, the noticeably lower-quality B12 marijuana that Liam was given became the norm instead of the aberration. Instead of coming with the names of known, established strains, our bins were now labeled with mysterious letter and number combinations like C13 and B5 and G7. It took only a few days for me to connect the dots and realize this was because neither the harvesters nor the managers knew what strain of marijuana they were handing us anymore. This told me that we were far closer to the end of the farm's harvest than any of us had predicted. Now that most of the bud we were given was smaller, leafier, and weighed less, I could trim all day and still manage to produce only a pound. It didn't matter if I brought up bags and bags of trimmed marijuana filled to the brim, I could tell just carrying the bags that they contained more volume than they did density. Acutely aware of the fact that our work could run out at any time, Liam and I worked harder than ever.

While Liam, our crew, and I worked our asses off, not everyone else in the shed felt the same sense of pressure. The king of joints, Arrow spent most of the day rolling up ridiculously large joints that he passed around the entire trimming shed to bring everyone working in the shed up to his same level of high. Liam and I were two of the people who didn't partake. Whenever I did take a hit off one of Arrow's joints, all his speeches suddenly made a lot more sense. Arrow's favorite subject to rant about was Bitcoin, which tied into a greater discourse about changing currencies and the economy of the future.

Taking a hit from his joint, Arrow would announce, "I'm telling you, man, blockchain is the way of the future. Just think, it's already given us Bitcoin, a fully digital currency that the government can't fuck with and the banks can't get their hands on. There's a whole revolution happening right under our noses, and this is just the beginning!"

As convinced as Arrow was of this so-called digital revolution, he struggled to explain what blockchain was exactly.

When pressed further, he would usually just end up telling us to watch some video on YouTube that could supposedly explain it better. I couldn't help but find it ironic listening to economic lectures coming from a man who'd spent most of his adult life homeless. Arrow would probably have argued that he was homeless by choice and that his time spent living on the streets had endowed him with a more pragmatic understanding of how our society operates. While I had a hard time taking Arrow seriously, his rather radical views drew some of the farm workers to him like moths to a flame. Strangely enough, Arrow's talks piqued the most interest from Chumani, Z's mother. Although Chumani was much more soft-spoken than Arrow when it came to expressing her own views, she listened to whatever Arrow had to say with rapt attention.

For me, this was when Chumani's carefully painted façade began to chip away in places. Something about the way Chumani presented herself reminded me of my first impression of Maya. Both women exuded an ultrafeminine, motherly sort of energy. They spoke in soft, sweet voices and stared up at you with big eyes as they spoke. As women, their outward sweetness made me more inclined to trust them. However, it took less than a day of being around Maya to see the gaping holes in her sweet façade. Maya's holes came from deep-seated insecurities—insecurities that left her with an insatiable desire for the sense of power that she lacked within herself. I never got to know Chumani well enough to know what was eating away at her and creating these holes. What I noticed was that Chumani claimed to be there to save up money for her and her son but instead spent most of her time smoking weed and talking to Arrow. Once, I caught Chumani digging her fingernails into Z's arm as she pulled him along behind her. More than once, I heard her hiss angry words into Z's ear. Liam noticed all of this, too. We watched Chumani with increasing wariness, paying particular attention to the way she interacted with Arrow in hopes that this would solve the mystery she'd come to represent.

I wasn't able to keep as close tabs on Chumani or Z as I would have liked because of all the other changes happening on the farm. The change that hit me the hardest was Sierra's decision to leave the farm early to head up north to be with her lover, Luke. Sierra gave me and Luke the news before she told anyone else, but this didn't make saying goodbye to her any easier. One of the saddest things to me was that Liam and Sierra never really got to know each other except through the stories I'd told them about each other. All I could do was be grateful for the intimacy of the connection that Sierra and I had experienced on Halloween night. Realistically, I knew that my path and Sierra's would probably never cross again.

A few days after Sierra left us, we received a welcome distraction from the sadness her departure had stirred up in me. One of Aukai's friends who managed a nearby farm invited all the farm workers in the area to come to a party on the farm's property. The intention of the party was to give everyone a "mid-season chill break." For our farm, this party wound up being the last big hurrah at the end of our season, but we appreciated the break nonetheless.

The day of the party, there was a line in front of the outdoor shower stall all day long. The women on the farm changed out of their sweats into actual jeans or even dresses, and some even bothered to put on makeup. The men mostly looked the same as they always did, but they smelled a little better. Since very few people wanted to be designated drivers, we all shoved into as few vehicles as possible and caravanned over to the other farm together. We drove ten minutes and through two gates before pulling up to a rustic wood cabin, outside of which stood a hazy-eyed man with long, black dreads greeting all the new arrivals. This man had a growing circle of people standing around him, as he was holding the largest joint any of us had ever seen, a monster doobie that looked to be a foot long. He lit the joint solemnly, taking in a deep pull before exhaling a cloud of smoke that temporarily engulfed his whole head. The party-goers stared incredulously with dropped jaws, many of the people having taken out their phones to capture the epic moment.

Shaking his head in disbelief, Liam mouthed to me, "Only in California ..."

By the time the joint made its rounds and reached us, Liam and I each took a hit, more for the novelty than anything else. Even after taking a rather conservative hit, Liam fell into another one of his coughing spells, and I was immediately and irreversibly blazed, a state from which I didn't recover all evening. Even after we disbanded and trickled inside to join the rest of the party, I still had the feeling of being stuck inside a marijuana cloud. Everything appeared hazy and slightly out of focus, and I couldn't concentrate for very long on what anyone was saying. I drifted haphazardly from one conversation to the next, losing and refinding Liam again many times throughout the course of the evening. After hanging out inside the house for a while, I eventually headed outside to refill my beer from the keg. Everyone outside was gathered around a large stack of wood palettes that had been piled on top of each other and set ablaze.

On the other side of the fire from me, I locked eyes with Liam, who was talking to one of the newer trimmers on our farm. Catching my eye, Liam drifted off halfway through whatever thought he was in the middle of expressing. Taking advantage of this pause in their conversation, I walked over and nuzzled my way inside Liam's arms. The other trimmer took this as his cue and left to refill his own beer. Soaking in our first real moment alone together at the party, Liam tightened his arms around me as I leaned my head back to rest on his chest. Melting into each other, we stared wordlessly into the raging fire of blazing wood palettes. Being back with Liam again, I lost track of where we were, what was happening around us, or how much time was passing, if time was passing at all. After a short time or after a long time—I'm not sure which—Liam spun me around to face him. Carefully placing his hand underneath my chin, he tipped my head up until I was looking him in the eyes.

"Look at us. We're in California at this dope-ass house party. We both have jobs, at least for a little while. We've met all these amazing people. We made it. Or I should say, *you* made it."

For the first time in a long time, I felt the sense of safety that comes from knowing that all is as it should be. Squeezing Liam a little tighter, I rose up on my tiptoes to kiss him. I started to spin back around to face the fire, but Liam held me in place with his hand on my chin and his eyes locked into mine.

"I love you, Skye."

Staring into the blue of his eyes, I felt myself fall into Liam as if I'd suddenly plunged into a deep, cold body of water. My breath was taken away by the shock of it. Swimming through the waters of this vast inner ocean, I lost myself in this subaquatic world. In this world, all that existed was water, and everything was quiet. I kept swimming and kicking my way deeper, but there appeared to be no bottom to whatever hole I'd fallen into. The blue of the water around me darkened as I moved further away from the surface and the light above, holding my breath this whole time. I wanted to keep swimming, to see what I would find, but my lungs were burning and crying out for air. Resurfacing, I drew in a sharp inhale. All at once, I felt the warmth of the fire we were standing next to. I remembered that we were at a party on some stranger's property, surrounded by more strangers, lost deep in the woods of bum-fuck nowhere California. But more importantly, I remembered what I wanted to say back to Liam.

"I love you, too."

Liam let out the breath that I didn't realize he'd been holding. He looked relieved and exhausted all at the same time, as if he, too, had just braved a journey to and from some other world. I wondered if he felt the same longing that I did to dive back in.

As if in reply to my unvoiced question, Liam proposed, "What do you say, babe? Wanna get out of here?"

We spent the next few minutes asking around to see if anyone else was trying to leave the party and could give us a ride. Finally, we found another trimmer headed back to the farm and hopped into the back of that person's car. After getting dropped off at our tents, Liam and I happened upon a scene in which neither of us wanted to take part. Coming from the tent that we knew to be Chumani's and Z's, Arrow's voice rang out loud and clear. I had no idea what to make of this, as I could only assume that Z was there in the tent with them. The sound of Arrow's voice was followed by a succession of shuffling noises and hushed moans. Most of the moaning sounds were distinctly female. Liam sighed, shaking his head in dismay.

"Never a dull moment on this farm ..."

My good mood suddenly flipped on its head, I sighed back, "Poor Z ..."

Thinking of Z trapped inside that tent, the only thing I wanted to do in that moment was curl up in a ball inside our tent and close out everything going on outside of us. Seeing my face shut down, Liam pulled me onto his lap before my body closed down along with it. For the second time tonight, he tilted my face gently up toward his. As I peered up at him, his gaze slowly changed. The same look of love and adoration remained, but Liam's expression wasn't as soft as it was before. There was a hard glint in his eyes that shone out despite the tenderness he emanated. I knew Liam well enough to understand where this hard glint was coming from and what it meant for me. My body reacted to this look instantly. All my muscles relaxed. All thoughts left my mind. My whole being folded open in surrender.

Liam and I had made love countless times by then, but my whole body still shivered with pleasure at the sensation of his hardness beneath me and then, finally, inside me. That night especially, we took our time. We savored every moment, every position. We made love until we were too exhausted to move anymore. Cradling each other afterward, Liam and I were too tired to even carry on a conversation. Yet somehow, in the early morning hours long before our alarms went off, the two of us were re-awoken by the force of a desire that all our passionate love-making from earlier in the night couldn't satiate.

Rolling back on top of me, Liam confessed, "The moment that we stopped making love last night, I already couldn't wait to be back inside you."

Along with having sex all over again, we also exhausted ourselves all over again. We used up all the energy we'd managed to regain in the few hours that we'd slept. Dozing off again, we slept in without a care in the world about how much work we were missing.

chapter sixteen

HOW TO COUNT TO ONE THOUSAND WITH TWENTY DOLLAR BILLS

FROM OUR TENT, WE WERE CLOSE enough to Chumani's tent, which at night turned into Chumani and Arrow's tent, to hear Z crying.

"But Mommy," Z wailed, "I don't wanna leave!"

After Z carried on like this for a while, Chumani lost her patience and hissed a reply too quiet for us to make out. Whatever Chumani told Z effectively shut him up, at least enough to lower the volume of his wailing. Yet when we ran into Z playing outside later in the day, we were faced with a Zaire who was drained of his usual zest for life. For our last few days on the farm, Z spent most of his time in hiding, darting through the marijuana fields as if daring someone to catch him. While Z made a bigger show of it than the rest of us, he wasn't the only one whose crankiness increased in our last few days on the farm. The quality of the marijuana that Aukai gave us deteriorated so much that Liam and I worked from 7:00 a.m. to 11:00 p.m. and still didn't manage to trim one full pound of weed. Working such long hours to produce so few grams numbed my mind to the point that I felt like a marijuana-trimming robot. While I could temporarily accept feeling more machine than human, the one part of our situation that I couldn't accept was how terrible Liam's cough had gotten. In the mornings especially, Liam coughed and coughed and coughed until even his inhaler could do very little to help him. Although I insisted multiple times that we could ask to get paid out and leave the farm early, Liam, knowing how much I needed the money, immediately shut down this idea whenever it came up.

By the time Aukai finally announced our last day of work, we were both so relieved to be getting Liam out of the trimming shed and off the farm that neither of us even considered trying to find trimming work elsewhere. Our main priority at that point was resting and allowing Liam to heal from his bronchitis. The last bins of marijuana Aukai gave us were very light and didn't have much marijuana in them, so it took Liam and me less than half a day to trim the little weed we had left. On the same day we finished, Aukai made a trip to the farm owner's property to collect all the cash he would need to pay out the trimmers on the farm. While Liam napped, I packed up my tent and the rest of our belongings into the back of my car. Since we didn't have very much in the way of belongings, this didn't take me very long. Wanting to see who was still around, I headed down to hang out by the fire circle until Aukai got back. Although this was the last time I would see most of the workers on the farm, the hang-out circle felt as casual as it always did. A lot of the trimmers, including all my friends in the OG Crew, had gone to run errands in town. I never got to say a real goodbye to any of them.

Once all the trimmers vacated the property for good, this would leave only Penelope, Maya, Calista, Aukai, Pedro, and Luke on the farm together. From the beginning, Bill had been explicit about his intention to leave the farm as soon as possible to be with his family again. Eventually, Ganesha Wellness Community would totally shut down for the season. Even these six remaining people would leave the farm. I couldn't pretend to know what would happen to any of them after that. From what Luke and Sierra told me, my best guess was that all six of them would go their separate ways. With that, the end of the season would mostly likely also mark the dissolution of Maya and Aukai's relationship.

The end of trimming season also brought other changes. In our final days on the farm, Chumani turned a cold shoulder to Arrow. She made it abundantly clear that her illicit relationship with Arrow would not survive beyond their days working together. On our last day of work, Chumani's husband, the large Hawaiian with the slight limp and booming voice, pulled up to the farm in his large diesel pickup truck, abruptly reinserting himself into his wife's and son's lives. With alarming speed, he helped Chumani and Z throw all their belongings into the back of his truck, loaded them into the truck with him, and set off back down the dirt road. The whole time he was there, Chumani didn't so much as deign to look in Arrow's direction. Arrow was so despondent after Chumani and Z left that he could hardly even muster up the motivation to get high.

Hardly able to stand seeing such a young child get carted around like this, I couldn't have gotten off that property soon enough. Of everyone I'd worked with on the farm, the only two people I put in the effort to wish a proper goodbye to were Luke and Bill. Per usual, I found Luke out in the fields. We hugged each other for a long time. After parting ways with Luke, I found Bill and Pedro deep-cleaning the kitchen. Grateful for any excuse to take a break from this project, they stopped what they were doing upon my arrival. They greeted me as warmly as if I were visiting royalty.

"Skye!" Bill exclaimed, "I was hoping you'd come to rescue us from this damn kitchen, but judging from the look on your face, I'm afraid you're leaving us instead. Am I right?"

"You're not wrong. We're waiting for Aukai to get back to the farm and pay us, though. In the meantime, I'd be happy to help you guys out. Want me to take over doing dishes for a bit?"

Bill relinquished his cleaning duties to me with such eagerness that I couldn't help but wonder for how long I'd just committed to doing dishes.

Reading my mind, or perhaps just the worried expression on my face, Pedro assured me, "I just talked to Aukai, and he should be back within the hour. Feel free to leave before then if you need to finish packing up. I'm not expecting this kitchen to get totally clean in just one day, so I'm trying to be leisurely about the whole process."

The person who was feeling the most leisurely about this process was clearly Bill, who sidled over to slump down at the wooden booth in the corner of the kitchen. Chuckling at Bill under his breath, Pedro headed to the back of the kitchen to start rearranging the most disorganized pantry I'd ever seen.

As soon as Pedro was out of earshot, Bill said quietly, "I'm on the same page as you. I'm getting the hell out of here as soon as I can. Hopefully in a day or two, I'll get to go back to being a boring old dad for a while. I can't tell you how nice that sounds."

Bill paused, daydreaming about a return to fatherly duties, mundane routines, and legal activities. When he snapped out of his trance, he turned his gaze back to me with a sense of focus that was almost disconcerting.

"How about you? Do you and Liam have a plan for when you leave?"

Laughing a little at his concerned parental tone, I admitted, "*Plan* is a strong word for me these days. I'm just glad that Liam and I figured out where we're going for Thanksgiving. We have some *ideas* for what we want to do beyond that, but nothing super solid yet."

Liam and I had decided that after we traveled around northern California for a little bit we would head down south to Los Angeles to celebrate Thanksgiving with Jake and a few of my other friends. After this, we had until the first week of December together before Liam had to fly back to Texas to babysit his younger brothers for a week while his parents went on vacation. Following this week back home, Liam would fly back out to California to drive up north to Oregon to visit a friend who was interested in hiring him on as a manager of his marijuana farm the next year. Beyond December, Liam had promised his dad he would spend the first three months of the new year living and working with him in Dallas. Since

Liam's dad hadn't been around for most of Liam's childhood, Liam was hoping that this intensive period of time together would allow them to finally get to know one another. After living under his dad's roof for a few months, Liam would have to decide between moving up to Oregon to manage his friend's farm or staying in Dallas to work for a startup that a different friend of his wanted to launch.

When it came to my own plans and goals, I had none. I was simply making up each subsequent step as I went along. I had absolutely no idea what I would be doing with my life beyond spending these next few weeks with Liam and returning to Colorado to spend Christmas with my family. My primary motivation for working so hard at Ganesha Wellness Community was to save up enough money to move someplace new and settle down somewhere for a while. If I was ever to make a new home for myself, I would need enough money to put down a security deposit, start paying rent and other bills, and feed myself until I could get a real job again. I knew I would always be a wanderer, but it was my dream of living and staying in one place for a while that inspired me to wake up so early and trim until so late every night. All I could do was pray that wherever my new home was, it would include Liam, although this limited my prospects for places where I could move to either Texas or Oregon. As long as I was in California and still reeling in the newness of this experience, the names of those two states sounded a lot more like interesting places to visit than potential future homes.

The wheels turning in his head, Bill pondered out loud, "Liam's too sick to work on another marijuana farm at this point, right?"

Without a trace of disappointment, I nodded. If I were alone, the easiest thing to do would have been to follow some of the other trimmers to a different marijuana farm. Yet if it meant spending more time with Liam, I felt no sadness walking away from those potential earnings. Since we couldn't continue trimming, Liam and I had come up with a lot of fun ideas on how to spend our remaining time together in California.

Sharing some of these ideas with Bill, I explained, "We may just explore California for a while. Or we've talked about WWOOFing on a local farm or trying to find a different kind of temporary work somewhere. We'll see what opportunities come up, I guess."

Hearing the word WWOOFing, Worldwide Opportunities on Organic Farms, Bill's ears perked up.

"A good friend of mine named Rebecca owns a goat farm a few hours north of here. She's pretty close to Nevada City, actually. While I have you here, why don't I call her and see if she needs any help right now? Rebecca's amazing. I know her all the way back from our early days as pioneers in California's fledgling, underground marijuana industry. Rebecca is also an amazing farmer when it comes to growing legal crops. You and she would get along just swell."

Sensing how badly Bill wanted to help us out, I gave him the OK to call Rebecca. I wasn't sure how I felt about immediately going to work on another farm, but the lure of free food and lodging was appealing. Surprisingly enough, Rebecca answered Bill's call after the second or third ring. After a few minutes of casual chitchat, Bill finally got down to asking Rebecca how things on her farm were going. When Rebecca told Bill that she had two female WWOOFers living and working on her farm, Bill took this as his chance to ask her if she had enough room for two more.

"Why sure!" Rebecca replied in a sweet, Southern-sounding drawl. "You know how it is running a farm. I could always use more help. There's always some project waiting around that I just can't seem to get around to."

Rebecca offered to let us onto her land, and Bill was far more enthused by this idea than I was. Nonetheless, I agreed to take down Rebecca's number. I promised to give Rebecca a call back after Thanksgiving with whatever decision Liam and I came to. Around the time that I finished hugging and thanking Bill, I heard Aukai's truck pull up in front of the processing shed. After Aukai parked his truck, he made multiple trips from his pickup truck to the processing shed. Each trip, his arms were filled with stacks of heavy-looking boxes. Once Aukai finished unloading his truck, he disappeared inside the processing shed for a while. I cleaned dishes for as long as I could possibly stand it before poking my head inside the shed. Although Aukai wasn't done tallying up the cash, he agreed to pay Liam and me out now as a courtesy to us. Watching Aukai sort through more cash than I'd ever seen in my life, I was unable to contain my exhilaration as I sprinted up the farm road to wake up Liam. I also grabbed my phone with the pictures of my trim log before running back down the hill. In the three or so weeks that I'd worked on the farm, I'd trimmed over thirty pounds of marijuana. This amounted to about four grand in wages.

After double-checking that my trimming log matched his official one, Aukai pointed to a large stack of twenty dollar bills that he'd set aside for me.

"Want to double-check my count?"

I began my count of twenties by separating them into piles of one hundred dollars. By the time I reached four hundred, I'd already confused myself somehow.

"May I offer a suggestion?" Aukai asked me as he casually counted out a smaller stack of twenty dollar bills intended for Liam.

Having lost count a long time ago, I acquiesced with no small amount of desperation.

"There are fifty twenties in one thousand. So I'd suggest separating your cash out into stacks of fifty. Make sense?"

Totally clueless when it came to handling this amount of cash, I thanked Aukai for the tip. Then, I focused my attention back on re-counting all the twenties. By that point, Liam had come down the hill to join us. Aukai handed Liam his own stack of twenties to double-check. For a few minutes, the only sounds in the processing shed were the three of us counting under our breaths and the shuffling of paper against paper. After spending a good few minutes double-checking Aukai's count, I confirmed that he had counted the money correctly. Aukai slid my entire pile of twenty dollar bills into a paper bag, folded over the top a few times, and handed the bag back to me. After Liam was given his own sandwich bag of cash, we wished Aukai goodbye, the last of our goodbyes to the Ganesha Wellness crew.

Once back at my car, I had no idea what to do with the paper bags full of all these illegally obtained twenty dollar bills—bills that I was too nervous to deposit at my bank. I ended up putting one hundred dollars in my wallet and locking the rest in my glove box. For the next few months of my life, my glove box would also serve as my unofficial bank. As far as my real bank knew, I didn't make or spend any money for over three months. Considering the capitalist, consumerist society that we live in, I practically no longer existed.

chapter seventeen

THE VULNERABILITY
OF HAPPINESS

WE LAY NAKED TOGETHER on a queen bed in a heated room with walls around us and a ceiling above us. The room was lit by warm, yellow light bulbs connected to electricity, and we had access to a shower and bathtub with hot, running water. The family we were staying with offered to let us use their washing machine and dryer, so our bodies and clothes were cleaner than they'd been in weeks. As amazing as it felt to be this clean again, even more amazing was being someplace warm enough for Liam and me to be able to sleep together naked. Having slept outside in my tent for over a month now, I'd become accustomed to sleeping in all my warmest layers. Whenever Liam and I made love, I couldn't help but recoil from the initial contact of Liam's hands against my skin, hands as cold as ice running up and down my body. To me, pleasure became associated with the feeling of a slow, languid shiver rolling up my spine. I never realized that Liam noticed my instinctive shudder when he first touched me at night. However, as we lay naked together on top of silk sheets surrounded by pillows, Liam reached over and gently stroked the whole length of my body. Instead of recoiling this time, I pressed my body into his. Eyes closed and smiling in bliss, I tried and failed to suppress the soft moan of pleasure that escaped my lips.

Nuzzling his face into my hair, Liam's lips brushed against my ear as he whispered, "It feels so good to be able to touch you without having you pull away from me."

By way of response, I rolled on top of Liam, pressing the whole front of my body into the front of his. A small voice in the back of my head told me that I shouldn't be doing this, that it was disrespectful to our hosts. I ignored this voice. Liam and I were so wrapped up in the decadence of this moment, this room, this bed, that we were unable to help ourselves from making love. Out of respect for our hosts, we moved slowly and quietly, careful to avoid any movement that could cause the bed to creak. When I could no longer hold my pleasure back a second longer, I bit down on Liam's hand to muffle the sounds of my orgasm. Afterward, we lay unmoving for a while with Liam still inside of me. Again, Liam stroked me as one would a kitten. I smiled and purred back at him. Pressed together like this, our bodies generated so much heat that Liam pulled back out of me to get up and open the window. A cool breeze floated in from the open window, cooling us down enough for us to eventually crawl underneath the sheets.

Lying together in the warmth and safety of this cloud of pillows and silk sheets, the trials of yesterday felt a world away from the reality of today. Just a day before this, Liam and I were sleeping in the back of Liam's car in Nevada City, struggling to decide where to go next. Being in Nevada City was a mixed experience for both of us. Liam's bronchitis was still so bad that he was coughing almost constantly. Walking up and down over the hills of the town, we had to take frequent breaks for Liam to catch his breath again. While I don't know how much Liam was able to appreciate Nevada City, he couldn't help but find inspiration in the unreal beauty of the Yuba River. We stood together for a long time on top of the bridge that crosses over one of the river's largest waterfalls, its mist splashing up onto our faces. Tearing his eyes away from the splendor of the turquoise blue water cascading below us, Liam rested his gaze on me.

So softly that I had to read the words in the movement of his lips, Liam mouthed to me, "I love you."

This made for the third time that Liam had spoken these

words out loud to me. It was all I could do not to melt into a puddle of water and leak down through the planks of the bridge to join the water crashing down below us. The rest of our time in Nevada City, Liam was the one struggling to hold himself together, struggling to breathe. To limit any unnecessary walking, we drove straight back from the Yuba River to the one establishment in town that I wanted to make sure Liam got to see, Elixart. No other place so perfectly captured the essence of Nevada City. After all, there aren't many other bars in the world that have a Bitcoin ATM at their front entrance and that sell healing tonics and elixirs instead of alcohol. Once there, Liam ordered a soothing, immune-boosting tonic, which the barista confirmed was particularly powerful for clearing the lungs. Healing elixir in hand, Liam and I moseyed over to lounge on the cushions in the corner booth of the bar. After a few minutes of sitting down, some of the color returned to Liam's face. I wasn't sure if this was the effect of the tonic or simply sitting down and not moving for a while.

A few minutes late but right on cue, Moon walked in through Elixart's front door, just in time to save us from sinking dangerously deep into the booth's cushions. Moon's presence imbued me with some much-needed vital energy. Unable to muster the same enthusiasm, Liam mostly just listened to Moon and me talk with half-closed eyes. As Moon filled me in on the latest government conspiracy he was digging into,

I caught him shooting occasional confused glances in Liam's direction. I'm sure Moon was wondering who this mysterious, mostly silent, and gravely ill boyfriend was. As inexplicable as this sudden apparition of a boyfriend may have seemed, Moon accepted this new reality with his usual grace and discretion. After the three of us finished our drinks, Moon invited us to camp on his land again for as long as we needed to. As kind as Moon's offer was, we stayed on Red Mountain for only one night. The bitter cold at night aggravated Liam's bronchitis to the point that sleeping indoors became a requirement.

After camping overnight on Moon's land, we spent the morning at my favorite coffee shop in Nevada City, looking up Airbnbs in San Francisco, almost all of which were out of our price range. Having daydreamed about visiting San Francisco my whole life, I started reaching out to anybody and everybody I could think of who was connected to the city to see if we could find some sort of alternate lodging solution. Just when we were about to give up on going to San Francisco at all, Liam's friend, Tyler, who was also Evelyn's ex-boyfriend, rescued us with a phone call. As luck would have it, Tyler just so happened to be from the Bay Area. He happily offered up his family home as a free place for us to stay. Ironically, Evie had also visited Tyler's childhood home the summer after our freshman year of college. I remember Evie complaining to me because Tyler's parents made them sleep in separate bedrooms. Even worse,

Tyler's mom never forgave Evie for spilling some of her blueberry smoothie on their white carpet. Six years after Evie's visit, I was about to see with my own eyes the infamous blue stain that forever marred the family's white living room carpet.

When we pulled up at the Lamorinda address that Tyler gave us, neither of us could contain our surprise at the affluence of Tyler's neighborhood. Having spent the past few months living in a tent only made the house seem more impressive. The next big surprise came in meeting Tyler's parents, the Ericksons. Although they didn't know what to make of me at first, Tyler's parents greeted Liam as warm-heartedly as if he were their own family. When I explained that I knew Tyler from freshman year of college and their younger son, Reid, from having worked for the same rafting company, the Ericksons visibly warmed up to me. Within the first ten minutes of meeting the Ericksons, it became evident that they both just missed their sons and were happy to have young people in the house again. Eager for any updates on how their sons were doing, the Ericksons peppered us with questions until late into the evening. Mr. Erickson made us all gin and tonics, which also helped get the conversation flowing. Although I tried to answer their questions as best I could, Liam put a heroic effort into talking and joking around with the Ericksons like he usually would. Despite his voice being an octave lower and much hoarser than it usually sounded, Liam somehow still managed to flaunt the full force of his Texas charm, wooing the Ericksons and me right along with them.

By the time we were all ready to go to bed, Liam had put the Ericksons so much at ease that they asked us if we would like to share the same room. As the Ericksons led us down a long hallway to show us to our room, Liam glanced back at me with a grin of triumph. I grinned back at him but lingered behind the group for a moment to shoot a quick glance in the direction of the living room floor. Sure enough, I could just barely make out a bluish stain near the couch.

The next few days were so heart-wrenchingly perfect that I almost wonder if my mind made up problems just to complicate things. During this time, I was reminded of the tremendous vulnerability that comes with happiness. When things are going well for an extended period of time, the anxious mind starts asking all sorts of questions: How long will this happiness last? Is this some kind of trap? How can I possibly deserve this? However, there were moments, like when I fell asleep with my head on Liam's chest, listening to the sound of his heartbeat, or when I woke up and Liam's face was the first thing I saw in the morning, when I was able to silence the questioning of my anxious mind. In these moments, I practiced learning how to bear happiness. When I sat with my joy instead of flinching away from it, I began to understand joy in a whole new way. To me, joy isn't about having everything feel good. It's about experiencing the fullness of life. When experienced fully, every experience is mixed and multidimensional. Nothing in life is so simple as to just be one way.

In the days Liam and I spent in San Francisco, all my emotions became so entangled as to become almost indistinguishable from one another. As overwhelming as this fusion of emotion was, the background to all my emotions was gratitude. More than anything, I was grateful for the opportunity that Liam and I had been given to rest, and for Liam, especially, to heal. Even just a few days of sleeping in a comfortable bed in a house with heating did wonders to heal Liam's bronchitis. Waking up warm and naked next to a Liam who was able to breathe again, I felt such a strong surge of gratitude as to almost be suffocated by it. From the moment we dragged ourselves out of the comfort of this bed, I was given no chance to catch my breath. Upon exiting our bedroom, we found Mrs. Erickson waiting for us in the kitchen with hot coffee and steaming plates of breakfast. We filled up on eggs and toast and more advice for things to do in San Francisco than either of us could possibly remember.

As jam-packed as each day was with amazing culture, food, sightseeing, and people-watching, the one day I'll never forget was the day Liam and I went to visit the San Francisco Museum of Modern Art. The entire time that we wandered around the art museum, I was as happy as I'd ever been. I couldn't imagine a more perfect start to a day. Although Liam's idea of a perfect day probably wouldn't revolve around going to an art museum, we had fun comparing and admiring each of our favorite art pieces. We spent an absurd amount of time on the top floor of the museum, which showcased a multisensory, interactive digital art exhibit. Our favorite exhibit in the whole museum was Ragnar Kjartansson's piece called *The Visitors*. *The Visitors* was set up in a large, dark room with nine projector screens hanging. Each screen featured a musician playing an instrument in a different room of the same house. Separately but simultaneously, all the musicians performed the same song. One screen featured the artist Kjartansson himself strumming a guitar naked in a bathtub, singing the song's main refrain over and over again.

With all eight of the other musicians playing and singing in unison with him, Kjartansson crooned, "*Once again, I fall into my feminine ways.*"

The simple power of this one refrain sank in through my skin and settled down into my bones. By the time Liam and I emerged from the dark room, the beauty of his piece had stunned us into silence. To shake ourselves out of this stupor, we took a cab across the city to the Buena Vista Café, the birthplace of Irish coffee. Since one cup of Irish coffee cost fifteen dollars, we resigned ourselves to sharing one small cup between the two of us. The Buena Vista Café wasn't the only place in San Francisco with ridiculously jacked-up prices. It was only our second day in San Francisco, but Liam and I were already well-acquainted with how expensive everything was.

Taking small, measured sips from our shared Irish coffee, Liam joked, "If it weren't for the Ericksons, I'd say, babe, this place is great, but we need to get the hell out of here."

I laughed in nervous agreement. San Francisco had almost ruined itself for me with how intimidatingly expensive every-thing was. Determined to make the most of our time there regardless, we set out to explore more of the city and spend more of our hard-earned trimming money. As if the Irish coffee wasn't decadent enough, we headed toward the Ghirardelli chocolate factory, where we got suckered into splitting a chocolate chip cookie sundae. All we did that whole day was eat and look at pretty things. I hardly felt capable of taking in any more exter-nal stimulation of any kind. Because of this, I had a hard time knowing how to handle the argument that Liam and I stumbled into on our way back to the BART station. The argument started with us looking at a map and trying to figure out how to get back to the station. I wanted to walk through San Francisco's crooked Lombard Street. However, we'd already been walking for hours, and the street was definitely out of our way. With the sun setting on us, Liam was focused on getting us to the BART station so we could make it back to the Ericksons for dinner. I was so full that I couldn't imagine eating anything else, so making it back to the Ericksons in time for dinner was less appealing to me.

At some point during this whole debate, Liam made a comment about how I can be, "aggressive in my decision-making."

This was the comment that sparked the whole argument. Hearing Liam use the word *aggressive* toward me, all sorts of triggers within me activated. My whole life, I'd been criticized for being too intense, too passionate, too assertive ... *too much*. In subtle, indirect ways, I'd been told to think, to be smaller, to shrink myself so as not to threaten those around me. One of the things that bothered me the most about this—something I noticed as a little girl—was that the boys around me were allowed to want things and to express what they wanted. The same quality that was censured in me was praised in the boys and men around me. As a girl, I was encouraged to keep quiet, to want less, to be smaller. This pressure to take up less space was both physical and psychological. On one hand, women are encouraged to make themselves physically smaller using whatever means we have at our disposal, including deprivation and starvation. We are also pressured to stay small in the way we express ourselves, to desire less, or at the very least to keep our desires contained.

On a physical level, I never quite figured out how to do this. I always had a large appetite for all things in life. As a child, my dad used to joke that I had a hollow leg. Somehow, I managed to devour large quantities of food while staying as skinny as a rail, until I hit high school that is. As a fifteen-year-old struggling with raging hormones and irremediable acne, I felt every new pound of my acquired bigness as if it were ten pounds instead of one. As terrified as I was of becoming fat, I never managed to stave off my hunger. I continued eating as much as I did before and dealt with the aftereffects of hating myself after every meal. Being around Liam 24-7 for the past few weeks also meant eating all my meals around Liam, something that still made me self-conscious. With the amount of food that we'd eaten already that day, I was feeling particularly disposed to hating my body. Losing touch with the reality of my actual size, I imagined my body swelling up like a dense, bloated balloon.

Feeling larger than I was and hearing Liam call me out of for this largeness, I was overcome with the urge to hide. I retreated back into what had been my go-to hiding spot since I was a young girl: silence. While I may never have gotten a handle on how to eat less or want less, I knew how to keep quiet. My penchant for silence was both a gift and a curse. More than anything, it became a part of who I am. On one hand, my quietness bestowed me with the capacity to listen, to empathize, and to hold space for people. Yet when I traced my tendency toward silence back to its origins, I hit upon something dark and almost sinister.

"No one really wants to hear what you have to say."

This was the root belief out of which my silence had grown. It was the belief that what I have to say is of less value than what others have to say. It was a doubt about whether I had value at all. From this secret, innermost secret place of self-loathing, from these dark and twisted roots, the tree of my silence had grown. This tree grew to bear me ripe fruit that has fed and nourished me throughout the course of my life—the fruit of open-mindedness, curiosity, and an insatiable yearning for growth. Yet, so long as the root of this silence remained below ground, unacknowledged, my way of thinking and my way of viewing myself remained poisoned.

Sensing that something was deeply wrong, Liam broke my silence with a question that was meant to be caring but came out sounding invasive.

"Is this about me calling you aggressive?"

"You don't know what that word means to me ..."

Unable to finish what I started, I retreated back into my silence.

His voice a degree softer, Liam asked, "Can you explain what it means to you?"

No longer able to hold in my shame, I fired back, "How about you explain what you meant by using that word?"

Sensing the need for caution, Liam explained, "It just feels like everything we've been doing these past few days has been your idea. Don't get me wrong; I've enjoyed almost all of it. The one thing I had a hard time with was our trip up to Nevada City. It was just so damn cold up there, and I was so damn sick. That being said, I've been happy to go along with what you wanted to do. Seeing you happy makes me happy."

Thinking back on our past week since leaving the weed farm, I realized that most of what we'd done, including coming out to San Francisco and most of the activities that we'd done since getting there, had been my idea. Feeling another flash of heat and shame, this was the moment when I would have normally apologized and gone silent again. However, this was Liam I was talking to—the Liam I loved, the Liam who'd told me that he loved me, too.

Steadying my voice as best I could, I asked, "If you're so happy doing what makes me happy, why you are accusing me of being aggressive? I don't really care what we do either, Liam. I'd never want to do something that made you feel uncomfortable."

Hanging his head, Liam apologized, "I didn't mean for it to come out that way ..."

"But it did," I continued, "and it hurt me. Aggressive is the last thing I want to be around you."

Then, I was the one left with my head hanging, overcome by the longing to disappear.

Sensing me withdrawing again, Liam clarified, "It's not that you're aggressive. That's the wrong word, I promise. It's just that you know what you want, and you aren't afraid to say it. I'm not always as clear on what I want. I should have spoken up earlier about some of the things that I didn't want to do, but I didn't say anything because I wanted to make you happy. Now, I've taken this out on you, and that's fucked up."

Even as I listened to Liam apologize, I still felt like the whole situation was my fault. Perhaps I'd grown too comfortable around him. I'd failed at my duty to contain myself, to keep myself small, palatable, and desirable. If Liam saw me as bossy or aggressive, if he no longer felt comfortable expressing himself around me because I expressed myself too much or too passionately, then I feared it would be only a matter of time before he stopped wanting me.

Inconsolable, I insisted, "I'm the one who fucked up. I don't know how I managed to get this all so wrong ..."

By that point, I could longer contain my devastation enough to express myself coherently. Cornered into a trap of my own making, I was terrified. I was terrified by the idea that Liam truly saw me, all sides of me, even the ugly *bigness* that I'd done my best to hide from him. Now that he saw me, I was terrified that Liam would leave me. Maybe not right then, but eventually. I felt the fear of losing him almost as acutely as if I were actually losing him. Just as I was about to fall irretrievably deep into the black hole of my fear, Liam called me back to him. Stopping in the middle of the sidewalk, Liam pulled me into him.

With both arms wrapped tightly around me, he murmured, "You haven't done anything wrong. Nothing's been lost here."

To check that he'd made himself clear, Liam pulled away from me just enough to look me in the eyes. His eyes took in all of me. Unable to hide or shrink away, I felt as exposed as if I were standing stark naked in the middle of a crowded city block in SoMa. Sensing my vulnerability, Liam took me back into his arms.

"I love you, Skye. Don't forget that," he insisted. "Your passion is one of the things that I love the most about you."

Taking in a deep breath, I sighed, "I love you, too."

I let go more out of resignation than conviction that Liam meant the words he said. Pulling away from him, I signaled to him that I was ready to start walking again. At that point, there wasn't much more I could say. Very little of what I was feeling was rational. As we started walking again, Liam reached out to grab my hand, re-establishing a connection between us.

On our walk back through the city, Liam refused to let go of me, maintaining this connection at all times. His hand was the rope that I used to pull myself back out of my darkness. Liam remained so calm this whole time that I had to wonder how much this stress and high emotion was in my head, coming from a made-up story that I'd been telling myself. This story was no longer serving me and maybe never had. Now, the time had come for me to let go of it, but I didn't know how. Before I had the time to process this any further, Liam and I found ourselves back at the BART station by the Ericksons' house. Once at the Ericksons, Liam and I had only a few minutes to ourselves before the Ericksons were expecting us to join them for dinner. With how much we'd eaten already, I was anxious about this dinner and the guilt that was sure to follow it.

As soon as Liam shut our bedroom door behind us, I whispered to him, "We've eaten so much today. I don't know if ..."

Before I could finish my thought, Liam cut me short.

"Listen, babe," Liam told me in complete earnestness. "Whatever Mrs. Erickson makes is going to be delicious. Let's just let ourselves enjoy this one, OK?"

By the time we sat down at the dinner table, taking Liam's advice proved to be a lot easier than I would have thought. The food was so good and the company was so pleasant that I was able to savor our last dinner with the Ericksons with only minor pangs of guilt. After we finished eating, we sat around the dining table for a while longer, chatting and sipping away at our gin and tonics. Our time with the Ericksons had been so wonderfully comfortable that I felt like I was visiting the home of a distant aunt and uncle whom I'd only just found out existed. As lovely as our stay had been, San Francisco was too expensive for Liam and me to stay for long, even with the

Ericksons hosting and feeding us. It was time for us to make our way down to Los Angeles, where we would spend Thanksgiving with my friends. The Ericksons offered to let me park my car in their driveway for the time being so Liam and I could drive his car down together.

The next morning, after we packed all my stuff into Liam's car and said goodbye, Liam looked up driving directions to the Golden Gate Bridge. Taking another piece of advice from the Ericksons, we pulled off before the bridge to go on a short hike at the Golden Gate Bridge Recreation Area. After taking in the stunning views from this higher vantage point, we drove down to the bridge itself. We spent over an hour walking up and down the bridge and taking goofy pictures on it together. By the time we made it out of San Francisco another hour or so later, Liam and I breathed a sigh of relief. While my sigh was a means of releasing some of the stress from our argument yesterday, I didn't know what provoked Liam's sigh. It didn't take me long to second-guess how much Liam's stress had to do with me. My fear of being *too much* bubbled back up to the surface again, drowning out all of Liam's reassurances from yesterday.

Sounding disappointed enough to exacerbate my fears, Liam said, "Damn. You know what I just realized?"

Before I had time to come up with the most awful potential answer to this question, Liam saved me by answering his own question.

Sighing even more emphatically, Liam lamented, "We left the Ericksons this morning without making love in their bed one last time ..."

~⁀‿

This was the first year that I'd ever had a *Friendsgiving* away from my family. I never knew how relaxing the holiday could be. Besides Jake, whom I met rafting, the four other friends present were all people whom I'd met in college. We'd graduated two years ago, and most of us hadn't seen each other since then. Despite these friends being some of the most outdoorsy people I'd met in college, they'd ironically all found their way to Los Angeles. Then again, Los Angeles was the last place that I expected to end up, particularly on Thanksgiving. Yet there we were, staying at one of my friend's apartment right next to Hollywood Boulevard. Although the apartment was a refuge of calm and quiet, we were reminded of our proximity to Hollywood Boulevard by the noise and chaos surrounding us. Inside, we may as well have been back in Colorado together with pine trees and mountains outside our windows instead of tall buildings and busy streets.

During the many hours we spent packed into my friend's small kitchen together, we laughed over old stories and caught each other up on the important new ones. When we finally sat down to eat our Thanksgiving meal, it was almost eight o'clock. By then, we'd burned through a couple of joints and were about ready to crack open our second and third beers. As hungry and as blazed as we all were, we took our time savoring each of the dishes that we'd put so much time into preparing. We lingered at the dinner table long after we finished eating, trying to adjust from being uncomfortably hungry to uncomfortably full. No matter the amount of food that I'd just ingested, I refused to feel guilty over my appetite. The space that my friends had created inside this simple but cozy apartment in downtown Los Angeles felt so safe and judgment-free that I was able to let go of my usual self-judgment.

Once we managed to get up from the dining table, all seven of us cozied up on my friend's couch to watch a mindless comedy together. By the time the movie ended, it was a little past one in the morning. The two of my friends who were a couple headed to their bedroom upstairs while Jake and my other friends laid out their sleeping pads wherever floor space was available. Since we were the first to show up, Liam and I claimed the large couch in the living room for ourselves. Although this couch was super plush and comfortable to sit on, neither Liam nor I foresaw how hard sleeping on it would be on our backs. Too uncomfortable to fall into a deep sleep, we were easily awakened by the fight that erupted in the apartment next door. If we'd forgotten for a second that we were in Los

Angeles, we were acutely reminded of this as we lay listening to the neighbors scream at each other all night long. From two until dawn, the yelling continued unabated, interrupted only by the occasional thump or loud crashing sound. The crashing noises made it sound like furniture, or perhaps even human bodies, were being hurled across the room and against the walls. Throughout all of this, we could hear almost every word that was exchanged between the two women. Every once in a while, a third male voice chimed in. The woman who started the argument sobbed hysterically about how everything was ruined and how everyone hated her. She threatened to kill herself a few times, by which point I was ready to call the police. The other woman alternated between trying to calm her friend and shouting out poisonous accusations that riled her up even further. Everyone involved in the fight was clearly on some kind of drug.

After an hour of this, I became legitimately worried about the safety of the people involved. Yet none of my friends who lived in the apartment said anything or got up. This left me to wonder if this kind of thing was considered a run-of-the-mill occurrence in this city. As hard as it was for me to ignore my instincts urging me to call the police, Liam was afraid that this would make things worse. Unsure what to do, we tossed and turned on my friend's saggy couch until we woke up to a quiet house in the morning and realized we'd somehow managed to fall asleep. We took our time clearing the fog in our heads, slowly sipping away at one cup, and then another, of coffee. By the time we felt hungry again, we pulled the Thanksgiving leftovers out of the fridge for breakfast.

Whenever we got hungry throughout the day, we haphazardly munched on a piece of turkey or a spoonful of mashed potatoes. The most ambitious thing we did all day was leave the apartment to stroll down Hollywood Boulevard. On our walk, I was so overwhelmed by all the different lights and sounds and smells and clashing sensations bombarding me that it didn't take me long to yearn for the tranquility of my friend's apartment. Taking the rear of our group, I watched from behind as this simply dressed, strangely calm, and far too happy pack of misfits weaved their way in and out of the craziness surrounding them. I was grateful to belong to the pack of people who don't belong. When we made it back to my friend's apartment, we took some time to recover from all the stimulation. I took advantage of the break to step outside and call Alice. The little walk that I took around the block while talking to Alice was the first time Liam and I had been out of each other's sight for weeks. I used this time to catch Alice up on everything that had happened since we left trim camp. After I relayed the story of our argument in San Francisco and my subsequent emotional blowup, Alice heaved out a shaky sigh. Even before Alice spoke, I knew from her sigh that she understood.

"I live with it, too," Alice admitted after some time, "that constant pressure to be small. Ever since we were little girls, everyone—our family, our friends, our teachers, the media— encouraged us to stay small, mostly in indirect ways. It feels good to hear you say it so directly. Even if we can't make the desire to be small go away, maybe we can reclaim some of our power by acknowledging that this desire exists."

Echoing Alice's sentiment, I admitted, "I'm just scared that if I stop making myself small, no one will want me. I'm scared that Liam won't want me ..."

Before I could finish this sentence, Alice assured me, "You, Skye, will never end up alone. I love you as you are, and I always will. So many people love you for you, and it sounds like Liam is one of them. Maybe the reason that this is coming up in your relationship right now to is to offer you a chance to heal. As uncomfortable as this may feel, see if you can open yourself up and allow Liam to see you in all your fullness. See if you can be yourself around him, fully yourself. See if you can untame and unmute yourself around him. Whenever this gets scary, just remember that I see you for who you are, and I cherish you for it."

Hearing these words, I was so overcome with emotion that I was unable to carry on the conversation. After thanking Alice, I took another walk around the block to collect myself before venturing back inside. I found Liam sitting outside on their front porch, deep in a phone conversation of his own. Keeping my face averted to hide my puffy eyes, I glided past Liam. Jake and the rest of my friends were getting ready to head back to their own apartments in the city. They waited for Liam to get off the phone before leaving, after which we all reluctantly hugged goodbye. None of us knew when we would see each other next, but we trusted life's strange and miraculous ways to bring us back together.

Once most of my friends left and the couple who lived in this apartment went to bed, Liam and I were left to ourselves. As he always did, Liam asked me about my phone call with Alice and how she was doing, who he still hadn't met but knew to be one of the most important people in my life. The person Liam was speaking to on the phone was Sal, Liam's best friend since early childhood. Back when Nate and I were dating, I'd met Sal a handful of times. I liked Sal from the moment I met him. Then again, so did everyone. Sal was not only the life of the party, he was the creator of it. Sal was the person who always made sure everyone else was happy. In the party setting, this role is usually taken by the person supplying the alcohol and drugs, a role that Sal had presided over since high school. Although he had ambitions of becoming a big-time hockey player, Sal injured himself too many times while playing in high school. Instead, he ended up as a big-time marijuana dealer in Dallas. It was Sal who connected Liam with the friend in

Oregon who offered Liam the job managing his marijuana farm. Having invested a lot of money into this farm to buy his way into the legal marijuana market, Sal was personally invested in the success of the farm. Sal had called to persuade Liam that going to Oregon was the right decision. From the preoccupied look on his face, I could tell that this phone call, and this impeding decision, was all Liam could think about.

Deliberating out loud, Liam mused, "It seems like too good an opportunity to pass up. But Sal's friend needs me up there by January or February. That means that I'd be skipping out on my promise to work for my dad for three months. With this late notice, I'd seriously be screwing my dad over. And before I see any real profit, I would be working long hours every day for months. It's a gamble to say the least ..."

Liam rambled on for a while after this. I did my best to follow him, although I got lost at some point with all the marijuana industry-related technical jargon. As it turned out, this phone conversation with Sal was only the first of many. Throughout the rest of our time in California together, Sal called Liam on an almost daily basis. The two of them spent hours over the phone brainstorming potential business plans for the farm in Oregon and other marijuana-related ventures. I have wondered, but will never know, how much these calls influenced the course of so many of the events yet to come.

For the time being, my anxiety over tomorrow's

uncertainties made it hard for me to focus on Liam's long-term concerns. Reeling ourselves back to the present moment, we put this conversation on hold to figure out what our next move would be. Liam and I agreed that neither of us were ready to work again just yet. More than anything, we wanted to spend some time together without worrying about anything or anyone else. After our cold night in Nevada City, we also agreed that wherever we went had to be someplace warm. Poring over my large road atlas of California, our eyes naturally trailed down south. They stopped at Joshua Tree National Park. We used Liam's smart phone to pull up freecampsites. net and browsed the site until we found a free campsite close to the park. This campsite was where we ended up spending most of Liam's remaining days in California before driving back up north to pick up my car and drop Liam and his car off at the Sacramento airport.

While this plan took us in the opposite direction of Rebecca's goat farm, my instinct told me that I should find a way to at least visit her farm before leaving California. Considering how effortlessly the opportunity had fallen into my lap, I felt like Rebecca and I were meant to meet each other. Even when Liam and I decided to head south to Joshua Tree, I called Rebecca back anyway. I let her know of our change in plans, and I asked if it would be OK if I came to help out on her farm a few weeks from then. Grateful for any help I could offer, Rebecca assured me that I was free to come and go on her farm whenever I pleased. She told me to call her back a day or two before I was planning on being there so she could give me directions to her property. With everything settled for the next few weeks at least, Liam and I snuggled back into the couch's saggy cushions for another try at a good night's sleep. As uncomfortable as the couch was, I was grateful that the neighbors kept quiet.

chapter eighteen

DESERT DA(Y)ZE: MOJAVE DESERT – JOSHUA TREE, CALIFORNIA

THE BLM LAND WITH FREE CAMPING near Joshua Tree National Park turned out to be nothing more than a dusty, desolate dirt lot a few miles out of town. For one week, this dusty lot became our home and the tumbleweed our new neighbors. After purchasing a national park pass for Liam and me to share for the next year, our goal was to spend zero dollars for the remainder of our stay in Joshua Tree. The first six of the seven days we camped there we managed to meet our goal. We lived entirely off of Thanksgiving leftovers and the groceries we bought before leaving LA. After a week of hard climbs and long hikes, we caved in on our last night and bought ourselves each a tall boy PBR from the nearest gas station. As simple as this lifestyle was, Liam and I preferred it this way. We had what felt like an entire desert to ourselves.

At liberty to do whatever we pleased with our time, Liam and I relied on the sun to wake us up in the morning. Although daytime in the desert was quite warm, the winter reminded us of its presence by the drastic drop in temperature as soon as the sun set every night. Craving warm things to offset the briskness of the morning, the first thing I did in the morning was boil water for coffee and oatmeal. Once we'd polished off a french press of coffee, the sun was usually high enough in the sky to chase away the morning cold. Liam dedicated the time it took for us to eat breakfast to researching new routes to climb each day. With the multitude of climbing routes that exist in the park, I have no idea how Liam picked out the routes we ended up on. Since Liam and I had only enough gear for sports climbing, this at least limited our options to a more approachable selection of routes that already had bolts fixed into the wall. The sport routes that Liam found usually required hiking a few miles and scrambling up large piles of boulders to get to the base of the route.

Each morning, Liam and I spent hours squinting up at massive, indistinguishable rock faces in search of the glint of metal that indicated bolts going up a wall. All the times that we got lost searching for a specific climbing route served as an excellent way to get to know the more remote and isolated parts of Joshua Tree National Park. Our quest to find specific routes took us to parts of the park so remote that we seldom even ran into other climbers. For example, our favorite climbing area in the park was a section of Joshua Tree called Outer Mongolia, which was part of a larger rock climbing area known as the Wonderland of Rocks. Once we got to the Wonderland of Rocks, we hunted for the North Wonderland. Within the North Wonderland, we had to find the climbing area designated as the Middle Kingdom. Within the Middle Kingdom, we kept looking for an even smaller climbing area called Outer Mongolia. Even when we found the small sign pointing us toward Outer Mongolia, the search continued until we found the specific wall within Outer Mongolia called the Siberian Corridor.

Finding the route that Liam had researched was only the beginning of our day. Although Liam would disagree with me on this, the hardest part of our day for me was not finding the route but climbing it. Although I did my best to mask my trepidation, Liam noticed my change in mood whenever we got to the route we were climbing for the day.

On our second day of climbing, Liam ventured to ask me, "Do you think you could be just a little afraid of heights?"

Despite my initial inclination to protest, I had to admit that Liam had a point. For reasons mostly having to do with pride, I never equated my fear of climbing with a fear of heights. As slow as I may have been to concede my fear, Liam recognized this from when we went climbing together on one of our first dates that summer. Our first day of climbing in Joshua Tree brought back all kinds of memories of that first camping trip together. That was the weekend when I took the risk of trusting Liam, at least trusting him enough to let him take me out climbing. I no longer questioned my trust in Liam. The challenge on this trip was trusting myself. Since Liam led most of the routes, I was the one who had to clean the route after we climbed it. While I enjoyed climbing to the top of a route, cleaning the route and removing all the gear that Liam set up to make an anchor at the top was a whole other ordeal. When it came time for me to clip into the bolts at the top with my own gear and untie the rope from the anchor that Liam had set up, my hands were shaking so badly that I was afraid I would drop the rope. As I grew more comfortable climbing over the week we spent in Joshua Tree, the solution that Liam and I found to minimize my anxiety was for me to lead the routes and for him to clean them. Never mind that leading the route should have been a lot scarier considering the higher likelihood that

I would fall a few feet. I still found this easier than dangling fifty to one hundred feet up in the air and having to untie and retie the rope securing me to the wall.

Once Liam and I had climbed four or five routes in a day, my hands were so tired that I could barely open and close my fingers. By the time my hands stopped working, I'd spent so many hours battling my fear that my mind had numbed itself into a state of vacancy. As sympathetic as Liam was toward my fear of heights, it wasn't a fear he shared. Climbing for Liam was a much more casual, laid-back activity than it was for me. By the time we called it quits at the end of the day, Liam could have probably still climbed another route or two. However, when he sensed that I'd reached my physical and emotional limit for the day, Liam packed up his rope and the rest of his climbing gear without me having to say anything. Back at camp, I got to work on cooking us a little feast on my Coleman stove. Liam alternated between helping me with the cooking and building a fire. After dinner, we sat together in the one camping chair that I'd brought, Liam happily scooping me up into his lap. Savoring our hard-earned relaxation, we alternated between staring into the flames of our fire or up at the stars in the night sky above us.

Eventually, I'd crack open my book, *Désert* by J.M.G. Le Clézio. Liam would dive into his own book, a biography on Hemingway's life. I loved *Désert* so much that I read it as slowly as possibly, dreading the day when I ran out of pages. My favorite part of every day was getting to reunite with my new and dear friend, Lalla, who quickly became one my favorite fictional characters. Parts of Lalla shone out like a pure, unfiltered version of the most essential parts of myself. Lalla moved about her world instinctively, feeling her way through the richness of life's mysteries. She trusted her intuition as an internal guide to navigate through life's challenges. Reading a few pages of life from Lalla's perspective taught me how to trust myself again. Together, our souls flew like birds across untamed expanses of emptiness, an emptiness that Lalla showed me how to appreciate instead of fear. Wherever we went, we yearned for the desert, always.

After a few consecutive days of climbing, even Liam reached a level of exhaustion that required us to take a day off. We researched different day hikes in the park and settled on a seven-mile hike that ended at the largest fan palm oasis in California. The hike started out on an open mesa that overlooked the Fortynine Palms Canyon below us and the Salton Sea to the south of us. The trail was speckled with vibrant red, orange, yellow, green, and pink hues from the bizarre collection of plant life that populated this northernmost region of

the park. Liam and I took our time admiring the long, scrag-
gly fingers of the ocotillo cactus reaching up toward the sky
like outstretched hands; the shimmering yellow spines of the
fuzzy teddy bear cholla cactus; the curled, deep red spines
of the red barrel cactus; and the spineless, flattened pads of
the beavertail cactus adorned at their tops with pink prickly
pear fruit. We were so entranced by the strangeness of our
surrounding scenery that the four miles out to the oasis flew
by before we were ready for them to end. We stopped for a
short break to enjoy the shade of the large fan palms before
continuing farther down into the Fortynine Palms Canyon.
Driven forward by the exhilaration of our remoteness, Liam
and I scrambled down into parts of the canyon that few people
ever lay their eyes on.

When we were too tired to go any farther, Liam and I
picked out a large rock to lounge on for the afternoon. Our
rock was high enough up to give us a panorama of the whole
valley below us. By the time we got settled on the rock, I was
already down to my sports bra and shorts, and Liam was shirtless. It took only a few seconds for us to strip off our remaining
clothing. With the sun beating down on us so intensely, it was
easy to forget that it was almost December. Since we weren't in
a rush to get anywhere in particular, Liam and I let the heat of
the afternoon sun lull us to sleep. When I woke up from my nap
an unknown amount of time later, I was parched and glistening

in sweat. Despite my dehydration, I basked in the warmth of the desert sun. Reconnecting to my inner lizard, I imagined myself as some kind of cold-blooded reptile that could use the sunlight to raise my internal body temperature in preparation for the cold that must eventually return.

As I lay baking, I reflected in gratitude upon how much of this fall I'd spent desert-hopping around the globe. Making my escape from a more stable life of work and routine in Durango, the first place I sought refuge was my favorite of all places, the desert of southeastern Utah. It was in this desert that I had started my acquaintance with uncertainty and fear. Wandering alone through mazes of colossal, burnt red sandstone rock, I lost myself to find myself. My wandering didn't end in Utah, nor did the cyclical process of finding and losing myself. From Utah, I wandered halfway across the world to the grandest, most hostile desert of them all, the Sahara herself. Confronted by her raw power and singeing heat, I fell to my knees in humble recognition of my smallness in a space so big. And there I was, having wandered my way back home and then farther west to a desert that was relatively new to me. It took only a few days of exploring this new desert for me to appreciate the uniqueness of her scrubby landscape sprinkled with spiky trees and jumbo granite rock piles. Already, my feet had traveled miles on her sandy soil. My hands had been scraped by her rocks. My eyes had opened wider to take in her peculiar beauty.

What I appreciate the most about the desert is the unique feeling of being simultaneously removed from the world and more intimately connected to it than ever before. Being in the desert allowed me to disconnect from the parts of the world and our society that I had the hardest time dealing with anyway. The desert was too brutal a place for any sort of falsehood to survive. The glaring light of the desert sun exposed a person's true face. I could no longer run or hide or pretend to be anything other than what I was. Yet as I lay out naked on a rock, totally exposed for the world to see, I felt safer there than anywhere else. I felt safe because I'd found the one place where I didn't have to hide, the one place where I could take up however much space I wanted to.

Luxuriating in the warmth of the sun on my skin and the inner warmth from the gratitude glowing within me, I reclined back on our rock. I lay with my eyes closed for a while, neither awake nor asleep. I was content to drift in and out of reality until Liam woke up. When Liam finally did, he sat up and reached for his own water bottle. Squinting against the brightness of the still blazing sun, I blinked my eyes open. Searching through the initial blurriness of the scene around me, I landed upon the pair of bright blue eyes I was looking for.

These blue eyes sparkled with a brilliant mischievousness as Liam asked me, "Are you thinking what I'm thinking?"

Without Liam needing to say anything more, I read in his

eyes the real question he was hinting at. My mind flashed back to the memory of Liam and I lying naked on a different rock underneath God's Bridge in Morocco. Half expecting another rock to come flying down at us, I scanned the horizon for any tricksters spying on us from above. This time, the rock that Liam and I had chosen was high enough up that we were the ones looking down on everything around us. All we could see below us were more piles of gargantuan boulders. Lowering my guard, I mirrored back to Liam the same look that he always gave me, except I wasn't able to pull off the look as effectively because I've never been able to lift just one eyebrow. Taking in both raised eyebrows, Liam grinned a smile wide enough to split his whole face open.

Unable to resist the charm of that smile, I crawled over until I was on top of Liam, straddling him. By then, the smile on Liam's face had faded. A much more solemn expression took its place—the facial expression of Liam's that I'd come to associate with intense focus or concentration. Closing the small gap of space that remained between us, I took Liam's face in both of my hands and leaned in to kiss him. Together, Liam and I breathed the same breath. We moved to the same silent rhythm. Our sweat mingled together, glistening on each other's bodies like salty tears that our skin wept out of joy. This close up, the blue of Liam's eyes was so dazzling that I couldn't look into them for long. Eventually, I gave in and closed my eyes. Yet even as I was hit by wave after wave of steadily building ecstasy, I never forgot where we were. While I was able to retain my sense of space and time, my sense of myself as a separate entity within this space and time slipped away. I was still the same Skye I was before, but I was also so much more. I was the body that moved against me and the granite boulder below me and the blue sky above me and the air that hovered between all these things, connecting them all together.

chapter nineteen

RESPITE FOR THE WEARY TRAVELER

AFTER DROPPING OFF LIAM at the Sacramento airport and his car in long-term parking, it was all I could do to drive the hour plus back east to Nevada City without collapsing on my steering wheel. I wasn't so much sad that Liam had left again. More than anything, I was tired. I was tired of all the change and the moving and the starting over again and the feeling that time was like sand slipping through my clenched fists, moving against my will until I was left empty-handed and clueless yet again. I drove without fully knowing where I was going, so I was surprised to find that I'd somehow stopped and parked in front of my old-time favorite, the Curly Wolf Espresso House. I ordered a cappuccino and sat down at a table by the window. Staring out the window, scooping up the foam at the top of the cappuccino with my tongue, I felt somewhat revived, not so much by the espresso, but by the simple relief that I could afford to order a coffee and sit by myself in silence.

The longer I sat, the more I was able to unwind. This unwinding wasn't necessarily a conscious process. I wasn't thinking about much for the majority of the time I spent sitting there. I mostly just watched the people in the street and the clouds in the sky float by me. This was the first time Liam and I had been apart in over a month, the first time I'd been alone in over a month. I wasn't sure what I would find in coming back to myself again, but I had a sense that I was searching inside myself for something, groping in the darkness for the doorknob that, when opened, would lead me into the next stage of my life. Instead of moving forward, I felt myself falling back. I fell back in time to the one place where time seemed to stop. As clearly as if I were still there, I saw myself lounging on a sandy rug under a circus-like tent in the middle of the desert, struggling to breathe in the oppressive midafternoon heat, sweating out all the water that I'd drank that day, swatting half-heartedly at those goddamn flies.

Unable to shake this image from my head, unsure what to do about the very real physical heat building up within my body, I stood up to refill my glass of water. I drank the whole glass in one quick gulp, filled the cup again, and sat back down at my table. I didn't know what to make of the intensity of sensation building up inside me. I was afraid I would lose my grip on reality if I let these sensations overwhelm me. In an attempt to move these sensations out from inside of me, I pulled my journal out of my backpack and put pen to paper. I tried my best to paint this vision and all its accompanying sensations with my words. When I first started writing, my only intention was to describe this one, unforgettable image of the Sahara on which I had become fixated. But here we are, countless pages later. By the time I finished my frantic scribbling of those first few pages, I felt satisfied enough to close my journal and contemplate moving forward again. This satisfaction wouldn't last long, but I didn't know that then.

What I knew is that I'd promised to help someone out—never mind that this someone was a stranger and that I didn't have a clear idea exactly what I would be doing to help her. After glancing over the directions I'd jotted down on how to get to Rebecca's farm, I picked myself up and got back on the road. Rebecca's farm was closer to *the ridge*, and that quasi-abandoned café that served as an outpost for the homeless, than it was to Nevada City. Driving by myself out to the middle of nowhere again to work on a different stranger's farm—this time for free—I had some serious questions about my mental lucidity. Yet when I pulled up to the address I'd written down and walked through the gate into a large garden, I was immediately greeted by the same syrupy southern drawl that had won me over on the telephone. The owner of the voice was a woman about the same age as my mom with a sleek mane of long silver hair, a dimpled smile, and deep, dark-brown eyes.

"You must be Skye!" the woman beamed at me, giving me the motherly up-and-down. "Welcome to the farm, child. Would you like me to show you around?"

Most of what being shown around entailed was being introduced to all the various farm animals. I counted two dogs, four cats, six bunnies, around fifteen chickens, over thirty goats, and three humans, which included Rebecca and two other WWOOFERs, Amber and Olivia. Olivia was younger than me, around twenty, astonishingly pretty and seemingly unaware of this. She had straight brown hair, green eyes, and freckled skin. She looked like she'd stepped straight out of an old-school Coca-Cola advertisement. Amber, on the other hand, was a few years older than me and perhaps less conventionally pretty but with features distinct and sharp enough to etch themselves permanently into my memory. She'd just cut her hair to a chin-length blond bob and, even on the first day I arrived, was openly questioning if having such short hair made her seem too masculine. I loved Amber's short hair and the chiseled jawline it highlighted, although no amount of reassurances from anyone could convince her not to regret the loss of her formerly waist-length hair.

All three of the women on the farm were beautiful in a way that required no makeup or superfluous adornment. All three of them seemed genuinely happy to have me there, which left me as the most noticeably guarded of the bunch. Sensing my need for space, Rebecca left me alone to unpack in the smaller side house that I would be sharing with Amber and Olivia. A bed had already been prepared for me and a fire started in the wood-burning stove. Although she seemed somewhat reluctant to go, Olivia eventually left to spend the night with her new boyfriend, a cute blond hippie boy who lived on a farm a few properties over. After eating a bowl of chili with Rebecca in the main house, Amber and I were left alone for the night to take turns tending the fire and swapping stories of how we'd landed upon this farm. After Amber shared that she specialized in natural building and had come to the farm to help Rebecca build an extension to her home, I had a hard time not feeling intimidated by how much unmistakably cooler Amber was than me.

Sensing my self-consciousness, Amber dropped her line of questioning regarding my life's direction and purpose in coming to this farm. She relieved me of my awkwardness by proposing that we watch a movie together. We settled on a Miyazaki film I hadn't seen before, *Laputa: Castle in the Sky*. The incredible detail and beauty of the animation took me out of myself and my own story, providing just the escape I needed to relax and let go a little. Although I was hesitant to trust it just yet, my gut told me this was a safe place to relax more than just a little.

After I was on the farm a few days, Rebecca began to delegate more tasks to me specifically. Amber worked most of her days mixing clay, sand, and straw to make cob, which she then used to build up the extension to Rebecca's home. Olivia had a particular knack for categorizing and organizing things. She spent most of her days in Rebecca's large tool shed, trying to impose a sense of order amid the chaos. I'd been assigned the project of tending to the greenhouse, watering all the plants, weeding, and rebuilding walkable pathways to connect one end of the greenhouse to the other. On one particular day, I spent four hours playing with and learning from peas. Kneeling in the dirt, I helped guide their little vines up to the netting that I'd installed for them earlier that morning. Despite how delicate this plant seemed, I'd come to admire peas for their ambition. As long as peas have something for their vines to cling to, they will grow infinitely upward. Whenever I grew tired of squatting in front of the peas, I took a break and sat back on the hay behind me. The yellow, big-bellied farm cat came to join me in the greenhouse that day. With a lot of loud meowing, he demanded that I rub his belly whenever I took a break, a request with which I was all too happy to comply.

Besides a brief conversation with Rebeca, Olivia, and Amber over breakfast that morning, I'd spent more time that day talking to plants and animals than to humans. Before getting to work on my list of morning chores, the first stop I made in the morning was to visit Sage, the farm horse. Sage was slow to warm up to new people. She still didn't like me very much, a fact I was trying to change by bringing her a banana peel to munch on every morning. With time, Sage became comfortable enough with me to let me take her for a walk along the dirt road behind the farm. However, I never got up the courage to try riding her.

After courting Sage with snacks, my first chore in the morning was to feed the chickens and rake the poop in their coop. For the length of my stay on the farm, Rebecca designated me as the person in charge of taking care of the chickens. I developed a special bond with my feathered friends. I especially loved the littlest rooster, whom I named Roger. Roger was about half the size of the biggest rooster. He cock-a-doodle-dooed twice as loud every morning to compensate for this. Ignoring all the racket Roger made, the hens in the coop continued pecking at the seeds on the ground, making it quite obvious that Roger wasn't worth their attention. To make up for this, I gave Roger extra attention every morning. I talked out loud to him while I fed the chickens, consoling him with reassurances that his worth had nothing to do with his size. The whole time I talked to him, Roger pecked at seeds on the ground and ignored me as the chickens did him. I didn't take this personally.

In between my chores, I always made time to stop and love on the two farm dogs, B and Maddie, both of whom liked to follow us humans throughout the work day. Even the cats, especially the fat, yellow cat, would follow me around. More than anything, the yellow cat loved to lounge with me in the warmth of the greenhouse. Hanging out in the greenhouse also provided him protection from Maddie, who loved nothing more than a good cat chase. Luckily for the fat, yellow cat, B didn't tolerate this kind of behavior. When Maddie bounded out the front door first thing in the morning looking for a cat to chase, B followed right behind on her heels. Whimpering in protest, B nipped at Maddie's heels to keep her from catching up with any of the cats. I'd never seen a dog step up for a cat like his, but B was no ordinary dog. As a rescue dog, perhaps B herself had been chased down and bullied too many times in her life. Now, she could no longer bear to witness this kind of treatment toward other animals. Whatever her motives were for protecting the cats, B kept Maddie in line. She provided the four cats on the farm with peaceful, albeit somewhat lazy, lives.

Olivia was the one in charge of feeding the rabbits, but I still liked to stop and say hi to the fluff balls every morning. However, I didn't dare stop for long. As soon as they saw us out and about, the goats commenced their bleating to be fed. There were so many goats that Olivia, Amber, and I all helped out with feeding them and raking their poop. Rebecca had split up the goats into three separate grazing areas, the bucks in one, the does in another, and the kids in the pen adjacent to their mothers. The bucks were smellier than the rest and liked to fight each other, but they also smiled a lot more and acted particularly silly. The babes were cautious, still afraid of most things. They cuddled together in clumps and stared at passersby with big, fearful eyes, which only made them more endearing. Most of Rebecca's goats were Nigerian Dwarf goats, so the babes were as small as lap dogs. As adorable as the little ones were, their mothers' intelligence impressed me the most. The does were also the friendliest of the three groups. Whenever I entered their pen, the does bleated at me and nudged me with their heads until I gave them a good scratch behind their ears. Their slit-shaped, alien eyes betrayed a foreign, other-worldly intelligence. Since Rebecca milked the does every day, she'd given every one of the twenty or so female goats a name. All Rebecca had to do was shout out a particular doe's name, and this doe would come running to the milking station, grateful for any opportunity to be close to Rebecca.

Most humans had a similar reaction to Rebecca. Although I was still getting to know her, I could already appreciate why every human and animal around adored her so. Ever present, Rebecca brought her full attention to whatever she was doing. This depth of awareness allowed her to tap into forces greater than herself as easily as an ordinary person would call up their friends on the telephone. The primary tool that Rebecca used to reconnect with her *spirit guides*, as she liked to call them, was a red pendant necklace she wore every day. Whenever Rebecca was feeling stuck or indecisive, she'd stop what she was doing. Coming to complete stillness, Rebecca swung the red pendant necklace back and forth on its chain. Invoking the help of her spirit guides, Rebecca internally chanted the words *yes* and *no* until the pendant swung in one direction and gave her the answer she'd been seeking. As I moved about the farm through-out the workday, I eventually stopped being surprised when I would run into Rebecca, silver hair blowing in swirls around her face, eyes closed, lips moving almost imperceptibly, having paused in the middle of her task to commune with her guides.

That's how Rebeca was. She was as mystical as she was grounded. She wasn't afraid to embody both of these polarities. Her ability to tap into otherworldly intuition, and her gift for nurturing and restoring life to all those around her, made up the quintessential Mother Nature that Rebecca so effortlessly embodied. Rebecca had four children of her own and two young grandchildren, but she acted as mother to all those around her. No matter how much was asked of her, Rebecca never turned anyone away. The door to her home was always open. Over the years of accepting WWOOFers onto her land, Rebecca had hosted people from all corners of the world and walks of life. Normally, Rebecca had somewhere between eight and twelve workers living and working on her land. We three were the smallest number of WWOOFers that Rebecca had hosted in years.

I was grateful to have come to the farm during a quieter time. I also loved being surrounded exclusively by women. This was the first time in my life that I'd been part of a female-only environment that was supportive and cooperative instead of competitive and catty. In so many ways, our society trains its women to view each other as competition instead of allies. Witnessing this level of cooperation among women healed something within me that I hadn't realized was broken, especially after my experiences of toxic female rivalry on the weed farm. Here, each of the women on the farm embodied her own flavor of authenticity. At times, our ways of being clashed; however, we upheld an unspoken respect for our differences. Most of the time, Rebecca refrained from offering her own advice and opinions, opting to listen and ask questions instead. Through the sheer power of her attentiveness, Rebecca guided people to their own realizations. When she did share her point of view, Rebecca wasn't one to mince words or spare feelings. In contrast with this was Amber, who loved to talk. She had no qualms about sharing her feelings. Like a prospector sifting through silt to find the gold that sinks heavy to the bottom of the pan, Amber rambled out loud as a way to sort through her feelings on a matter. Although Amber sometimes lost track of what she was saying, she always made it back to her original point.

While Rebecca and Amber had refined these communication styles over time, Olivia was still in the process of finding her voice. Six months before, Olivia left her small hometown in Minnesota and came to work on this farm as a means of escaping from an unhealthy family situation. Probably ingrained in her from the unhealthy communication styles of her family, Olivia had a penchant to hold her tongue when she shouldn't. However, Olivia became much more open in the presence of food, as if the food imbued her with a greater sense of security. It also helped that Rebecca was an extraordinary cook. All the food we ate was grown on Rebecca's land or a neighboring farm. Most of our meals consisted of fruit and vegetables that Rebecca cooked up in creative ways or blended into delicious smoothies and soups. Every morning for breakfast, Rebecca poured us each a cup of fresh goat milk. I'd never before tried coffee with goat milk, but Rebecca got me hooked. The biggest meal of the day on the farm was lunch. Lunch brought us all back together from our separate projects and provided everyone a nice respite in the middle of the day. It was usually toward the end of our long lunches that Olivia shared more of what was going on in her world. When Olivia did speak her mind, she left nothing out. She often stunned me with the acuity of her insights.

While our communication styles differed, what we shared in common was a general love for communication. This helped a lot when it came to working through miscommunications. As four very emotional, sensitive women living and working together on a small piece of land, some amount of conflict was inevitable. Along with working together during the day, Olivia, Amber, and I also shared the same bedroom in the side house. Every night, we took turns tending the wood-burning stove. On some of the coldest nights, we all cuddled together in the same bed for warmth. While I created some space for myself by going on long runs and taking trips to visit Moon on Red Mountain, these were short, stolen moments. Nonetheless, I appreciated all the women on the farm so much that I didn't mind my relative lack of privacy. Never before had I been in an environment as richly emotional and deeply textured as this one. Whenever the four of us gathered in Rebecca's kitchen to eat a meal together, we took the time to talk through any feelings that had come up for us throughout the day. Rebecca was usually the one to initiate this conversation.

Rebecca opened with something along the lines of, "The wind has me feeling restless today. Have any of you picked up on a strange energy in the air?"

The openness with which Rebecca invited each of us to share our thoughts and emotions relieved me of what would have otherwise remained pent-up anxiety. As idyllic as life on Rebecca's farm was, my life to follow was completely unknown. Ever since I'd dropped him off at the airport, Liam and I still hadn't had the chance to discuss our future together. I had to leave the farm just to get cell phone service, so it was hard to discuss much of anything with Liam at the moment. Even before my arrival on the goat farm, I'd been floating blindly through life for months, pushed every which way by forces that felt out of my control. Since the end of summer, the closest thing I'd had to a home was my tent. I'd spent most of my nights sleeping outside on the ground. Even now, most of my days were spent working outside, covered in goat poop and dirt, at the mercy of whatever elements the sky had in store for us. The only shower on the farm was also outside, so even the process of bathing myself happened outdoors. With only a wood-burning stove to keep us warm at night, it was hard to tell the difference between being inside and outside even when I did have a roof over my head. Although I'd had the luxury of desert-hopping across the globe for months, winter had at last caught up to me in the cold, wet forests of Northern California. The part of me that was tired of the roughness of outdoor living daydreamed of a return to warm indoor spaces and more familiar territory. Simply put, I was homesick, or sick with longing to have a home.

At first, I struggled to express these feelings to the other women on the farm. As Rebecca, Amber, and Olivia took their turns expressing their own feelings in their own unique ways, I clung to my defense mechanism of listening more than I spoke. I didn't want my homesickness to come across as me being ungrateful for the opportunity of being on the farm. Yet as I opened up more under Rebecca's gentle prodding, the guilt I felt in sharing my own feelings slowly began to dissipate with the attention and care that these women showered upon me. The biggest relief in all of this was that none of the women expressed any judgment when I was honest about the difficulties I was experiencing. Their support gave me the strength to continue accepting discomfort and anxiety in exchange for fulfillment and expansion. Regardless of my uneasiness, I recognized what a miracle it was that I'd landed on this beautiful little goat farm. The greatest blessing of all was the women who surrounded me.

chapter twenty

FROM YOU,
I HAVE LEARNED

"IS THERE SOMETHING you're running away from?"

Olivia asked me this as casually as if she'd just asked how I was feeling that day.

She asked the question as if the answer was already a foregone conclusion, because, and I could imagine her thinking exactly these words, "We're all running away from something, aren't we?"

About a week into my stay on the farm, Olivia and I had hunkered down together under her thick comforter, waiting to feel the heat from the new log that we'd thrown into the wood-burning stove. Amber had gone to town for a few drinks, so it was just the two of us hanging out for the evening. When Amber first left, Olivia was quieter than usual, which I guessed had something to do with the argument she and Rebecca had gotten into earlier that day. Olivia and Rebecca had a complex, raw, and at times messy relationship. Having been on the farm for six months, Olivia had been living and working alone on the farm with Rebecca for four months before Amber arrived. Rebecca's farm was also the first place Olivia had ever lived besides her family home. Although undeniably close, Rebecca and Olivia didn't always see eye to eye. Olivia wasn't afraid to talk back to Rebecca, and she wasn't particularly good at admitting when she was wrong. While too stubborn to stand down to this kind of attitude, Rebecca was also patient enough to stick with their arguments until they reached some kind of understanding.

Originally, I'd assumed that Olivia's attitude toward Rebecca was a reflection of how Olivia treated her own mother. That night, as we huddled together against the cold and the dark, Olivia proved my assumption wrong. With time and patience, the wood-burning stove did its job of warming up the room. As the feeling returned to our fingers and toes, something within Olivia thawed. Instead of continuing to silently stew over her argument with Rebecca, Olivia conceded out loud that she couldn't stop thinking about it. Even as Olivia explained more of what had happened, the source of the disagreement remained unclear to me. What mattered in this case wasn't so much how the argument had started but how it had been left. While Olivia initially tried to defend her position in the argument, she dropped her defenses after it became clear that I had no stakes in the argument. As Olivia shifted from being defensive and closed to more honest and vulnerable, her voice became quieter and quieter, as if the strain of opening up was threatening to take her voice away. By the time Olivia started sharing more about her mother and her mother's problems with addiction, I had to strain my ears to hear her voice over the sound of the wind raging outside our room.

"Back home," she murmured, "I didn't dare speak out against mama. You never knew how she was going to react to something—scream, cry, walk out the door, or use again ... Whatever happened always felt like my fault. So I got quiet. I stopped saying much of anything."

As if falling back into her old habit, Olivia fell silent after this. As a means of holding space, I held the silence with her. Over my life, I too had come to associate silence with safety. To some degree at least, I understood the forces that had pressured Olivia to keep quiet—that had taught her that speaking out was unsafe. In our shared silence, Olivia found the confidence she needed to continue.

Beginning again, Olivia confessed, "Now that I'm here, I can't seem to stop myself from speaking out. I don't even mean what I say half the time. I just get so angry … and then I get scared of how angry I am, and I say something stupid or hurtful."

In Olivia's sigh, I recognized the sound of shame. Yet shame can only endure unseen and unspoken. As Olivia inhaled the courage to continue, she extinguished this shame by openly conceding to it.

"Sometimes, I wonder if this anger is what I'm really running away from. Sure, I'm also running away from having to worry about who's paying rent and how, or where papa went this time, or what happens when mama relapses again. But that's not the biggest thing I'm afraid of. I'm afraid of this anger inside of me that I can't put out. I'm afraid that no matter how far I run, it will just keep on catching up to me …"

Emboldened by having finally put a name to the fear that tries to convince you that it is nameless, Olivia turned the conversation around to focus on me. This was when she'd asked me what I was running away from, leaving me as clueless and answerless as ever. I knew that, most of the time, Olivia was right. Almost everyone has skeletons buried deep in the soil of their subconscious that they will do almost anything to avoid digging up. Yet, at least on a conscious level, I couldn't identify any one thing from which I was actively trying to get away. More than moving forward of my own volition, I felt like I was being pulled *toward* something. Thinking back to Halloween, I remembered the conversation that I'd had with Sierra when she'd brought up the idea of magnetism. I tried explaining this concept to Olivia, or at least my version of it, searching my mind for words to explain an idea that hadn't fully formed yet.

"It doesn't always feel like I have a say in where I'm going. I can't be sure that I chose any of this. One opportunity leads to another. When I connect all of these opportunities together, everything starts to feel inevitable. I'm not saying the choices we make don't matter, because they do. I just don't think that we have nearly as much control over our lives as we'd like to believe. We don't just live by ourselves in our own little worlds, you know? We're all connected to each other, to something bigger. Those connections exert their own pull; they have their own influence."

As usual, the first feeling that came up for me after any attempt to genuinely speak my mind was self-consciousness. While I berated myself for having said too much or for having said something I wasn't supposed to, Olivia wasn't judging my words so much as taking the time to process them. All my awkwardness was relieved when Olivia let out a high-pitched, unrestrained giggle a second or two later.

"So when you stopped running away from anything, that's when you lost control over your life? If that's the way it works, I may just keep running."

While I sometimes struggled to find the words to explain myself to Olivia, Amber often explained myself for me. Not only were Amber and I very similar in a lot of ways, but she was also a few years older and had been living this kind of vagabond lifestyle for a lot longer than I had. In a way, Amber reminded me of a more developed, exaggerated version of myself. While the deepest part of me would always long for the desert and the freedom it represented, I also had to contend with the side of me that yearned to put down roots and have a home. If these desires existed within Amber, she was very good at ignoring them. Remaining free of constraints and outside pressure was Amber's MO.

One of my days on the farm, Rebecca gave me permission to take a break from the greenhouse and help Amber out with the building project. As we worked alongside one another that morning, I asked Amber how she'd gotten into sustainable building.

Slapping a fistful of cob onto the house's exterior wall, Amber replied, "Well, I get in my head a lot, so having a really physical job helps balance that out. I also like working on projects where I can see immediate, tangible results from the work I put into it. I'm not patient enough to stick around anywhere for long. Or I guess you could say that I'm bad at commitment.

Either way, it helps having these concrete projects where I can work really hard at something for a relatively short period of time, see the project done, and then move on."

Nodding my understanding, I slapped my own fistful of cob onto my side of the wall. I too loved the tactile nature of this kind of work. I loved the feeling of the clay and straw mixing in my hands, the satisfaction that came with pounding the clay against the wall, the focus that came with patting and smoothing it down. For me, a tired body also meant a calmer mind. The more hours we worked, the deeper I dropped into the space of thoughtless calm. The passing of time and the onset of weariness had a similarly relaxing effect on Amber. While my exhaustion helped to still my thoughts, Amber's thoughts flowed more freely. For most of the time that we worked together, Amber rambled on, her voice as smooth and steady as a babbling brook, lulling me into a trance. Listening to Amber talk reminded me a lot of my conversations with Rudy on the weed farm. As similar as they were, I'd never heard a woman speak with such unfettered freedom about living her life the way she wanted to.

At different points, I lost track of what Amber was telling me, as I was more focused on the feeling behind her words than the words themselves. I tuned back in upon hearing a word that I hadn't expected—*fiancé*. Paying closer attention, I listened as Amber told me the story of a trip she had taken to Mexico, trying to grasp the connection between these two seemingly unrelated things.

Finally, I asked, "Sorry if I missed something, but are you engaged? How does Mexico fit into this?"

Chuckling, Amber glanced sideways at me through her newly cut bangs.

"I'm not engaged anymore. Mexico is where I fucked it all up ..."

I had so many questions that I wasn't sure where to start.

Keeping it simple, I stuck with asking, "Who is this guy? And can I ask what happened?"

Flippantly, as was her way, Amber replied, "He's a friend I've known and loved my whole life. He's one of the only people who I kept in touch with no matter where I ended up. Now, of course, we don't talk anymore. Anyway, we started dating, or really just hooking up, when I was going to college in New York. I had no illusions about my ability to stick with a long-distance relationship, so all of that ended when I decided to make my way out west. But it just so happened that he got this big tech job in the Bay Area right around the time that I made it out to Cali. We got together again, and I moved in with him for what was supposed to be a short while. I was in between jobs at the time and got a part-time job at a nearby coffee shop that was run by this dope nonprofit. Then, a short while turned into a longer while. Before I knew it, over a year had passed, which is the longest I've stayed in one place for quite some time."

"Carson—that's his name—knew my ways. The whole time we were together, there was always this part of him that was afraid of losing me. He was right not to trust me. I'm not the kind of person who will ever fully belong to someone else. When Carson proposed, I knew, even as it was happening, that this was his way of trying to keep me. I loved Carson very much, and I didn't want to hurt him, so I said yes. I stayed, and we were engaged for a whole other year, which is, again, a very long time for me. We even made some rudimentary plans for the wedding. Because he knew this excited me more, Carson and I daydreamed a lot about our honeymoon, about sailing around the Mediterranean Sea, swimming all day, lying naked and making love out on the sailboat deck, drinking too much wine ..."

I was so mesmerized by her story that I realized that Amber was crying only when she stopped talking. While Olivia responded best to time and space, I didn't hesitate with Amber to walk over and give her a hug. By that point, we were both covered in clay and sand and had hay sticking out of our hair. Laughing at the stickiness of our rather sweaty, muddy hug, Amber brushed away her tears, streaking a line of clay underneath her eyes, unknowingly decorating herself with what looked like warrior stripes.

Making fun of herself, Amber joked, "Me being who I am, it should have come as no surprise that I quit my coffee shop job out of the blue one day and disappeared on a weekend trip to Mexico. But I was so in love with Carson at the time that I even surprised myself. All in all, I was gone only four days. All I really did was lie on the beach, chat up some locals, and drink too much tequila. The problem was, I didn't tell Carson where I was going. I just left."

"Whatever trust we'd built was gone after that. The thought that I could disappear again like that was too much for Carson. He told me that I needed to move out. We didn't officially break up or cancel the engagement right then. Our pretense for me leaving was that we were giving the relationship some space. But if you give me too much space, I won't come back again. I found another building project, and then a few more, and then I wound up here on Rebecca's farm. By the time I reached out to Carson, a month or two had gone by. He didn't answer my call, but he sent me a text that he wasn't ready to talk yet. It's been the same thing every other time I've tried to call. I miss him, so I keep calling, but I'm starting to wonder if I'm just being selfish ..."

Amber trailed off. For once, she was at a loss for words. In this moment, I felt my hunger and weariness hit me stronger than ever. I suggested that we take a break to sit in the shade and drink some water or maybe see if Rebecca would make us one of her famous smoothies. Sensing our need for a pick-me-up, Rebecca was all too happy to oblige. She hand-delivered two strawberry and banana smoothies to us a few minutes later. Feeling myself come back to life with the extra dose of sugar and calories, I watched Amber's head perk up and her shoulders move down away from her ears, like a flower opening its heart up again. While Amber didn't bring Carson's name up again in our conversation, I could feel his presence as if he were sitting under the tree with us. Before we went back to work, Amber turned to me, her eyes sad but her chin lifted, her prominent jaw fixed and resolute.

"There's a price you pay for freedom. I've paid it."

Amber was just as covered in clay and sand as I was, her face still streaked from the reddish clay, her short hair tangled and falling into her face. To me, she looked wild and proud and beautiful.

After so much quality girl-on-girl bonding time, I felt like I was breaking some sort of implicit code by asking Rebecca if Liam could come stay on the farm for a few days. Liam had been gone for a little over a week to help his family out back home. He'd come back to the west coast for only a week or so before the holidays, his primary purpose being to check out his friend's weed farm in Oregon. Yet two days ago, he had called to ask if he could spend a few days with me on the farm before driving up north. It took me a day to get up the courage to ask Rebecca what she thought of this, even though I should have known better than to be nervous.

Her eyes gleaming with mischief, Rebecca replied, "Well, I can certainly think of a few projects around the farm that could use a man's touch!"

I didn't dare ask too many more questions about what projects Rebecca had in mind, although I made a mental note to warn Liam that he would be working to earn his stay.

After Rebecca and I cleared up a few of the details about when and how long Liam would be staying, Rebecca settled the matter by proclaiming, "This all sounds perfect! Depending on how late he gets in, we'll have a little celebration tomorrow night or the night after that. I have all the ingredients to make my special vegan, gluten-free, sugar-free pumpkin pie. So don't you worry, honey. Any friend of yours is welcome on my land."

Hardly able to stand so much sweetness, even the sugar-free kind, I hugged Rebecca in gratitude. The next day and night passed in a blur. On the day Liam was due to arrive, I danced and sung my way through my chores. I made such a ruckus with all my prancing about that even Roger the rooster condescended to lift up his head and glower at me. After I finished my chores, I headed into town to wait for Liam at the Curly Wolf. He arrived around the time that the sun was setting and the coffee shop was closing. I met him outside, glad to be back in Nevada City again with a Liam who was fully able to breathe. As he lifted me up to twirl me in the air, I myself took in a big breath of him. Liam and I had separated and come back together so many times by then that my dreams at night were almost always filled with some kind of reunion scene with him. It took me breathing in Liam's unmistakable scent to believe that he was real this time.

After taking in a few full breaths, I let Liam go and had him follow me back to the farm in his car. Early to rise and early to bed, Rebecca had already gone to sleep by the time we got back. Amber and Olivia had lit a fire in the wood stove of the side house. Per usual, they were cuddled up together under our warmest comforter, watching a movie on Olivia's computer. They paused the movie to say hi to Liam, after which Liam and I made our way up the stairs to the attic of the side house.

The side house attic had walls only on three of its four sides. The missing wall provided views overlooking the goat pens and the fields beyond them. This open exposure and total lack of insulation made for very cold nights. Yet the privacy the attic afforded us was well-worth the exposure to the elements. The open space and the windows all around us also came with spectacular views of the night sky. To Liam and me, this dusty, unused attic felt like our own private suite. For a moment, I was reminded what it had felt like on my first night in Morocco when Aamir gave us the keys to the hostel's honeymoon suite. Neither of us felt the same shyness that we did then. We romped around in our new bed until we'd worked up enough heat to welcome the draftiness of the attic to cool us down.

As forewarned, Rebecca put Liam to work first thing the next morning. Amber, Olivia, and I went about our usual round of chores feeding the animals and raking their poop. Rebecca gave Liam the job of tearing down the thorny cluster of blackberry bushes that were threatening to take over the outer perimeter of the farm. When he wasn't wrestling the barbed bushes, Rebecca had him haul furniture from the side house into the main house. With Rebecca ordering him around this whole time, Liam made a large stack of mattresses and other heavy, cumbersome items for Rebecca to sort through. After a few hours of Liam doing this back-breaking work, Rebecca took mercy on him. She ordered him to take a break in the shade and made us all one of her classic smoothies. Still trying to catch his breath, Liam came to drink his smoothie in the greenhouse with me. We lounged back on the hay together. The yellow, fat-bellied cat came to lay between us. None of us moved for a while. The cat was the only one that spoke, meowing occasionally for good measure. When Liam had enough energy to stand up again, we went back to work for a few hours before Rebecca called us in for lunch.

Rebecca rewarded us for all our hard work by preparing her delicious home-made hummus, which she complemented with a smorgasbord of fresh veggies and homemade farinata bread. When we made it to the end of the day, an especially long and grueling day for Liam, Rebecca served each of us a slice of her highly anticipated gluten-free, sugar-free, vegan pumpkin pie. Liam was so hungry that he could have eaten half the pie by himself. Grinning knowingly, Rebecca readily offered him a second, heaping slice. Considering that this pie contained no dairy, refined sugar, or wheat, I wasn't sure what Rebecca put in it to make it taste so good. Fairy dust, perhaps.

After celebrating his arrival with everyone over dinner and pie, Liam and I headed straight up to the attic for the evening. Snuggling in bed together, we laughed over the ridiculousness of the tasks Rebecca had assigned him.

As we quieted down from our giggling, Liam swore to me, "That woman really cares for you."

"You think?"

"Definitely," he reaffirmed. "With all of this wrestling blackberry bushes and moving mattresses and shit, I feel like she's testing me for my worthiness."

If Liam was right, the test was by no means over. The next day brought more of the same. Rebecca even hired the neighbor's boy for the day to help Liam with the tasks that were challenging enough to require two people. All day long, Liam and the neighbor's son hacked away at the ground with shovels, moved more furniture, and finally tore out the last of the invasive blackberry bushes.

When I caught him on a rare break, Liam whispered under his breath to me, "I'll be sad to leave you tomorrow, babe, but I don't know how many more days of this I could handle."

To make matters worse, we realized at some point during the afternoon that one of the bucks had managed to wriggle its way into the mamas' pen. Rebecca, Olivia, Amber, Liam, the neighbor's son, and I all stopped what we were doing to address this issue immediately. All six of us frantically ran around the does' goat pen with ropes and handkerchiefs in an attempt to wrangle the stray buck and lead him back into his proper pen. The whole time we were chasing after him, the defiant buck was having the time of his life. It took him almost an hour to tire from our game of chase. After order on the farm had been restored, Liam and I retreated back to the quiet of our attic to take a nap, which inevitably turned into us making love again. Only after we tired from our love-making did Liam and I catch a true moment's rest. After our nap, I made us each a cup of Rebecca's extra strong black tea to keep us awake through dinner. The caffeine helped. We managed to stay up late enough to play a round of gin rummy with Rebecca, Olivia, and Amber in the main house.

Rebecca was smiling and jovial all throughout our game.

Partway through the first round, she got up to make us all hot toddies as a special treat. If Rebecca was indeed putting Liam through some kind of test, he'd passed with flying colors. He had worked hard for two days straight without complaint. Even then, sitting in a kitchen among a group of four very talkative, emotional women, Liam remained relaxed and undaunted. He listened with such care and was so thoughtful when he did contribute to the conversation that every woman in the room appreciated his presence. By the end of the night, Liam was more tired than ever, and I was happier than ever. The only thing capable of tainting my happiness was the knowledge that Liam would leave for Oregon the following morning. Yet when the dreaded time of Liam's departure came, our goodbye was not nearly as heart-wrenching as I'd imagined.

Before hitting the road, Liam asked me, "What day will you be getting back to Breckenridge?"

"December 17th, I think. Why?"

Even as I said it, I could hardly believe that this date was real. December 17 was less than a week away.

As I tried to process this, Liam replied, "How about I meet you in Breckenridge on December 17th? I'd love to see you, and it'd be nice to break up the drive from Oregon back to Texas."

Squealing, I threw my arms around Liam's neck in delight. Knowing that I would see him in less than a week, I was no longer as despondent to see him go. This gave me one more week to soak up as much precious time as I could with all the women on the farm.

~⌒○

Amid all this coming and going, this talk of freedom and escape, only Rebecca remained still, as still and mighty as the great Pacific madrone. Her roots firmly planted in the wet Northern California soil, Rebecca's generosity extended out from the core of her being like branches reaching out to shelter and protect all those around her. Having so much land to take care of and so many animals and humans dependent on her, Rebecca could rarely afford to leave the farm. Every single day, the farm received numerous visitors, from people coming to buy goat milk, to neighbors dropping by for a chat, to family members and friends coming to drop off their kids for Rebecca to babysit. Just thinking about having to bear the responsibility of so many people relying on me gave me a mild case of claustrophobia. Nonetheless, Rebecca bore this responsibility with that special grace that only mothers can embody. After all, Rebecca had spent more years caring for other people and animals than I had been alive.

When I asked Rebecca how she kept going like this, spending day after day of her life taking care of other things and people, she admitted, "There's a reason I go to bed so early every night. Most mornings, my body wakes me up at four. It knows those are the only hours I'll have for myself in the day. So I get up, make myself some tea, and listen to an audiobook."

"What do you listen to?" I asked, happy to hear Rebecca talking about herself for once.

A dreamy look in her eyes, Rebecca sighed, "Truth is, I love nothing more than a good fantasy novel. I've listened to the whole Wheel of Time series at least three times by now. I know the characters so well that they feel like old friends. I also like a good mystery novel from time to time, or really any story that's good enough to take me out of this world and into a different one for a while. As I'm listening, I'll watch the sunrise. Watching the light spread over the farm in the morning and listening to the animals wake up ... the beauty of that makes me feel OK about coming back to our world for the rest of the day."

Rebecca paused, giving me a sly side glance and a little smile.

"Now, don't you go telling everyone my little secret, OK? Otherwise, I'll have people knocking on my door starting at four in the morning."

I could all too easily imagine a long line of people standing out in front of Rebecca's front gate, each holding a ticket that allotted them a certain amount of her time. Taking in the mildly horrified look on my face, Rebecca interrupted my imaginings with a deep belly laugh.

"Don't you worry. I like my life just the way it is. You see, the people I give to give back to me. Now, it may not always seem equal. Some people have more or less to give. But when I really get to know someone, I understand that, coming from a certain person, a genuine smile may be all they have to give. And sometimes, someone special will come around, someone who has a whole lot to give back. When that happens, it's like the balance has been restored."

As she spoke, the features on Rebecca's face smoothed over, and I felt a deep sense of peace emanating from within her. Then, Rebecca fixed her warm, dark-brown eyes directly on me. I felt like I'd been caught in an especially bright beam of sunlight.

"Like you, my dear," Rebecca continued softly. "You've brought a certain kind of balance back to this farm. You have a way of holding space for people, child."

Something about the word *space* triggered me, piercing through to an issue that I'd been half-contemplating, half-avoiding for weeks. Against my will, I felt tears collecting in the corners of my eyes.

Looking down as if this would make my tears less noticeable, I admitted, "I think I know the space you're talking about. I get lost in it sometimes. It's like I hollow out and become empty inside, like I'm nothing more than this empty container to be filled with other people's experiences and emotions. I lose track of what I feel or want. It scares me."

As if the words she was looking for would come if she searched hard enough, Rebecca peered beyond me out into the distance. For a minute or two, she said nothing, softly humming a song that sounded vaguely familiar.

Musing out loud, Rebecca uttered, "We come from space, and to space we shall return ... Even while we're here, what if, deep down inside, we're all just empty space? Each space has its own texture and color to it. Some spaces feel more dense or more light than others. To me, your space just seems to be more open and more easily entered by others. It reminds me of this Trampled by Turtles song that my youngest boy, Tucker, used to play me on the guitar. It's a lovely little bluegrass tune about a window that got stuck wide open."

Connecting her words to the song that Rebecca was humming earlier, I exclaimed, "'Again!' That's the name of the song ... 'Again.'"

Her face splitting into a smile, Rebecca agreed, "Yes, that's it! You're like that window, stuck wide open, and all the braver for it. With time, you'll learn how to open and close the window when you need to. You'll develop a little more control of what comes in and out of your space. You'll have to trust me on that, OK?"

Her smile fading, Rebecca looked upon me with those wise and intuitive brown eyes. She waited until I nodded to indicate my understanding before continuing.

With a voice that was both somber and soft, Rebecca insisted, "In the meantime, just promise me you'll take care of yourself. It's like he sings in that song—*Don't let it burn you out*, child. As best you can, stay open."

—◦

The wind blew hard the first day that I showed up on the farm. The last day before I was to leave, it blew hard at the pages of this journal, threatening to tear them away from me. On that first day, I heard gunshots ring out from Rebecca's next-door neighbor's property. Another chorus of them were fired off that morning, again without explanation. B still followed me everywhere with her favorite stick, and Maddie curled up at my feet as I wrote this. Just as when I'd arrived, I felt scatterbrained that day. I kept leaving things in random places and forgetting what I was supposed to be doing. The winds of change had brought me there, and away with the wind I would go. Part of my mind had left already. The part of my mind that was still there lingered over all of this, reluctant to move on. This part of my mind urged me to take this moment to process and reflect. I sat quietly with my gratitude until it became too much for me to bear. Finding release in writing, I let my happiness flow through me and out of me. By the time I was done writing, I felt empty in the best of ways. As a token of my appreciation,

I ripped out the page of my journal that the wind was trying to steal from me anyway. On this page was a hastily scribbled poem, which I titled "From You I Have Learned." Before I left Rebecca's farm at five the following morning, I left this poem on her kitchen table. From what I can remember, it went something like this.

From you, I have learned the grace of being able to empathize with a chicken.

I have learned to admire peas for their ambition, for they are better climbers than I will ever be.

I have learned that waste is an imaginary concept invented by the laziness of men, for all used things can be given new life again—even poop.

I have learned that goats will come when you call them out by name and to respect the intelligence behind those alien eyes, for intelligence comes in many forms.

I have learned from baby seedlings how it is possible to be both delicate and strong.

I have learned the devotion that it takes to commit oneself fully to a piece of land, and I have seen how the land repays this devotion.

I have learned that, if one is big-hearted enough to keep one's door open, it is possible to travel the world while staying in the same place.

I have learned that there are dogs who protect cats, that even among other species in the animal kingdom, cooperation can replace competition.

I have learned of the earth's abundance, that a home may be built with a simple mixture of clay and straw. I have also learned that the greatest thing that one can ever build is a community. Imperfect though every community may be, it is the people around us who give our lives meaning.

I have learned how to talk to and befriend a horse. I still hope to learn more about how a horse talks back!

I have learned the discipline of routine, but also the flexibility that makes one's routine sustainable long-term.

I have learned how powerful it is when women work together, and I have been reminded daily of the many forms that femininity may take.

I have learned that something as simple as swinging a necklace can open up a doorway to divine intuition if one listens closely enough.

From you, I have learned all that one human is capable of, that generosity can be limitless, that the only limits binding us are the ones that we imagine for ourselves.

chapter twenty-one

QUARTER-LIFE CRISIS

THE TWO DAYS LIAM SPENT WITH ME in Breckenridge
floated by like a dream. To finally be back home again and to
have Liam there with me—how could both of these things
be true at the same time? To add to the dream-like qualities
of these two days was the fact that Liam and I had the whole
house to ourselves, as my mom had left on a short trip down
to Denver. Liam and I spent the majority of these two days
hiding away in my old upstairs bedroom. There was something about the familiarity of my old bed, the thickness of
my comforter, and the abundance of pillows surrounding us
that felt like sleeping on a cloud. For the two days Liam was

with me, we descended from our cloud only to eat, shower, and once to walk around the town of Breckenridge. Our walk was snowy and beautiful, but I spent most of it consumed by the longing to return to our high-floating cloud of ecstasy. Once we made it back, it felt as if we'd never left. Time up on our cloud worked in funny ways. Although I knew this was impossible, it felt as if we spent these entire two days making love without rest or interruption.

His head spinning from the effects of the strange time warp we'd fallen into, Liam asked me, "Do you ever reach a point when we're making love when you can't imagine doing anything else?"

When he asked me this, he was still inside me, and I could hardly process what he was saying. Did he mean to tell me that other things in this world existed beyond just me, him, and this mattress?

Even when Liam left for Dallas a few days later and this reality proved to be temporary, as all realities do, I felt secure in knowing that Liam and I would be meeting up again to spend New Year's in Austin with Sal, Nate, and a few of our other friends. In the meantime, I was blessed to spend a lovely white Christmas in Breckenridge with my mom and Alice, who came up to Breck shortly after Liam left town. After our Christmas morning brunch, Alice and I snuck outside to go snowshoeing around the neighborhood. When we got home from our trek, we took turns soaking in the bathtub and munching on the brunch leftovers. After a glorious day of hanging out just the three of us, my mom, Alice, and I drove down to Denver in the evening to have our Christmas dinner with the rest of our extended family.

As grateful as I was to be back home, surrounded by friends and family, I had trouble relaxing completely. I'd been on the move for so long that I'd forgotten how to be comfortable. It didn't help that I had no idea what I was doing beyond New Year's. Sticking with my one-step-at-a-time approach to life, I called Liam two days after Christmas to figure out the details for New Year's. We spent the first part of the conversation trying to work out the best way for me to get down to Austin by New Year's Eve. As the conversation went on, I felt more and more like I was the only one trying to come up with solutions.

Frustrated, I eventually asked Liam, "Do you even want me to come down to Austin?"

In the pause that came after this question, I heard the answer that I'd been dreading all along.

After some time, Liam replied, "I don't know if it makes sense for you to spend all this money just to come down to Austin for three days. At this point, it doesn't seem worth it."

My voice icy cool, I reminded Liam, "I am perfectly capable of deciding for myself what is worth spending my money on."

I attacked the minor point in Liam's argument because I wasn't ready to face the bigger issue at hand, which was that

Liam didn't want me to come down to Austin to be with him. In my head, this idea quickly condensed down to the single phrase—*Liam doesn't want me.*

The ice in my voice melting into a pathetic, lukewarm puddle, I asked Liam, "Why didn't you say anything earlier?"

"I was afraid of disappointing you."

This was a sentiment that I'd heard before, a refrain that had repeated itself throughout our relationship. Up until this point, I'd spent so much energy trying to prove Liam wrong that I hadn't really listened to what he was saying. For the first time, I wondered if Liam wasn't voicing a fear of his, but rather trying to issue a warning.

In a last-ditch effort to fight back against the truth that I didn't want to accept, I asked, "When will I get to see you again?"

Again, I was left to sit with an awful silence on the other end of the line.

Unable to bear the silence any longer, I told Liam, "I love you, Liam. To me, our relationship is magic. It's absolutely worth fighting for. But I can't keep fighting for you if you're not willing to fight for me. And here's the thing. You've never expressed appreciation for me being willing to move to wherever you end up, which makes me think that you don't actually want me to move somewhere for you. If that's true, I don't know what you want."

Forcing himself to speak, Liam elaborated, "I don't know

how to explain this to you because I still can't make sense of it myself. But in the past few weeks, something in me changed. What I want is different now. I know this sounds ridiculous, but I feel like I'm having some kind of quarter-life crisis or something. I was lost for so long, but I've finally regained a sense of focus. Now that this focus has returned, it's hard for me to see anything else."

Not wanting to believe the words I was hearing, I stammered, "I don't understand. What changed? What is it that you want now?"

"You're not going to like any honest answer that I give you," Liam warned me.

With more judgment than I intended, I snapped back, "Is it money? Success? Status? Is that what you're chasing?"

"You're not wrong. But it's more than that. I want to build something for myself, something that has my name on it, something that I can look back on with pride. Until I've done that, I don't know how much I have to offer to anyone."

"And then what? What happens after you've built your empire? What will you do with all your money and success?"

With a hint of impatience, Liam sighed, "I don't know, Skye. All I know is that my priorities are different now. My focus is ... single-pointed."

My stomach sank. I couldn't see any other way that Liam's aimless pursuit of success would end except with regret. For

Liam's sake, I prayed that his chase would end somewhere. I prayed that Liam would finally arrive at some point where he said, "OK, this is enough. *I* am enough." But that point in time, if it even existed, felt far enough away to be unreachable. Before these terrible thoughts and premonitions took over my mind, I forced myself to speak out.

"With this new focus that you've found, what am I to you now? A distraction? A burden?"

Liam started to deny this, but his voice sounded tired and half-hearted. Before long, I cut him off. No matter what Liam said in this moment, I wouldn't have believed him anyway.

Sensing that this was one of my last opportunities to stand up for myself, I asserted, "You have this fear of disappointing me, Liam. I feel like it's prevented you from being fully honest with me. A lot of the time, it feels like you're lying to protect me from something. Now all this energy that you've put into protecting me has turned me into a burden. I'm worried that you think I'm more fragile than I am."

His voice strained, Liam acknowledged, "You're not wrong..."

I heard in his voice the amount of willpower it took for him to concede to just that one sentence. As much as Liam didn't want to talk about this, I wasn't finished.

Somewhere in the back of my head, Alice's voice rang out, urging me to untame and unmute myself, challenging me to,

"See if you can be yourself around him, *fully* yourself."

Stepping up to meet this challenge, I told Liam, "I understand where your assumptions are coming from. A part of what I love about being with you is that I feel safe to be soft around you. By nature, I'm a sensitive person, and the softness I feel around you brings that out even more. I know you're aware of how sensitive I am because of all of the beautiful, gentle ways you accommodate it. On top of my sensitivity, you've had to deal with my heightened anxiety from all the uncertainty of these past few months. You've carried a lot. With all you've been carrying, I'm worried that you may be overlooking the power behind my softness. So I want to clarify something."

As I had already done many times, I thought back to my conversation with Sierra when I'd tried to explain to her how and why I'd been living my life the way I had. I thought of all that I'd said, and all that I'd failed to express. Now, the time had come for me to either speak my truth or miss out on what could be my last real opportunity to do so. Gathering together all the thoughts that had been left hanging in my mind, every little truth that remained unspoken, I took a deep breath, and I spoke.

"The amount of fear I've been struggling with doesn't make me weak or a coward. To me, cowardice isn't about feeling fear, it's about avoiding it. Courage is about being big enough to let the whole world in, fear included. Courage is my choice to see and feel all of it. Every day, I practice sitting with what I see and feel, no matter how scary or how painful it may be. Every day, I practice not running away. By opening myself up like this, the things and people around me affect me a lot more. As easily affected as I may be, I still consider my sensitivity one of my biggest strengths. It's a kind of *soft* power.

"Being this sensitive, I've also had to learn how to protect myself when I need to. I'm good at giving myself what I need. I don't expect you to protect me, to be strong for me, or to have your shit figured out for me. The only thing that I want from you is to be with you, just as you are now. I love you unconditionally. I love you so much that, if you need me to, I can even let you go."

I remained strangely calm throughout the delivery of this message. There was a part of me that didn't believe these last words coming out of my mouth even as I said them.

Choosing his words carefully, Liam replied, "For now, I think we'd be better off as friends. I still want you in my life. I just can't give you what you need. Everything that you're talking about—sensitivity, openness, vulnerability—I can't do that right now. Any of it."

Choking on the words as I said them, I asked, "Are you breaking up with me?"

I heard the hard edge in Liam's voice as he told me, "It's for the best, Skye ..."

For a long minute, neither of us spoke. Not knowing

when we would speak again, neither of us dared to hang up either. Knowing that this was my last chance to scrape out some small peace of mind for myself, I asked the question burning in my mind.

"Do you not love me anymore?"

Sounding appalled, Liam protested, "What are you talking about? Of course I still love you."

"So you just don't care anymore about the fact that you love me?"

This time, Liam had nothing to say for himself. Again, the suffocating silence returned. Unable to make sense of how someone could decide to not care about love anymore, I assumed that something else must be wrong. Everything I'd been taught to believe about myself and my worth as a woman came down to this one, last, awful question.

"So is it that ... you aren't attracted to me anymore?"

This time, Liam actually laughed, a shocked, almost-bitter laugh.

"Are you kidding me? Of course I'm still attracted to you. Why would that change?"

Then, I was the one left speechless. I was more confused than ever, but I'd run out of questions to ask. Although it offered little consolation, I wasn't the only one who was confused. When Liam spoke up again, he sounded confused to the point of frustration.

"Goddamn, Skye. I ..."

Thinking better of whatever he'd been about to say, Liam stopped himself midsentence.

Instead, he insisted, "I have to go. I'm afraid I'll change my mind if I talk to you any longer."

Perhaps this was my grand opportunity to make one final case for myself, to defend myself one last time. Heartbroken as I was, I didn't have the willpower to fight any longer.

The last thing I told him was, "Just remember, I love you, Liam. Unconditionally."

"I love you, too," Liam echoed back.

Then, Liam hung up, leaving me to drown in that terrible silence.

If I had to paint the progression of my emotions on a normal day, I would paint a scene of soft, rolling hills. Over the next few days, these rolling hills turned into a series of jagged mountains and steep valleys. I jumped from shock to anger to grief to denial back to anger and finally to numbness. Numbness was the valley in which I settled down to stay. When the anger came back, I went for long runs and stayed up late drinking too much wine with Evie. Lost in a wine-fueled haze, I dreamed of disappearing, of vanishing off the map, of getting as lost as

I felt lost inside. I dreamed of spending what was left of my trimming money to buy myself an RV. I dreamed of returning to the desert and parking my new RV out in the middle of nowhere, someplace safe where I would be totally alone. I dreamed of a simple, sun-drenched life in which I went on long hikes and read and wrote voraciously. When I was ready to emerge from the desert and my self-imposed solitude, I dreamed of traveling across the U.S. and driving south to New Orleans, my favorite American city. I dreamed of parking my RV in someone's driveway there and finding a gig as a dancer at some club downtown. I dreamed of dying my hair pink, of transforming myself until I became unrecognizable. I didn't know if any of this would actually be good for me. I didn't know what was good for me anymore. The only person with whom I dared share these fantasies was Evie.

Rather than trying to talk me out of it, Evie offered, "Dying your hair pink is easy enough. I can help with that if you want."

The two of us spent the next hour online researching at-home hair dye kits. We ordered a kit to be shipped to her Denver apartment in two days. After I came down from the burst of endorphins that this small act of rebellion provided me, I was hit by a sense of loss stronger than before. I was incapable of doing anything besides going to sleep. I woke up the next morning with a pounding headache, still exhausted after a full night's sleep. However, I didn't dare close my eyes again because

I was afraid of waking up and remembering all over again that Liam was gone. I felt the shock wearing off. I could no longer count on it to cushion my grief. The tears that I couldn't cry earlier leaked out of my eyes in twin rivers that streamed down my face, pooled together at the tip of my chin, and dripped down to mix in with my now lukewarm cup of coffee.

I love Evie because she didn't try to pick up my broken pieces. Evie simply bore witness to my brokenness. She held me tight to remind me that I may have been broken, but I wasn't alone. When I was lucid enough to listen to her, Evie read out loud to me from Rupi Kaur's newest book of poetry. Hearing the heartbreak that resonated throughout so many of the poems, I wondered if Rupi had lost a Liam of her own. She asked all the same questions that haunted me throughout my days. Rupi's voice was so distinct and so personal that I could almost imagine her curled up on the couch with me and Evie. I imagined the three of us holding each other as Rupi whispered her poems in our ears as reassurances. While Rupi may not have had an answer to the questions that haunted me, it helped me to know that someone else was asking the same questions. Crying out to no one in particular, I wondered—what happens to a love that is left to die? How long does it take for love to wither up and fade away? Does the pain wither up and fade away along with it? What will happen to Liam when the last of the love binding us together has faded? Will he be OK? Will I?

Worse than all of these terrible questions that I couldn't stop asking myself were the questions asked of me by others. Their questions were of a more logistical nature. They mostly had to do with my plans. I still hadn't come up with a good way of telling people that I had no plan, so these questions made for terribly awkward conversations. Like a scared, cornered animal, I spent these conversations searching for an escape route. Most people couldn't fathom the terrifying amount of freedom I was facing in that moment. Now that Liam was out of my life, the last tether tying me to anything or anyone had been cut. Uprooted and unanchored, I had no obligations to anyone. There was no place that I needed to be. There was nothing in particular that I needed to do.

In a desperate attempt to save myself, I reached out to the one person who I'd always been able to count on for impartial advice. Although my dad lived abroad and we didn't talk much, he had a way of cutting straight through to the heart of an issue. He refused to tolerate bullshit of any kind. To some extent, this trait lived on in me, as well. When I told my dad about my recent breakup with Liam, my dad was surprisingly empathetic. No matter the space between us, my dad was still just a man listening to his daughter cry to him over the telephone.

"It's going to get better, Skye. There's always a way forward."

My dad sounded so sure of this that I was almost inclined to believe him.

Continuing on with his trademark confidence, my dad said, "Let me be honest with you. You're not in a good place to be making any big decisions for yourself, especially not decisions with long-term consequences. What you need is to buy yourself some more time. Is there something constructive you can do for the next few months before you settle down anywhere? And, no, living out of your car in the desert does not count."

Reluctant to let go of my desert fantasy, I forced myself to review the list of dreams and goals that I used to care about. Most of these goals were outdated and no longer felt relevant. The one goal that still called out to me was obtaining my yoga teaching certification. I had a larger dream of moving toward a career in mental health and mindfulness, and becoming a yoga teacher felt like a concrete step in the right direction. I shared this with my dad, and he jumped on the idea.

"That sounds perfect. Why don't you do some research on yoga schools you could attend at the beginning of the new year? When you find a program that looks appealing, let me know. I'll help out with some of the cost."

Before my dad had the chance to change his mind about this offer, I spent the rest of the day researching yoga teacher trainings in Central America. Not only were the trainings in Central America more affordable, but it was also a place where no one knew me and to which I had no previous connections. After a few hours of research, I stumbled upon a therapeutic yoga teacher training in Nicaragua, a program with which I instinctively resonated. Even more perfect, the program started in the middle of January and lasted only three weeks. Once the program was over, I'd have some time to travel around Nicaragua and practice my Spanish and my newly acquired yoga teaching skills. First thing the next morning, I bought a one-way ticket to Nicaragua departing on January 10, just under two weeks away.

Come New Year's Eve, Evie and I were forced to emerge from the cave that was her apartment. Some of our high school friends in Denver were throwing a party—a party they insisted we couldn't miss. This would be my first appearance in public since the breakup. The rawness of my heartbreak showed, but the holiday at least gave us an excuse to get fucked up. Fortunately, we got to my friends' house early enough that most of the other guests hadn't showed up yet. Upon our arrival, Valeria, one of the party hosts, invited a small group of six of us into the kitchen. Valeria led us all over to a large pot she had simmering on the stove. She lifted the lid and gave the soup-like contents of the pot a good stir. This brought a few clearly visible mushrooms floating to the top of her concoction.

Valeria winked at us, "Who wants a cup?"

Before helping myself to a cup of Valeria's infamously strong mushroom tea, I glanced over at Evie. We shared a guilty, furtive look.

Ultimately, Evie shrugged and looked away as if to say, "Fuck it."

Mugs in hand, the six of us drifted out of the kitchen and re-integrated with the rest of the people joining the party. Although I was OK with separating from the rest of our group, I didn't let Evie out of my sight. Arms linked to signal our inseparability, the two of us headed downstairs in search of a quieter space to hang out. One of our good friends who'd also drank the mushroom tea followed us downstairs. Much to our delight, she took over DJ-ing for the basement area. This friend had such exquisite taste in hip-hop that Evie and I lost any desire to return upstairs. It turned out that we wouldn't need to go anywhere anyway. Sooner or later, everyone came to us. The slow trickle of people coming down to the basement was nice because it allowed Evie and me to be social without having to put in much effort. However, we also had to deal with a lot of persistent, unwanted visitors, almost all of whom were men. The man who settled down beside me was particularly intolerable. He leaned far enough into me to practically be laying on top of me. Casually chatting with one of his friends on the other side of the couch, he stretched out his legs on the coffee table in front of us. I was so shocked at this total disregard for my personal space that I couldn't even come up with the words to object.

After tolerating several uncomfortable minutes of this man leaning on me like this, the man finally asked me, "It's OK that I'm laying on you, right?"

Ignoring my lack of response, the man went back to talking to his friend. Through his body language, the man was sending a clear message to the other men at the party that I belonged to him. This was absurd, because I didn't even know his name. The nonconsensual ownership that this man had claimed over me made me so uncomfortable as to temporarily paralyze me. Thankfully, Evie read the discomfort written all over my face and body.

Leaning into me, Evie murmured, "Do you want me to make him move?"

Staring up at her with big, pleading eyes, I nodded. Without another word, Evie picked up her sharp stiletto heel and planted it directly into the unwelcome intruder's back. With one swift kick, she pushed the man off of me. The man stumbled to his feet, holding the spot on his back where Evie had dug her heel into him. Putting on a deliberate show of innocence, the man glared back at Evie with an indignant expression.

Disregarding him completely, Evie looked over at me and said, "You see, I wore these heels tonight for a reason."

Just as our intruder was sitting before, Evie kicked up her feet and set them down on the coffee table in front of us.

Without Evie needing to say anything, the heels said every-thing—*this bitch is mine, boys. Back off.*

Taking advantage of the space Evie had earned us, I whispered to her, "Why won't they just leave us alone?"

Perhaps because I was tripping, admittedly pretty hard at that point, all the men sitting around us began to looks like sharks. Drawn to the bloodiness of my recent heartbreak, the men circled around Evie and me like we were easy, wounded prey. It was as if they could smell how vulnerable I was. This time, I was not the empowered, open-hearted kind of vulnerable. I was the kind of vulnerable that needed protecting.

Sensing this much herself, Evie muttered back, "Maybe try keeping your eyes down. Or just look at me for a while. The mushroom tea is making your pupils all huge and dilated. And you already have big eyes. I know that you're not meaning to do this, but I feel like something in your eyes is drawing all these men in. Whatever the fuck it is, they can't get enough of it."

Flinching, I immediately glanced down. Looking back on the night so far, I saw where Evie was coming from. Every time I caught one of the men's stares, I felt something within them latch onto me and refuse to let go. No matter if I never glanced their way again, I could feel the men's gazes lingering on me. If I accidentally looked one of them in the eyes again, I was stunned by the neediness I saw there.

"Let me complete you," the eyes of these men implored me.

If I could have found my voice, I would have answered, "You're the one who needs completing, not me."

I may have been lost, but what if I wanted to be lost alone? I certainly didn't want to help these men find themselves. How could I help someone else find himself when I didn't even feel like myself? Newly single, I no longer had a man attached to me to prove or reinforce my value. Nonetheless, I was done being valued as an accessory to a man. I was not an accessory. I was not a commodity. I was entirely my own. As empty and broken as I felt, my shoulders were strong. My shoulders bore the weight of freedom that would crush most people with its magnitude. I stood in this freedom now, even if the most overt gesture I could make to signal my freedom was to avert my eyes from the gazes of the men encircling me. Left with few options for safe directions to look in, I turned my whole body toward Evie. I let myself be mesmerized by the complexity of her hazel green eyes—eyes whose pupils were also remarkably large.

Shrugging, Evie joked, "At least the music is good, right?"

I had to laugh at this. My laughter provided me with some much-needed relief. The sound of it drew my real friends in. Squeezing past the men around us, Val and the four other friends who'd drank the mushroom tea claimed their spots on the couch beside us. We were all tripping hard at that point, so just about everything was funny. We laughed until we didn't know what we were laughing at anymore. No one else at the party had any idea what was going on except that we seemed to be having a lot more fun than everyone else.

The day before I left for Nicaragua, Evie and I invited Valeria and a few of our other closest friends over to Evie's apartment for a hair-dying party. The at-home hair dye kit that we'd ordered had arrived in the mail a few days before, and Evie and I went out and bought all the other supplies we needed. Neither of us had ever tried dying hair before. Despite her inexperience, Evie dedicated herself to doing the most professional job she could with the tools at her disposal. She worked through my hair in carefully partitioned sections. In order for the pink dye to hold, she started off by bleaching my hair. While Evie got to work, my friends trickled in to join us. They took their seats in the kitchen around us and watched entranced as my hair transformed from a darker blond to an almost-white platinum blond.

Throughout the whole bleaching process, my friends and I were having a grand old time together. They asked me all sorts of questions about Nicaragua and the yoga school that I'd signed up for. They knew me well enough to not bother asking questions about my future beyond that. They also avoided directly asking about Liam, not wanting to dampen my fragile, newly reclaimed sense of optimism. After so many weeks of struggling to come up with any plan at all, I was grateful just to be moving forward again. I even felt like I was starting to move on from Liam, although I could have just been running away from him. The last contact I'd had with Liam was a message he'd sent me on New Year's Day.

His message said, "Happy New Year's, Skye! Last year was amazing because of you. Wishing you the best in this year to come."

Not only did I ignore this message, but I also ignored his birthday six days later. I made it abundantly clear that I had no desire to be friends. Since our breakup, one of my only sources of satisfaction came from the fact that Liam knew absolutely nothing about my life since we'd last talked. His request that we remain friends, and his expectation that this would happen instantly, bordered on offensive to me. Why would I want to remain friends with someone whom I no longer trusted? Whenever I thought through my relationship with Liam and how it had ended, my mind kept coming back to one of two explanations. Option A was that Liam had told the truth about still loving me. That being said, he was just as lost as I was—perhaps more—and hell-bent on pretending that he wasn't. Determined to keep up appearances, Liam had chosen one path, the path of success, and decided to stick with this path at all costs. Anything that deterred him from this path was a distraction and a weakness, which turned Liam's love for me into a weakness. If this option was true, leaving me probably felt to Liam like he was standing in his own power again. Option B was simply that Liam was an asshole. If I believed this option, then I had to accept that he had been leading me on for quite some time and that he'd never intended to commit to our relationship. Looking back now, I see an Option C. Option C is that Liam was lost and insecure, and this insecurity is what made him an asshole.

For my own peace of mind, I like to think that Liam really did love me. However, his insecurity was like this growing black hole that slowly ate away at whatever love he had to give me until eventually his love ran out. As lost and insecure of an asshole as he may have been, I meant the last words I'd said to him over the phone. I loved Liam just as he was, without conditions, regardless of how much he'd hurt me, regardless of whether he loved me back. Some part of me would probably always go on loving him. Like a window stuck wide open, I'd let him all in. As Trampled by Turtles sang in their song that had become a sort of soundtrack to my life, I was left with one final haunting question: *Will I see you again?*

That night, surrounded by Evie and all my friends, I did my best to empty my mind of all these pointless questions. As the night went on, this became easier. I became increasingly absorbed by what was happening above my head instead of inside of it. Most of my friends made it only through the bleaching process and the beginning of Evie dying my hair pink. Since it was a weeknight, they all had jobs to report to early the following morning. Fortunately, this meant that Evie and I were the only ones who witnessed when things started to go wrong. Our problem was a simple one. I hadn't ordered enough pink dye to be able to dye all my hair. My hair fell down to my hips, so I should have known that one tube of pink dye wouldn't be enough for my whole head. Nevertheless, Evie did her best with the dye we had. She spent all night preening over my hair with her brushes and combs. The moment of truth came when I went to the bathroom and rinsed out all the dye that Evie had let sit in my hair.

Instead of the bubblegum pink advertised on the hair dye kit, my hair came out as a blaringly bright yellow. Upon closer inspection, this yellow contained some subtle pink hues. Despite all the effort that I put into reassuring Evie of the amazing job she'd done, the color was so atrocious that I couldn't look in the mirror for long. Thankfully, I didn't know anyone in Nicaragua. Upon landing in Managua, the capital city of Nicaragua, the first thing I did was book an appointment at one of the city's most reputable hair salons. In this case, it didn't matter that my Spanish was rusty. All I had to do was point at my head and say, "Ayuda!"

Three hours and another bleaching session later, I walked

out of the Managua salon with my hair dyed the exact shade of bubblegum pink I was going for. Throughout my entire walk from the salon back to my hostel, not a minute went by without the men driving by catcalling to me from their cars. One thing that I hadn't considered before dying my hair was how having bright pink hair would affect my safety while traveling alone as a young woman in a developing country. After all the time and money I'd spent dying my hair just the right shade of pink, I didn't dare leave my hostel again without throwing a scarf over my head. However, I didn't mind this so much. After all, I dyed my hair pink for myself and no one else.

chapter twenty-two

TWO HUNDRED HOURS OF YOGA

AS I WALKED AROUND THE CITY of León, I had the strangest feeling that I'd been there before. I couldn't shake the feeling of déjà vu. As random and last-minute as this trip was, something about these streets felt familiar. In the few hours that I'd spent wandering the city, I came to know it like the back of my hand. I wondered if it wasn't so much the place itself that I recognized but the feeling of being there. I was well-acquainted with what it feels like to be a traveler, a backpacker, a young woman traveling alone, a noticeably pale-skinned foreigner, a combination of privileged elite and vagabond bum.

I hadn't expected to be traveling again quite so soon, but there I was. Already, I'd fallen back on the old habits I'd built to make traveling feel less like lonely wandering and more like purposeful exploration. I didn't go anywhere without a book in hand. I used every occasion I was given to practice the local language. I shed my introversion and talked to as many new people as I could, especially the locals. I tried any experience and food offered to me, provided that there was a minimum of safety involved. I took pictures of all the little things that I found beautiful, whether it was a bougainvillea bush in bloom or the deep fuchsia color painted on so many of the houses. I meditated. I wrote. I walked a lot. As well-worn as these habits were, and as familiar as this place felt, what felt unfamiliar was me within this place.

Whenever I caught a glimpse of my shockingly pink hair in the mirror, I asked myself, "Who's she?"

Watching the confidence and ease that I projected outwardly while traveling, I had an even harder time recognizing myself. My pink hair made me appear even bolder than I was. That being said, there's a certain amount of validity to the phrase, "Fake it until you make it." Having bright pink hair instilled in me the confidence to sign up to go sledding down the side of the Cerro Negro volcano, a popular tourist activity in León. The most worthwhile moment that came with having pink hair was the picture I took of myself standing on top of the volcano with ski goggles on my head and my sled hitched onto my back. Everything about the picture, my stance, my facial expression, said *fuck it*. This perfectly summed up the reason why I'd dyed my hair pink in the first place. As fun as it was to wear this slogan on the top of my head, it came nowhere near capturing my true life philosophy, which would be something more along the lines of *embrace it*. For this reason, it took me only a few days to tire of having such brightly colored hair. When people first saw me, they had a much easier time fitting me into neat, labeled boxes. I watched people mentally stamp my forehead with labels like free spirit, hippie, rebel. None of these labels or boxes felt like home. I missed being able to disguise myself behind the plainness of my natural dirty blond hair.

However, there was no going back on any of this. After my third day in León, I hopped on what the locals call a chicken bus to the small town of Las Peñitas, where my yoga course was taking place. The bus was so packed that I had to stand in the back with my backpack between my feet. The crowd on the back of the bus was mostly male and very rowdy. One of the men in particular, a man who was standing regrettably close to me, was so drunk that he could barely hold himself upright. Halfway through the bus ride, I noticed a small, yellow puddle pooling at his feet. Not taking any chances, I picked up my backpack from the floor and slung it back over my shoulders.

I spent the rest of the ride carefully monitoring the progression of the yellow puddle across the bus floor. Whenever the bus careened hard to one side, I shuffled my feet to avoid getting inundated by the man's pee.

Although this portion of the journey seemed to go on forever, the whole ride was worth it for my final destination. Las Peñitas was a quiet, relatively undiscovered surfing town that bordered the Pacific Ocean. The hostel where I was staying for the next three weeks was right on the beach on the outskirts of town. The hostel itself consisted of little more than a roof covering a few guest rooms. The only walls were the ones separating the rooms for privacy. The rest of the hostel was a large, open space with hammocks strung up everywhere. Outside the main building, there was also a second-story, open-air platform right in front of the beach. For the next twenty-two days, I woke up and watched the sun rise every morning from atop this platform. Staring out at blue-gray waves and lilac-colored skies, I watched the pelicans fly over the wave break. The pelicans liked to show off their fine fishing skills by dive-bombing into the waves. The audaciousness of this plunge took my breath away every time. When I could no longer stand just looking at the Pacific Ocean, I dove in to test for myself the force behind its waves. If anything could heal me of my broken heart, it was the power of these ocean waves and the bright equatorial sun rising high above them.

After arriving at my hostel, one of the first things I discovered was that I wasn't the only one in our program with crazy-colored hair. The person sleeping in the bunk bed above mine was a young woman from Switzerland with dark purple hair. Somewhat ironically, this woman's name was Candy. Besides Candy and me, everyone else in the program appeared relatively normal. A Canadian woman named Quincy settled down into the bunk bed across the room. Quincy was an older, very sweet, self-effacing woman. She signed up for this program looking to transition from her life-long career as a nurse and midwife into a less demanding profession. Quincy was the type of person who I could imagine myself growing into by the time I reached her age. The two of us hit it off right from the start.

The person who I had the hardest time with was an American man in his early thirties named Dean who slept in the bunk above Quincy's. With his long, flowing blond hair, well-trimmed beard, and crystal blue eyes, Dean looked a lot like a Viking warrior who had been converted to the yogic discipline. He was strikingly handsome and had a larger-than-usual ego to show for it. This ego extended beyond Dean's good looks into his spiritual outlook, as well. Nonetheless, in the course of the intensive three weeks we spent together, I developed a lot more compassion for the shaky foundations that

Dean's ego was built upon. This helped soften my initial judgment toward him, although Dean's need to be right in every debate still grated on my nerves. The fifth and final person in our program was the only student who didn't live at the hostel and share the same dorm room with the rest of us, Mila. Mila was also in her midtwenties and had moved to Nicaragua from Belgium to be with her boyfriend, who ran a different hostel in Las Peñitas. Mila's incentive for studying yoga was to be able to teach yoga and meditation classes out of her boyfriend's hostel.

Although other students occasionally dropped in on our classes, the five of us formed the small core group that had signed up to participate in the yoga school's full two-hundred-hour program. The two women who founded our school were Raina, a middle-aged French woman, and Juliette, a younger Canadian woman. Raina and Juliette had dedicated their lives to yoga, which showed in the passion with which they taught their classes. Raina had spent most of her adult life studying and teaching yoga in India. She brought to the program a wealth of practical knowledge on the correct form of each pose and how to safely guide students into these poses. As both a yoga teacher and physical therapist, Juliette's expertise was more focused on human anatomy and the therapeutic benefits of the poses. Our third teacher was an Italian man named Salvo, whom Raina and Juliette hired to teach us the history and philosophy of yoga.

All our classes were taught in the building adjacent to our hostel. Our classroom was a cement platform with a grass roof overlooking the beach. Getting to stare out at the ocean during class made it a lot easier to study yoga for ten hours every day. Monday through Saturday, we were expected to show up for our first yoga class at six a.m. We practiced for two hours, took a short break for a breakfast, and then returned for theory class with Salvo. Apart from our hour-long lunch break, we spent the rest of the day in class. With Raina, we studied the form and application of the primary poses of yoga. In the afternoon, Juliette taught us about human anatomy and the science behind yoga. Our day ended with Juliette guiding us in another two-hour sunset yoga practice.

During our opening ceremony on the first day of class, we were all instructed to set an intention for the rest of the course. The intention I chose was clarity. Although I still wrestled with fear and uncertainty every day, each day there brought me new clarity. Thinking about what came next for me after this course, I narrowed my options down to two choices. The first, more comfortable, option was to move back to Denver. The second, more adventurous, option was to move to a new city in California. On one hand, settling down in California would satisfy my lifelong dream of living by the ocean. On the other hand, the mountains of Colorado were the place where I felt the most at home. For the time being, my intuition about which choice was the most right for me lay dormant. With all these future decisions looming on the horizon, I was grateful to have made it where I was. Amid heartbreak and loss, I'd somehow found my way to this magical tropical oasis. Every day, I got to practice yoga with the rising and setting of the sun. With a small cohort of fellow practitioners, I delved into my spiritual practice as I never had before.

Spending so much time studying yoga and meditation also meant spending a lot of time studying myself. This wasn't always a pleasant experience. Along with asking us to set an intention for the program, our teachers also invited us to choose one thing that we wished to let go. I chose my broken heart. Yet, before I could feel whole again, I first had to accept my current state of brokenness. Only by embracing myself as I was in that moment, emotionally unstable and still hurting terribly, was I able to find the love within myself that I needed to heal and move on. I learned many things from taking this time to consciously sit with my grief. I learned that grief is a cyclical thing. Every day, I was subject to the ebbs and flows of its changing tides. Some mornings, I woke up and watched the pelicans playing in the waves at sunrise, and my heart felt as light as the pelicans floating above the waves. Other mornings, I could barely make myself get out of bed. On these days, I identified more with the pelicans dive-bombing head-first into cold water. Subject to the unpredictability of these mood swings,

I wondered how many of my experiences were governed, like the tide, by forces as invisible and immutable as gravity.

Staring up at the moon at night, I pondered, "Are you the one to blame?"

When it came to healing from grief, blame was hardly relevant. Regardless of how I got into this emotional mess, the mess was mine to clean up. On bad days, I saw no end to the job in front of me. Face-to-face with what appeared to be an insurmountable mountain of sadness, my instinct was to recoil in fear. Fighting this instinct, I held myself together until I could find some quiet time alone. Whenever we got a break from class, I set off by myself for long walks down the beach. On these walks, I let loss have its way with me. Oftentimes, these walks began with a sense of nostalgia. Losing myself to my happiest memories, I reveled in the beauty of what once was. Before long, each memory faded away. My happiness faded along with them. Feeling how full my heart once was, I was left feeling emptier than ever before. This emptiness was the feeling I had to sit with, or in this case, take out on long walks along the beach. During the time I spent processing these feelings, I didn't have much of a sense of progress. The peak of the mountain I was climbing remained out of sight.

Thankfully, not all of my healing needed to be done alone or involved pain. Some of my greatest breakthroughs happened in the presence of my fellow yogis. When it came to leading group meditations, our Italian teacher, Salvo, was particularly gifted. One of my favorites was an exercise he called the "Just Like Me Meditation." This meditation is an eye-gazing practice during which two people hold eye contact and repeat the same mantra. The practice of eye-gazing is designed to help people connect with each other on a deep, soul level. Repeating the same mantra is simply a way of keeping both participants present enough for this connection to happen. What amazed me the most about this meditation was how different my experience was with each partner with whom I practiced.

Looking into Candy's eyes was like looking into the eyes of a doe or some other innocent baby animal. The frailty within Candy's eyes made me wish I could reach out through my own eyes and assure her that everything would be all right. In the first few seconds of sitting with Quincy, I could immediately tell that I was looking into the eyes of a healer. These were the eyes of a sage old woman, a woman who'd learned the ways of the world the hard way. These were eyes that pierce through people and experiences and see straight into the heart of things. I could only imagine what they saw in me. Staring into Mila's eyes made for a much lighter experience. Mila's eyes radiated warmth and cheerfulness. After peering into the depths of Quincy's eyes, looking into Mila's eyes was almost soothing. Mila's eyes were still so full of hope. These were the eyes of a young dreamer who believed that anything was possible and had yet to be proven otherwise.

In contrast with Mila's youthful optimism was the unexpected darkness that I encountered looking into Dean's eyes. At first, staring into Dean's eyes felt like walking into a wall. Given how open-minded Dean presented himself to be, I was surprised by the fierceness of his defenses. Later, as we all sat in a group and dissected our eye-gazing experiences, Dean quietly told me the horror story of his childhood. Taking into account the amount of abuse he had suffered at the hands of his family, Dean never really got a childhood. From the age of fourteen on, he had to fend for himself. However, I didn't have any of this information during our eye-gazing practice. All I knew was that I was face-to-face with a wall that I had to figure out how to climb over. Intuitively, I sensed that what Dean needed the most was softness. Tapping into the inner mother within me, the nurturing force within all women, I sent a simple message from my eyes out to Dean's.

"You are safe here."

Dean later told me that he saw swirling patterns of baby blue and soft pink as he stared into my eyes. The softness of these colors put him at ease. Dean's once-solid wall melted to the ground like a block of ice melting down to a pool of water. Once his wall was down, I had to take deep breaths to be able to sit with what I saw. Leaking out from Dean's eyes was an almost overwhelming amount of raw, unprocessed pain. For the remainder of the meditation, I sat with this pain, wishing I could take some small amount of it away from Dean and onto myself. In my mind, I imagined myself as Rebecca had seen me, as a window beyond which lay infinite amounts of space. Looking into Dean's eyes, I opened up this window, and I took it all in. Because I was the one choosing to open this time, I didn't feel burdened by the pain I let inside of me. As much pain or emotion as I let inside of me, there would always be more space. This space no longer felt empty, but rich and full with potential.

Coming to the final hours in my two-hundred-hour yoga teacher training program, I chuckled, looking back on the intentions that I'd set at the beginning of this journey. Beneath these intentions lay so many hidden expectations. In setting the intention of healing my broken heart, I was expecting this healing process to feel good. I was also expecting that it would bring about some kind of miraculous, newfound clarity. Given all this time and space to look inward, I was expecting to find myself again. When I first reconnected with myself, it felt like something within me had been broken. Assuming that this brokenness was fixable, I went to work to heal myself. Each time I reconnected to myself, I noticed a trend. The self who I was yesterday is not the same self who I am today. The self who I am tomorrow will not be the same as the self who I am today. This is when I started to understand the truth about myself. The truth is not that I have been broken. The truth is that I am constantly breaking.

Before this, the word *break* used to connote something negative to me. Hearing this word, my natural urge was to reach out as if to catch a falling glass before it hit the ground. I believed that breaking was something that should be prevented whenever possible. If breaking couldn't be prevented, then the mess it created should be cleaned up and cleared out of sight as quickly as possible. This was no longer how I saw it. My capacity to break was not a burden or a punishment. It was my gift. My gift was to dare to be broken open again and again. Each time I broke, I became less fragile. Through the process of breaking down, I was also building up. I was building my capacity for courage, patience, and trust. The self who I was coming to know through this process was a not a contained, static object but an ongoing, ever-changing event. When I was present, I experienced every moment as a breaking point.

One of the final meditations that Salvo led us in further detached me from any solid sense of self. At the end of a particularly demanding two-hour yoga class, Salvo instructed us to lie down on our mats in Savasana, or corpse pose. When Salvo warned us that he was going to lead us into a disembodiment meditation, I knew I was in for quite the trip.

Salvo began the meditation by guiding us to "Feel your toes with your full awareness. Imagine each of your toes melting into the ground. Slowly, work your way up your feet until nothing is left of your feet besides two small puddles on the ground. From there, move your attention up from your feet toward your ankles and calves. Slowly, slowly, imagine your entire leg melting into the ground. Once you have melted your legs into the ground, move your focus up to your hips. Now, I'd like you to ..."

Salvo carried on like this for a long time. However, his main instruction remained clear. *Melt*. Moving from my toes up to the crown of my head, "slowly, slowly," as Salvo liked to say, I melted my entire body into a puddle on the ground below me. Where my belly once was, I imagined a light blue orb hovering above the ground. No longer bound to my physical body, I took this orb and sent it flying up to join the line of pelicans catching fish in the ocean. I dove with the bats as they plunged for bugs in the air. I tumbled with the ocean waves as they crashed against the sandy shore. With no restrictions as to where I could go or what I could be, I could have played like this forever. As much fun as I was having, the sound of Salvo's voice brought me back.

"Now that you have melted your body away, I would like you to crystallize the droplets of your body into solid particles of sand. What was once your body is now sand blowing in the wind. Let the wind do with you what it pleases. Let it take you wherever it wishes you to go."

All it took was for Salvo to say the word *sand*, and I was instantly transported back to the Sahara Desert. Everything around me turned the color yellow—yellow that shimmered on the dunes and hung like a thick haze in the sky. Just as Salvo instructed, I imagined the sand particles that formed my being blowing every which way in the wind. As random as the movements of the wind seemed, I watched them long enough to detect a pattern behind the randomness. These patterns formed images—images broadcast against the grayish-yellow screen of the sky. These images told the story of my life. Watching this story play out, I told myself that I wasn't this story. I did my best to disassociate from it. Still, I clung to it. As detached as I felt in that moment, I wasn't ready for this story to end. I wasn't ready to die. Mesmerized by the beauty of my own life story, I was jolted out of my trance by a voice that I had to strain to recognize. I no longer remembered who the owner of this voice was, but something told me I should pay attention to what it had to say.

Echoing across the Sahara dunes, this voice proclaimed, "Within this disembodied state of being lies a golden opportunity. This is your chance to ask a question, any question. This may be one of the only times when you can count on yourself to give you a detached, unbiased answer. Whatever your question may be, take some time to sit with it and see what comes up."

Without having to think about it, I knew what question I wanted to ask. This question ricocheted off the sand dunes encircling me, reverberating for miles in every direction.

"*Why am I here?*"

Again, the wind moved the sand in patterns that painted images across the sky. These images mirrored back to me all of my past stories and future stories yet unlived. I couldn't see the future stories consciously. As soon as they appeared in the sky, they disappeared from my conscious memory. The only thing I remember from these future images was that my life would unfailingly take me down the path I least expected. Gaping up at the sky in awe, I watched as my story extended beyond my present-day understanding of myself to encompass more stories than my brain could retain or comprehend. Although I didn't recognize these stories or identify them as my own, they were all somehow a part of me. Seeing how all these stories connected with one another, I cried at the beauty of the visual tapestry painted for me across the sky. Without needing to hear an answer to my question, these images told me all I needed to know. *I am here to witness beauty.*

Unable to help inserting itself in the matter, my mind cried, "I'm not just here to witness. I am also here to create!"

Now, this is simply my own answer to a universal but

uniquely personal question. Putting the two pieces of my answer together, I found my version of peace.

"*I am here to witness and to create beauty.*"

From where I lay, melting into the ground in corpse pose, everything was beautiful.

chapter twenty-three

LAND OF MISTY CITIES
AND SECLUDED BEACHES

AFTER THE STRUCTURE AND RIGOR of our yoga-teaching program, I was itching for a return to the independent lifestyle to which I'd become accustomed. As much as I enjoyed the intimacy of our yoga school's small group setting, I was ready to delve into the even deeper intimacy that came with spending time alone. Sitting there in my tiny but private bedroom at Hotel Primavera in Jinotega, I was very aware of my aloneness. There was nothing in my room besides the twin bed that I was sitting on to write this, a trash can, and a cheap plastic chair. The fluorescent light above me buzzed slightly as I wrote. Having come up north to visit Nicaragua's coffee country, I'd officially made it off the beaten path. Throughout my time in Jinotega so far, I'd seen only one other foreigner. This foreigner was a very sunburnt white man in a business suit, pacing back and forth while talking on the phone in German. Given our remote location in Nicaragua's northern coffee country, I assumed he was somehow involved with the coffee industry.

When the man saw me walking down the street, he gave me a funny look as if to say, "I know why I'm here. Why are you?"

While I had no official business with the coffee industry, I was there for my own coffee-related reasons. Although Nicaragua was becoming increasingly known around the world for the quality of its coffee, most of the coffee that I'd tried during my time there had been mediocre to subpar. After a little digging, I found out this was because the Nicaraguan coffee farmers made so much more money exporting their coffee that they kept only the lowest-quality beans to sell in their own country. By traveling north to the region where most Nicaraguan coffee was grown, I was hoping to buy some of the good stuff before it was shipped off to be sold abroad. I was drawn to the town of Jinotega in particular by the allure of its nickname, the City of Mists. I found very little written about Jinotega online, which confirmed the fact that it was not well-known among tourists. The occasional foreigners who came through were mostly missionaries or businessmen. They were certainly not pink-haired coffee freaks. Thankfully, after three weeks of swimming in the ocean every day, the pink dye in my hair had faded to a much subtler hue. From far away, my hair just looked like a shimmering platinum blond. To avoid attracting too much attention, I still wore a scarf over my head while traveling.

It took me an entire day from dawn to dusk and four different chicken buses to make it all the way up north to this isolated mountain town. Now that I was there, no one—myself included—knew what to do with me. On top of my obvious foreignness, I was also a young, single woman traveling alone. This made me quite the puzzle for all the locals with whom I interacted.

The most common question the locals asked me was, "Where is your husband? Did you leave your children at home with him?"

The fact that I was twenty-four and didn't have a husband or children was incomprehensible to most of the people there. The locals' judgments aside, I was excited for this solo adventure. Taking matters into my own hands, I organized my own coffee tours. I spent hours online studying maps of the area and learning which bus routes would take me where I wanted to go. Once I was on the bus, I had to pay very close attention to where we were going so as not to miss my stop. Most of the time, my stop was nothing more than a gas station on the side of a dirt road in the middle of nowhere. To find the farm I was looking for, I then walked for miles up a remote, unnamed dirt road. I had no map, no smart phone, and no way of knowing for sure that I'd picked the right dirt road to walk along. Somehow, my good luck held. I always made it where I intended to go. Without knowing quite how, I suddenly seemed to have become a seasoned and courageous traveler. If there was somewhere I wanted to go, I figured out a way to get there—never mind the risks I was taking by going on these missions alone.

When I wasn't out on a mission to find a particular coffee plantation, I kicked back and enjoyed some of the amazing coffee in Jinotega's coffee houses. Every day I was there, I drank at least three cups of coffee, each from a different farm or coffee shop. Every night, I visited my favorite local bakery and brought home a different baked good. For reasons that I couldn't fathom, the Jinotega bakery I fell in love with opened only after nightfall. Despite its unusual hours, the bakery was always packed. Since the owner of the Primavera Hotel locked the doors at eight, I had to sprint back to the hotel with my baked goods in hand to make it back before she locked me out for the night. Since I was unaccustomed to having a curfew, and such an early one at that, the hostel owner reminded me of an over-protective grandmotherly figure. The breakfasts she cooked every morning more than made up for the lack of freedom I put up with at night.

Come morning, I escaped outside again to revel in the stunning three-hundred-and-sixty-degree views of the misty mountains after which the city had been named. The mountains encircling Jinotega were blanketed with a lush green flora that was home to an outstanding variety of birds and insects. As I took in the splendor of Jinotega's natural scenery, it was a wonder to me that the city had managed to stay off the backpackers' circuit for so long. As things were at the time, Jinotega was doing just fine without tourism. The town bustled with a productive, industrious energy, which I assumed was connected to the strength of the coffee produced there. For five days, I hid away from the Western world in this uncorrupted piece of paradise. Not wanting to spoil my hidden treasure, I did my best to remain as discreet as possible during my time there. Considering that I'd made it to the ripe old age of twenty-four and had no husband or children back home to worry about, just being there was a privilege.

The last coffee tour I went on before leaving my beloved City of Mists was much more well-organized than any of the others. It was the only tour that I managed to organize beforehand, which also meant it was the only tour I actually paid for. During my time wandering the streets of Jinotega, I met a mapmaker who was trying to put Jinotega on the map by literally making maps of Jinotega. Geared toward tourists, his maps showcased all the city's most alluring attractions with bright pictures and featured ads of prominent local businesses. One of the ads on the map was for a tour of a nearby coffee plantation. I asked the mapmaker how I might get in touch with the person who organized the tour.

"It's easy! We can walk over to his house right now. I'm sure he'll be happy to take you tomorrow!"

Although I was skeptical of the mapmaker's claims, I let him lead me on a brisk walk across town. Just when I was starting to think that the mapmaker was pulling my leg, we stopped in front of a large, bright pink house. By Jinotega's standards, this house was quite luxurious. It was enclosed by a high cement fence topped with barbed wire. A twelve-year-old girl with braces answered the door. She turned out to be the youngest daughter of the coffee plantation owner. The girl told us that her father wasn't home, but that she was happy to set up the tour for me. The daughter proceeded to negotiate a deal with me in a manner so fluid and practiced that I wondered if having his daughter talk to potential customers was part of her father's business strategy. Smiling her charming, metallic smile, the girl gave me a limp handshake to seal the deal.

"Someone will be by tomorrow morning at eight to pick you up. Está bien?"

I assured the girl that eight was just fine. The following morning, the person who picked me up turned out to be Humberto himself, the owner of the coffee plantation and the father of the young girl. Humberto drove me in his pickup truck high into the mountains of the Northern Highlands. We made a few stops along the way for Humberto to pick up some snacks and to visit a local church that was famous in the region for its murals. One of these murals depicted a devil whose face looked eerily similar to Daniel Ortega, Nicaragua's current president, or dictator, depending upon which way you look at it. Besides pointing out this mural to me, Humberto said very little. Out of the corner of my eye, I caught the smirk that he tried to hide. Later, when we were stopped by a police blockade farther down the road, all of Humberto's quiet subversion vanished. Humberto made a big show of getting out of his car to greet the head police officer, whom he knew by name. Humberto clapped him on the back as one would greet an old friend. This was when I realized just how smart a man Humberto was. So far, he was the only farm-owner I'd met who was from Nicaragua. Despite receiving many offers from wealthy foreigners looking to take over his coffee operation, Humberto had stubbornly held onto his land. This land had been in his family for three generations. Outside of the pressure that Humberto dealt with from international buyers, he'd also weathered a good deal of national conflict. When Daniel

Ortega was first elected president in the 1979 post-Sandinista revolution, a lot of the land in the country was nationalized and turned into cooperatives, Humberto's farm included.

As Humberto told the story, "My family and I finished lunch and were about to go rest for our afternoon siesta when a family of strangers came knocking on our door. 'We are the new owners of this land,' the father of the family told me. He held up an official document to prove it. Not knowing what else to do, I welcomed this family onto my land and treated them as if they were my guests. For six months, I housed and fed this entire family, which included the husband and wife and all five of their children. In time, we became friends and developed a mutual respect for one another. This respect went so deep that the father of the family agreed to accompany me to the capital, where we petitioned to get the land re-signed in my name. Once the documents were signed, the man packed up all his things and left with his family to go back to who knows where. I never saw them again.

"No matter what is going on around us, no one can convince me to give up my farm. My grandfather spent all of the money he had to buy this land. Then, he spent all the remaining years of his life building a coffee plantation on this land. When he could carry on no longer, my grandfather passed the land on to my father, who later passed it on to me. When I can carry on no longer, I intend to pass on the land to my eldest son. This land is my family's legacy. It is all that will remain of me when I go."

Upon making this last point, Humberto went silent. He spoke again only to point out when we passed the fence that marked the beginning of his land. When we arrived at the farmhouse, I got to meet Humberto's eldest son, who managed the land in his father's absence. Clad in leather cowboy boots and a broad-brimmed hat, this eldest son looked like a younger version of Humberto. I recognized these men as *Nicaragüense* cowboys. They reminded me of my late grandfather, who was an American cowboy. I'm sure my grandpa would have loved nothing more than the opportunity to sit down over a cup of coffee with Humberto and talk business. Despite my being a young woman, and a single one at that, Humberto was surprisingly open with me about how he ran his farm, as well as his plans for expansion in the future. He took me on a tour on foot of the trails around his farm. The tour ended at a large complex of buildings that hosted his coffee-roasting equipment. What impressed me more than the machinery itself was the agility that Humberto displayed throughout the entire tour. Here was a man well into his sixties who was clambering over steep, muddy slopes and bushwhacking through thick jungle, all the while carrying on a steady conversation about how he planned to attract more tourists to his farm.

The only time Humberto conceded to having physical limitations of any kind was toward the end of our tour.

"Now, for the grand finale of the tour!" he announced with gusto. "This is where I leave you."

Without offering much else in the way of explanation, Humberto walked me over to the building adjacent to us, which turned out to be the stables. A young man wearing a well-worn cowboy hat and a mischievous smile helped me up onto a horse that was all saddled up and ready to ride.

After I was already seated on the horse, Humberto confirmed with me, "You've ridden a horse before, yes?"

With the young cowboy taking the lead, we set off on a trot before I had time to qualify that I'd been horseback riding only a couple of times before this, and ten years ago at that. After we made it up our first hill, the young cowboy with the mischievous smile turned back to make sure I was still on my horse. Despite the fact that I'd never trotted on a horse before, I was doing my best to appear calm. I'd heard that horses can detect fear in their riders, and that fear can make a horse skittish. Although my hands had gone white from gripping the reins, I put my bravest face forward. Taking in my outwardly calm demeanor, the young cowboy guide smiled a little bigger and winked back at me.

Turning back around, the cowboy clucked loudly. He kicked his heels into his horse's flanks. Before I had time to prepare myself, my horse thrust forward at a full gallop, almost sending me flying off her backside. With my nameless cowboy leading the way, we flew up and over hills, skirted around fences, and jumped over streams. Most of the time we rode, we weren't on a road and didn't seem to be following any particular trail. I had no idea how far we'd gone or how long this would go on. This worried me, because I didn't know how much longer I could hold onto the reins like this. Were I in the United States, who knows how many waivers I would have had to sign to even go for a tame stroll on horseback down a farm road.

While I can't say that I was able to take in much of the surrounding scenery, I made it back to the stable without falling off my horse. The cowboy helped me get off the horse and stand on my feet again. Once I no longer appeared at risk of falling over, the cowboy tipped his hat at me and headed back to more serious work. Smiling in approval, Humberto greeted me with another cup of coffee. For one of the first times in my life, I refused. My heart wasn't yet strong enough to handle another dose of caffeine. Thinking that I must be tired, Humberto offered to drive me back home in his truck. The whole ride back home, Humberto told me all kinds of stories about life in Nicaragua. Despite my exhaustion, I did my best to follow his rapid-fire Spanish. Humberto's stories painted an honest picture of what it was like to live in a country with such a messy history and high propensity for political upheaval. These bone-chilling stories made my horseback riding adventure seem like a peaceful walk around the park. However much I admired Humberto for all that he and his family had gone through, he made me vow not to repeat any of the stories he told me.

Before dropping me off at my hotel, Humberto insisted, "Now don't go telling all of this to your American friends back home! No, you must tell them how beautiful my country is. Tell them to come visit my land! Above all, Nicaragua is a magnificent country."

By the time I made it to my final destination in Nicaragua, no one in the world knew where I was, not even my mother. After Jinotega, I made my way down south to Playa Popoyo, a remote beach town on the southwestern coast of Nicaragua. Playa Popoyo was my last hideaway from the world before I flew back to rejoin the world in five days. Before returning to Colorado, I would fly out to San Francisco and spend a week exploring California's most alluring coastal cities. In this week of exploration, I was hoping to gather enough information to decide once and for all whether I was moving out to California or back to Colorado. Before any of this happened, I had a few more days to ride the waves of Playa Popoyo.

In order to get there, I took four more chicken buses and

hitched an hour-long ride on the back of some guy's motor-cycle. Riding on the back of a motorcycle at high speeds on a bumpy dirt road with a heavy backpack on my back was not an experience that I am keen on repeating. My whole body was sore from how tightly I had to hold on to stay on the man's motorcycle. Hoping to walk off some of this soreness, the first thing I did upon arrival was go for a stroll down the beach at sunset. Playa Popoyo was so isolated that I ran into only two other humans and a stray band of dogs on my walk. One of these dogs, a shaggy yellow dog with big brown eyes, took a liking to me. For the rest of my time in Playa Popoyo, this dog followed me wherever I went. This dog's presence by my side was a comforting reminder that I wasn't alone. As I sat watching the sunset from a rocky outcropping at the far end of the beach, my new canine friend cuddled right up by my side. Together, we watched, entranced as the big ball of fire that lights our sky slowly drowned in the ocean.

As gorgeous as this beach was, I couldn't decide whether Popoyo felt more like heaven or hell to me. I vacillated between states of total bliss and soul-crushing loneliness. As perfect as this place was, I had no one with whom to enjoy this perfec-tion. I was alone there, totally cut off from the world. Before the end of my relationship with Liam and my decision to come to Nicaragua, I had no interest in traveling alone. I wasn't that interested in traveling in general. All I really wanted was a place to call home. Instead, my path had led me in the opposite direction of what I imagined. I felt more lost now than ever before. I'd fallen off of the map completely.

As haphazard as the events leading to me coming there were, I counter-balanced this haphazardness by choosing one thing to focus on during my time there—surfing. Surfing became my entire purpose. While very few people know about Popoyo's existence, almost all of the people who do are serious surfers. Now, I am no serious surfer. Fortunately for me, there was a smaller wave break farther down the beach that I practiced catching to avoid getting humiliated on the wave that Playa Popoyo was named after, the Popoyo main break. Every morning I spent in Popoyo, I woke up at sunrise to surf my little wave. I returned again sometime after lunch when the tides were low. Regardless of how many waves I caught during a day or how many times I fell, I went to sleep at the end of every night exhausted and satisfied. As humbling and terrifying as surfing was for me, it wiped my mind clean of the sorrows that haunted me.

It is the finite nature of every moment that makes our time here precious. This was my last day in Playa Popoyo and my second-to-last in Nicaragua. In two days, I would be back in the States. The period of time that I'd bought myself to heal and process would come to an end. With so many major life decisions looming on the horizon, I reeled my attention back in to focus on the horizon in front of me. I watched the pale yellow sun rise above the cliffs of Playa Popoyo, grateful for the imminent warmth that its presence represented. Even with my wetsuit on, the ocean water felt particularly cold that morning. If it weren't for the company of my new friend sitting on the board next to me, I would have already headed back to my hostel for breakfast.

My new friend's name was Ari, short for Ariel. I met Ari because he worked at the surf shop that I rented my surfboard from every day. With his dark, curly hair, startling green eyes, and shy smile, Ari made quite the first impression on me. I must have stood out to Ari, as well. From the moment I entered his shop, I could feel his beautiful green eyes following me wherever I went. As handsome as Ari was, I can't quite say that I was attracted to him. My heart was still too closed for this to be possible. That being said, something about Ari drew me to him. It was this fascination that finally prompted me to accept Ari's offer to surf together. Little did I know, this early morning surfing session was just the beginning of Ari's plan.

When neither of us could brave the cold any longer, we caught one last wave back to shore. After dropping off our boards at his shop, Ari offered to take me on a tour of the area on the back of his motorbike. We split ways long enough for me to walk back to my hostel, put dry clothes on, and scarf down a quick breakfast. As I finished my last few bites, Ari pulled up on his bike at the front entrance of my hostel. I couldn't help the giddiness I felt as I put on the helmet he offered me and we zoomed off down Popoyo's one and only dirt road. Twenty minutes later, this giddiness turned to panic when Ari pulled his motorbike off to the side of the road.

Turning around to flash me those big green eyes, Ari declared, "It's your turn now."

Ignoring my protests, Ari hopped off the motorbike and gave me a brief rundown of how to operate the bike. He made me move to the front of the motorbike and sat down behind me. When I insisted that I had no idea what I was doing, Ari reached his arms around me, resting his hands on the brakes as backup insurance.

"Try not to worry so much. We can take it slow. If we really need to stop, I will pull on the brakes. OK?"

The path of least resistance in this situation was to succumb to Ari's optimism. After my initial panic subsided, I was grateful to have succumbed. Operating the motorbike was much more intuitive than I would have guessed. Riding high on adrenaline, I slowly picked up speed as I learned to trust myself and the motorbike. I was having so much fun that I was actually disappointed when we reached our intended destination—another small town in the area called Playa Gigante. While Playa Popoyo is known for its epic wave break, the tranquility of Playa Gigante's waters was what made this town so beautiful. Pulling into the town on Ari's motorbike felt like unexpectedly pulling into a small French town along the Mediterranean Sea. Verdant cliffs encircled a small bay where pristine white sailboats floated above still, turquoise waters. Toward the far end of the bay, a large rock jutted out of the water. This rock must have been home to all the pelicans in the area, for every square inch of the rock's surface was covered by a sleeping bird. As enamored as I was by Playa Popoyo, the beauty of this place was something else entirely, something out of a dream.

Innocently enough, Ari asked if I wanted to go for a swim with him. This was when I realized that I'd somehow forgotten to bring a bathing suit. All that I had on was a long, flowy summer dress. Underneath it, I was wearing a thong and no bra, which eliminated the possibility of going swimming in my underwear. I didn't let this stop me. There was no way I could sit on this beach and stare at such bright blue waters without diving into them. Since I had no other option, I committed to going swimming in my dress. Shaking his head at me, Ari followed behind me as I waded into the water. Each step I took became increasingly difficult as the heaviness of my dress weighed me down. Eventually, I gave in to the water and let myself fall forward. Holding my breath, I took a few strokes underwater. My long dress opened up like a parachute behind me, and I had to kick hard to keep moving forward. When I came up for air, Ari stepped forward to help me.

Taking me in his arms, Ari bid me, "Lie back, relax. Just float with me for a while."

As I lay floating on my back, Ari held me up and spun me around him in slow circles. Gazing up at the sky, I wondered how on earth I'd gotten myself into such a ridiculous situation. I felt like I'd stumbled onto the set of a cheesy teenage romance movie, a movie in which I'd become an unwilling protagonist. When I couldn't bear the cheesiness any longer, I asked Ari to put me down. We waded back to the beach and took a seat on the sand. Ari lit up a joint that he had pre-rolled for the occasion. We passed the joint back and forth between us a few times without saying much. Ari sat dangerously close to me, and he kept staring at me with those big green eyes. I cringed away from him in anticipation of the moment when he would inevitably lean in to kiss me. Before this happened, I felt obliged to tell Ari that I wasn't interested in him. Too disappointed to let this go right away, Ari pushed back a little.

"Did I do something wrong? Did something happen to make you feel uncomfortable?"

Trying to explain my reticence, I assured him, "You didn't do anything wrong. In fact, you've done everything right. I'm just not ready for this yet."

Scrutinizing me with sad, dreamy eyes, Ari pressed me, "Ready for what—love? How can we ever be ready for love?"

Without blinking, I concurred, "We can't. We also can't prepare ourselves for when it ends."

Ari nodded in reluctant understanding. Before saying anything else, he relit the joint and took another hit. When he glanced back at me, I could tell from the wistful look in his eyes that he knew what it meant to have his heart broken.

Exhaling a cloud of smoke, Ari sighed, "I wish that we were meeting at another time. Someday in the future when you are ready."

"That would be nice," I agreed. "Right now, it's just too soon. My boyfriend broke up with me a few weeks ago. As much as I wish I could let go of him and move on, everything still feels really fresh."

Instead of pushing me any further, Ari simply stated, "Your boyfriend was crazy to let you go. You are a princess, a real-life princess. Do not forget this, no matter what crazy thoughts your boyfriend put into your head."

Hearing the sincerity behind Ari's words, I hovered on the brink of tears. Watching the intensity of emotion playing out across my face, Ari's face twisted in sympathy. His green eyes clouded over a little.

Easing me back onto his towel, Ari again instructed me, "Just lie back, relax."

Gently, Ariel flipped me over so I was laying on my stomach, where he proceeded to give me a massage. The passage of Ari's hands across my back and shoulders tingled, covering my skin in goose bumps. I felt a strange mixture of heat from the sun shining down on my back and coolness from the dampness of my dress against my skin. I was also feeling the high from the hits I'd taken off the joint. All these mixed sensations made it hard for me to relax at first. Nonetheless, Ari kept working away at the knots he found in my back. With each knot that Ari released, I felt my muscles gradually relaxing. Even with all the time that I'd spent on the beach these past two months, this was the first time I'd truly been able to "lie back and relax," as Ari kept telling me.

I relaxed so deeply that I eventually fell asleep. I don't know how long I slept. When I opened my eyes, I somehow found myself standing in the security line at the airport with my backpack on ... or so it felt. With the passing of time, it was becoming harder for me to distinguish between my dreaming and waking moments. Sometimes, time crept by me in slow motion. I felt like I was swimming through water with a heavy, soaking wet dress trailing behind me. Other times, I blinked, and whole days seemed to vanish. In this way, my waking life sometimes felt more unbelievable than my dreams. When I dreamed at night, Liam was almost always with me. When I woke up in the morning, he was gone. If it weren't for how relaxed the muscles in my back felt, I would have some serious doubts as to whether meeting Ari was even real. Yet when we said goodbye in front of my hostel, Ari made me promise not to forget what he told me on the beach.

"*Eres una princesa. No lo olvides.*"

When Ari drove off on his motorbike, I was relieved of the duty to continue playacting as the reluctant protagonist in our cheesy teenage romance movie. Some dreams are better left to Hollywood, which, ironically, was very close to where I was headed next.

~⌐

author's note:

Skye left Nicaragua at the end of February 2018, shortly after which political unrest took over the country. On April 18 of that same year, strife spread throughout the land. In protest against President Ortega's social security reforms, thousands of citizens took to the streets. Within five days of the protests beginning, Ortega's men killed almost 30 people. Defying Ortega's orders that the protestors stand down, the opposition against Ortega continued to spread across the country. Conflict continued throughout the spring and summer months as Ortega refused to forfeit his presidency. In September 2018, Ortega made a new law declaring political protests to be "illegal" in Nicaragua. Ortega authorized his police and paramilitary forces to use live ammunition to fire on any protestors. Ortega has also expelled multiple international human rights organizations from the country and censored all of the media within Nicaragua. Although his hold on power is more tenuous than ever, Ortega refuses to let go.

During my process of writing and editing this book over the past three years, Daniel Ortega has maintained his monopoly on violence in Nicaragua, and, with that, his presidency. Since the government crackdown, human rights groups estimate that over 300 people have been killed, over 2,000 have been injured, hundreds have been arbitrarily arrested and prosecuted, and more than 103,000 people have been driven to seek asylum abroad. Freedom of expression remains severely limited, active discrimination is practiced against anyone who supports the opposition, and an increase in stringency on abortion laws has led to a decrease in women's rights and protection for rape victims. Since President Ortega has seized the assets of local NGOs and civil society groups and expelled a number of international aid agencies, the citizens of this country have been left to fend for themselves during the COVID-19 health crisis.

By the time this book reaches your hands, I am not sure how much will have changed in Nicaragua's political climate.

This note is written as a prayer for the safety and well-being of the Nicaraguan people. May Nicaragua soon find its way back to peace again, and may time help heal the wounds that this conflict has inflicted on the Nicaraguan people.

chapter twenty-four

DESERT DA(Y)ZE: COLORADO PLATEAU – CEDAR MESA, UTAH

SONORAN DESERT – SEDONA, ARIZONA

MOJAVE DESERT – PALM SPRINGS, CALIFORNIA

I SAT AT THE SAN DIEGO AIRPORT, waiting for my Denver flight to be called. I dreaded the moment when the flight attendants would announce that it was time for me to board. After spending almost two months in Nicaragua and then two weeks visiting various cities in California, I figured that I'd had more than enough time to process and reflect. Sick and tired of my own indecision, I'd given myself the flight back to Denver to make up my mind about whether I was moving back to Denver or out to San Diego, my favorite of the cities I'd visited in California. As soon as I got on the plane, I would have only two hours and twenty minutes to come to a decision. There was nothing else I could do to stall this decision except miss my flight. If I couldn't get myself to stand up from this seat, that could be a real possibility. Now that the time had come for me to make up my mind, I was scared to the point of paralysis. Regardless of which option I chose, they all ended the same way, with me alone. I longed for the days when I cared strongly enough about something or someone that none of the other options mattered to me. Now, all I saw were options, like stepping into a hall of mirrors that reflected back to me infinite variations of my aloneness.

The island that I'd pretended to be for so long was slowly being inundated. Standing on the last piece of dry land, the last piece of sanity I had left, I watched the ocean level of my anxiety slowly rise. Soon, I feared, my entire island would disappear underwater. In a last-ditch effort to save myself, I clutched at the only line of support I had left. Moving of their own accord, my fingers dialed the number of the one person who'd kept me afloat all these years.

"Alice?" I croaked when she answered the phone.

"Skye?"

Hearing her voice, I could clearly imagine Alice's face in front of me. I saw the way her eyebrows bunch together in worry. I saw the effort she made to smooth out her brow, but the slight downturn of her mouth gave her away. I knew I had to say something, anything, to take that worried look off Alice's face.

"I don't know what to do ..."

Taking a deep breath, Alice replied, "Well, you can start by telling me about San Diego. What did you like about it so much?"

Just thinking through my response helped ground me back in a more concrete reality.

"Part of what I like so much about San Diego is how much it reminds me of Denver. It's like a Denver by the ocean. There are coffee shops and breweries everywhere, beautiful parks and amazing hikes within city limits, and hip young people strolling around everywhere, living the good life."

Alice sighed, and I was surprised to catch the note of longing contained within that exhale. Ever since Alice had decided not to move to Denver with me that past summer, she'd dedicated herself to building up her community in Fort Collins, the town she'd called home for the past four years.

That's why I didn't expect the genuine curiosity I heard in

Alice's voice when she asked me, "And the beaches? What are they like?"

With as much detail as possible, I painted a picture for Alice of the beach near my friend's house in Encinitas, California, just north of San Diego. I told Alice about paddle boarding out from this beach with my friend. We'd paddled so far out into the ocean that I worried about whether we would be able to make it back to shore. I described to Alice what I imagined it would feel like to live next to the Pacific Ocean, to be connected through this great body of water to all the far-away places this ocean's water touches.

"San Diego is a beautiful city," I concluded, "but I don't know if I have it in me to move somewhere alone. I'll probably end up back in Denver, which is fine. I like Denver. But you know how it is with me. Anything too comfortable feels like I'm settling."

Alice took a moment to mull this over before coming out with a confession of her own.

"I'm sick of feeling alone, too. What if..."

Hesitating, Alice used the full length of a breath to check in with herself before finishing this sentence. In the finality of her exhale, I heard the sound of commitment.

"What if we moved to San Diego together?"

Just like that, Alice rescued me from my man-made island. In one instant, all the uncertainty and heartbreak of the past ten months became worth it. In this way, the end of my story brought me back to its beginning. What started with a phone call ended with another one. For once, the voice on the other end of the line wasn't delivering bad news. My relief was so strong that it numbed out all other emotions.

All I could think was, "Thank God, it's over."

One month later ...

I planned four stops on my road trip out to San Diego. My first stop was Durango. I met Hayley there on my way out to my second stop in Cedar Mesa, Utah. Cedar Mesa was my favorite place in my favorite-of-all places, the Utah desert. Years ago, a friend recommended that I check out this particular camping spot in Cedar Mesa. My friend described this spot as *the best campsite ever*, which I mistakenly took as hyperbole. Driving up to this campsite for the first time, I understood the sentiments that prompted my friend to make such a grandiose statement. This campsite was situated on top of a cliff that looks out west over the undulating, snakelike San Juan River. To the south of this campsite was the Valley of the Gods. Beyond this valley, the plains of the Navajo reservation stretched out for miles until they came to meet the colossal sandstone towers of Monument Valley. Hayley and I were blessed to watch the sun rise and set from atop this most astounding cliff, a blessing I was reluctant to relinquish. Hayley didn't want to relinquish me either. She did her best to convince me to stay and come with her on a rafting trip that her friends had planned down the San Juan River. Looking down on this river from our cliff-top viewpoint, I imagined myself on one of the rafts that we saw floating by below us. I imagined what it would feel like to let go and float just a little bit longer.

Letting Hayley down as gently as I could, I told her, "I've been floating for almost a year now. I can't float any longer."

So much work lay ahead of me before I could call San Diego my home. I was driving out to San Diego two weeks before Alice to hunt for apartments and apply for jobs. My task was to find an apartment for us, after which Alice would drive out with a U-Haul full of our stuff. I had no idea if I would be able to find an apartment in two weeks. I had no idea what we would do with all of our stuff if I didn't. Considering how much I was worrying about this already, I didn't have it in me to submit myself to four more days of lying around. Swallowing her disappointment, Hayley gave me a long hug before we drove our separate ways. I headed south toward the sandstone mammoths glistening beyond the plains. Although I'd stared at Monument Valley for years from atop Cedar Mesa, this was my first time driving through it. The closer I got to these towering sandstones buttes, the harder time I had believing they were real. The contrast of the rich, red sandstone against the bright, blue sky made my heart soar. Someday, I imagined, I would come back and make this place my final home. For now, I kept on driving.

As Monument Valley receded in my rearview mirror, I steadily picked up speed. My next stop was Sedona, Arizona, another place that I'd wanted to visit for years. I couldn't help my disappointment when I arrived. The whole town was grid-locked with traffic. Like ants on an anthill, tourists crawled all over Sedona's streets. I was so overwhelmed by the number of people there that I drove straight through the town without stopping. Instead, I followed the directions I'd written down to a nearby free campsite. Once I got there, I hoped to find some peace and quiet to be able to appreciate the brilliant sandstone cliffs and ponderosa pine forests for which Sedona is known. Turning off onto a dirt road, I passed a promising sign: "4x4 Vehicles Only." I didn't slow down to consider whether my 1997 RAV4 qualified for this kind of journey. Only after driving a mile up this five-mile road did I grasp what a mess I'd gotten myself into. It turned out that this was the most popular road in the area for local tour companies to take their customers off-roading on 4x4 Jeep tours. The road was narrow, windy, and steep. It was peppered with holes the size of small canyons and boulders as big as dinosaur eggs. There was one Toyota Tacoma driving behind me that eventually passed in front of me, but every other car that passed by me was a lifted commercial Jeep filled with tourists. Gaping at me from their open windows, the tourists shouted out unsolicited advice as they drove by.

"Turn back while you still can!" or "It only gets worse!" or simply, "You're crazy!"

Having made my way two miles up the road, I didn't know if I could turn around even if I wanted to. No matter how big of a mess I'd gotten myself into, the only way to go was forward. Following the closest Jeep in front of me, I circled around the holes in which they got stuck and dodged the boulders that brought their progress to a temporary halt. The Jeep hit all the worst parts of the road before I did, which provided me with some warning as to what lay ahead. In the end, it took me almost an hour and a half to make it up this one five-mile stretch of road. The entire time I played the same hip-hop song on repeat, "Missed Calls" by EarthGang, my heart pounding in rhythm with its beat. Just as everyone in the Jeeps had warned me while yelling at me from their windows, the last mile was the gnarliest mile of them all. I have no idea how my old RAV4 made it to the top of the road. But if I was good at anything, it was diving into a situation headfirst, totally unprepared, and figuring out my shit along the way. After a couple of near heart attacks, I made it to the top of the mesa. All the passengers of the Jeeps in front of me cheered wildly to see me round the last bend in the road, pumping their fists out the Jeep windows.

As much as I appreciated their enthusiasm, I'd driven all this way to get away from people, not to be surrounded by a frenzied mob of them. I kept driving down the dirt road past the top of the mesa, looking for a suitably quiet spot to set up camp. It turns out that almost no one continues down this road after reaching the first viewpoint, so I didn't have to drive far. The campsite I chose was about a ten-minute walk from the mesa rim, surrounded by ponderosa pines, with just enough space for me to park my car and set up my tent. As soon as I'd pitched my tent, I took advantage of my last few hours of sunlight and set off on a walk along the mesa rim. I walked in the opposite direction of the road, carefully picking my way over rocks and boulders, taking care not to leave a trace of my trail. When I noticed the sun hovering just a few inches above the horizon, I stopped, turning to face the valley to the west of me. The burnt red rocks and sandstone formations of the Sonoran Desert were greener and more lushly forested than I was used to, almost as if I was looking out over a carpeted version of my most beloved desert. Despite the differences in scenery, what remained familiar was the vast amounts of space stretching out all around me and the freeing insignificance of myself within this space.

Losing myself all over again in the desert's magnificence, I stared on in awe as the setting sun burned the surrounding sandstone cliffs a deeper orange and turned the pine needles atop the towering Ponderosa pines a golden yellow. Over the valley, two turkey vultures soared, the black feathers at the tips of their long wings translucent and shimmering in the golden light of the setting sun. Standing at the edge of this cliff as I watched the buzzards surf the thermal currents, my mind glided back on the winds of time to that first desert sunset I'd witnessed at the end of the summer, right after I'd quit my job and left my home behind. The sunset this evening marked an end to the wandering phase of my life that began with that first desert sunset over seven months ago. It also signaled the beginning of a new phase of my life that I couldn't fully imagine for myself yet, but that I hoped would at least feel more rooted and calm.

Drawing this circle closed in my mind, I glanced around to double-check that the coast was clear, and then I pulled my shirt up over my head. Then came my bra, hiking shorts, and underwear, until I was left standing completely naked with only my hiking boots still on at the top of this cliff in the middle of nowhere.

"*Here I am*," I thought, offering myself up to the desert. "*Here is all of me.*"

Arms hanging open by my side, I stood unmoving as the wind blew my hair around my face. With each inhale, I breathed in the sweet dusty smell of the desert. My skin drank in every last drop of energy that the setting sun had to give. When the sun finally dropped below the western horizon, the temperature of the air immediately dropped along with it. My skin covered in goose bumps, I hastily slipped back into my clothing and headed back to camp to make a fire. After making myself an easy ramen dinner, I fished out a half-empty bottle of whiskey from the depths of my trunk. For all I knew, this would be my last night in a long time sleeping outside with no walls around me and only the sky above me as my ceiling. I didn't feel much like sleeping, so I kept my small fire going and sipped at my whiskey every so often to keep warm. The moon was so bright and full that night that it blocked out most of the light from the stars. Tending to my little fire, I watched the moon make its slow arc across the night sky, bathing the pine trees around me in a ghostly white light. Or perhaps I was the ghost there among these hundred-year-old trees and million-year-old rocks, a mere desert apparition, quick to arrive and just as soon to leave. *We come from space, and to space we shall return ...*

On that last night out in the desert, I wasn't consciously processing these thoughts or consciously thinking about much of anything. I simply sat by my fire in my sleeping bag, observing the night unfold around me and listening to the silence as it deepened. This was the last night of March and the first morning of April. On that morning, I remember that the full moon set within twenty minutes of the sun rising, both moonset and sunrise taking place just a little after seven in the morning. As the sun took the moon's place in the sky, the light slowly changed, and whatever spell the moon had cast on the forest was lifted. I had run out of whiskey a while ago and let my fire die, but I was still reluctant to move or get up from my chair. Over the course of the past few months, I'd said so many goodbyes. I'd had my heart broken so many times, in big and small ways. With this goodbye, I felt like I was leaving behind a part of myself. All I could do was trust the breaking and move forward to greet this newest version of myself, whoever she was and whatever form she decided to take. The first step in this was simply to rise to my feet, after which all the subsequent steps felt a lot easier.

Not having used my tent, I took down my temporary home. I boiled water for coffee and packed my things into the back of my car as the grinds steeped in my french press. After this, my final stop before San Diego was Los Angeles, where I would get to stay with Evie for a few days at her new apartment. As luck would have it, Evie had moved to Woodland Hills shortly after New Year's. The anticipation of getting to see her again after three months apart made me far less tired than I should have been, and my extra strong coffee carried me the rest of the way. To avoid having to return down that awful, boulder-strewn road, I took the longer back road off the mesa before reconnecting with the nearest major highway. Blasting hip-hop out of my stereo to keep myself awake, I drove without stopping for as long as I could, letting out a whoop of glee as I passed the sign welcoming me to California.

My glee plummeted into a dull sense of dread when I noticed how dangerously close my gas tank was to empty. Sure enough, I ran out of gas a mile from the top of Chiriaco Summit, less than an hour out from Palm Springs. Thank goodness for AAA, whose number I called to request roadside assistance. Once I made the call, there was nothing I could do besides sit in the shade of my rapidly heating car. Rolling all my windows down, I reclined my seat as far back as it would go. The only thing I could see in any direction was the color brown. I looked out upon dark brown mountains; lighter brown dirt; and brown, dirt-stained shrubs and cacti. I had no idea how long I would be stranded in this brown-hued purgatory, so I closed my eyes to wait. I waited for sleep or the tow truck to come, whichever got there first.

This is where I will leave you, waiting alongside me on this desolate desert road. Although it was more gold than brown, the desert is the first place I brought you on this journey. For my own sense of completion, the desert is where my journey will end. After all, it's never really over.

about the author

SUMMER SHULTZ lives in Denver, Colorado, at least for now.

Summer has been writing ever since she first learned how. She finished her first book, a young adult fantasy novel, at age 14. *Stuck Wide Open* is Summer's first published book.

Summer is a rare millennial who does not use social media, but you can connect with her at summershultz.com.